CW00517574

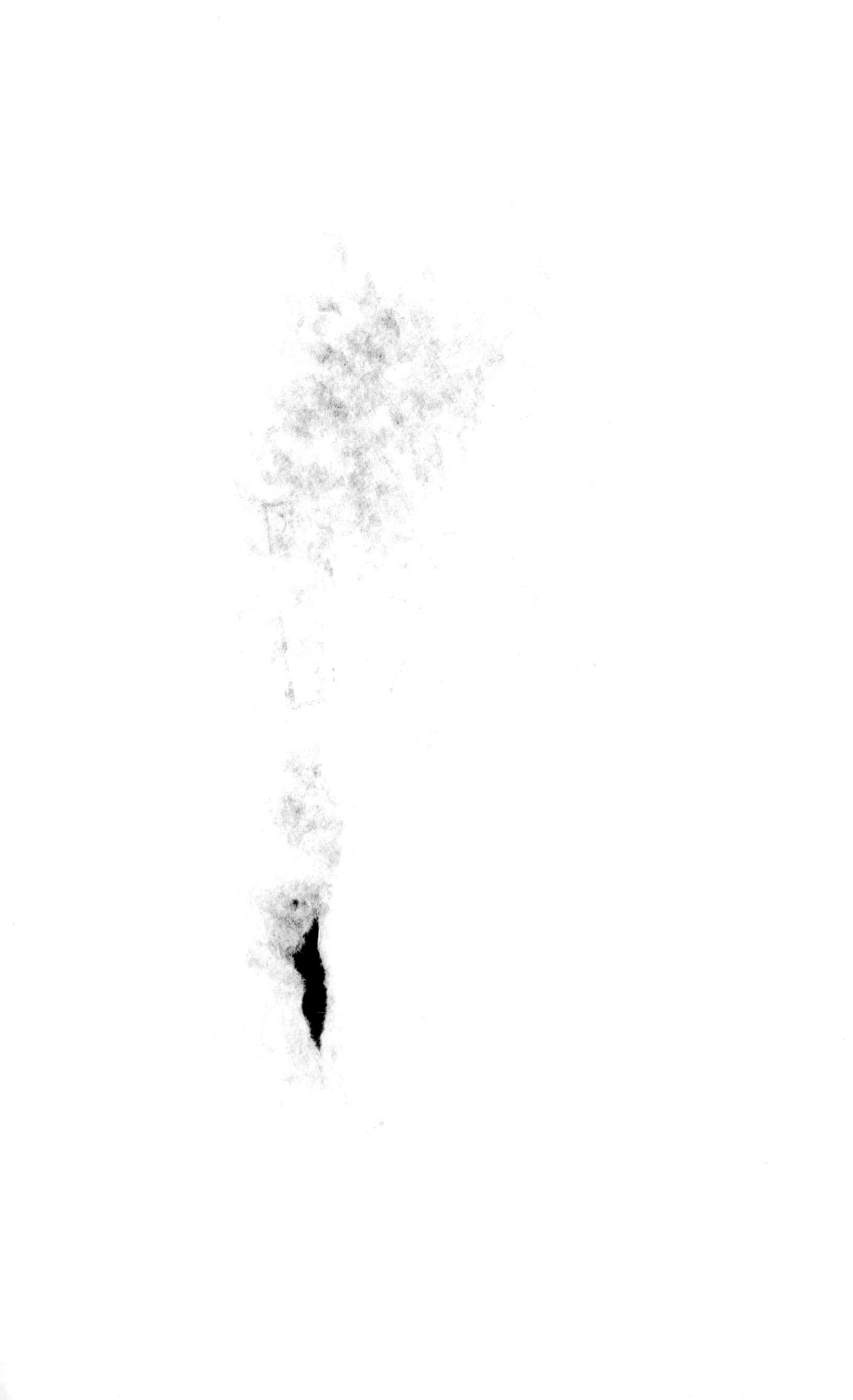

Intimate Enemy

BY THE SAME AUTHOR

Bird of Paradise
The Indiscretion
Friends and Other Enemies
The Wilder Side of Life
Don't Look Back

INTIMATE ENEMY

Diana Stainforth

C

CENTURY · LONDON

First published by Century in 1996

1 3 5 7 9 10 8 6 4 2

First published in the United Kingdom in 1996 by Century Ltd
Random House, 20 Vauxhall Bridge Road, London SW1V 2SA
Random House Australia (Pty) Limited
16, Dalmore Drive, Scoresby
Victoria 3179 Australia
Random House New Zealand Limited
18 Poland Road, Glenfield
Auckland 10, New Zealand
Random House South Africa (Pty) Limited
PO Box 2263, Rosebank 2121, South Africa
Random House UK Limited Reg. No. 954009

A CIP catalogue record for this book is available from the British Library

ISBN 0 7126 76244

Papers used by Random House UK are natural, recyclable products made from wood grown in sustainable forests. The manufacturing processes conform to the environmental regulations of the country of origin.

Phototypeset by Intype London Limited
Printed and bound by Mackays of Chatham plc, Chatham, Kent

ACKNOWLEDGEMENTS

MANY PEOPLE GAVE up their valuable time to help me research this book. Their expertise has given credibility to my story. They made it fascinating – and fun.

For his hours of help, my special thanks to David Walker.

For their insights into the City and the money-markets, I am grateful, alphabetically, to: Geoffrey Bunting, Emma da Cruz, Susan Hill, Michael Hintze, Richard Morley, Diarmuid O'Hegarty, Malise Reid-Scott, Christopher Stainforth – and to many others.

In the world of newspaper publishing, I am indebted to John Jay and Judy Bevan.

I thank Charles Cousins and Dick Rogoff for their invaluable contacts.

I am also grateful to Trudy Gold for her knowledge of history, and to Deenagh Brook and Duncan Buyers for their computer assistance.

Diana Stainforth
February 1996

I

March 1993

JOANNA PAID THE taxi driver with a twenty pound note, told him to keep the change, and sashayed up the steps towards Broadgate Circle. He eyed her legs and liked what he saw. She walked exuding confidence.

He did not see that her knuckles, clamped around the handle of her briefcase, were white with tension across the bone and that she shivered beneath her black cashmere suit.

She separated herself from the waves of smartly dressed money-market employees and paused in the shadows of the circle. Above her, green-leafed creepers cascaded from its upper floors. Below, on the ice rink, a lone skater was executing figures of eight, the morning light glinting on the blades of his skates.

Taking a compact from her bag, she checked her make-up. She had a face of contrasts. Her classically sculpted cheekbones were at odds with the irregular trail of freckles across the bridge of her nose, and her straight, serious eyebrows made her grey eyes seem softer – bedroom eyes, Peter had called them.

Her determined jawline was emphasised by a new hairstyle. It was a short, shiny auburn bob which left her neck feeling unfamiliarly cold. Until Saturday it had been below her shoulders, but she'd had it cut to look more businesslike.

She flicked a speck of dust from the lapel of her tailored jacket and smoothed down her short, straight skirt. It was a little tight. Since she'd given up smoking she'd put on weight, snacking on chocolate and crisps. Now, she resolved to stop.

Taking a deep breath, she counted to three and stepped out into the fray. As she did so, she was reminded of Christopher. She didn't want to think of him today, but she couldn't help it.

He slipped into her thoughts, as he so often did, taking her back to that April afternoon, the day before she had commenced her last term at university, when they'd walked across the Quantocks, just the two of them, above the quarry where as a child she had seen a stag cornered by hounds.

'Life is just starting for us,' he'd said, laughing and fearless, the wind tousling his blond hair. 'You now, Jo. Me next year.'

Only life had not begun for Christopher. Perhaps that was why Joanna had taken so long to leave Fittertons. New beginnings held terrible memories.

II

THE FIRST CLARENCE Tower was fifteen storeys of tinted glass and marble whose pinkish hue had been chosen, according to rival banks, to hide the blood when First Clarence Bank employees stabbed each other in the back.

As soon as Joanna stepped through the swing doors into the domed, marble hall, her nerves subsided. She became exhilarated and confident, reminding herself that First Clarence had approached her – not the other way round.

Vanessa, the fiercely aggressive personnel officer, was standing beside the front desk admonishing one of the six receptionists. The girl appeared on the verge of tears.

The Joanna of five minutes earlier would have apologised for being late, even though she was on time. This Joanna said an efficient, 'Good morning.'

Vanessa turned her back on the receptionist and stepped forward, beaming. 'Welcome to First Clarence, Joanna.'

'I'm delighted to be here,' Joanna wondered if Vanessa knew that she had applied to First Clarence from university but they hadn't even granted her an interview.

They took an empty lift to the fifth floor.

'Did you have time to read our manual?' asked Vanessa.

'Of course,' Joanna patted her briefcase. She had spent all weekend trying to master the myriad First Clarence employee regulations.

As the lift reached its destination, Vanessa handed Joanna a bar-coded name tag. 'You'll need this to access the trading floor,' she explained, adding in little more than a whisper, 'You'll find Jeremy a very dynamic head of sales but I'd better warn you that he refers to all salespersons as salesmen – even the women. I don't agree with it, of course, but he refuses to change – and since his desk makes a great deal of money, I'm afraid we women have to live with it.'

'That doesn't worry me – so long as we have the same opportunities. Old Mr Fitterton called us all "my young chaps".'

Vanessa frowned. 'Did no one complain?'

'He's a charming, elderly gentleman and he meant no disrespect.' Joanna smiled pleasantly. 'That's what matters, isn't it?'

'Perhaps . . . but I prefer regulations.' Vanessa ushered her through the electronic doors and into the vast, bustling equity trading room.

At Fittertons, the trading room had been as sedate as a public library. At First Clarence it was a frenzied market place with over three hundred institutional salesmen and market-makers clawing for business against the other investment banks.

The floor was divided into countries, with each desk seating a dozen salesmen whose eyes flicked constantly between their three monitors: one for the UK stock market, one reporting up-to-the-minute world news, and a third for the foreign markets – yesterday's Wall Street closing prices, last night's Far East prices, the movement on the Japanese Nikkei, Sydney's All Ordinary and Hong Kong's Hang Seng.

The market-makers – traders who set the share prices – had finished their morning meeting and were updating their prices in line with overnight world events whilst keeping up a bawdy repartee about their personal night-time successes.

'She gives the best telephone sex of any woman I know,' one trader was regaling his colleagues. 'Just to hear her voice is enough to make me so hard that . . .' He caught sight of Joanna and called out, 'Hey, Vanessa, aren't you going to introduce me? I'm free tonight. I have a window – after midnight.' He gave Joanna a cheeky grin.

'Harry, cut it out!' Vanessa turned to Joanna. 'Ignore them. It's the best way.'

The traders laughed. Joanna tried to look cool, but a faint blush touched her cheeks. No one had behaved like this at Fittertons.

She'd already met Jeremy, her boss. He looked like a large cuddly teddy bear, with tightly kinked reddish hair, a slight paunch, pale amber eyes, and heavy rimmed glasses.

'Welcome to the fray, Joanna.' He rose, beaming, and shook her by the hand, crushing her fingers with the power of his grip.

'Thank you.' She tried not to wince as she retrieved her squashed hand.

'I'll take over, Vanessa.' He waved the personnel officer away as though she were of little importance and focused his attention on Joanna, saying, 'There's no point in you meeting everyone on your first day. Too bloody confusing. We'll stick to your sector.' He led her to a nearby desk where a dozen or so salesmen specialised in communications and computer shares, mainly in the Footsie 100 – the *Financial Times*' top one hundred companies.

'Team, meet Joanna Templeton.' Jeremy allocated her to a spare seat near the end of the desk and introduced her to her new colleagues, starting with her neighbour, Simon, whose mop of golden hair and clean-cut boyish face reminded her of Christopher.

'Hello there.' Simon gave her a friendly smile. 'If you need to know anything, don't hesitate to ask me.'

'Thanks.' Joanna warmed instantly to him.

Next to Simon was Karen, a fast-talking New Yorker with a chiselled face, who paused in the middle of a telephone call to mouth, 'Hi.'

Further down the desk was Rupert, who had joined First Clarence the previous month. Thin, pale and aristocratically handsome, Rupert chewed nervously on a solid gold pencil. He looked up. 'Hello. Didn't we meet at Lady Cobthorne's?'

Joanna shook her head. 'I'm afraid not.'

'Rupert, stop name-dropping!' Vikram, whom Joanna guessed to be of Indian descent, gave her a conspiratorial wink.

At the far end was a supercilious strawberry blonde called Charlotte. She gave Joanna a bored, bland glance. 'Oh . . . er . . . I didn't catch your name.'

The put-down was not lost on Joanna – or on the desk – and she was aware that everyone was waiting to see how she coped.

'Templeton, Joanna.' She smiled innocently. 'I'm afraid I didn't catch your name either.'

There were shouts of laughter, except from Charlotte, and Joanna sensed that she had passed a test. She was gratified, but at the same time horrified. She wasn't accustomed to open hostility from colleagues. At Fittertons, they'd all been friends.

'Where have you come from, Joanna?' enquired Simon.

'Fittertons.'

'How long did you work there?' asked Vikram.

'Five years.'

'You mean, you've abandoned civilisation for this tribe of cannibals? Aren't you scared of being eaten alive?'

Joanna's eyes lighted on Charlotte. 'I think I can defend myself.'

There were more smiles.

The desk filled up until just one space remained, opposite Joanna.

'Here come the boffins,' said Simon as the clock touched seven-thirty and the analysts filed in, carrying their notes, to take their places at a long table beneath the podium. Silence fell as the Head Boffin, a tall, bearded man, stepped up to the microphone – known as the 'hoot and holler'. Before he began to speak, a pretty girl with black curly hair and a very red mouth hurried across the room and slipped into the seat opposite Joanna.

Jeremy glared at her. 'Rebecca! You're bloody late again. This is your place of work – not the local branch of Relate.'

Rebecca flushed. 'I'm sorry.'

'Sorry isn't good enough. Next time, you get an official warning. Three warnings – and you're out.'

Rebecca bit her lower lip and stared down at her hands. From the puffiness around her eyes, it was obvious to Joanna that she'd been crying.

The Head Boffin spoke and Joanna – like all the salesmen – took notes. He recapped on the recent budget, saying, 'In our opinion it won't hold back the rise in the UK stock market.' He touched on Hong Kong, explaining, 'The Hang Seng has taken a knock following China's disagreement with the Governor but we expect it to be temporary.' He ran through the main company news and gave his recommendations on their shares – to buy, sell or hold. Finally, he outlined the Government reports due that day.

After the Head Boffin had finished speaking, each of the boffins rose in turn to give detailed reports on various companies. The last boffin to take the podium was young and clearly nervous. He eyed the listening salesmen as though expecting them to tear him to pieces.

'Restbreak Motels.' He cleared his throat. 'When I phoned the company last month I was given to believe that their results would be in . . . ummm . . . line with my figures. As a result of this, I . . . er . . . recommended the shares as a strong buy. But the figures are . . . umm . . . considerably lower. I . . . umm . . . therefore downgrade Restbreak to a sell.'

The salesmen groaned as they anticipated their clients' displeasure. The young boffin stumbled on in an attempt to excuse himself, but no one listened. Finally, he abandoned the podium.

The Head Boffin marched out of the trading room. The other analysts followed, the youngest slinking along behind. As he went out of the room, he let the trading-room door slam. It created a deafening bang.

From the market-makers' desk, Harry quipped, 'He jumped.'

'No,' replied Vikram. 'He's a gentleman. He shot himself.'

Everyone laughed.

Joanna couldn't help feeling sorry for the young analyst. One mistake – and he was out.

At eight a.m., some salesmen began to make their calls, trading in the premarket – the half hour before the official opening of the stock market. Others studied their notes, exchanged information or asked Jeremy's opinion. Joanna watched. It was familiar, and yet different. At First Clarence there was a feeling of urgency, of living on a knife edge, which had been lacking at Fittertons.

Eight-twenty-nine a.m. There was a tense lull. Around the circumference of the trading room, the ticker-tape moved like a long black ribbon giving a constant update of share prices and currencies.

Eight-thirty a.m. The market opened. The noise level increased, monitors flashed, prices moved – blue for risers, red for fallers. Some salesmen shouted at market-makers demanding prices. Others hunched over their telephones, trying to pacify irate clients and explain away the young analyst's mistake.

Jeremy sat at the head of the desk, next to Joanna. Unlike Mr Fitterton, who'd remained in his office waiting for employees to approach him with their queries, he was a hands-on Head of Sales.

'Here's a client list for you to get your teeth into. They're already loaded into your machine.' He handed Joanna the names of some twenty companies, mainly small investment funds or trusts – the major funds would be looked after by experienced salesmen. 'We do, of course, expect you to prospect for new clients,' he added, picking up his headset to listen in to Rupert's phone call, then hissing at him to be more aggressive.

He returned to Joanna. 'So . . . familiarise yourself with each client's portfolio – and then "smile and dial", as we say.'

Jeremy went to congratulate a salesman who'd landed a huge order, leaving Simon to explain that to safeguard against industrial espionage each desk shared a password with which to access their computers. This was changed monthly.

'We can only call up our clients,' said Simon, 'but Jeremy, as Head of Sales, can access the main computer. His code has an extra four digits which only he knows.'

'Bound to be the day and month of his birth,' cut in Vikram. 'Vain people never choose their year of birth.'

Simon continued with his explanation. 'Our code for this month is Maynard – like Maynard Keynes – followed by our sector code.' He listed eight digits.

Joanna nodded.

'Don't you need to write them down?'

She repeated the numbers back to him.

'I'm impressed. Good luck.' Simon returned to his own work.

Joanna keyed in the code and called up each of her clients, studying their transactions for shares bought or sold through First Clarence – she had no idea what deals they had done through other banks. Her list contained a handful of offshore companies, companies registered and managed outside the UK, usually to avoid UK tax. Of these there were three – Kathpeach Trust of Liechtenstein, Società Hadini of Monte Carlo and New Aldren Fund of Grand Cayman – which were marked '*Await instructions only*'.

'Is this normal?' she asked Jeremy when he returned.

He glanced at her screen. 'If that's what the client wants, why not?'

She nodded, although she'd never experienced this at Fittertons.

He reached for his headset. 'Try Sternhold at the Durable Savings Trust.'

Joanna did her best to forget Jeremy's presence. Mentally, she ran through her spiel as she dialled.

'Sternhold,' barked a gruff voice with a strong Scottish accent.

'Good morning, Mr Sternhold, my name is Joanna Templeton of First Clarence Bank and I have been assigned to look after the special relationship between yourself and First Clarence.'

'How many times do I have to tell you people to stop bothering me?'

Joanna gulped. She was so stunned that she almost put the phone down but managed to stop herself. 'I am . . . umm . . . sorry to hear that you're annoyed,' she stammered, hoping to diffuse his hostility. 'Perhaps we could discuss your complaints over lunch.'

'Didn't you hear what I said?' Mr Sternhold demanded.

'Of course I don't expect you to change your mind about First Clarence,' she persevered, 'but it would help us enormously to know where we have gone wrong.'

'Miss Templeton, my fund lost a lot of money following your analysts' advice and the salesman I dealt with couldn't have cared less.'

Sensing that he was on the point of slamming down the receiver, she cut in quickly, 'A client who gives me constructive criticism is of great value. I do hope you'll reconsider lunch.'

There was a pause. 'I'll think about it.' He put the phone down.

As Joanna came off the line, Jeremy gave her the thumbs up. 'You'll do well.'

He moved to another desk. His task was to inspire his salesmen and, since his bonus was directly related to their profits, he drove them hard.

'Jeremy always makes the new intake phone Sternhold,' Simon confided to Joanna. 'It's his way of discovering if you can take the heat.'

'What an initiation!' Joanna sank back into her chair. She was already exhausted.

The stock market rose and the atmosphere in the trading room was exuberant. Joanna dialled, introduced herself, and fixed meetings. Of the directors named on her list, one was dead, one had gone bankrupt, one had emigrated, and a fourth demanded to know why he was no longer dealing with Rosalind.

'Who is Rosalind?' Joanna asked Jeremy, not recalling a colleague of that name.

'Rosalind left because she couldn't sell.'

Joanna wished she hadn't asked.

At lunchtime she ordered in a sandwich, as did most of her colleagues.

'If you go out, you have to log out so Jeremy can switch your calls and faxes to his machine,' explained Simon, showing her a book in which each salesman listed his time of departure and the reason – usually the name of the client he or she planned to meet.

There was a few entries for 'doctor' or 'dentist' and even fewer for 'personal'.

All afternoon Joanna continued to telephone her clients, hoping that one of them would place an order. None did.

Jeremy returned to her side just before the end of trading. 'Done any business?' he asked her.

She tried not to look defeatist as she shook her head.

'Don't worry.' He gave her a reassuring smile. 'Only a few people sell on their first day.'

'I wanted to be one of them.'

'That's the right attitude. Determination.'

At four-thirty p.m. the market closed. The Footsie had risen twenty points. The salesmen chatted happily.

'My wife will be pleased if this continues.' Simon stretched to relieve the tension across the back of his neck. 'She's expecting twins,' he explained to Joanna, 'and we'd like a house with a bigger garden.'

'Congratulations.' She smiled and tried to look contented, but she wished she could have had one order. In spite of what Jeremy said, not having done any business made her feel vulnerable. She couldn't help recalling Rosalind.

Some of Joanna's desk went to meet clients, others were going for a drink at Corney & Barrow in Broadgate Circle. Not wanting to appear intrusive, Joanna collected up her belongings and said goodnight.

'Aren't you coming with us?' asked Simon, looking disappointed.

'Of course Joanna's coming,' said Vikram. 'We always chew the cud at the end of the day. Hurry up, Rupert! I know you're invited to a smart dinner party, but the women will seem a lot more exciting if you arrive drunk. Hey, Harry!' he shouted at the trader's desk. 'Coming for a drink?'

Harry winked at Joanna. 'Wish I could, but not tonight. I have to see my grandmother.'

Vikram flicked a rubber band at Harry. 'Liar!'

'It's true. I promise.' Harry held up two fingers in the Scouts' salute.

They left the First Clarence Tower and walked through Broadgate Circle, past the black granite façade of St Leonard's Commercial Banking Group, First Clarence's major competitor. The air was cold and crisp with the last sting of winter. From every building, people poured out into the evening, buttoning up their coats.

Rebecca accompanied them as far as the steps which led up to the wine bar. 'I'd better go straight home,' she said.

'Patrick not found another job yet?' asked Simon, sympathetically.

Rebecca shook her head. 'He's so bitter about being made redundant and, of course, he feels worse because I'm at work all day. We used to be very happy but now . . . well . . . everything I do, even the way I brush my hair, is wrong.'

Joanna remembered how Peter had constantly corrected her grammar during the year after they left university, when he'd taken longer than she had to find a job.

They went upstairs to the bar which was packed with celebrating traders.

Vikram laid his credit card on the bar. 'Drinks are on me.'

The others protested.

'I've had my best day all year,' he insisted, ordering a couple of bottles of Bollinger although he drank only orange juice.

'You want to watch your back with Charlotte,' he warned Joanna as he passed her a glass of champagne. 'She's horizontally upwardly mobile.'

Joanna was mystified. 'She's what?'

'She's having an affair with Sebastian Deveraux, head of corporate finance. Be warned! She tells him everything – and he passes it on to Jeremy. They're thick as thieves, same public school and all that. I'm sure it's Charlotte who informed Jeremy that Rebecca's having boyfriend problems which make her late.'

They gossiped about First Clarence, telling Joanna who was trustworthy and who to avoid. After an hour or so, they separated, each going their different ways. Simon and Joanna shared a taxi as far as Sloane Square, where he grabbed another for Clapham and she went on to the pretty, ground-floor flat in South Kensington which she had bought the previous summer, when prices were rock bottom.

Felicity, her flatmate and closest friend from university, worked as a fiction editor with a small publishing house. She was curled up on the sofa, reading a manuscript, her jolly, round face resting on her hand, the remains of a Lean Cuisine meal and a Mars bar wrapper on a plate beside her.

'How's the new job?' she asked, happily putting aside the manuscript in order to chat.

'Exciting and terrifying.' Joanna kicked off her shoes and removed her jacket. 'The market shot up. Everyone did lots of business – except me. Not one of my miserly clients placed an order. Oh, God, I hope I do better tomorrow.'

'You will.' Felicity tucked a strand of fair hair behind her ear.

'Supposing I don't? First Clarence's probationary period only lasts three months and the personnel officer informed me that they can tell if you're any good within one week.'

'Jo, it isn't like you to panic. First Clarence wouldn't have offered you the job if they didn't believe you were capable.'

'I know, but I've never worked anywhere so cut-throat.' She recounted Charlotte's attempt to belittle her.

Felicity was horrified. 'What a bitch! Why didn't your boss intervene?'

'Because I'm meant to be able to stand up for myself – I suppose.'

'Which you did – brilliantly. If Charlotte attacked you, it means she feels threatened. She knows you're going to be better than her.' Felicity smiled encouragingly.

'Thanks. You've cheered me up.' Joanna glanced down at the remnants of Felicity's supper, and laughed.

'I just *had* to have some chocolate.' Felicity's smile turned to a guilty grin.

The telephone rang. Joanna answered. It was Tom, Felicity's American fiancé, calling from Washington.

Joanna wandered into the kitchen, opened the fridge and grazed on cheese and pâté. She ate some chocolate before she remembered that she was meant to be on a diet.

From the sitting room Felicity's voice, warm and tender, was asking Tom about his day. Hearing her, Joanna felt a sudden and acute hunger for the intimacy she had shared with Peter. He'd been a part of her life, off and on, for six years. They had lived together in this flat, briefly, and she missed his presence although their relationship had been dead long before either of them would admit it.

Nevertheless, on this evening, she longed for his friendly voice, to go to bed and feel the security of his familiar body. She wanted the affectionate but unadventurous lovemaking which had become their habit. She craved the safety in his lack of passion.

She wondered if he was still living in his cousin's flat in the Barbican where she had forwarded his mail, or had he bought the house he'd told her about when they last spoke? Was the cousin's number ex-directory or could she obtain it from enquiries? Would Peter be home now?

She pulled herself up sharply. She mustn't contact him. She had to let him go. He wasn't right for her any more than she was for him. He didn't stand up to her. It had taken her a long time to accept the end, in the same way that it had taken her years to leave Fittertons.

III

THAT FIRST WEEK, Joanna did no business. She phoned her clients, discussed the latest market news and gave them the First Clarence analysts' view. They thanked her politely, but placed no orders. By Friday she was desperate. 'I told you to sound more confident,' said Jeremy, no longer bothering to mask his disappointment in her. It was he who had suggested to personnel that First Clarence should approach Joanna Templeton after friends at Fittertons had told him she was their brightest rising star.

Joanna did her best to follow Jeremy's advice, but it was hard to sound positive when each time she failed to deal he turned his pale amber eyes on her.

'Try to relax,' said Simon, with an encouraging smile. 'All you need is one deal and you'll be brimming with optimism.'

'Don't worry so much,' advised Rebecca. 'Lots of people don't deal during their first week.'

'Did you?'

'Yes – but I was lucky.'

Joanna felt even worse.

On Friday evening she didn't join her colleagues for an after-work drink: she was too ashamed of her failure. Instead she went home.

Outside her house she met Bertrand and Sylvie, her French neighbours who owned an antique shop. They were loading a chiffonier on to their van.

'How's the new job?' Bertrand asked Joanna.

Joanna pulled a face. 'Not great.'

He smiled sympathetically. 'It's a tough life. I used to work in insurance. How I hated it.'

'Oh, I don't hate it,' said Joanna, recalling the excitement of the trading room.

That evening she confided in Felicity. 'Maybe I'm not good enough for First Clarence.'

'Jo, you haven't given it time.'

'I'll probably be fired on Monday.' Joanna flopped down on to the sofa. 'Do you think that God, if he exists, is punishing me because I wanted to earn more? Is this my just deserts for succumbing to greed?'

Felicity was laughing. 'You're crazy!'

'I will be, if I don't get an order. I shall be carried away in a strait-jacket, muttering, "I have been assigned the special relationship between . . ." Maybe I should have stayed at Fittertons.'

'You were bored to tears.' Felicity went to the kitchen to fetch a couple of diet Cokes. As an afterthought, she included two bags of crisps. 'No point in being too abstemious.' She tossed one bag to Joanna.

Crunching her crisps, Joanna recalled that old Mr Fitterton had barely trusted her to buy 1,000 ICI shares without fearing she'd bankrupt the firm or contravene the Stock Exchange Regulations.

'You're right. I was bored,' she admitted. 'But at least I was safe.'

On Monday morning, Joanna arrived at work with renewed determination.

The first client she contacted was Miss Samson, a fund manager at Foxham Trust. 'Our analysts feel that the swing to the right in the French elections opens an ideal opportunity for Rampayne Communications to expand in Europe,' she began.

'Well . . . er . . . Miss Templeton.'

'Please call me Joanna.'

'Joanna, we're already sufficiently exposed to Rampayne. For the time being Foxham are watching the market. Thank you.' The phone went down.

'You should have suggested Inter-Picture as an alternative,' said Jeremy crossly.

Joanna nodded, and tried the next client. And the next. But not one of her contacts gave her an order that day, although the market rose again and all her colleagues dealt constantly.

By that evening, Joanna was completely disheartened. Each time Jeremy spoke to her, she was convinced she was about to be fired. When she left the trading room, Harry didn't even glance her way. She sensed that the word had gone out; Joanna Templeton does no business. She's useless.

She went home. Felicity was out. She made herself some scrambled eggs, but after one mouthful she could eat no more.

In the morning she stood on the scales. She'd lost five pounds since starting at First Clarence, but even that didn't raise her spirits. She could barely swallow her coffee. She was nauseous with nerves.

That evening she took her first client out to dinner.

'Colin Rottingdean places small orders, but they accumulate,' Jeremy told her as she prepared to leave her desk. 'Talk about golf. Don't hard sell. He'll place an order.'

She had booked a table at a nearby restaurant recommended by Simon. Mr Rottingdean arrived ten minutes late, by which time Joanna had begun to fear he wasn't coming. He was a beaky little man with thatched hair and thick, round pebble spectacles.

'What happened to Rosalind?' he asked as soon as he sat down.

'She . . . er . . . left.'

Joanne passed him the wine list. She was quite capable of ordering but he was a small man and she wanted to make him feel in control.

'You people have such a turnover. Clients prefer to deal with the same person, you know.'

'You're absolutely right, and I intend to remain at First Clarence for many years.' She wondered what he would say if he knew she might not survive the week.

Since First Clarence were paying, Mr Rottingdean chose the most expensive bottle of claret. Joanna didn't care so long as she got her order.

'Jeremy tells me you play golf,' she said. 'I've always wanted to learn.'

Two hours later, Mr Rottingdean was still talking about the day he had almost had a hole in one. Suddenly, he glanced at his watch. 'Nine o'clock. Oh, I must run. My train leaves in twenty minutes. I have enjoyed myself . . . Joanna.' He stood up.

She rose, expecting him to give her his order.

'Thanks for dinner.' He held out his hand. 'We're not buyers at present. We already have a good spread of investments, but you'll hear from me when we decide to make some changes.'

He scuttled out of the restaurant. Joanna was near to tears as she called for the bill.

Disconsolately, she walked through Finsbury Circus, rehearsing her explanation to Jeremy. As she searched for a taxi, she noticed Charlotte standing beside a parked car, talking to a tall, blond, ruggedly handsome man. He was fingering his gold watch, only half-listening to Charlotte whilst his eyes roved over any passing woman. Joanna gave Charlotte a quick nod. In return, she received a blank stare.

Too disheartened to go straight home, Joanna stopped at a public phone booth in Liverpool Street Station. She rang Max, a close friend from university and her solicitor, but he was out. She tried Sophie, a former colleague at Fittertons, but she was in Australia. Finally, in desperation, she took a taxi to the Barbican.

She had to wait beside the underground car park whilst the porter contacted Peter.

'Is he at home?' she asked, anxiously pacing up and down.

'Yes, miss.'

A moment later a door opened and Peter stepped out of the building. His brown curly hair was standing on end and he was wearing his favourite green jumper and yet he looked different to how Joanna remembered him – less like a little boy, more like a man.

He gaped at her in astonishment. Clearly, he had expected someone else. 'Oh . . . hello . . . Jo.'

She took a step towards him. 'Peter, I know I shouldn't have come, but I had to speak to someone.'

He shook his head. 'Thanks. That makes me feel really special.'

'I didn't mean it like that.' There was a break in her voice and she could feel tears biting at her eyelids. 'I think I'm . . . about to get the sack.'

He hesitated, frowning. 'You'd better come up for a drink.'

'Not if you'd prefer I didn't.' She realised how selfish she'd been in coming.

'No! Come up.' He held the door for her.

In silence, he led the way up several flights of steps and along an open walkway next to an artificial lake, into a second building where he unlocked a door. The flat was small, with a galley kitchen adjoined to a sitting area whose window looked out over the lake.

'Wine all right for you?' he asked, producing an already open bottle.

'Yes, thanks.' She leaned against the fridge and watched him pour it, noticing that his hands were unsteady.

He passed her a glass and their fingers touched. They drew back sharply, conscious of each other in a way that they hadn't been for years.

'I'm sorry about your job,' he said.

She smiled ruefully. 'Thanks.'

'Of course you always were over-ambitious. Maybe you should have stayed at Fittertons.'

'Peter, I was so bored.'

'As you were with me.'

'That's not true.' The lie to spare his feelings came automatically, as it often had in the latter part of their time together.

'Isn't it?' He looked deep into her eyes.

She was shocked to find herself aroused by him. 'No.'

They stared at each other.

'I was very upset when you told me to move out,' he said.

She swallowed hard.

'I've had a fucking awful time since we split.'

She felt far guiltier now than she had when she'd asked him to leave. 'I'm sorry,' she whispered.

He put down his glass and removed hers. Then he placed his hands on her shoulders. 'You shouldn't have come, Jo,' he said hoarsely.

'I wanted to see you.'

He pushed her back against the fridge, his body pressed against hers, his mouth on hers, his tongue probing. She responded, as aroused by him as she had been in the early days of their relationship. She moved her hips and he stiffened, hard against her. She reached for his zip, wanting him to take her there, in the discomfort of the kitchen. He ran his hands up the inside of her leg, lifting her skirt, tugging at the thin lace of her pants.

'Come here!' he said, leading her into the bedroom.

Not bothering to undress first, they fell on the bed and on each other. Their clothes became entangled as they attempted to remove them. He unbuttoned her shirt and unfastened her bra.

'I like to hold your breasts,' he said, placing his hands on them. 'Have you forgotten?'

'No, of course not.'

He pulled her on top of him, manoeuvring her till she sat astride him, riding him. 'I like to see your face when you come,' he said. 'Have you forgotten that?'

'Of course not.'

She moved rhythmically as he caressed her breasts. She moved faster. He seized her buttocks and thrust himself upwards, as though he wanted to hurt her. She arched her back and gasped with pleasure. He held her on to him, digging his fingers into her as he shook with the spasms of his own orgasm.

Immediately, they rolled apart and lay in silence, not looking at each other. Peter rose, leaving Joanna half-naked and curled in a foetal position. He returned wearing his dressing-gown.

'I know this might sound callous after what we've . . . er . . . just done, Jo,' he said, avoiding her gaze, 'but I've had a lot of time to think. I've hated being on my own. A clean break is best – easiest for me.' He paused. 'And . . . er . . . as a matter of fact, I've met someone recently. I'm not sure what I feel about her, but if I keep seeing you, we won't stand a chance.'

Joanna tried not to mind. 'It's all right, Peter.' She forced a smile. 'I understand.'

She slipped off the bed, picked up her clothing and went into the bathroom. Her face in the mirror looked debauched. Her mascara had smudged and her lips were swollen. She felt sad and flat, and wished she'd stayed away. As she adjusted her skirt, she noticed a piece of paper beside the telephone. On it was written 'Judy', followed by a number.

'I've called you a cab,' Peter told her when she came out of the bathroom.

'Thanks. I'll wait for it downstairs.'

They looked at each other with sorrowful eyes.

'Goodbye, Peter,' she whispered.

He did not reply.

She kissed him quickly on the cheek and walked out. She couldn't reproach him for rejecting her now, she'd hurt him enough in the past. Nor did she blame him for needing to bury the ghost of their relationship before he began with someone new.

IV

On the following morning Joanna arrived at work feeling sick with dread.

'How did it go with Rottingdean?' asked Jeremy.

She forced herself to look him in the eyes. 'Fine – but he isn't dealing at present.'

'For God's sake!' Before Jeremy could give vent to further frustration, the analysts filed in. 'I'll speak to you later, Joanna,' he hissed.

She wondered if she should give in her notice now or wait to be fired.

The analysts gave their usual update, at the end of which the Head Boffin said, 'Now Sebastian Deveraux of Corporate Finance will talk to you about the Merantum Building Company flotation – First Clarence's big news of the day.'

The ruggedly handsome blond man whom Joanna had seen with Charlotte in Finsbury Circus strode into the trading room, heading for the podium. She glanced at Charlotte, who was watching him with barely concealed bitterness etched into her normally bland face.

'Here comes Mr Sexpot.' Vikram purposefully raised his voice. 'Be warned, Joanna, women fall like flies – and he's there to catch them!'

Joanna smiled non-committally. She was far too worried about losing her job to think about men.

Sebastian Deveraux stepped up to the podium. 'As you all know, First Clarence has underwritten the Merantum Building Company flotation,' he said with a proud smile. 'Merantum has great growth potential. The recession is ending and all indicators point to a rise in the commercial property market. If you read the *Sunday Chronicle* at the weekend you will have seen Adam

Hunter's upbeat article about Merantum. The *Sunday Chronicle* doesn't have the bite it used to, but Hunter's acerbic pen is well known and he's not a journalist to back a flotation unless he believes in it. We've priced the shares at one hundred and forty. Dealing on the open market will start in two weeks. I want all of you salesmen to phone your clients immediately and get them to commit to buy the shares. We want this issue sub-underwritten within the hour. We need to spread the risk.' He paused, then added with a grin, 'Not that there is a risk. Merantum is a winner.'

'Deveraux needs his bonus to pay for all his wives, women and polo ponies,' said Vikram, reaching for the telephone to call his first client.

Jeremy stiffened, but to Joanna's surprise he didn't remonstrate with Vikram. Instead, he left the desk.

She consulted her client list and, after uttering a silent prayer, called Miss Samson at Foxham Trust – but Miss Samson wasn't interested in building shares. She tried Mr Rottingdean, who preferred to buy after the flotation. She rang all of her clients, even Mr Sternhold, but not one of them was interested in Merantum.

Jeremy returned. 'How are you getting on?'

'Er . . . nothing so far.'

'Jesus Christ! What's wrong with you?'

She flushed. 'I haven't rung them all yet.'

'Then get on and do so.'

'Do you mean I should try . . . absolutely all of my clients?'

'Are you deaf as well?' he snapped.

Scarlet with humiliation, Joanna tapped out Kathpeach's number in Liechtenstein. There was a short pause as the overseas call registered.

'Yes,' said a man's voice.

'Mr Bilsham?'

'Bilsham,' he replied.

'This is Joanna Templeton from First Clarence. I realise that you prefer us to await your instructions but we have a very interesting new issue.' She gave him a brief but upbeat description of Merantum, ending with, 'It would be an excellent investment.'

'Excellent investment,' he repeated.

She could hardly believe her ears. 'Let me suggest a commitment of . . . four hundred thousand shares.' She expected him to reduce the amount.

'Four hundred thousand,' he said.

'Or we could round it up to half a million,' she ventured.

'Round it up.'

Joanna could hardly contain her excitement. Her voice quavered as she confirmed his order. 'Five hundred thousand Merantum Building Company at one hundred and forty per share. Thank you.'

Mr Bilsham repeated it back to her, word for word, adding his thank you. This struck her as being extra cautious, but she didn't care. She had finally done some business.

She came off the line and turned to Jeremy. 'I've had a sale. Half a million!'

He clapped his hands. 'Brilliant! I knew you could do it.'

'Congratulations,' said Rebecca, with genuine delight.

Around the desk, Simon gave Joanna the thumbs up, Vikram whistled, Karen smiled, and Rupert saluted. They were visibly pleased that she'd made it, and she was touched by their reactions.

'Which client?' asked Jeremy, glancing at her list.

'Kathpeach.'

His face froze. 'I told you not to call Kathpeach.' He pointed to 'Await instructions only'. 'For God's sake, can't you bloody read?'

Joanna was stunned. So were her colleagues. They stared at Jeremy in astonishment.

'My conversation was recorded, as are all our calls.' She was determined to defend her only sale. 'Mr Bilsham even repeated the order to me. If you don't believe me, play it back.'

Jeremy hesitated. Then he turned away from her, picked up his yellow telephone and quickly tapped out a number, speaking quietly to whoever answered, whilst Joanna and her colleagues exchanged mystified glances.

'Any problems?' asked Sebastian Deveraux, hurrying over to Joanna's desk when he saw the salesmen sitting motionless.

Before any of them could reply, Jeremy came off the line. 'Not at all. We're doing damned well. Joanna Templeton, our newest salesman, has just placed half a million.'

'Well done, Joanna.' Sebastian gave her his perfect smile. 'We're glad to have you with us.'

She thanked him, glowing with pride – and relief.

As Sebastian moved away, Jeremy informed her, 'I've spoken to Kathpeach and luckily they were on the point of giving you an order. But in future you must adhere to a client's instructions.'

'Of course. I'm sorry.'

Joanna telephoned the remainder of her clients. Having succeeded once, she had gained confidence and it was reflected in her voice. She placed a further 100,000 shares.

In the late afternoon she went back to Miss Samson at Foxham Trust to update her on Rampayne Communications, whose price had started to rise on rumours of a merger.

'What price for a hundred thousand?' asked Miss Samson, without revealing if she already possessed the shares or if she was a buyer.

Joanna checked the yellow strip on her screen which gave her the best three prices on offer. The St Leonard's Commercial Banking Group were quoting 266 to sell and 270 to buy, First Clarence quoted 266–271.

Obliged to give Foxham 'best execution', even if that meant placing the order with another bank, Joanna called to Harry, 'What price Rampayne?'

He frowned, calculated, and matched St Leonard's Commercial.

'Two sixty-six to two seventy,' Joanna told Miss Samson.

'I'll buy a hundred thousand at two seventy.'

Joanna repeated the order, thanked Miss Samson, and shouted, 'Harry, a hundred thousand Rampayne to buy at two seventy.'

Then she smiled at Simon. 'You were right. It only takes one deal.'

Joanna earned more commission on that one day than she had in a month at Fittertons. Nevertheless, she remained apprehensive. She couldn't forget the terrifying sense of inadequacy when she had failed to do any business. Nor did she forget Jeremy's violent reaction to her sale to Kathpeach.

V

IT WAS SEVERAL weeks before Joanna could relax. As her fear of failure subsided, she began to enjoy First Clarence. She relished the buzz, the cut and thrust, the exhilaration – and the money.

Harry continued to show blatant interest in her, to the amusement of the other traders. When she sashayed through the trading room, he demanded to know what she had done the previous night. If she went to the coffee machine, more often than not he joined her. His attention was very public, and Joanna parried it with humour, although secretly she found him attractive. His barrow-boy chutzpah was appealing. He made her laugh – and he had a way of walking which made her think he'd be good in bed.

One evening he followed her into the lift and pressed 'door close'.

'How about having dinner with me tonight?' he asked, stepping towards her as they plummeted to the ground.

She held her briefcase in front of her in an act of mock protection. 'Harry, we work together.'

'So what? I fancy you – and I don't think you're indifferent to me.'

She was about to deny it, but said, 'I've no intention of becoming the butt of trading-room gossip, like Charlotte.'

'Joanna, no one would ever know. I promise you.' He gave her his most earnest and beguiling smile.

She recalled the way he'd recounted his adventures to his colleagues, and laughed aloud. 'Harry, you're such a liar!'

The lift stopped at the ground floor, and she stepped out of it, still laughing.

To give Harry his due, he laughed too.

One morning, when the Head Boffin had talked enthusiastically about the economic development of China and the opportunity for British firms to participate in huge contracts, Joanna braved Mr Sternhold.

'I do hope you have reconsidered my lunch invitation,' she said. 'I'd really like to know where I can improve our service.'

'I won't use First Clarence again so it'll be a waste of your time, young lady.'

'Mr Sternhold, it will be most useful.'

He was silent for a moment. 'Oh, very well, but I'm a busy man.'

She booked a sedate restaurant, not popular with noisy traders, and arrived ten minutes early. To her consternation, Mr Sternhold was already seated. He was a large, crusty, balding man in his late fifties.

'I have only thirty minutes, so I've already ordered,' he told Joanna brusquely.

'I'm grateful for whatever time you can spare.' She smiled sweetly and handed him the wine list. 'Please choose.'

He passed it back. 'I'm a teetotaller, Miss Templeton.'

'Oh . . . er . . . how healthy,' she stammered, wondering how she was going to survive the next half hour.

'Drink is a curse, Miss Templeton. So are drugs.' He paused whilst the waiter brought his plain, steamed fish. 'I'm a Glaswegian and it breaks my heart to see what these evils have done to my home city. I caught my grandson smoking in the garden and he's only sixteen.'

'My brother used to smoke behind the potting shed in my parents' garden,' she told him. 'I smoked from my teens onwards and nothing my parents said or did could stop me.'

'But you gave up?'

'Only three months ago – and only because I was determined to stop.' She didn't add that she would have loved a cigarette at that moment.

They continued to talk about his grandson. Mr Sternhold didn't place an order – they barely discussed business – but when they left the restaurant, he smiled at Joanna for the first time.

'You are very tenacious, Miss Templeton,' he said. 'I had no intention of meeting you, and here I am. You must have Scottish blood in your veins. That's a compliment.'

She laughed. 'Thank you.'

They shook hands.

'May I telephone you?' she asked.

'You will – whatever I say.' He was chuckling as he walked away.

Returning to First Clarence, she met Jeremy in the lift. 'You look pleased with yourself,' he said, adding with disbelief, 'Don't tell me you seduced old Sternhold into placing an order.'

She smiled. 'Not yet – but I will.'

Joanna, Charlotte and Rupert attended a lunch given by Rampayne Communications. They prospected for new clients, and to Joanna's gratification she made contact with Hugo Porter, the recently promoted fund manager at LinkFund, a specialist fund investing in communications shares.

Returning to the office, she reported her success to Jeremy. 'I couldn't pin him down to lunch but I'm sure he wants to hear from me.' She produced Hugo's card from her bag. On the reverse, he'd written the number of his private line.

'Well done!' Jeremy beamed at her. 'LinkFund have attracted huge sums and Hugo is going places fast. I was at school with his younger brother. The whole family's brilliant.'

They were interrupted by Charlotte. 'I'm sorry to spoil your triumph, Joanna, but Hugo wishes to be my client. You talked to him – as did every salesman – but he prefers to deal through me.'

Joanna flushed. 'Did he say so?'

'No . . . but it's obvious. I am more senior. You are still on probation. I too have his card.' Charlotte laid it on Jeremy's desk, next to the one which Hugo had given Joanna.

There was silence. Joanna knew that she was being outmanoeuvred. She was angry and disappointed – with herself as much as with Charlotte. Then, on impulse, she reached for Charlotte's card and turned it over. The reverse was blank. With a flourish, she revealed her own – with Hugo's neat handwriting.

'I'd say he wishes to deal through me,' she said.

'And what Hugo wants, he gets,' added Jeremy firmly.

Without another word, Charlotte retreated. Across the desk Joanna caught Rebecca's eye. They exchanged a triumphant wink.

Jeremy sent LinkFund's details straight to Credit Clearance, urging them to authorise trading by the following morning.

That evening Joanna and Rebecca took some clients to the National Theatre. Afterwards the two women walked back across

Waterloo Bridge. It was the first warm evening of the year and there was a feel of approaching summer in the air. Halfway across the bridge, they stopped to look down at the dark, greasy water.

'The way you defeated Charlotte was brilliant,' said Rebecca. 'I wanted to clap. It serves her right. She's always poaching other people's contacts. She tried the same trick on Rupert when he first arrived. Unfortunately, she succeeded. But you want to watch your back, especially during your probation period. If you slip up, she'll ensure Jeremy knows.'

'How can I protect myself?' asked Joanna, wondering how she could ever perform well if she had to worry about Charlotte.

'Jeremy will ignore her so long as your figures are high. His only concern is money.' Rebecca paused. 'Did Rupert pick up any new clients at the lunch?'

'I'm not sure. Why?'

'His probation period ends in a couple of weeks and he confided to me yesterday that his figures are down. He did very well initially but he seems to have lost his nerve.'

Joanna pictured Rupert chewing apprehensively on his gold pencil. 'I'm not surprised, with people like Charlotte around. I'll be anxious too when the time comes for me to be offered a contract – or not.'

'Oh, you'll be all right,' Rebecca assured her. 'You won back old Sternhold.'

They continued across the bridge, walking slowly, relishing the leisure to chat.

'How are things with Patrick?' asked Joanna.

'He's moving out,' Rebecca sighed. 'He says it's because I make him feel inadequate, but I think he's met someone else. I just wish he'd tell me the truth.'

'I'm sorry.' Joanna recalled how hurt she'd been when Peter had confessed to a one-night stand, blaming her because she'd been working late and he'd felt neglected.

'Of course, my mother is delighted,' Rebecca went on. 'She never approved of Patrick because he's a Catholic and she wants me to marry a nice Jewish boy. Can you believe it? She's already phoned her friends to find out whose son is still available.'

Joanna couldn't help laughing.

When they reached the Strand, they stood on the corner gossiping until, reluctantly, they said goodnight and hailed separate taxis.

Joanna was on the point of making her first call to Hugo Porter when she noticed that LinkFund hadn't yet been authorised by Credit Clearance.

'If I don't contact Hugo today, I'll lose him,' she protested to Jeremy.

He picked up his internal extension. 'Credit?' he shouted. 'Why isn't LinkFund cleared? What! You haven't done it yet? What the hell do you think you're playing at. Joanna Templeton has worked her butt off to win this client. Don't you understand that every fund manager has scores of salesmen chasing after him, trying to do business? How can Joanna compete if you hold her up?' He slammed down the receiver.

An hour later LinkFund were cleared to deal and Hugo bought a million shares through Joanna, which she purchased in-house from Harry. It was her biggest commission to date and she felt immensely proud of herself.

That evening as she crossed the trading room, the market-makers clapped.

At Easter, Joanna visited her parents, who lived in Somerset, in a pretty village on the edge of the Quantock Hills. She drove down on Saturday morning – she would have travelled late on Friday but because Christopher had been killed at night her mother worried if Joanna drove after dark.

She arrived to find her father in the garden, standing unsteadily on the lower rungs of a ladder as he attempted to prune back the ivy which threatened to swamp the whole house. He was a small man, slightly balding, with fair fluffy sideburns which gave him a military air although he had never been in the army.

'Hello, there.' He waved his secateurs in her direction – and almost fell.

'Be careful!' she called.

'I'm all right.' With obvious relief he climbed down. 'Want a hand with your luggage?'

'No thanks. I can manage.'

She slung her bag over her shoulder. As she walked across the lawn towards him, her mother's long-haired dachshund raced to meet her.

'How are you, Mischief?' Joanna ran her hand down the length of his warm, round body, which made him wriggle with delight.

Her father gave her a whiskery kiss on the cheek. 'So glad

you've come, darling. You do us all good. We're longing to hear about the job. James, my new partner, is very impressed to hear you're with First Clarence. Apparently he tried to get in on their legal side after he qualified but they turned him down.' He stood back and studied Joanna. 'You've lost weight.'

'Only a few pounds, but it's a start.'

'Don't get too thin. You looked better . . . rounded. I keep telling that to Alice. Oh, by the way, she's hoping you'll help her with her maths A-level revision.' He paused, then added, 'Your mother's been a bit down again lately. Tenth anniversary soon.' He squeezed Joanna's hand.

She glanced towards the kitchen, fearful of what she might find. Her father had used those same words nine years earlier when her mother had had a breakdown. 'I'll go in,' she said.

He patted her shoulder. 'Yes, darling, you do that.' He returned to the ladder.

'Don't climb up,' she called after him. 'I'll cut the top.'

'No, darling, it's my job. I've always looked after the garden – and I want to.' He placed his foot on the lowest rung.

Knowing that it was pointless to argue, Joanna continued towards the house. She found her mother basting a roast chicken. Tall and very slim, she was bent over the open oven, her thick grey hair falling forward over her face like a safety curtain.

Joanna took a deep breath. 'Hello, Mum, how are you? Can I help?'

Her mother straightened up. 'Oh, hello, darling, I didn't hear you arrive. Have you seen Daddy? He's pruning the ivy. I do hope he doesn't fall.' She lowered her voice. 'Please tell him about your new job. He's a little . . . down today. The distraction would do him good.'

'Yes, Mum. Of course.' Joanna had been through this many times. 'I'll tell him about it at lunch.'

She went upstairs to find Alice, who was listening to the radio and gazing dreamily out of the window, text books unopened on the desk in front of her. 'Jo!' Alice jumped guiltily and reached for her revision.

'Day dreamer!' Joanna gave Alice's auburn pony-tail a gentle tug.

Alice pulled a face. 'I'm bored with revising, but Mum and Dad will be so upset if I don't pass every subject. You know what they're like.'

Joanna nodded. 'Since Christopher, they can't bear even the smallest setback. But don't worry. You'll pass. You're bright.'

'No, Jo, I'm not. At least, not like you. Mr Birtwhistle still refers to you as "our school's success".'

'There were lots of clever girls, but it's a dozy school. I'll help you with your maths.'

'This afternoon?'

'Whenever you like.' Joanna went next door and dumped her bag on one of the single beds in the spare room, which had been her bedroom before she left home. The window looked up towards the Quantocks. During her childhood Joanna had spent hours with her nose pressed against the pane as she watched the wild ponies grazing on the hills.

Over lunch she described her new job, omitting the sexual banter and the blatant greed which her parents would have found offensive.

Afterwards, when they were stacking the dishwasher, her mother asked, 'Have you patched things up with Peter yet?'

'No, this time it's for good.' She wondered how he was getting on with Judy.

Her mother looked distressed. 'I'm sorry. I was fond of him. Christopher liked him too.'

Joanna wanted to protest that she couldn't spend her life with Peter simply because he'd known Christopher, but she kept quiet for her mother's sake.

She passed the afternoon helping Alice with her maths. After tea they took Mischief for a walk. The air smelled of spring and the valleys were lush and green. From time to time they caught glimpses of deer moving through the tall, waving bracken.

'Lindsay hasn't been home for weeks,' Alice confided as they climbed up the stony path, away from the village. 'Mum thinks she has a new boyfriend. You know she got rid of James because he refused to become a vegetarian? She caught him eating meat in secret.'

Joanna giggled. 'I didn't know that.' She avoided the lethal thorns of a gorse bush. 'Lindsay and I hardly speak. When we do talk, she finds fault with what I say. We have nothing in common. It's a shame, but that's the truth.'

'Daddy says that Lindsay always felt excluded by you and Christopher.'

Joanna frowned. 'I hadn't thought of that. What about you, Alice? Did you feel left out?'

'Yes . . . but it didn't matter so much. I'm the youngest so I was used to being left with Mum. Lindsay felt humiliated when you two used to disappear on your ponies.'

'But she wouldn't ride.'

'She was frightened.'

They walked on in silence. Joanna thought about Alice's words.

'I suppose it was hard for Lindsay,' she said after a while. 'Christopher and I were yearners and Lindsay is . . . different. She's so pessimistic. He was full of life.' Joanna felt tears prick her eyes as she looked up at the windswept hill, and thought of the many times when they had walked across the hills and talked of their glorious futures. It had never occurred to them to include Lindsay.

VI

THE CORPORATE FINANCE department was to host an evening reception to celebrate the successful flotation of the Merantum Building Company. Any salesman who had placed over 50,000 shares was invited to attend. On Joanna's desk, only Rupert had failed.

The issue had been popular with private investors and institutions. On the first day of trading the price rose to 170p – a large enough premium to please investors but not so great that Sebastian Deveraux and his team could be accused of undervaluing the company.

Joanna had an exceptionally busy afternoon. At one point Jeremy had to divert her faxes to his own desk because she was too occupied to deal with them. At five to six, she hurried into the ladies' cloakroom, splashed cold water on her face to revive herself, retouched her make-up and ran a comb through her hair. Then she stepped back to examine herself in the full-length mirror. Her new suit of ice blue raw silk was extremely smart. The skirt, calf length with a slit up the front, looked demure until she sat down, when the slit revealed a flattering length of leg. It was a little daring for work, but she felt good in it – and she looked good. She knew that from the extra appreciative glances that morning as she crossed the trading room.

Only her face betrayed her exhaustion. Her eyes were hollow from stress and shortage of sleep. Her skin was deathly white from tiredness and lack of daylight. She took out her rouge and added more to her cheeks. Then she decided that she'd applied too much and rubbed some of it off with a tissue.

'Joanna!' Rebecca called from the corridor. 'Are you coming? We're waiting.'

'Yes . . . sorry.' She hurried to join her colleagues in the lift, arriving in time to hear Jeremy warn them, 'The Managing Director of Merantum has insisted on inviting some journalists. He's a great admirer of Adam Hunter at the *Sunday Chronicle*, especially after that upbeat article. Hunter will ferret out anything, so for Christ's sake be careful what you say – not that First Clarence has anything to hide!'

They all laughed politely.

The lift carried them to the fifteenth floor, where they stepped out into the sumptuous First Clarence entertaining suite. The party had only just begun but already the room was filling up, with waiters bearing trays of champagne circulating amidst dark-suited City figures, and the roar of predominantly male voices echoing out over the floodlit terrace to the roof-tops of London.

Joanna's colleagues dispersed to speak to their clients, leaving her alone. She didn't recognise anyone and for a moment she was assailed by the same gripping shyness she had experienced that first morning on her way to work, when she'd hidden in the shadows to recover her composure. Then, to her relief, she saw old Mr Fitterton waving to her. She hurried to him.

'Joanna! How's my brightest girl?' he asked, beaming.

'Very well, thank you. How are you? How is everyone?'

'Missing you, though I don't expect you think of us, not with all this extravaganza.'

'I missed Fittertons greatly at first,' she told him truthfully, recalling the terrifying days when she had failed to deal.

'But you're happy now?'

'Yes. Very.' She modified her pleasure so as not to hurt his feelings.

'Good.' He patted her arm. 'What a party! Even Quentin Brocklebank is here. I remember when he was just a junior barrister.' Mr Fitterton waved to the eminent Queen's Counsel, who stood nearly a head above the next tallest man in the room.

Joanna remained talking to Mr Fitterton until a client demanded his attention. As she moved away, Vikram intercepted her.

'Guess what I've heard,' he said, his eyes glittering over his orange juice. 'Sebastian has ditched Charlotte because she telephoned his wife.'

'Poor wife!'

'Don't waste your sympathy. His wife did the same to the previous Mrs Deveraux – and she had four children.'

'You're very censorious,' said Joanna.

'I don't believe in adultery.' Vikram glanced around the room. 'Oh, look! Karen has been accosted by that animal Bryan Rawdale.'

Joanna saw a large, redheaded man bending to speak to Karen whose chiselled face was turned away in disgust. 'If you were a gentleman, you'd rescue her,' she told Vikram.

'And incur the wrath of "those who really matter"?'

'What do you mean?'

'Bryan Rawdale is very important to First Clarence.'

'That man is a sex-pest. He was banned from Fittertons after he molested the receptionist.'

'He'll never be banned from First Clarence so long as he's useful. He's one of the sharpest Mergers and Acquisitions lawyers around and he's tolerated for the same reason that Jeremy tolerates me! Money! That's what it's all about, Joanna. Money – and sex.' Vikram lowered his voice and watched her expression as he added, 'What's all this about you and Harry?'

Joanna looked him straight in the eye. 'Nothing! And if I catch you inventing stories about me, Vikram, you'll be very sorry.'

Irritated by his muck-raking, Joanna moved on. As she did so, she noticed Sebastian Deveraux hurriedly break away from a group in order to greet a familiar-looking man in a beautifully tailored grey suit who had entered the room. He was powerfully built, with broad shoulders and large, expressive hands. The upper part of his face was handsomely elegant, the lower part was heavy, almost as though it belonged to someone else. He lifted his hand to run his fingers through his black hair, streaked with silver, whilst his dark eyes swept the room from beneath hooded, cobra lids.

The eyes landed on Jeremy. The two men looked at each other. Then Jeremy followed Sebastian to the stranger's side though, to Joanna's surprise, he walked slowly.

She turned away to talk to a client. When she looked back, Sebastian had disappeared. Jeremy alone was speaking to the stranger. He glanced in Joanna's direction, said something to the man, then beckoned to her.

She hesitated, thinking he wanted someone else nearby. He beckoned again. Still unsure, she crossed the room.

'Oliver,' he said, 'may I introduce Joanna Templeton, our newest star, whom I told you about on the telephone. Joanna, I don't think you have met Oliver Safarov.'

'No.' She blushed with pleasure, flattered at being singled out to meet such a highly respected City figure. 'But of course I have heard of you, Mr Safarov. Congratulations on your new appointment with Invest-Est Europe.'

'Thank you. Please call me Oliver.' He had a clipped, almost Germanic accent. 'Tell me, Joanna, what do you really think of the property market as a long-term investment?'

'Oh, the commercial property market is bound to pick up now the recession is ending – and Merantum have the capacity to be a major developer,' she replied eagerly, whilst Jeremy nodded his approval.

Oliver smiled at her enthusiasm. 'I hope you're right. I bought half a million.'

Whilst Jeremy repeated to Oliver how delighted First Clarence was to be involved with the Merantum flotation, Joanna tried to remember all she'd read about him.

A well-known name in financial circles, Oliver Safarov remained something of an enigma. Russian by birth, he'd been educated in England and France. He was a director of several medium-sized companies, as well as being chairman of Invest-Est Europe – an investment fund specialising in the least developed regions of Eastern Europe. He was known as a patron of the arts, especially Russian. At Christmas Joanna had read an article about a forthcoming exhibition of Russian icons. Beneath one of the illustrations had been printed: '*Reproduced with the kind permission of O. Safarov Esq.*'.

Jeremy was called away, and he excused himself to Oliver. With regret, Joanna took a step backwards, conscious that a circle of important people were waiting to speak to Oliver.

'Don't abandon me yet, Joanna,' he said, to her surprise. 'I want to talk to you.'

She was pleased, but a little uneasy. 'I ought not to monopolise you.' She indicated those waiting nearby.

'Your opinions interest me. Do you think the residential property market will surge ahead too?'

'Personally, no – at least, not as it has in the past.'

'Why is that?'

'Because there are fewer eighteen-year-olds today than there were in the sixties, so supply will satisfy demand. That's merely my own opinion,' she added quickly.

'If you're right, I shall invite you to lunch.'

'Oh . . . thank you.' She could hardly believe this was happening. A month earlier she'd been on the verge of dismissal. Now she was being invited to lunch by one of First Clarence's major private clients.

They were interrupted by Sebastian Deveraux. Joanna took her cue and slipped away. As she skirted around the room, seeking familiar faces, she was accosted by Bryan Rawdale.

'My compliments to the sexiest girl in this room,' he said, beckoning to a waiter to bring him another glass of champagne.

'Thank you.' She walked on.

'Oh, don't go!' He barred her path. 'I want you to have dinner with me.'

'Thank you, Mr Rawdale, but I already have an appointment.' She stepped smartly to one side, but her escape was blocked by a pedestal flower arrangement.

He reached out for her. 'What the bloody hell's the matter with you women? Don't you know you're only employed for sex?'

She pushed his arm away. 'Not with you, thank goodness!'

A tall, rangy man with a hawkish face, a shock of dark brown hair, and piercing blue eyes stepped between them. 'Leave her alone, Rawdale,' he ordered, with a touch of the north in his accent.

The lawyer flushed angrily, his face puce against his red hair. 'Don't you speak to me like that, you bloody snoop.'

The younger man moved closer. 'Fuck off!'

Joanna was shocked. People at City parties didn't talk to each other like that – even when they meant it. Bryan Rawdale was equally stunned. His mouth had dropped open like a goldfish. Without another word, he walked away.

'Thank you for saving me,' she told the stranger.

'Rawdale's a bully with a charming wife whom he doesn't deserve.'

'But you shouldn't say . . . er . . .'

'Fuck off?' He laughed at her discomfiture. 'Why not?'

'Because it's rude.'

'It's what I meant – and I always say what I mean.' He pushed up the sleeves of his blazer, and held out his arms in front of

Joanna. 'Would you fasten my cufflinks? I didn't have time before I left home. I'm always running late.'

She bent to secure them. 'They're beautiful,' she said, touching the oval of gold, plain except for the inscription 'R.H.'.

He watched her face, solemn as she concentrated. 'I cherish them greatly.'

'Why did Rawdale call you a snoop?'

'I'm a journalist.' He held out his right hand. 'Adam Hunter of the *Sunday Chronicle*.'

'Joanna Templeton.'

They shook hands. She glanced at the inscription on the cufflinks, and assumed they'd belonged to his father or grandfather.

'I enjoy your articles,' she told him. 'I was especially interested in the one you wrote last winter about the risk and reward of investing in emerging markets.'

'Thank you.' Adam was genuinely pleased.

'You were right about China and Turkey.'

'What a relief! You should see the vitriolic letters which swamp our postroom when I'm wrong.'

'Do readers blame you if they lose their money?'

'Naturally.'

'Do they thank you if they make a killing?'

'Of course not! They congratulate themselves on their financial acumen.'

She enjoyed his self-deprecatory reply. 'You write with such authority. That's why people believe you.'

Adam's eyes softened. 'I had a brilliant teacher.'

He turned to scrutinise the room, gazing over Joanna's head, an action which she found extremely rude. She noticed that Oliver was watching her from the far side of the room, and she smiled at him, thinking what good manners he had – unlike this rough, tough, barely civilised street-fighter.

'Oliver Safarov is a fascinating character,' Adam remarked casually.

'Yes – and very polite.'

Adam laughed at her rebuke. 'Do you know him well?'

'I had never met him before tonight.'

'He seems very interested in you.'

She was pleased but tried not to show it, shrugging off the compliment. 'Oh, I'm just a younger woman who's fascinated by his world.'

'Don't belittle yourself. Oliver Safarov is attracted by your intelligence. He could get a hundred younger, prettier women.'

Joanna flushed. 'Have you thought of attending a charm school?'

'You're too bright to be offended by the truth.'

'There's a difference between honesty and rudeness.'

He chuckled at her response. 'I imagine Safarov's invited to most of First Clarence's parties.'

'I don't know. I've only been here a month.'

'Congratulations! First Clarence are top league. Of course that's why Safarov seldom does business through anyone else. Very loyal of him, don't you agree?'

'If we're the best, why not stick with us?'

'Good point!'

She was marginally mollified by his praise.

'He must earn some lucky person a lot of commission,' Adam went on. 'Does he also deal on the institutional side?'

Joanna looked up sharply. Adam's eyes were fixed on Oliver. Appalled, she realised that this was no idle chat.

'I am not allowed to give interviews to the press,' she said, crisply.

'Don't worry! I always protect my sources.'

'You are totally unprincipled. By praising First Clarence, you attempted to lull me into discussing a client.'

'I'm a journalist. I seek information.'

'You're a bloody snoop. Bryan Rawdale was right.' She walked away, reproaching herself for being such a fool – and praying that she hadn't been indiscreet.

Joanna spent the remainder of the party worrying over her conversation with Adam Hunter. She would have confided in Felicity when she reached home, but she found her flatmate entertaining Max, with whom they'd shared a house during their final year at university. He was accompanied by his girlfriend, Emma.

'Hey, you look terrific!' Max enveloped Joanna in a bear hug. 'Who'd believe that you used to buy your clothes from Oxfam?'

'You look pretty prosperous yourself.' Joanna patted his navy cashmere sweater, stretched a little too tight over his broadening chest. 'Rich lawyer! Client lunches! No more economy tins of baked beans divided between the three of us.'

They laughed at the memory of their frugal student days.

Joanna took off her jacket, kicked off her shoes, and flopped into a chair. 'Have you seen Peter?' she asked Max, thinking how strange it was to enquire about the man with whom she'd spent half a decade.

'I had lunch with him yesterday.'

'Is he . . . all right?' She wondered if Peter had told Max about her visit.

'Er . . . yes. He's fine.'

Joanna would have liked to hear more, such as whether Peter was happy with his new girlfriend, but she sensed that Max didn't want to be questioned. 'It's OK. I'm not going to grill you,' she assured him. 'I know you want to remain friends with both of us.'

Max looked relieved. 'I do. I'm sorry that things didn't work between you, but Peter's a good chap.'

'He is,' she agreed, thinking how apt those words were.

They talked of other things: of Max's new flat, Emma's new job, and Felicity's new author. The evening was reminiscent of many they had shared at university – the endless discussions about the meaning of life around the kitchen table of their scruffy terraced house, the chaotic all-night parties drinking wine so cheap it could have doubled as paint-stripper, and, finally, the frenzied all-night revising.

For once, Joanna didn't talk much. She preferred to listen. But every so often her thoughts returned to the party, to her interrogation by Adam Hunter – and to Oliver Safarov.

VII

ON THE MORNING after the party, Joanna answered her telephone to Adam Hunter. 'I want to see you,' he said.

She was thrown off guard by his direct approach. 'I . . . er . . . can't.'

'I promise to attend that charm school.'

Joanna was very conscious of Jeremy seated beside her. 'I'm not allowed to talk to the press,' she replied. 'Please don't phone me again.'

'Adam Hunter?' asked Jeremy, as she came off the line.

She nodded.

'You did the right thing. I saw him corner you last night and I intended to warn you about him.' Jeremy moved off to speak to another salesman.

Joanna's phone rang again.

'Templeton,' she answered crisply, fearing that it was Adam, being persistent.

'Joanna? Is that you?'

It took her a moment to recognise the clipped tones of Oliver Safarov.

'Have I called at a bad moment?' he enquired.

She saw Jeremy leave the trading room. 'No. Absolutely not.'

'You sounded so fierce.'

'I had been dealing with a difficult call.'

'How tiresome.'

He paused. Silence hung between them. She waited, intrigued. Did he want Jeremy? Did he wish to deal? Did he want her?

'I enjoyed our talk,' he continued eventually.

So that was it. He wanted her. She felt a stir of excitement. 'I enjoyed it too.'

'I'd like you to lunch with me.'

'Has the residential property market proved me right already?'

He chuckled. 'Are you free next Tuesday? One o'clock, at my club?'

Joanna was flattered. Nevertheless, she hesitated. Lunch meant logging her absence from the desk, but she didn't want to explain that to Oliver because it would make her sound very junior – and she could hardly say that dinner would suit her better.

'Thank you,' she replied. 'I'd love to.'

She had the weekend in which to decide what to tell Jeremy.

Oliver gave her the address of The Archimedes, a famous and exclusive gentleman's club off St James's whose membership – Joanna had once read – was so select that most applicants died whilst still on the waiting list.

That evening, Joanna arrived home to find Felicity wading through a pile of ironing whilst watching the video of *Pretty Woman* for the fourth time.

'I have a problem,' she confided. 'I've met a man through work – a very important player – and he's invited me to lunch.'

Felicity put the video on hold. 'How exciting! Who is he?'

'Don't tell anyone – Oliver Safarov.'

'Heavens! He was mentioned in the *Interrogator* only last week. I was reading about him on the way to work. Or was it in *Private Eye*? No, it was the *Interrogator*.'

'What did they say?'

'Oh, nothing scandalous. Just that he was the epitome of the cultured European and that he spoke six languages fluently, a skill which more British businessmen should master.' Felicity held the iron aloft. 'What's he like?'

'Fascinating and incredibly powerful.' Joanna leaned against the back of the sofa. 'You can't imagine the contacts a man like that has, people I'd never normally meet.'

'You mercenary creature!'

'I work in a mercenary world. But I'm not having lunch with him solely for the good he could do my career. I like him.' Joanna paused, then confessed with a laugh, 'Though, in truth, I'd go even if I didn't. Oliver Safarov is a big name, and I'd be mad to refuse.'

Felicity studied Joanna's animated face. 'You find him attractive, don't you?'

'Yes. Who was it who said "power is the greatest aphrodisiac"?'

'I can't remember.' Felicity looked concerned. 'Jo, isn't Oliver Safarov a bit old for you?'

'I like older men.'

'You've never had one.'

'That's why I like them!'

Felicity shook her head and continued ironing. 'So, what's the dilemma?'

'I'm meant to log out at lunchtime and name the client I'm meeting. That is First Clarence's policy. Oliver isn't my client, but he's a bank client and I don't want everyone on the desk gossiping – not that there's anything to gossip about.'

'Not yet!' Felicity gave Joanna an exaggerated wink.

Joanna tossed a cushion in her direction. 'Don't look at me like that! We're only having lunch.'

'All affairs have to start somewhere.'

'I wouldn't risk my job.' Joanna spoke with more conviction than she felt.

When Joanna stepped from her taxi outside The Archimedes, she found Oliver waiting for her.

'I am so glad you could come,' he said, taking her by the elbow to escort her inside.

'So am I.' Felicity was wrong. He didn't seem too old.

He ushered her across the beautiful, flagged hall and into the oak-panelled dining room – the only room where ladies were permitted.

'This club was founded by an eighteenth-century devotee of Greece,' he explained. 'New members still have to recite, in ancient Greek, this Archimedean saying.' He pointed at the inscription over the door, and translated, 'Give me somewhere to stand, and I will move the earth'. Then he lowered his voice as they passed two elderly gentlemen. 'I think some members are past moving.'

Joanna laughed. There was something in the way Oliver confided this little aside to her which suggested that he would not say it to everyone.

He had reserved a table in an alcove near the window and, from the way in which he spoke to the waiter about the menu, he clearly lunched there often. After carefully questioning Joanna about the kind of food she liked, he ordered for her – something she'd never allowed Peter to do – proposing a cold coriander soup followed by poached salmon, the exact dishes she would have chosen for herself.

Finally, he selected a very light white wine, explaining, 'I know you have to work this afternoon.'

She smiled. 'I do – unfortunately.'

'I saw you being harassed by that bore, Bryan Rawdale,' he said, as soon as the waiter retreated. 'I was on the point of coming to save you when you sent him packing.'

'Bryan Rawdale is a renowned pest.' She was surprised that Oliver hadn't noticed Adam's intervention.

'Why don't First Clarence ban him?'

'Because he's . . .' Joanna stopped, not wanting to criticise her bank. 'I don't know.'

'Because he's the best lawyer in his field and he makes them money, so they turn a blind eye?' Oliver finished her sentence, repeating Vikram's sentiments.

Joanna felt awkward. 'I wasn't criticising First Clarence.'

'No,' he replied. 'I said it, and I think it's disrespectful to you women to invite a man like that.' He fixed her with his dark eyes. 'Do you play chess, Joanna?'

She had been thinking how unusual he was to be so concerned, and his sudden change of subject threw her. 'Yes . . . I do . . . but not well.'

'Rawdale is like the Bishop – so bent he can only move diagonally.'

She laughed, but she was shocked. 'Surely he isn't dishonest?'

'Of course not. I was joking.' He leaned back in his chair to allow the waiter to remove his plate. 'Chess is the greatest game in the world. It's like life. The best player wins. There is no luck, just skill.'

'Don't you believe in luck?'

'I believe some people are born lucky, but without skill they make no use of it.'

He asked where she had grown up and she told him about her parents, the village, the Quantocks, Christopher, her sisters.

'You were born lucky,' he said, which stunned her – because of Christopher, she saw her family as wounded. 'How I envy you that safe childhood. I was born in Riga, at the end of the German occupation of Latvia. It wasn't a pleasant time or place to be.'

'I thought you were Russian.'

'I consider myself Russian because my father's family were. My grandfather came from St Petersburg. He was a committed liberal, not a state of mind appreciated by the Tsar or the Soviets. When Latvia became independent in 1920, he escaped to Riga. Have you been there?'

She shook her head.

'Latvia's one of those endlessly invaded countries. It had only twenty years of independence before being annexed by Russia in 1940, then invaded by Germany in 1941. So my wretched grandfather spent all his life in fear of arrest by one side or the other.' Oliver picked up a bread roll and turned it slowly before tearing it in half. 'The insecurity and fears brought about by such a history are incomprehensible for you, British islanders.'

Joanna was beginning to feel guilty because England had not been invaded since William the Conqueror. 'How did you get to the West?' she asked.

'My mother is French and she had kept her passport – thank God! At the end of the war, she managed to escape on a boat to Sweden.'

'And your father?'

'He was dead.'

'How sad for her.'

'She has her memories.'

'A poor substitute for reality.'

'That depends. My mother met my father when she was teaching French to the children of a Swedish diplomat in Riga. She was eighteen and very beautiful – she still is.' He smiled fondly. 'When the Swedish family fled at the outbreak of war, she refused to leave. She moved in with my grandfather, who taught her Russian – we always speak Russian together.'

'Where was your father?' asked Joanna, picturing her own father, solemnly pondering the minor legal problems of a small village.

'He was away . . . fighting . . . somewhere.'

'That must've been awful for your mother.'

'It was! The Germans commandeered my grandfather's house. He and my mother had to live in a freezing basement with no fuel and little food. When I was born, he delivered me.'

'Did you . . . know your father?'

Oliver frowned. 'He saw me once, towards the end of the war, just after I was born. He died soon afterwards.'

'How tragic for your mother. To go through the whole war, and then lose the man she loved.'

He gave a thin smile. 'Perhaps – but she hardly knew him. They'd never lived together. He might not have been . . . as she imagined.'

They fell silent whilst the waiter brought their coffee. Joanna had a feeling that she'd offended Oliver, although she wasn't sure how. It was simply that the warmth with which he had greeted her on the doorstep of the club had been replaced by a certain distance.

'How did you come to live in England?' she enquired, in an attempt to regain the harmony.

'My mother married an English officer, a widower.'

'Did you like England?'

'No, I hated it. I was sent to boarding school.'

Silence fell again. Oliver stared into the distance, his face stiff, his expression one of distaste. This time, Joanna gave up.

'But I was very fond of my stepfather.' Oliver suddenly relaxed. 'He made my mother happy and gave her security – and he left me three thousand pounds, which was a lot of money thirty years ago. I placed it all on the stock market – and quadrupled my investment!'

Joanna laughed – in part at his story and in part because the dark cloud had lifted.

'I ought to go,' she said, reluctantly consulting her watch. 'Heavens! It's after three.'

'Jeremy won't mind.'

'Actually . . . I haven't told him that I'm lunching with you. Trading rooms are hives of gossip, so I pretended I was meeting a friend.' She blushed, afraid that she sounded silly and presumptuous.

'I understand and I agree,' he replied. 'I hate tittle-tattle. We'll say nothing – to anyone. It's our secret.'

'Thank you.'

He asked the waiter to call her a taxi, rose, and held her chair.

'I didn't know Oliver was a Russian name,' she remarked as they retraced their steps across the flagstoned hall.

'My real name is Arkady, as was my father's and his father's but I changed it when I came to England. By then Russia was England's enemy – the evil empire, the nuclear threat. It was not pleasant being a small Russian boy in an English boarding school.'

'Why choose Oliver?'

'Because *Oliver Twist* was the first English book I read – and Oliver always wanted more.'

They stepped out into the street. She thanked him for lunch. He handed her into the taxi, which swept her back to the City. But she was barely aware of the journey. She went over her conversation with Oliver – she couldn't help feeling deflated that he hadn't suggested a further meeting.

VIII

BY THE TIME Joanna reached First Clarence, she was reproaching herself for having been so unwise as to risk Jeremy's wrath. She decided to tell him the truth about her lunch appointment, but when she reached the trading room she saw that his seat was empty. Her colleagues were busy dealing. The market was rocketing, fuelled by an upbeat set of trade figures. No one appeared to have noticed her long absence.

She slipped into her chair and, almost immediately, received a fax from Mr Frederick at New Aldren Fund, one of her offshore clients in Grand Cayman. He instructed her to purchase 150,000 shares in a large, ailing computer components company called Fact-Select. The shares, currently quoted at 40p, had halved in the past two months and the company had been down-graded by nearly every analyst.

'Someone thinks Fact-Select is worth a punt,' she remarked to Simon as she faxed confirmation of the deal to Mr Frederick, imagining him a sun-roasted, slick businessman lying under a palm tree drinking rum.

He glanced at his screen. 'They've just moved up to forty-one pence. Can't think why.'

She shrugged. 'Nor can I. The Head Boffin said they might go to the wall.'

Jeremy returned in an excellent mood. 'I've ordered a birthday present.' He beamed excitedly. 'A top of the range BMW.'

'Many happy returns.' She decided that if Jeremy didn't ask why she'd been away so long, it was pointless to volunteer the information.

'Thanks,' he replied, 'but it's not till Sunday. Don't ask how old I am. That's becoming a sore point.'

Five minutes before the market closed, Joanna's fax machine

whirred into action. It was a buying order from Mr Lawrence at Società Hadini in Monte Carlo for 200,000 Fact-Select maximum price 42p. Quickly, she checked the yellow strip. First Clarence were giving the best price, so she placed the deal in-house.

'That's two buyers for Fact-Select,' she told Jeremy. 'I wonder what's going on.'

'Oh . . . who bought?'

'New Aldren Fund and Società Hadini, two of my offshore companies.'

'What's their maximum loss if Fact-Select goes down the tube?'

'Sixty grand for New Aldren Fund and eighty plus for Società Hadini.'

He yawned. 'Oh . . . they're just speculating. Fact-Select has good software but it's underfunded and badly managed.'

'The kind of company which could attract a buyer?'

'Possibly.'

Shortly afterwards, Jeremy called Rupert into a side office. When Rupert returned, he looked even paler than usual.

'Are you all right?' enquired Joanna, thinking he was ill.

Rupert pulled a face. 'I'm on probation for another three months.'

'Bad luck – but at least you're still here,' she said, in an attempt to make him feel better.

'Yes. That's something.' He slumped dejectedly into his seat.

Joanna carried on with her work – and tried not to worry about her own contract. Her probation period would be up in June. Would she be offered a permanent position, an extension – or nothing?

Several hours later, as she prepared to go home, Jeremy's secretary appeared in the trading room carrying an enormous bouquet of white lilies.

'Joanna,' she called. 'These are for you.' With a sigh of envy, she laid the exquisite blooms on Joanna's desk.

The market-makers looked up from their screens and whistled.

'You've broken my heart,' called Harry. 'You've been unfaithful to me. You women are all the same.'

'So are you men,' responded Joanna, laughing.

She wondered if the flowers were from Oliver, but that seemed unlikely. Then she thought of Peter. He'd sent her white lilies as a peace offering after he'd confessed to being unfaithful.

'Someone appreciates you, Joanna,' said Jeremy, looking amused.

'They certainly do.' Rebecca leaned over the desk to admire them. 'They're beautiful. Who are they from?'

Joanna could see a small white envelope nestling among the stems. Carefully, she extracted it from the Cellophane wrapping and slit the top. Inside was Oliver's own embossed card on which he had written '*Thank you for lunch*'.

'Come on! Tell us!' urged Rebecca.

Joanna tried to sound unfazed. 'Oh . . . just someone I used to know.'

She picked up her briefcase and her bouquet, and sauntered out of the trading room to accompanying cheers and wolf whistles.

Joanna did her best to discover Oliver's home address so that she could thank him, but he wasn't listed in the telephone directory and she didn't want to court curiosity by enquiring at First Clarence. She was extremely occupied at work, both during the day and in the evening. Nevertheless, she was more disappointed than she cared to admit when the days passed and she heard nothing more from Oliver.

One morning the Head Boffin evaluated a rumour that someone was about to bid for Fact-Select. 'We've phoned the company, but they refuse to confirm or deny it,' he told the meeting. 'So we rate Fact-Select as a very high-risk buy.'

Joanna was in a dilemma. She wanted to give Mr Sternhold a really profitable tip so as to re-establish his belief in First Clarence, but she was afraid to jeopardise his tentative goodwill by recommending a speculative venture. On the other hand, if she didn't tell him about Fact-Select some other salesman would.

Eventually she telephoned him, heavily emphasising the risk.

'Are you trying to persuade me not to buy?' he asked her gruffly.

'Oh, no, Mr Sternhold. It's just that I . . . er . . . don't want you to make a loss through me.'

He was silent and thoughtful. Then he said, 'I'll buy a hundred thousand at fifty pence, Miss Templeton, but if you're wrong I never want to hear from you again.'

Joanna repeated his instruction, almost wishing that he hadn't given her an order.

To increase her fears, next morning as she ate a hurried breakfast whilst listening to 'Dawn Traders', she heard a well-known City analyst give an interview in which he said the rumoured bid for Fact-Select was nothing more than speculation.

When the market opened, the shares had dropped back to 45p.

Her first phone call was from Mr Sternhold. 'Your analysts are useless,' he barked at her. 'My holding has fallen by ten per cent in one day.'

She was determined not to be bullied. 'Mr Sternhold, I did warn you that Fact-Select were high-risk.'

'Miss Templeton, if these shares crash I shall expect you to dump them without charge.' He slammed down the receiver.

Joanna turned to Jeremy. 'That was Sternhold. He wants me to sell without commission. Can I do it? If I don't, I'll lose him.'

'Not on this deal. You told him that Fact-Select were high-risk. Sternhold's an experienced fund manager. He knows the game.'

'But I hate to lose a client – especially one I've tried so hard to recapture.'

'That's why you're a good salesman.'

'Thank you.' She was gratified. Perhaps she would be offered a full contract.

By the end of the day Fact-Select had plummeted to 30p. Each time Joanna answered a call, she expected a verbal lashing from Mr Sternhold, but he didn't phone.

She arrived home exhausted, thankful to have a rare evening to herself. No sooner she had relaxed into a bath with a glass of wine and the radio than the telephone rang. She reached for the receiver, her wet arm dripping on the carpet.

'Hello,' she answered, splashing as she leaned back into the scented warm water.

'Joanna?'

'Yes.' She thought she recognised Oliver's voice but was afraid to say his name in case she was wrong.

'This is Oliver Safarov. We seem to have a bad line. I can hear water.'

She gave an embarrassed laugh. 'I'm in the bath.'

'Would you prefer me to ring back later?'

She nearly said yes, then she changed her mind. This was no business call. 'Not at all,' she replied. 'Thank you so much for the beautiful flowers.'

'I would have had them delivered to your home but I wasn't

sure if anyone would be there to receive them. I hope I didn't embarrass you by sending them to First Clarence.'

'My female colleagues were wildly envious. They kept asking me who'd sent them.'

'But you didn't say?'

'Of course not.' She was glad that he didn't know about the traders' ribald remarks. 'I would have written to thank you, but I couldn't find your address.'

'Isn't it on First Clarence's computer?'

'Yes, on the central system – I imagine – but only heads of sections can see that.'

'How ethical of you not to look.'

She didn't tell him that she lacked the code.

'I want to hear about your day,' he told her. 'I hope you're making lots of money, but not having to work too hard.'

'Oh, this afternoon was frantic. There's great speculation about Fact-Select.' She wasn't revealing anything which was not common knowledge.

'Do you think they'll be taken over?'

'Impossible to say, but they're ripe for it. They have a good product. They're just underfunded.'

'Exactly my opinion.'

She was pleased, and wondered if he'd bought shares in Fact-Select, but she didn't like to ask.

'I believe that Jeremy is a great motivator,' he went on.

'Yes, he is.' She was too discreet to add that he could also be a pig.

'Quite different from old Mr Fitterton?'

She was surprised. 'How did you know I used to work at Fittertons?'

'Joanna, you told me.'

'Did I?' She didn't recall having done so.

They discussed the market further, and she couldn't help remembering how Peter had never wanted to hear about her work.

'I'll have to say goodbye in a minute,' he said. 'I'm due to give a talk this afternoon.'

'This afternoon!' she repeated, puzzled.

'I'm calling from Boston. Didn't I tell you? I'm visiting my eldest daughter who's at university here and I've been asked to speak to the economics students.'

'Are you . . . still married?' she asked, wishing to discover how the land lay.

'I have been divorced for seven years. If I were still married, I would have told you. I wouldn't invite a woman to dine with me under false pretences.'

She sank lower into the scented water. 'You haven't asked me to dinner.'

'I am now.'

She was suddenly uncertain whether he had intended to invite her, or if she'd put him in a position where he couldn't do otherwise without being rude.

'I'd love to come, but I'm sure you must be terribly busy,' she said, proferring him an escape.

He ignored her offer. 'Let's say . . . Thursday night.'

'Thank you.' Clearly, he had meant it.

'We'll dine at my home. Do you know anything about Russian art?'

'I'm afraid not.'

'Good. I look forward to teaching you. Shall I send my chauffeur to collect you at eight?'

She was on the verge of accepting, when past experiences reminded her that it was preferable to have her own transport. Even the most eagerly anticipated evening could prove a disaster.

'Please don't worry,' she replied. 'I'll drive myself.'

He didn't persist but gave her his address, naming one of the smartest streets in Holland Park.

After they had said goodbye, Joanna lay back in the bath, sipping her wine, smiling. This powerful, influential man was interested in her and he made her feel important. She pictured him in sedate Boston, where she had once been caught in a snowstorm, and realised that if his daughter was at university, she must be older than Alice. That put Oliver in the same decade as her mother. This seemed incredible. Oliver was sensuous and exciting, a man whom she found increasingly attractive. Her parents were parents.

Joanna hadn't had many lovers because she had been with Peter for so long. Other men had come into her life only when she and Peter were in their 'off' periods. All had been the product of her failing relationship: used to get away from Peter or to get her own back or to fill the lonely gap. Oliver was different. He was a man of the world.

She had an added sparkle in her eyes when she arrived at work next morning.

'Who's my lucky rival?' asked Harry, as she passed his desk.

She laughed – and walked on.

'Love makes up for the bad news on Fact-Select, eh?'

She backtracked. 'What news?'

'They're opening at twenty-five pence. Don't you read the papers? They all think Fact-Select are a goner.'

'Oh, no!' She hurried to her desk. Her screen confirmed Harry's words. She opened her paper and scanned the pages for news. The editorial decried the plague of unfounded rumours in the market, saying '*No one on this newspaper has forgotten the tragedy of Carthew Instruments*.'

'What was the story behind Carthew?' she asked Jeremy, as she tried to recall the details.

'The editor of the *Sunday Chronicle* was a manic depressive, only no one there seemed to realise. God knows why! A couple of years ago he had a breakdown and wrote an article, based on sheer rumour, downgrading Carthew, which then went bankrupt.'

'Because of that one article?'

Jeremy shrugged. 'Richard Holdfast was brilliant. His word counted as fact. Carthew's bank panicked and foreclosed.'

'What happened to Holdfast?'

'He shot himself.'

'I remember now. How sad!' Joanna thought of the way Adam Hunter's face had softened when he'd said, 'I had a brilliant teacher,' and wondered if he'd been referring to Richard Holdfast.

Fact-Select opened at 25p. Deciding that it was preferable to confront Sternhold rather than wait for his irate call, Joanna tapped out his number.

'I'm surprised at your courage,' he said. 'I didn't expect to hear from you again.'

'You're my client, Mr Sternhold. It's my responsibility to keep you informed.' She gave him the analysts' view, trying to make it sound less gloomy.

He allowed her to finish without interruption. 'You've lost half of my money, Miss Templeton. Advise me immediately of any further adverse news.' As usual, he cut her off without saying goodbye.

'At least Sternhold hasn't sold yet.' Joanna recounted the call to Jeremy. 'To hear him speak, you'd think I'd prised the money from his clenched fists.'

He smiled. 'Oh, Sternhold's a canny old devil. He must have believed Fact-Select were a good risk. In any case, you've done well. This is the first time he's dealt through us for months.'

'I don't want it to be the last.'

By mid-morning Fact-Select had dropped another two points.

'They're going to the wall,' shouted Vikram. 'We're in for a bloodbath.' Quickly, he moved to warn his clients.

Feeling slightly sick, Joanna steeled herself to speak to Sternhold. As she keyed in his number for the second time, her screen flashed.

News Update. Confirmed bid of 50p per share for Fact-Select.

'Someone up there definitely loves me!' she exclaimed, laughing with sheer relief as she watched the price start to rise. When it touched 50p, she telephoned Mr Sternhold.

'The bid has been confirmed,' she told him triumphantly.

'Miss Templeton, the shares stand at exactly what I paid for them. I want to see a profit.'

'They'll go up, Mr Sternhold.'

'They'd better, Miss Templeton.' This time he said goodbye.

Fact-Select turned down the initial offer, but after a few days of stand-off they accepted a revised bid of 70p per share. Società Hadini and New Aldren Fund made a healthy profit. Mr Sternhold made 20,000 pounds. It was a small gain, but Joanna was delighted – and intensely relieved.

IX

JOANNA WORE A plain black linen dress for her dinner with Oliver. She'd bought it in Rome the previous autumn. She had gone there with Felicity – Peter disliked Mediterranean countries – and they'd spotted the dress in the window of a boutique in Via Condotti. It has cost her a fortune, even in the sale, and she'd never worn it. By the time they returned to London it was too cold and after she gave up smoking she'd put on weight. Now, at last, she could fit into it again.

'Do I look all right?' she asked Felicity, emerging from her bedroom.

Felicity put aside a manuscript she was editing. 'Perfect. Sexy, but elegant. Oliver will be drooling.'

'Jewellery?' Joanna held a thin gold chain around her neck to see the effect.

'Subtle. Or maybe none.' Felicity wiggled her eyebrows suggestively. 'So he'll take the hint and buy you some.'

Joanna swiped the air in her direction. 'I am *not* interested in Oliver's money.'

'Then what is the attraction? Power or sex?'

'Both!'

'You brazen hussy! What would poor old Peter say?'

'I dread to think.' Joanna retouched her red lipstick. 'Why shouldn't I have an adventure? I haven't had sex since . . .' She stopped, recalling her last encounter with Peter. 'Do you remember at university, when we used to huddle around one paraffin heater and joke about meeting rich men who'd whisk us away to hot countries?'

'And hot dinners.'

'Yes. No more shared tins of beans. Well, Oliver Safarov is that dream rich man. But I also like him. He's fascinating.'

'Am I to understand that I should put the chain on the door when I go to bed?'

'Definitely not!' Joanna replied emphatically. 'He hasn't even kissed me on the cheek. In any case, I'm still concerned about him being a client. I'd hate anyone at work to find out. Luckily, he feels the same way.'

'He seems to like you a great deal,' said Felicity.

'Yes, I *think* he does, though sometimes he seems very distant and I'm not sure why.' Joanna snapped her bag shut, picked up her jacket and her car keys, and headed for the door. There, she halted. 'I'm nervous,' she confessed.

Felicity smiled encouragingly. 'You'll be fine when you get there. You always are.'

'Thanks.' Joanna said goodnight and hurried out before she could succumb to another attack of uncertainty.

Oliver's house was a magnificent, pillared, detached residence set back from the road, with its own circular driveway of immaculately swept gravel. There were two cars parked outside, a black Bentley and a red E-type Jaguar. As Joanna drove in, the front door opened and Oliver hurried down the steps to greet her.

'I've been looking forward to this evening,' he said.

'So have I.' Felicity was right. Now that she'd arrived, she felt perfectly confident.

Oliver held the car door as Joanna stepped out. 'That dress looks Italian.'

She smiled. 'You're right. How did you guess?'

'Because I love Italian clothes.'

He ushered her up the wide front steps and into a mirrored hall where an elderly but ramrod-straight butler took her jacket.

'This is Withers, without whom my life would be in chaos,' Oliver introduced him.

'Good evening.' Joanna smiled at the butler, thinking what a luxury it must be to have your home run like a five-star hotel.

'Good evening, Miss.' Withers gave her a small, almost military bow.

Oliver led the way into the drawing room. It was extremely opulent, with windows draped in heavy red velvet curtains and walls so densely covered in gold and silver icons that there was hardly an inch between their frames. The furniture was equally ornate. The antique chaise-longue was upholstered in heavy gold brocade, the highly polished tables displayed silver samovars and amber figurines, and on the mantelpiece, either side of an intricate ormolu clock, were six Fabergé eggs. Joanna found it intriguing and very foreign.

'It's fascinating,' she said, looking around her.

'I'm glad you approve.' Oliver handed her a glass of champagne without asking her what she would like to drink. 'One of the most famous icons is the Virgin of Kazan. This is a particularly valuable version.' He pointed to a small, exquisite representation of the Virgin Mary, her mosaic-haloed head inclined towards a child who looked more like a ten-year-old boy than a baby. 'The gold covering which leaves just the hands and face bare is called a riza.'

Joanna studied the icon closely. 'It's beautiful.'

Oliver looked up at the face of the Virgin. 'She belonged to my grandfather's family. This icon was the only item of value he took with him when he left Russia. My mother brought it with her when she left Latvia. She planned to use it to bribe her way out if she was stopped, but luckily she didn't have to.' He was silent for a moment, lost in thought, then he took Joanna by the arm and led her to the chaise-longue, saying, 'I want to hear all your news. How's the market? What do you think of the Fact-Select takeover?'

She was on familiar ground. 'I'm glad for my more speculative clients.'

'Do you have many?'

'Oh . . . some.'

'Surely they knew the risks?' he said.

'Of course. Fact-Select wasn't a wild punt. The potential for profit was clear.'

'I totally agree.' His smile praised her.

'Did you . . . buy any?' she ventured, hoping he didn't think her question impertinent.

He shook his head. 'I wish I had, but by the time I became aware of the rumoured bid, the price had moved.'

She recalled Mr Sternhold's rage. 'It went down again.'

'Yes, but I was too slow. Unlike you, I'm not able to attend the analysts' meeting.'

His choice of words made Joanna feel slightly awkward. She was unsure if they were merely a comment, or a hint that he'd like her to pass him details of the morning meetings. As a First

Clarence client he had a right to information – but from his own broker on the private client side, not from her.

Dinner was served by Withers in a similarly luxuriant dining room. Oliver and Joanna sat at one end of a rich mahogany table, and dined by the light of twenty silver candles. The food was delicious but Joanna was very conscious of Withers' presence, although Oliver did his best to put her at ease. He regaled her with stories about famous Wall Street characters, making her laugh.

As soon as Withers withdrew, Oliver reached across the table and laid his hand on top of Joanna's. 'I wasn't suggesting that you should give me confidential information,' he said.

'Oh . . . I know you weren't.' She reproached herself for being so suspicious.

He smiled. 'Good. Now let's have some coffee.' Only then did he remove his hand.

They returned to the drawing room. Joanna settled herself on the chaise-longue, and crossed her legs provocatively. She watched Oliver pour the coffee. She liked the way he held the delicate cups in his large hands,.

'I find you very attractive, Joanna,' he said, looking serious.

'Thank you.' She leaned back, and her skirt rode up her thighs.

He sat down beside her. They drank their coffee.

Then he removed the cup and saucer from her hand. 'In fact, I find you irresistible.'

She turned to him and smiled, purposely inviting. He put his arm around her and drew her close. She lifted her face to him and he kissed her gently, his mouth covering hers. She responded, parting her lips beneath his. He kissed her hard, hungrily, crushing her to him. Briefly she thought of the morning – she had an even earlier start than usual – but what the hell! She wanted him. She wanted sex.

He laid his hand on her thigh. She uncrossed her legs. His fingers moved higher; he touched the lace edging of her pants.

The ormolu clock struck midnight. They stared at it.

'I ought to go,' she said, without meaning it.

'I want you to stay.' His voice was hoarse. 'But you're right. We must be sensible. It's late. You have to work tomorrow and I'm on an early flight to Moscow.'

She was disappointed – and surprised – but told herself that it was for the best.

Oliver rose and held out his hand to her. 'Do you mind if I don't accompany you home? My chauffeur will follow you in my car to make sure you are safe.'

'Thank you.' She didn't say that she frequently drove around on her own at night.

He slipped his arms around her waist and drew her close to give her a farewell kiss, but when their lips touched he pulled her fiercely to him so that she felt him stiff and hard against her. She moved her hips, and he stroked his forefingers up the backs of her legs. Then, suddenly, he seized her buttocks, squeezing them so hard that he hurt her – or, almost.

'If you don't stop, I shall refuse to leave,' she whispered against his mouth.

'You're irresistible.' He held her at arm's length, astonishing her with his self-control.

He escorted her out to her car. The chauffeur was already waiting beside the Bentley – the E-type had gone.

'I'll be back as soon as I can,' Oliver assured her. Then he stepped aside to watch as she drove away.

Joanna didn't hear from Oliver for several days, during which time she began to fear that he had changed his mind – or that she'd scared him off by coming on too strong. Then he telephoned her at work from Moscow.

'I am flying back to London this evening, just for a couple of hours,' he said. 'I know it's short notice, but can you meet me? I want to attend a preview of an auction at Sotheby's. There's a particular icon I'm interested in. Can you come? Can you leave work early? I long to see you, Joanna.' His voice sent a shiver down her spine as she relived the moment when he had pulled her to him.

'I have a client meeting at six, but it shouldn't last for more than an hour.' She cursed her full diary.

'Come afterwards. But don't be too long. My flight leaves at eleven.'

'I'll escape as soon as I can.'

'I'll be waiting.'

For the remainder of that day, Joanna found it hard to concentrate on work.

She arrived at Sotheby's nearly an hour later than intended and found Oliver talking to an elegant silver-haired woman. He beckoned her to him, saying, 'Lady Fircroft, may I introduce Miss Templeton?'

'How do you do?' Lady Fircroft touched Joanna's hand with her tiny, gloved fingers. 'Are you an expert in Russian art too, dear? Such an interesting subject. Of course I'm indebted to Mr Safarov. He's so generous to my refugee children's charity.'

Oliver seemed embarrassed by her effusive praise. 'You give me too much credit.'

'Not at all. You deserve it. You're far too modest.' She patted him on the arm. 'Oh dear, there's that princess. What is her name? I can't remember, but I simply must talk to her. She's awfully dull but so benevolent – as you are, my dear Mr Safarov.' She patted Oliver again, and moved away.

Oliver turned to Joanna. 'I was worried. You're late. I have to leave in an hour.'

'I'm sorry. My client wanted a more detailed meeting than I'd anticipated.'

'It's all right. I understand. Your career is very important. I was only afraid that you would . . . let me down.'

'Of course I wouldn't!' She was stunned. 'I would have come – however late. Didn't I say I would?'

'Not everyone is as good as their word.'

'I am,' she said firmly.

'Which is why I like you, Joanna.'

He guided her to the far end of the room, his hand tucked under her elbow.

'The icon in which I am interested is top right,' he whispered. 'Glance at it casually, no more. I don't want the dealers to know I'm interested.'

Joanna pretended to study all the icons on the wall whilst focusing on the one which Oliver intended to bid for. It was a small, rather dark oil painting of St Nicholas with an unadorned gold riza.

'Do you like it?' he asked.

'I prefer your grandfather's.'

He looked genuinely touched. 'Thank you. I prefer it too. But this icon is rarer. It would be a good investment.'

Joanna recalled his drawing room, with barely an inch of wall space free. 'But would you ever sell it?'

He laughed. 'You've discovered my guilty secret. I'm a collector. I hate to part with anything.'

They left the party soon afterwards. As they were walking towards the Bond Street exit, Oliver suddenly stopped. Outside, on the pavement, there were a couple of photographers.

'Could we leave by another door?' he asked the porter.

'Er . . . of course, Mr Safarov.'

'It's for the lady's sake,' Oliver explained, putting a protective arm around Joanna. 'Could you tell my chauffeur to come round to the back.'

Joanna was a little embarrassed. 'I think the press are waiting for the princess, not us,' she whispered.

'Of course they are. But if the princess leaves by the back as well, then they might make do with a picture of us – and I wouldn't want you to be the subject of gossip at work.'

'Thank you.' She was pleased that he remembered and, as she confided to Felicity when she reached home, this fact reassured her.

X

JOANNA DIDN'T SEE Oliver for several weeks, although he telephoned her frequently from Moscow, St Petersburg, Prague, Krakow and Bratislava. On the one occasion when he did return to London, she had to take a client out to dinner and couldn't see him – much as she would have liked to.

On the first Friday in June, First Clarence were due to entertain clients at the Goodwood evening race meeting. That morning, as Joanna was about to leave for work, with her black Italian linen dress draped over her arm, Oliver telephoned.

'I'm coming to Goodwood tonight,' he said.

She felt a surge of excitement. 'That's wonderful! I didn't know you'd accepted.'

'I hadn't, but I've changed my mind. I want to see you.'

'I want to see you too,' she replied, reaching inside her cupboard to return the black dress. She could hardly wear the same thing twice. In its place she selected a cream suit and a pair of high heels which flattered her legs.

Late that afternoon, when the market had closed, she and Rebecca changed in the ladies' cloakroom.

'You're mad to wear those shoes,' said Rebecca, eyeing Joanna's heels. 'You'll sink into the grass.'

'Oh, they're really quite comfortable.' Joanna tried not to teeter as they hurried down to the waiting limousine.

They arrived at Goodwood as the sun dipped behind the stadium, casting long shadows across the velvety green lawn. It was a glorious early summer evening and the racecourse was filling up rapidly. The bars were packed with people drinking champagne and there were long queues at the windows in the betting area.

Jeremy was pacing up and down outside the hospitality suite.

He hurried over as soon as he saw his team. 'Can any of you ride?' he enquired.

'Why?' asked Vikram. 'Are they short of jockeys?'

Everyone laughed, then stopped when they saw that Jeremy was serious.

Rebecca shook her head, Simon said he'd ridden once, Vikram pulled a face.

'I had a pony when I was a child,' said Joanna.

'So did I,' said Rupert.

Jeremy did not hesitate in his choice. 'It will have to be you, Joanna. Harriet Cunningham of the Women's Finance Advisory, with whom – as you all know – we've been trying to do business for some time, has decided to attend after all. She's already here and we've promised that she'll have someone who knows about horses to look after her. She's tougher than old boots, has no small talk, and her sole interest – apart from money – is horses. If we'd known in advance that she was coming, we'd have lined up Charlotte but . . . er . . .' he glanced towards the suite where Sebastian was introducing his wife to a client . . . 'we can't call on Charlotte now. So, Joanna, it's your job to look after Harriet – and win her as a client.'

'I'll do my best.' Joanna gave him a breezy smile.

Beside her, Rupert twisted his fingers. She wished that she hadn't won against him, but she couldn't ignore a prospective client – she too was on probation.

She followed Jeremy into the hospitality suite where a large, prematurely grey woman was berating Sebastian for arranging dinner during the second race. 'We're here to see the racing,' she was saying. 'For God's sake, why else does one come to Goodwood?'

'Er . . . Harriet.' Even Jeremy appeared terrified of interrupting her. 'May I introduce Joanna Templeton? She's one of our brightest . . .'

'Jeremy, do stop wittering! Hello, Joanna.' Harriet shook her firmly by the hand. 'So you're the one who's horse-mad. Come on, let's get out of here. I want to see the paddock – and I'm sure you do too.' She strode out of the room.

'Horse-mad?' Joanna mouthed at Jeremy.

He grinned sheepishly. 'It was the only way to get her to stay.'

Joanna hurried after Harriet but it wasn't easy to walk fast in her straight skirt and unsuitable shoes. She reached the paddock to find Harriet leaning against the barrier, race card in one hand, binoculars in the other.

'Where do you keep your horse?' she asked Joanna.

'Well . . . er . . . I don't have one at present.' She wondered what Harriet would say if she knew her only experience of horses was Marbles, a scruffy little brown pony who had been buried under the daffodils at the bottom of her parents' garden for over fifteen years.

They watched the horses being led around the paddock.

'Interesting that the Government are to sell off nearly all their stake in BT,' Joanna commented as casually as she could.

'I refuse to discuss business when I'm racing.' Harriet opened her race card. 'Now, what are you going to back?'

'No Trump is my choice,' murmured a quiet voice behind Joanna.

She turned quickly. Oliver smiled and gave her a half wink, nodding towards Harriet's solid back to indicate that he understood the situation.

'Good evening, Joanna,' he said, loudly.

'Good evening.' Joanna kept a straight face. 'Harriet, may I introduce Mr Safarov?'

Harriet glanced round. 'We've met before. Good evening.' Her tone was polite but chilly.

'I saw your filly run at Doncaster,' said Oliver. 'She should have won.'

'Thank you.' Harriet continued to study her race card.

'How many horses do you have in training?' Oliver persisted.

'Three.'

'One of them is a great-great grandson of Northern Dancer, if I'm not mistaken?'

Harriet looked surprised. 'You're right. How did you know?'

'I'm interested in breeding. I have a couple of horses in training in France and intend to buy more.'

Harriet lowered her card. 'Have they run yet?'

'Next year – hopefully.' He continued to discuss horses with Harriet, slipping in the odd good word about First Clarence for which Joanna was grateful.

In the paddock, the jockeys were being given a leg up on to their mounts. One by one, they left for the starting stalls. Oliver, Harriet and Joanna returned to the hospitality suite, Joanna doing her utmost to prevent her heels from becoming stuck in the turf.

'You look very elegant,' Oliver told her when Harriet stopped to study the starting line through her binoculars.

'Thank you – and thanks for helping me with . . .' She nodded towards Harriet.

'She's a tough nut but I think we charmed her – in the end.'

'I hope so,' replied Joanna, although she had a feeling that Harriet had only partially mellowed towards Oliver.

At the end of the evening, Oliver offered Harriet and Joanna a lift back to London in his helicopter. As they left the hospitality suite, under the envious glances of those faced with the drive back to London, he clapped Jeremy on the back.

'Let's pray that no one from the Securities and Futures Association sees us,' he said.

Jeremy looked startled. 'Why?'

'They might think First Clarence was luring clients with excessive hospitality.'

'Oliver, the helicopter is your property.'

'I bought it with the profit made on my investments placed through First Clarence!'

'There's nothing illegal about that.'

Oliver laughed. 'Jeremy, I'm only teasing. Where's your famous British sense of humour? Come on, ladies!' He led the way to the limousine which was to take them to the helicopter pad on the far side of the racetrack.

As they settled into the back seat, Harriet remarked, 'Jeremy reacted oddly.'

'He's apt to be tight-lipped,' replied Oliver.

'Do you think so?' Joanna was astonished. 'In the trading room he's always either shouting abuse or yelling praise. I've never seen him lost for words.'

Oliver shrugged. 'Oh, people act differently when they're away from work.'

Joanna didn't pursue the argument. Oliver and Harriet were clients, and it would have been churlish to remind them that as far as Jeremy was concerned, Goodwood counted as work.

They landed at Battersea where they were met by Oliver's chauffeur, whom he instructed to drop Joanna first – for which she was grateful. She didn't want Harriet to suspect anything. When they drew up outside her flat, Oliver left the car to accompany her to her front door. As she removed her key from her bag, he took it from her, inserted it in the lock, and opened the door.

'Thank you for a lovely evening,' he said, placing the key in the palm of her hand.

'Thank you for bringing me home.' She returned the pressure on his fingers, excited by the knowledge that he longed to say more but was prevented by Harriet's presence.

Half an hour later, as Joanna slid under her duvet, the telephone rang.

'Can you come to France with me next weekend?' asked Oliver.

'I'd love to,' she replied, without hesitation.

'I have a villa in the hills behind Cannes,' he went on. 'It's very beautiful. I know you'll like it there. I designed the gardens and the swimming pool myself.'

She balanced the receiver on her pillow. 'It sounds wonderful.'

'Do you mind flying out on your own? I leave for Romania tomorrow and I'm afraid I won't have time to come back to London to collect you. But my chauffeur will take you to Heathrow – and I'll meet your flight in Nice.'

'That'll be fine.' She wondered what it would be like to spend two whole days alone with him.

'I'll phone you during the week with all the details.'

'I look forward to it.' She assumed that he often flew women out to join him.

He paused, then added softly, 'I can't wait for next weekend.'

'Nor can I.'

They said goodnight. As Joanna drifted off to sleep, she imagined herself making love with Oliver, on a sunlit terrace beside a sparkling blue pool.

XI

JOANNA HAD ASKED to take Friday afternoon off but, although Jeremy raised no objections, when the time came to leave she was too busy. Again, Jeremy had to divert some of her calls to himself in order to keep up with her clients' demands.

To Joanna's delight, Harriet Cunningham placed a large buying order for shares in the Hong Kong & Shanghai Bank. Then Mr Bilsham at Kathpeach faxed her to buy 200,000 Rampayne Communications at 90p a share. Rampayne wasn't a bad company but its shares had taken a knock since one of the directors had been charged with theft – he'd lavished 20,000 pounds of the firm's money on a holiday with his mistress.

It was mid afternoon when she finally reached home with less than fifteen minutes in which to shower, pack and dress before Oliver's chauffeur arrived to take her to the airport. Having no time to deliberate, she slipped on a smart but casual orange linen suit. She was zipping up the skirt when the doorbell sounded.

Three hours later she stepped out of the plane into a glorious, hot Mediterranean sunset. Oliver was waiting for her in the first-class lounge: he'd flown in shortly beforehand. He looked suntanned and debonair in an open-necked white shirt and dark trousers. She wondered how she could have worried that he was too old for her.

'We've waited far too long,' he said, kissing her on both cheeks.

'We have.' She smiled at him.

For the first time since Joanna had known Oliver, he drove himself, sweeping her along in his open-topped Corniche, away from the glittering sea and the coastal hotels and up into the purple hills. They passed luxury villas draped in red bougainvillaea, with swimming pools cut in exotic shapes. Joanna tipped back her head and relished the beauty of the inky blue sky above her. It was a world away from the bustle of the trading room.

Oliver took her hand and rested it on the inside of his thigh. 'Were you busy today?' he enquired.

'Very.' She circled her fingers, and tried not to mind that he'd brought her back to reality by asking her about work.

'Much gossip about Rampayne Communications?'

'Yes – and great contempt for the director who sacrificed everything for twenty grand.'

Oliver looked disapproving. 'Theft is theft, whether it's twenty thousand or twenty million.'

'Oh, I agree,' she replied quickly.

They were running along beside a high white wall. Suddenly Oliver swung the car sharply into a driveway, the wheels sending up a cloud of dust. Ahead of them were a pair of solid, studded iron gates with a security camera on either side. Oliver activated the gates electronically, and they opened to reveal a beautiful white villa set in perfectly manicured gardens. As they drew near it, Joanna was enveloped in the scent of jasmine which covered the sun terrace.

'What a glorious place.' She leaned towards him.

He kissed the corner of her mouth. 'I knew you'd like it.'

The front door opened and a small, white-haired woman, dressed in plain black, darted down the steps. Joanna assumed she was the housekeeper.

'Arkasha!' cried the woman.

Oliver removed Joanna's hand from his thigh and hurried from the car. 'Mama!' He enfolded his mother in an affectionate embrace.

Joanna was dumbfounded. In all Oliver's talk of their romantic weekend together, he had never once mentioned that his mother would be present. Although she was touched by their obvious fondness for each other, she felt extremely awkward. Stepping from the car, she hovered, waiting to be introduced – but they continued to hug each other and converse animatedly in Russian.

Finally, they separated. 'Mama, this is Joanna.' Oliver beckoned her forward.

Joanna held out her hand. 'How do you do, Madame.'

'You'll have to speak French,' said Oliver.

'I'll try.' Joanna stumbled out a few words.

'*Vous êtes bienvenue, Mademoiselle,*' his mother replied.

'*Merci, Madame.*' Joanna smiled politely, but she couldn't help wondering why she had to drag up her rusty French when Madame, who'd lived in England for over a decade, must speak passable English.

Oliver led the way into the house. The interior was high ceilinged and light, with floor of white marble and all the furniture in cream. The only colour came from the pictures, mainly French Impressionist, except for a dramatic blue Picasso which dominated the hall.

'It's so different from your London house,' remarked Joanna.

'Don't you like it?' He sounded offended.

'Very much.' She was surprised that he should be so sensitive. 'It's fabulous. By saying it was different, I didn't mean that as a criticism.'

'It's the contrast which I like.' He turned to his mother and said something in Russian, then to Joanna, 'I'll show you the gardens. As I told you, I designed them myself.'

As they went out on to the terrace, his mother slipped silently away.

'My mother's only happy in the kitchen,' said Oliver, linking his arm through Joanna's. 'You'll see. She's a marvellous cook.'

'I'm sure she is.'

She waited for him to explain why he hadn't told her about his mother. She wasn't upset, more disappointed. Having his mother at the villa was hardly conducive to a weekend of lust. Surely Oliver must realise that.

They wandered through the sumptuous gardens to the swimming pool, which was so cleverly designed that it appeared to be a natural lake. Oliver slid an arm around Joanna's waist. Again, she waited for him to speak.

'I'm afraid I have a couple of urgent business calls to make before dinner,' he told her as they returned to the villa. 'Would you mind if I ask Mother to show you to your room?'

'Er . . . of course not.' What else could she say?

'Dinner is at ten. We always eat late.' He gave her a warm look. 'I'll be up long before then.' He paused. 'I'm so glad you're here.'

She decided to make the best of it. 'So am I.'

When Joanna followed Madame up the wide staircase, she began to wonder if Oliver viewed their relationship more seriously than she did. She was flattered if that was true, but also a little concerned. She had no idea what she felt about him – beyond enjoying his company and wanting to make love.

Joanna had imagined they would share a room, but Madame escorted her to a large airy guest room. It had its own bathroom and walk-in cupboards, where she found her clothes already unpacked and arranged on hangers. She wondered if Madame had done this. She didn't like the idea of her lover's mother going through her suitcase, especially since she had packed her sexiest silk underwear and – after consultation with Felicity – two packets of condoms.

'It has a beautiful view,' Joanna stammered out in French.

'*Merci.*' Madame gave her shy smile, and withdrew.

Joanna bathed in scented water, slipped on her new peach silk dressing-gown, and stretched out on the bed. The air was warm. It caressed her limbs. She stroked one foot up the inside of her calf, sensuously, seductively, and waited for Oliver.

An hour passed, but there was no sign of him. She glanced at her watch. It was twenty to ten. She wondered if she'd done something to put him off. Or was it the presence of his mother? But he'd known about that when he'd invited her.

Feeling uneasy – and more than a little annoyed – she dressed for dinner, selecting a navy silk dress with a subtle yet sexy wrapover skirt. As she slipped on her gold sandals, there was a knock on one of the doors which she had assumed to be part of the wardrobe.

'Come in!' she called.

A key turned and Oliver stepped inside. 'Joanna, I'm so sorry to have abandoned you, but I've been waiting for an important call. It still hasn't come through. So irritating! But we'll forget about it now. You look wonderful. Let's go down to dinner – you must be hungry.' He held out his hand to her.

'I am.' She took it, linking her fingers through his.

Dinner was laid at one end of the terrace, at a round table shielded by a bower of jasmine. There was a plate of lobster, a platter of cold seafood, champagne on ice – and only two places.

'Isn't your mother eating with us?' asked Joanna, trying to conceal the hope in her voice.

'She prefers her room.' Oliver indicated a ground-floor annexe overlooking the swimming pool. 'She's accustomed to being here on her own.'

He held a chair for Joanna, poured her a glass of champagne and placed the dishes between them. 'I trust that you like lobster.'

'I love it.'

He sat very close to her, tore off a particularly succulent piece of meat with his fingers, and held it towards her. She opened her mouth and he slipped it inside, suggestively, his fingers touching her lips.

Oliver fed her another morsel, selecting the choicest piece.

'You must eat too.' She returned the compliment.

She asked him about the villa and how often he used it.

'It's my escape,' he replied. 'I come here whenever I can.'

'I don't blame you. It's magical.' She breathed the scent of jasmine. 'How long have you owned it?'

'I bought it just after I married Susan.'

It was the first time he had mentioned his wife by name and Joanna wished he hadn't, at least not at that moment. Then she chastised herself for being over-sensitive. Susan had been a part of Oliver's life. They'd loved each other and had children together. They shared a past.

'We only came here a couple of times,' he went on. 'Susan is American. We spent most of our time there. When I was a teenager, everything American appeared so much better, bigger, more exciting. They had Hollywood, rock and roll, oil wells, jazz. I was determined to marry an American.'

'How very strategic.'

'Did I say that I didn't love Susan?' He sounded angry.

'Oliver, I meant it in a general sense. I wasn't criticising you personally.'

'I'm glad to hear it – because of course I cared for the woman I married.'

Joanna said nothing. She wished she'd stayed at home. The whole situation was most odd. In London, Oliver had been amusing and urbane. Here he was peculiarly defensive. She wondered if he regretted having invited her.

Oliver left his chair and came round to her, took her face in his large hands, and kissed her softly on the mouth. 'You have every right to ask me questions and I have nothing to hide,' he said. 'Ask me anything you like.'

She smiled. 'I don't need to.'

He kissed her again. 'Come! Let's go to bed. We can eat more later – if we're hungry.'

He half-carried her up the stairs and into his room, which was almost clinical in its uncluttered whiteness, and dominated by his bed. They stood at the foot of the bed, kissing gently, tenderly. He slipped the dress from her shoulders. The silk whispered as it fell to the floor. He ran his mouth down her shoulders to her breasts, covering them with tiny butterfly kisses.

When she tried to respond, he shook his head. 'No! Let me make love to you.'

He undressed her gently, kissing each new area of skin as he laid it bare. He placed her on the bed, naked, her legs sprawled, and stood looking at her as he unbuttoned his shirt.

'You're much more beautiful without your clothes,' he said.

She smiled and watched him. He was bigger than she had imagined, with muscular shoulders and thick black curly hair covering his broad chest.

He came towards her. 'We must be sensible,' he said, opening a bedside cabinet and producing a packet of condoms.

Once again, he astonished Joanna with his self-control. She had forgotten all about them, but was relieved to be saved from having to broach the subject.

He lay down beside her and took her in his arms, stroking her breasts and neck. Aroused by his caresses, she turned to kiss him. Suddenly, he seized her by the wrists and stretched her arms above her head until her hands touched the headboard.

'Now you're mine,' he said, separating her thighs with his knee. 'Tell me you want me! Say it!' His voice was harsh, as though it belonged to a stranger.

Joanna was too stunned to reply.

Before she had time to react, Oliver's mood reverted. He became so tender that she wondered if she'd imagined the abrupt change in his behaviour. He kissed her eyelids, her eyebrows, her nose and her mouth. He aroused her until she ached for him, lifting her hips to him, wanting him. Gentle when he entered her, he pulled back almost immediately so as to prolong their enjoyment. Only then did he thrust harder, relished her cry of pleasure and the feel of her long legs wrapped around him.

'You're beautiful,' he whispered against her mouth. 'God, how I've wanted you.'

'I've wanted you too.' She raked her fingers down his wide shoulders.

The telephone rang. Oliver froze. It rang again. There was a click as the answering machine engaged.

'I'm sorry,' said Oliver.

To Joanna's astonishment, he withdrew from her, rose from the bed, and hurried into the adjoining dressing room where he picked up the receiver before the caller could leave a message.

She was bewildered. However important the call, Oliver could have rung back later. She lay on the bed, naked, waiting for his return. As the minutes passed, she became decidedly less aroused – and increasingly indignant.

She couldn't see him, just a full-length mirror reflecting a row of suits hung in colour order, but she could hear him talking quietly and, although she could not catch what he said, from the rhythm of the words she knew he was speaking English.

As she watched the open doorway, he stepped into the mirror's range. He had the receiver hooked under his chin and his hands were on his chest. He was studying his reflection. Still talking, he ran his hand down his upper thigh and caressed his belly. Then he turned to capture a rear view of himself, stroking his buttocks, separating them slightly. When he faced the mirror again, Joanna could see that he was as excited by looking at himself as he had been by making love to her – if not more so.

She was humiliated and angry. She'd waited long enough. Since he preferred himself, let him masturbate. She slipped out of bed, collected up her clothes and hurried from the room. Oliver didn't notice. He continued to talk.

If Joanna had been in England, she would have left immediately. She'd have phoned for a cab, taken a train, a bus, walked, anything to get away. Stuck in France, in the hills, escape wasn't so easy.

Wondering how she would survive the weekend, she climbed into her own bed, pulled the sheet up tight under her chin, and closed her eyes. Ten minutes later, she heard the door open and Oliver came in. He called her name but she kept her eyes firmly closed, forcing herself to breathe deeply and evenly as though asleep. To her relief, he didn't touch her. Instead, he crept out. Exhausted, she slept.

In the morning Oliver returned. She sensed his presence by her bed. Again, she didn't open her eyes. He whispered her name. She didn't move. He left, and shortly afterwards she heard him in the garden, talking Russian with his mother.

At midday, Joanna felt obliged to get up. She took a shower –

quickly in case Oliver came back – dressed in her least provocative knee-length shorts, and went downstairs.

It was very hot, and the sun was streaming down on to the terrace, heating the marble steps. Joanna crossed the lawn to the pool and put one foot into the water. It was deliciously cool.

Oliver's mother was laying lunch at a table in the shade of a vine.

'Good morning,' she called in English. 'Did you sleep well?'

'Er . . . yes . . . thank you. Good morning.'

'Why don't you take a swim? My son won't return for an hour. You have plenty of time.'

She was so friendly that Joanna concluded Oliver must have told her he was no longer interested in the English girl.

She hurried upstairs to change into her bikini – not the skimpy red one she'd bought to entice Oliver but her more modest navy blue. She returned to the pool and swam a few lengths. When she surfaced, Madame was waiting for her by the steps with a bathing towel.

'My son tells me you're very clever.'

'He did?' She wondered what else he'd said.

'He is a good judge of character.' Madame beamed with pride. 'Very loyal to those he loves and caring to his family. Would you like to see a picture of him as a baby?'

'Oh . . . er . . . yes.' Joanna could hardly refuse.

She followed Madame into the annexe, her wet feet leaving prints on the floor. Madame's sitting room was cosy and cluttered, with photographs and ornaments on every surface, and a faded picture of St Francis on one wall – not an expensive work of art such as Oliver owned, but a cheap print.

Madame sat down on the sofa and patted the seat next to her, indicating to Joanna to join her. From the many photographs of Oliver on a side table, she selected a framed black and white picture of a very fat, bald baby wrapped in a shawl.

'My Arkasha, taken by his father with a friend's camera,' she said. 'It was the only occasion on which Arkady saw his son.'

Joanna studied the photograph. 'How sad!'

'Life was tragic then.'

Madame went into the bedroom. Through the open door Joanna could see her take another photograph from her bedside table. She returned with it.

'Oliver's father.' She handed Joanna a second black and white photograph.

It was badly cracked down the centre where it had been folded, but in spite of this Joanna could see a striking man who bore a clear resemblance to Oliver. He was dressed in a uniform, with the jacket unbuttoned, and he appeared to be striding forward, his right hand raised as though he were hailing someone. His left arm had been cropped by the photograph. Behind him there was a fence, then a forest.

'He was very handsome,' said Joanna.

'He was my love.' Madame's voice shook. 'He died in the camp, at the end of the war. Nearly fifty years have passed but I shall never forget him.'

'I'm so sorry.' Joanna recalled her mother's intense, lasting grief for Christopher.

She passed the photograph back to Madame but the older woman's fingers were shaking so much that it slipped through them and fell to the floor. Joanna picked it up. As she did so, she noticed *Ponary 15.3.1944* was written on the back, in ink long faded.

'Why don't you have it framed, like the others?' she asked, nodding towards the many pictures of Oliver.

'Arkasha doesn't want me to. It upsets him that he can't remember his father. His first summer at the Sorbonne, he went to Riga. He wanted to meet his father's old friends. I was terrified that the Soviets would arrest him because his father had spoken out against communism. But you know my son, Mademoiselle, he's afraid of nothing. He planned to stay for a month, but he came home after one week. When he returned, he made me put this picture away. He said, 'If I can't know my father as a man, I do not want to see his image.'

With great care, Madame refolded the photograph.

They sat in silence for a moment. Madame was slumped in thought. Then she straightened up.

'That was my English husband,' she said, indicating a photograph of a fair-haired bespectacled man in a tweed suit. 'I expect Oliver has told you about Laurie?'

Joanna smiled. 'Who . . . is Laurie?'

Before Madame had time to reply, there was a shout from the pool. 'Joanna! Where are you?'

'I'm here, with your mother,' she replied, steeling herself for the moment when he demanded to know why she had left his bed.

Madame rose. 'You'd better go to him, Mademoiselle. Men are impatient.'

Joanna went out into the brilliant sunshine. Oliver was in the pool, swimming up and down, his powerful shoulders gleaming wet.

'What were you doing?' he asked pleasantly, with no hint that anything was wrong.

'I was seeing pictures of you as a baby.'

He laughed. 'A fat baby!'

'Very fat.' Joanna stretched out in a deck chair. 'Who's Laurie?' she asked, to keep the conversation general.

Oliver stopped in mid-stroke. 'My stepbrother.' He swam over to her, and added in a quiet, urgent voice, 'Please don't talk to Mother about Laurie. It upsets her to be reminded of happier days, when George was alive.'

Joanna was on the point of saying that she'd never heard of Laurie till his mother mentioned him, but she decided to leave it. If Oliver liked to think he was protecting his mother, it wasn't her business to interfere.

Closing her eyes, she relished the sun on her limbs, whilst Oliver continued to swim up and down the pool, stopping occasionally to chat. If only they could remain like this – companionable but with no sex – she could survive her visit and even enjoy it.

During the heat of the afternoon, they played chess in the shade of the vine. Joanna gave him a good run but he beat her easily, outmanoeuvring her queen with a bishop and a knight.

'I've been defeated,' she lamented to his mother, who had watched their contest from a distance.

'It is better for you that you lose, Mademoiselle. My son does not like to fail.'

Oliver laughed. 'She's right, Joanna. I don't believe in the Boy Scout idea of "It's playing the game which counts". That's rubbish! What matters is to win.'

'Someone had to lose,' said Joanna.

'Someone else – but not me.'

That evening Oliver decided that they'd have dinner down on the coast. He invited his mother to accompany them.

'Oh, yes, please do,' urged Joanna, thinking that his mother's presence would prevent their talk from becoming personal.

To her disappointment, Madame preferred to remain at home.

They drove to a small, exclusive restaurant overlooking the sea.

'It was so kind of you to suggest that Mother came too,' said Oliver. 'I could see that she was very touched.'

Joanna couldn't meet his gaze. She sensed that he'd guessed her true reason.

Oliver was well-known at the restaurant and many other diners stopped to chat. He was, as usual, an amusing host, telling Joanna snippets of gossip about everyone present, but as the evening progressed she became increasingly uncomfortable. Each time there was a lull in the conversation, she expected him to mention her escape.

Finally, she could bear the suspense no longer. 'I was very offended last night,' she told him. 'You stopped making love to me in order to answer the phone. Then you left me lying there, waiting, whilst you chatted. That's why I disappeared to my own room.'

He looked genuinely repentant. 'I'm sorry. It was an important call.'

She realised that he was unaware she had seen him in the mirror. 'Surely you didn't expect me to hang around for ever?'

'It won't happen again.' He leaned across the table and took her hand in his. 'I promise.'

Oliver assumed that his apology was sufficient, but for Joanna the subject was unresolved. During the drive home he insisted on holding her hand, whilst she debated mentally between making up some fantastic excuse so as not to have sex with him or giving it another go. Perhaps she'd been too critical. She often looked in the mirror, so why shouldn't he? She frequently examined her body. There was nothing wrong in that. But she didn't take phone calls in the middle of sex. That's what really galled her.

On the steps of the house, Oliver took her by the shoulders. Now was the moment to claim a migraine. But she recalled how much she had wanted him that night in London – and she decided to try again.

They went up to his room and he undressed her, but something in the way he moved his hands down her body seemed mechanical and detached – the caresses of a man who preferred a telephone call to sex. Her desire evaporated. She tried to respond but she felt nothing. She pretended to be aroused, hoping that she would become so – but she didn't.

Oliver appeared not to notice. He kissed her passionately, whispering how much he wanted her. But this time Joanna didn't relish his thrust. It was an invasion of her body, which she now regretted.

'What's wrong?' he asked, suddenly aware that she was passive.

'Nothing.' She lied to save his pride.

'You're not enjoying it.'

'Yes, I am.' There seemed no point in wounding him.

He redoubled his efforts.

In desperation, Joanna faked an orgasm to end the fiasco. Only then did Oliver allow himself to come.

To her relief, he fell asleep immediately. This time she remained in his bed – she could hardly creep away twice.

Early next morning she was woken by Oliver shaking her arm. She sat up, resolved that however angry he became she would never have sex with him again.

'I have bad news,' he said. 'I have to return to London this morning. I'm so sorry. You can stay here till this evening, if you like, and I'll arrange for a taxi to take you to a later plane.'

'Oh, no, I'll come with you.' She shot out of bed and raced to her room. She didn't care if she sounded delighted to leave, she couldn't wait to get home, but as she threw her clothes into her suitcase, she couldn't help wondering if Oliver also wanted to be rid of her.

Joanna arrived at the flat to find Felicity stretched out on the patio, trying to make her fair skin turn to a golden tan before she next saw Tom.

She looked up, startled. 'Jo! I didn't expect you. Why are you back so early? What happened?'

Joanna dropped her suitcase on the floor and collapsed on the rug beside Felicity. 'Thank God I'm home. It was ghastly.'

Felicity put on her sunglasses. 'What? His villa?'

'No, that was fabulous. But the situation was bizarre. His mother was there.'

'His mother!' repeated Felicity.

'Isn't it extraordinary? He'd never mentioned her presence, yet they're very close and she lives there all the time.'

'I thought you were flying off for a weekend of lust – not two days *en famille*.'

'So did I!'

'Maybe he thinks of you as the future Mrs Safarov?'

'Oh, no! I'm sure not. In truth, there were moments when I sensed he regretted having invited me.'

'Perhaps he felt vulnerable because you'd witnessed his fondness for his mother?'

'Then why did he take me there? He has other houses.' Joanna lowered her voice so that their neighbours couldn't hear. 'That wasn't the only peculiarity. The sex was . . . a nightmare.'

'What did he do?' Felicity sat up sharply. 'Was he . . . perverted?'

'No, but he was odd.' Joanna whispered the details of her first night with Oliver, ending with, 'Fancy getting up in the middle to answer the phone. I was so insulted. I was completely turned off.'

'I don't blame you. What did you do?'

'I went back to my own room.'

'Serves him right. Was he angry?'

'No. The next day he acted as though nothing was wrong. So I tackled him about it over dinner. He apologised, though he didn't seem to realise how pissed off I'd been. Anyhow, I decided to give it another go. I thought I might've been over-hasty.'

'What happened?'

'It was awful.'

'Was he rough again?'

'Not at all. But I couldn't forget that he'd preferred to chat on the phone than to make love to me.'

'How did you get out of it?'

'I didn't.'

'So what did you do?'

'I faked an orgasm.'

'Did he realise?'

'With an ego like his? You're joking!'

Felicity lay down. 'Do you think you'll hear from him again?'

Joanna shook her head. 'I wish I could keep him as a friend, but his pride would never allow that. It's a shame, because he's such stimulating company. Coming back on the plane, he was telling me a hilarious story about the head of a merchant bank – he wouldn't name the bank, of course, he's too discreet. I laughed till I cried. But when we reached London, he didn't even bring me home. He put me in a taxi. Not a good sign.' Joanna stretched out in the sun and closed her eyes. 'I just hope no one at First Clarence finds out.'

XII

Joanna had little time to think about her embarrassing weekend with Oliver. On her arrival at First Clarence on Monday morning, she met Rupert leaving the trading room.

'Good morning,' she said.

He walked on, tight-lipped.

She hurried to her desk. 'What's the matter with Rupert?' she asked Simon.

'He's been let go.'

'Poor Rupert!' She tried not to worry about her own contract.

That week, the big story in the market was that Rampayne Communications were fighting off a hostile takeover bid from Twinberrow, who were offering 110 per Rampayne share. The share price stood at 109 to sell and 111 to buy. Alongside the news of the bid came more revelations concerning the arrested director – his mistress was the wife of the company secretary who, angry and humiliated, had informed the police about his wife's lover.

Joanna was surprised to receive a fax from Mr Bilsham instructing her to increase Kathpeach's holding by 100,000 shares. 'Bilsham's buying at one eleven. That's above the bid price. He must be confident it won't go through,' she remarked to Jeremy.

He shrugged. 'Oh, Bilsham's quite a gambler. He goes on gut instinct. The most he can lose is our commission.'

On Friday morning, the giant US company Wardener Inc made a counter bid of 120 per Rampayne share. The market reacted strongly. The price rocketed, then dropped back with profit-taking before rising again to 125 as speculators tried to guess if Twinberrow would top Wardener's offer.

Joanna joined her colleagues for an after-work drink. They had invited Rupert, but he chose not to come. All around them, salesmen and traders were discussing Rampayne.

'One of my clients is very bullish about Rampayne,' Simon confided to Joanna and Rebecca.

'So is one of mine,' said Joanna, 'but Jeremy thinks they're just gambling. He says they always go on gut instinct.'

'That's exactly what he used to say about Donia & Co., one of my old offshore clients,' said Rebecca. 'They once bought shares just before a takeover was announced.'

Joanna stared at her. 'What happened to them?'

Rebecca pulled a face. 'They stopped using First Clarence, luckily just after I was out of probation. If not, I'd probably have been for the chop – like poor Rupert.'

Over the following days, Joanna found herself thinking of Oliver more than she had expected, wondering what he would say about this or if he would laugh at that.

One evening, she took thatch-haired Mr Rottingdean out to dinner.

'Rampayne's director is a bloody fool,' he confided. 'Fancy risking his career for a mere twenty grand!'

Joanna gave him an appalled look. 'But fraud is fraud – whatever the amount.'

Mr Rottingdean gulped, and hurriedly agreed with her.

She wished she could tell Oliver. How he would laugh.

Arriving home an hour later, she found Tom's briefcase on the kitchen table but no sign of him or Felicity – just a note that her father had rung to say he'd booked the caterers for her mother's sixtieth birthday party and Lindsay wanted to discuss their mother's present.

Joanna tapped out Lindsay's number.

Her sister answered in a sleepy voice. 'Hello.'

'Lindsay, it's me. Were you asleep?'

'Yes. You've woken me up. Why are you ringing so late?'

'I'm sorry, but it's only just after ten.'

'I go to bed at ten, you know I do.'

'Lindsay, I've apologised. Go back to sleep. I'll phone again tomorrow.'

Joanna came off the line feeling flat and depressed. Speaking to Lindsay, with whom she had nothing in common, never failed to remind her how much she had shared with Christopher.

She made herself a cup of coffee and mooched around the flat, adjusting ornaments and straightening pictures, her mind on Christopher. When she heard Tom and Felicity in the hall, she hurried into her room in order to give them some privacy.

On her dressing table there was a photograph of Christopher, the one she'd taken on their last walk. She studied his carefree face, as she had done so many times. There was nothing in it to suggest that he had only a short while to live.

Twinberrow increased their offer for Rampayne to 130. Everyone expected Wardener to top it. The shares crept up to 151 – 150 to sell, 152 to buy. Just as the market was about to close, to Joanna's surprise Kathpeach instructed her to sell.

Had they been any other client, she'd have phoned to discuss her analysts' advice – which was to hold for an expected higher offer. With Kathpeach, she didn't dare.

She wished she could consult Jeremy, but he was out of the office all afternoon and she couldn't delay dealing in case Rampayne's price dropped. Quickly, she keyed into Kathpeach's file and re-read 'Await instructions only'. Then she studied their fax. This was an instruction. But to be on the safe side, she didn't telephone them but faxed the analysts' advice.

It took Kathpeach an hour to fax back: 'Sell as instructed'.

Two days later Wardener backed off, leaving Twinberrow the winner. Kathpeach had almost doubled their profit by selling early.

'I can't help feeling they had a tip-off.' Joanna recounted the bare bones to Felicity, without mentioning any names.

'Sure you aren't just piqued because they didn't take your advice?'

Joanna thought about it. 'No, I'm genuinely concerned.'

'What are you going to do?'

'I'll tell Jeremy. That's company procedure.'

During a lull the following morning, she confided her fears to Jeremy.

'Good God! Are you certain?' he asked, looking worried.

'I'm not sure, but I'm unhappy about it.'

He ushered her into a side office, where she ran through the deal, after which he questioned her closely and made notes.

'Did you act immediately on their selling order?' he asked.

'No, I . . . umm . . . faxed the analysts' advice.'

He lowered his pen. 'Why? This is an "Await instructions only" client.'

She began to wish she had kept her mouth shut. 'I know, but theoretically they had instructed me so I believed I should update them. If you'd been here, I'd have checked with you.'

'Did they take the analysts' advice?' He looked even more anxious.

She shook her head. 'No, I'm glad to say.'

'That's something! They'd have been furious. Joanna, you must follow instructions. I've told you that before.'

'Yes, I'm sorry.' This was not at all the discussion she had intended. Instead of Kathpeach being under suspicion, she was under attack.

Jeremy reread his notes in silence. 'If you had an iota of proof, of course I would pursue this,' he said eventually. 'But you have nothing, only your vague doubts. In my opinion, Kathpeach have merely been lucky.'

She wasn't totally convinced – and it showed in her expression.

'They are a good, active client and it would be a shame to upset them unnecessarily,' he went on. 'We all know that clients have a way of sensing if they're under suspicion, even if they're investigated in secret.'

'Do you think so?' She'd never heard that before.

'I certainly do. We'll watch them and if it happens again, we'll act swiftly – and with more evidence.'

'I suppose you're right,' she said.

'I'm glad you're taking a sensible attitude, Joanna. There's far too much unwarranted scaremongering.' Jeremy paused. 'I believe your probation period is up at the end of next week.'

She swallowed nervously. 'Yes.'

'You've had a few up and downs.'

'I'm aware of that.'

'Your main problem is your failure to follow clients' exact instructions. You become over-eager.'

'Yes.' She had a sinking feeling that he was not going to keep her.

'But you're enthusiastic and your clients like you. Your sales figures are good, you've won new business, and you're popular with your colleagues – most of them!'

'Thank you.' She waited, her knuckles white with tension.

He noticed, and smiled. 'I won't keep you in suspense any

more. So long as you don't have any serious mishaps during the remainder of your trial period, I can tell you in strict confidence that I plan to recommend that we offer you a permanent contract. You'll make an excellent addition to the desk.'

'Thank you.' She was weak with relief.

For seven days Joanna did not tell anyone her good news, except for Felicity. On the eighth day, she received a confirmation letter from First Clarence.

'Joanna is now a permanent member of the desk,' Jeremy announced that morning. 'We're lucky to have her. Champagne on me after work.'

Her colleagues congratulated Joanna. Even Charlotte managed a thin smile. Joanna longed to tell her parents, knowing how pleased they'd be. At the same time, she couldn't help feeling that she had sold her soul to the devil. Old Mr Fitterton would never have ignored even the slightest whiff of dishonest dealing.

Flushed with success and champagne, Joanna arrived home that evening to find Felicity on the telephone.

'Oliver,' mouthed Felicity.

'You're joking!' Joanna took the receiver.

'I do apologise for not having phoned for so long,' he said, 'but my mother had a bad fall and I've been very worried about her.'

Joanna pictured the small, shy woman holding a faded black and white photograph. 'Oh, I'm sorry to hear that. Is she all right?'

'Yes, thank you. She's only a little bruised. I'm with her now. But I want to hear your news, Joanna. Have you been busy?' He spoke as though nothing was wrong.

Nonplussed but pleased, she replied in the same vein. 'I'm celebrating. First Clarence have offered me a permanent position.'

'That's marvellous – and well deserved. We must celebrate too. I'll be in London a week on Friday. Come to the opera with me. They're putting on one of my favourite productions of *Rigoletto*.'

'I'd love to,' she replied. Perhaps they could be friends after all.

They talked for a few more minutes – about Rampayne and the market.

'I'm amazed to hear from him again,' Joanna told Felicity as she replaced the receiver.

Felicity broke a Mars bar in two and gave half to Joanna. 'How will you avoid sex?'

'Trust you! Straight to the nitty-gritty!'

'He's bound to expect it.'

'He's not getting it. I shall make that clear.' Joanna munched on her chocolate. 'I don't believe he's desperate. He must have many women chasing him. He's rich, attractive and famous. He won't mind about losing me.'

'Maybe not,' said Felicity. 'But it's human nature to want the one who got away.'

On Sunday night, Simon's wife, Katie, produced twin girls. He telephoned Joanna with the news as she was leaving for work. His call meant that she arrived as the Head Boffin was beginning to speak.

Jeremy was sitting at Simon's desk. He tapped his watch. 'You're late.'

'Sorry. Simon phoned about the twins and . . .'

'Joanna, this is a job, not a maternity ward.'

She bit back an angry retort.

Across the desk Rebecca caught her eyes and mouthed, 'Vile mood.'

Jeremy spent the day handling Simon's clients, sifting through Simon's papers and listening in to Joanna's phone calls as though she were a beginner. She found it demeaning and off-putting, but decided to ignore it.

'What on earth's the matter with him?' whispered Rebecca when Jeremy went to the loo.

Joanna shrugged. 'God only knows! But something must be wrong.'

'Maybe his girlfriend dumped him?' Vikram suggested.

'Serve him bloody well right,' said Rebecca. 'He was so unsympathetic to me when Patrick and I split up.'

In the middle of making a call to Mr Sternhold, Joanna happened to glance at Simon's desk. On it was a piece of paper with some figures and '*See to Kathpeach*' scrawled across the top in Jeremy's handwriting.

When he returned, she braved his acid tongue. 'Is that note meant for me?' she asked.

'No. It's personal.' He removed it.

When Simon came back to work, the desk took him out for a celebratory meal. To their relief, Jeremy was busy.

The conversation soon turned to Jeremy's recent bad mood.

'My cousin was at school with him,' said Simon. 'He told me that Jeremy's always been consumed with envy because his elder brother stands to inherit the family estate.'

'It's not called Kathpeach, is it?' asked Joanna.

Simon flushed. 'Kathpeach is an offshore fund.'

'I know. Kathpeach is my client. It's just that I saw a note on Jeremy's desk and . . . oh, it means nothing.' She looked at him. 'What's wrong?'

'Only that . . .' Simon took a deep breath. 'Kathpeach used to be my client until they complained to Jeremy that I hadn't responded quickly enough to a sale order.'

Joanna was embarrassed. 'I'm so sorry. I had no idea.'

'It wasn't your fault, but I'm still annoyed about it.' Simon picked at his food. 'I can't understand why Kathpeach complained. I made them a good profit. They had bought shares in a tiny company called Bellamilly Natural Products, which was about to be taken over, and the fact that I sold their holding fifteen minutes late meant that they earned an extra two per cent. I shouldn't still be upset, but it really rankled.'

'You have every reason to be angry,' Joanna assured him.

'What I mean is that Kathpeach have a history of complaining. Prior to being with me, they were with Rosalind.'

'You mean the girl who couldn't sell?'

'That's not strictly true,' said Rebecca. 'Rosalind was just very argumentative. She queried everything. She wanted Jeremy to report one of her clients to the SFA.'

'Not Kathpeach?' enquired Joanna, feeling uneasy again.

'No. Another name. I can't remember who. Why?'

'Because Kathpeach made a profit on Rampayne and I was unhappy, so I spoke to Jeremy about it.'

'In his present mood I'm amazed you're still alive.'

'So am I. But he was very conscientious, only he reckons there's no reason to worry.'

'I hate to give him credit when he's being such a bastard to everyone, but he's probably right,' said Simon. 'Kathpeach could just be clever or lucky on the deals they've done through First Clarence but have made losses with the twenty other banks and brokers they use.'

Because Simon defended Kathpeach even though they'd

dumped him, Joanna decided to give them the benefit of the doubt.

XIII

ON THE DAY when Joanna was due to meet Oliver at the opera, Jeremy called her into a side office.

'What the hell did you do to upset Kathpeach?' He slapped a fax into her hand.

'I haven't done anything.' She glanced at it, then swallowed hard, horrified as she read, 'We regret to advise you that we will no longer be doing business with First Clarence due to the unsatisfactory performance of your employee, Miss Templeton.'

'Just because you're out of your probationary period it doesn't mean you can afford to lose a client,' he snapped.

'What did I do wrong?' she asked, bewildered.

'You were argumentative.'

'I never even spoke to them.'

'You queried their instruction to sell Rampayne.'

'I faxed them our analysts' advice. When they repeated their instruction, I executed it instantly. If Kathpeach are complaining, it's because they're used to getting away with it.'

'What do you mean?' he demanded.

She had to think quickly so as not to make trouble for Simon. 'Well . . . it's . . . er . . . obvious from the initials beside their previous deals that they've been looked after by various different salesmen, which indicates to me that they're fault-finders.'

Jeremy hesitated. 'Yes, I suppose they have been a bit tricky,' he conceded, taking the fax from her. 'But you must be more careful, Joanna. You're good, but you tend to get over-enthusiastic. I've told you before, never deviate from a client's instructions.'

'Yes, I know. I'm sorry.'

'You have a chance to exonerate yourself.' He handed her a piece of paper on which was written the details of another offshore company, the Redrey Trust in Bermuda. 'They're a new client and I want no complaints. Understood?'

'There won't be any. I promise.'

'Good. Now get back to work.'

'Thank you.' Her hand shook as she opened the door.

She tried to look composed when she crossed the trading floor, but realised she had failed when Simon asked, 'Anything wrong?'

'Kathpeach dumped me.'

'They're bastards.'

'I know – but it still hurts.'

'You can't help mourning the one that got away,' he said with feeling.

She recalled that was what Felicity had said about Oliver.

Joanna did no business all morning. Kathpeach's defection had cracked her confidence. Without it, she couldn't sell. By lunchtime she was completely dejected and haunted by memories of her early days at First Clarence. In the late afternoon, to her relief, Mr George of the Redrey Trust faxed a buying order for 50,000 shares in Inter-Picture, a photo-news agency. Joanna executed it promptly. The Redrey Trust must have no cause to complain about her.

Joanna was very badly shaken by the loss of Kathpeach and the last thing she wanted that evening was to see Oliver – or anyone. She longed to go home, crawl under her duvet and lick her wounds, but she couldn't cancel because she had no way of getting hold of him – he was somewhere between Zurich and London.

As arranged, she met him at the Opera House. Punctual as ever, he was waiting in the foyer, studying the arriving audience.

When he saw Joanna, his face lit up and he hurried to her. 'I've missed you.' He kissed her on both cheeks. Then he stood back to examine her. 'You look exhausted. I should have sent my car to collect you.'

'It's all right. I'm fine.' She forced a smile. 'How's your mother?'

'Much better, thank you. But I'm worried about you, Joanna.' He put his arm around her. 'You're working too hard. You need some champagne. After all, we must celebrate.'

She thanked him. It would have been churlish to say that celebration was the furthest thing from her mind.

He ushered her up to his box and handed her a glass of

champagne. After the stressful day which Joanna had experienced, the alcohol went straight to her head and she longed for sleep.

They had little time to talk before the music rolled and the curtain rose, and during each interval Oliver concentrated on his praise for the production.

'You are enjoying it, aren't you?' he enquired anxiously.

'Very much.' She tried to look enthusiastic.

It wasn't that she didn't like the opera, simply that, although she heard the toadying Rigoletto, the seducing duke and the sobbing Gilda, she was barely aware of their drama. Her mind was on Kathpeach.

When the audience rose after the last of many curtain calls, Joanna stood up.

'Let's wait a moment.' Oliver laid a restraining hand on her arm. 'I can't bear pushing my way through crowds.'

She sat down, and he spoke about a forthcoming production of *Tosca* until the mass had left the opera house.

They dined at a small, intimate restaurant. By now Joanna could hardly keep her eyes open and she was more than happy for Oliver to order.

'You looked so worried when you arrived,' he said. 'Have you had a bad day?'

She nodded. 'Ghastly.'

'I could see it in your face. Tell me about it. Let me help.'

She forced a smile. 'I wish I could.'

'Joanna, I wasn't suggesting that you reveal confidential information, but it can help to air a problem.' He paused, and added with a touch of modesty, 'I'm not exactly a stranger to the money-markets.'

'Oh, I know that. I wish I could confide in you.'

'Give me the bare bones, that's all.'

She hesitated. 'I'm upset because I lost a client.' She picked her words carefully, mentioning no names.

'Oh, no! I am so sorry.'

'They faxed First Clarence to complain about me.'

'They must be mad.' He reached for her hand and linked his fingers tightly through hers as if to give her all his support. 'You're excellent at your job. Jeremy told me so only last week. Does that make you feel better?'

'Yes. Thank you.' She thought for a moment. 'Did he telephone you?'

'No. Why?'

'I . . . er . . . thought you'd been abroad.'

He looked slightly uneasy, which made Joanna wonder if he'd been visiting another woman. 'I came back for just one day, but I didn't call you because I knew I had no time to see you. I was here for a very difficult meeting. When it ended, I had an hour to spare before returning to Heathrow and I felt like a game of squash. Jeremy and I belong to the same club – and he happened to be there. Satisfied?'

'I wasn't prying.' She could hardly tell him that she hoped he did have other women.

'I know you weren't.' He beckoned the waiter to bring another bottle of wine, although Joanna insisted she could drink no more.

They talked of other things; of his mother, France, the markets, and Rampayne.

'I suppose the client who complained made a loss and blamed you,' said Oliver sympathetically.

'No, not at all. In fact, they made a profit.'

'A healthy one?'

She nodded. 'Considerable.'

'You don't think . . .' he began. Then he stopped. 'No, I'm sure that's not the reason.'

'Tell me!' She leaned forward.

'That they are not strictly above board?'

Joanna flushed. 'Well . . . actually.' She stopped. 'Oliver, I can't tell you but . . .'

'Trust me! This conversation is in complete confidence.'

She hesitated, then continued, 'I can't give you any details, but . . . I did query their deal. They made quite a killing and I felt uneasy.'

He looked serious. 'What happened?'

'I followed our procedure and I informed my boss.'

'And he looked into it but decided there was no case?'

'Oliver, please don't ask me to tell you any more.'

'Of course not. I wouldn't dream of it.' He was silent for a moment, frowning at his half-filled glass before he went on. 'I must say, as a private investor with First Clarence I am very disturbed to think that they ignored a suspicion of insider trading.'

She was appalled. 'I didn't say that!'

'You implied it. Fraud is a very serious matter. I've been a client of First Clarence for many years, but if they're turning a blind eye to dishonesty I shall seriously consider moving all my business elsewhere – and I shall tell them why. I shall be seeing Sebastian Deveraux next week and . . .'

She was horrified. 'Thanks very much! What about my job? I wouldn't have told you anything about it if I'd known you'd take this attitude.'

'Joanna, it is the duty of everyone to take a firm stand against unethical practices.'

She'd lost Kathpeach, and now risked losing First Clarence their major private client. 'I agree, but I was wrong about Kath . . . the client. I was being over-imaginative.' In her anxiety, she nearly let slip their name.

'Are you sure?'

'Of course I am.' She was nearly in tears, from stress and exhaustion. 'Please don't say anything! Jeremy looked into it very thoroughly. My suspicions were completely unfounded. I promise you.' She had divulged far more detail than she had intended.

He thought for a moment. 'Very well. For your sake, I'll do nothing – so long as you keep me informed if you have any other cause for misgiving.'

'I . . . er . . .' She swallowed hard. 'I can't do that, Oliver. I have to advise Jeremy, my boss. That's company policy and the Stock Exchange ruling.'

'Joanna, stop worrying! I wouldn't dream of asking you to do anything unethical. I admire your loyalty to your clients and First Clarence. Naturally, you must follow the correct procedures. But I have a great deal more experience than you. If some racket is taking place, it could become very unpleasant. I just want to be sure that you aren't involved in anything dangerous.'

Joanna studied Oliver across the table. She'd witnessed his callous side. A few minutes earlier he hadn't given a damn about her position at First Clarence, he'd only thought of cutting his own links in case disaster fell. Of course, she'd realised he was ruthless. He wouldn't have got where he was otherwise. But, to his credit, he also seemed ruthlessly honest. She admired that.

'Very well,' she said.

'Good.' Oliver smiled. 'Now I'm going to take you home. You've had a terrible day and, much as I'd like to make love to you, I can see that you need your sleep.'

'Thank you.' She was greatly relieved to be spared further confrontation.

XIV

ON THE FOLLOWING Monday, Joanna was woken by the telephone. She grabbed the receiver, mumbling, 'What? Yes? Hello?'

'It's Simon. Have you heard the news? The Hang Seng is in free fall. There's a rumour that Deng Xiaoping has died.'

'Oh, hell!' Joanna struggled to sit up. 'What time is it?'

'Four o'clock. I thought you'd want to know.'

'Yes . . . thanks. How come you're up so early?'

'The twins have had a sleepless night – and so have we!' Simon gave an affectionate groan. 'See you later.'

'Thanks for the call.'

Joanna dragged herself out of bed. Her clients would expect her to be at her desk during a crisis. Many of the UK electronic and software companies in which they held shares were hoping for big contracts in developing China. An internal power struggle could delay these deals – and push the companies' shares down.

An hour later Joanna strode into the First Clarence Bank Tower, showed her identification to the two night porters, and took the lift up to the fifth floor. The normally frenetic trading room was deserted except for the thirty salesmen who worked on the Nikkei and two office cleaners wearing bright blue overalls labelled *BetterClean*.

As Joanna reached her desk, her phone rang.

'Joanna, Harriet Cunningham here. What's First Clarence's advice on China?'

'Good morning, Harriet,' replied Joanna, stalling for time as she thought of an acceptable reply. 'Our analysts are working on it at the moment. May I . . . umm . . . get back to you after I've heard their views?'

'I want your opinion now.'

Joanna had to go on instinct. 'I'd say that we shouldn't panic. This isn't the first time that Deng Xiaoping's death has been rumoured. To a certain extent the market has already discounted the effect of his demise. After all, he's an old man. His death can't be a surprise.' Joanna sat back in her chair. She didn't know whether she was speaking sense or waffling, but she hoped for the best.

'The recommendation I've had from a salesman at St Leonard's Commercial is that the Hang Seng is going to crash and we should sell now,' said Harriet.

Joanna hated it when clients quoted another salesman's differing opinion, but she kept cool and stuck to her guns.

'I think he's wrong. In fact, I'd say there would be some good buying opportunities when the market opens.'

Harriet was silent for a moment. 'Joanna, I'll go with your advice because you're the first salesman who has ever put me off dealing.'

'I'm not so commission-obsessed that I'd compromise my views,' replied Joanna, more bluntly than she intended.

'Glad to hear it. But I'll blame you if you're wrong.'

Joanna came off the line and uttered a prayer for Deng Xiaoping's good health. She couldn't afford to lose another client.

She went to fetch a cup of coffee. On her return she found a very young, exhausted-looking cleaner hoovering beside her desk.

'Don't worry about this area,' Joanna told her, anxious to check her other clients' Far East investments.

'I'm meant to vacuum everywhere,' said the cleaner timorously.

Joanna sat down. 'Not today, thank you. I'm working here.'

The cleaner hovered. 'Please, Miss! If I have another complaint, I'll lose my job. My husband's out of work and we have three children.'

Joanna was on the point of saying that her telephone calls were far more important than some wretched cleaning job when she saw the desperation in the girl's eyes.

She stood up. 'Yes, of course. Go ahead.'

The girl was tiny and very dark, probably Filipino, Joanna decided. She didn't look more than fifteen.

'Do you really have three children?' Joanna asked her.

'Yes.' The tired face broke into smiles. 'Maria, my eldest, is four today.'

The cleaner vacuumed around the desk, quickly and

thoroughly. Then she hurried away, so small that she looked like a lost child between the computer terminals.

Joanna picked up her bag and hurried after her. 'Excuse me!'

The cleaner turned. 'Yes, Miss?'

Joanna held out a twenty pound note. 'Please buy a birthday present for your daughter.'

'Oh, no . . . I couldn't take your money.'

'I insist.' Joanna pushed the note into the cleaner's hand.

Tears came into her eyes. 'Thank you,' she whispered. 'You are very kind.'

Joanna was embarrassed to think how often she'd blown twenty pounds on four glasses of champagne.

To her relief the Head Boffin backed up her intuition on China.

'The young Chinese have tasted consumer goods and progress – and they'll want more,' he told the morning meeting.

Joanna spent the next couple of hours on the telephone to her clients. Some opted to sell, but most took her advice. A few brave ones instructed her to buy. They were bottom-fishing – buying at bargain prices.

At noon there was another report of Deng's death and Hong Kong-related shares wobbled further. Joanna had an anxious moment when Harriet's holding slipped. She hunched over her screens, watching every movement. Suddenly there was a news flash.

'*Rumours of Deng's death greatly exaggerated. Chairman Deng Xiaoping appeared briefly in public this morning.*'

'Thank God for that!' Joanna leaned back in her chair and stretched her arms above her head to relieve the tension in her neck. All around her there were sighs of relief.

As she was recovering, Harriet telephoned. 'Well done,' she said. 'You kept a cool head – which is more than can be said for some.'

'Thank you.'

Joanna waited for Harriet to place an order, but she didn't. She had merely called to congratulate, which was unusual.

In the late afternoon, Joanna received a fax from the Redrey Trust instructing her to buy a further 50,000 shares in Inter-Picture. As she finished executing it, Jeremy's secretary arrived with another glorious bouquet of lilies for her. This time, she didn't need to open the card to know they were from Oliver.

When Joanna left the trading room, with the flowers in her arms, she felt on top of the world. The traders cheered and whistled. Harry swore he'd commit hara-kiri because she had another man. Even Jeremy complimented her. She was still smiling when she reached home. Friday had been hell. Today had been brilliant. On her next bad day, she promised to remind herself of Harriet's congratulations.

A couple of days later the market was rife with rumours that Inter-Picture was about to be taken over. The share price moved up. Joanna heard the news as she was travelling to work. She was pleased for the Redrey Trust – and relieved for herself.

When she reached her desk, she called them up on her screen to re-check their investment. The code beside their name showed that they had been introduced to First Clarence by Jeremy. She was about to exit their file when she noticed that they'd been authorised to trade for over a month – yet Jeremy had only just allocated them to her. She recalled how he'd harangued Credit Clearance when they were slow to sanction Hugo Porter's Link-Fund. Puzzled, she attempted to gain further information, but her screen flashed up that this was only available on the main computer.

'Joanna!'

She turned to find Jeremy watching her.

'What are you looking for?' he demanded.

'I was checking data on a client.'

'Why?'

She stared at him. She couldn't understand his question. Salesmen constantly monitored their clients' files.

'Why?' he persisted.

'I was . . . surprised that they hadn't traded before.'

'They've only just been cleared.'

It was a clumsy lie, and he realised that when he saw the expression on her face.

'I mean . . . I wasn't satisfied with their references until now,' he said, and he walked away.

Joanna returned to her screen, but she found it hard to focus on her work. She glanced up, and met Jeremy's stare. Five minutes later she looked up again. He was still watching her. She felt uneasy – and angry. If Jeremy was involved in some racket, his actions would have a detrimental effect not only on First Clarence but on her desk. Maybe Oliver was right. She did need his help.

When Jeremy went to lunch, Joanna telephoned Oliver. He was out, so she left a message with Withers asking him to call her at home – not at work. After the market closed, she was obliged to attend a talk given by Mr Sternhold. Normally she would have taken the opportunity to prospect for new clients. Tonight, she hurried home.

She arrived at the flat to find Felicity drying her hair in a rush before taking a new author to dinner with the buyer of a chain of bookshops.

'Has Oliver phoned?' Joanna shouted over the buzz of the hairdryer.

Felicity shook her head. 'You're not . . . interested in him, are you?' she asked.

'No. I want his advice.'

Felicity switched off the dryer. 'What's wrong?'

'I have an awful suspicion that Jeremy is up to something crooked.' Joanna started to explain about Kathpeach and the Redrey Trust, but was cut short by the arrival of Felicity's taxi.

'I'll ring you in the morning,' said Felicity, picking up her jacket and bag. 'I'm going up north tomorrow afternoon to visit a couple of authors who live near my father, so I'm staying with him on his houseboat. No telephone. No electricity.' She grimaced, then chuckled fondly. 'Dear Dad, why are you so eccentric?'

For once Joanna was too preoccupied to empathise. 'Don't phone me at work,' she said quickly. 'All our calls are recorded.'

Felicity looked horrified. 'What a mistrustful place! Do be careful.'

'That's why I need Oliver.'

Alone in the flat, Joanna waited for Oliver's call. She had a bath, made herself a salad, and did her ironing in front of the television. Halfway through the nine o'clock news, the phone rang.

She lifted the receiver. 'Hello.'

'Jo, it's Bertrand. Sorry to disturb you, but we've been to an auction in Dorset and the damned van has broken down so we can't get back tonight. Could you feed the cats?'

'Yes, of course.' She was loath to leave her flat but she could hardly refuse.

Switching on the answering machine, she dashed next door. As she opened the tin of cat food, she heard the muffled ring of her phone through the wall. But when she returned home, to her frustration the only message was for Felicity from Tom.

She contemplated ringing Oliver again, but decided against it. Withers was so efficient. She couldn't imagine that he'd forget her message.

In the morning she rose even earlier than usual. Knowing that she'd be unable to talk freely all day, she wrote Oliver a brief note, outlining her suspicions without including names. Then she drove to Holland Park and posted her letter through his front door. The curtains were drawn. The house was silent and sleeping. As she turned out of the driveway, she inadvertently clipped one gatepost. Cursing, she stopped to examine the damage. She'd only scratched the paint-work – not enough spoilage to warrant waking the household.

She drove on to the City, parked near Liverpool Street and walked through to Broadgate. The ice-rink had long since melted, replaced by a sand and straw arena where a band played and prancing horses displayed their paces in the lunch hour. Ahead of her, she saw Simon.

She hurried after him. 'Have you time for a quick coffee?'

'Of course. Let's go into the station.' He paused, and studied her face. 'What's wrong? You look pale.'

'I'll tell you in a minute.'

They ordered cappuccinos and stood to one side to drink them.

'I think Jeremy's involved in something dishonest,' Joanna confided in little more than a whisper.

He lowered his cup. 'You're not serious?'

'I am. Remember I told you that I'd reported my suspicions about Kathpeach?'

Simon nodded.

'I'm convinced the reason he took it no further is that Kathpeach – and, possibly, a new client he has given me – are dealing on inside information and he knows it.'

Simon glanced around as though afraid of eavesdroppers. 'Joanna, for God's sake don't go spreading this rumour. To mistrust a client is one thing. To point the finger at our Head of Sales is another. Why on earth would Jeremy risk his career – not to mention prison?'

'Money.'

'Jeremy earns a fortune.'

'Simon, listen to me. After I voiced my suspicion of Kathpeach, they dumped me. OK, I know what I'm saying sounds like sour grapes but . . . I just have this feeling. You see, as soon as I told Jeremy that I knew Kathpeach were difficult – no, I didn't drop you in it – he back-tracked and allocated me another offshore client.'

'So what?'

'It felt like a . . . buy-off.'

'Don't you think you're being over-imaginative?'

'This other client bought Inter-Picture *before* the rumours of the takeover.'

Simon said nothing.

'They were cleared to trade a month ago but hadn't been allocated a salesman,' she continued. 'That is odd.'

Simon frowned. 'OK, I agree. That's not like Jeremy.'

'I discovered this when I was checking their data. Jeremy saw me and demanded to know what I was doing. I told him what I'd found out, and he lied. He made out that their initial references had been unsatisfactory.'

'It could be true,' said Simon.

'Yes – only why was he so hostile? I don't mean in his normal aggressive way, but he kept watching me. Simon, I don't know what to do. Our procedure is that if I have doubts, I have to report to Jeremy. What's the point if he is involved? It's obvious he wouldn't take it any further. What would you do, Simon? Would you go over his head?'

Simon stirred his coffee thoughtfully. 'How much do you value your career at First Clarence?'

'Enormously.'

'Then I would think very carefully before you act. No one thanks a whistle-blower. If you go over Jeremy's head, whatever the circumstances, you'll never get promotion at First Clarence – or anywhere else.'

'But we have to take a stand against dishonesty,' protested Joanna.

He smiled sadly. 'You may, but I have Katie and the twins to consider. Rosalind used to query every transaction – and she was fired. Did I tell you that I bumped into her before Easter?'

Joanna shook her head – and tried not to look impatient.

'I stopped to buy petrol at a garage near home. Rosalind was working behind the till on the weekend night shift. I couldn't believe my eyes, but she told me that Jeremy had refused to give her a reference. Without one, she'd been unable to get another job in the City. I can't afford to take a stand, Joanna, especially when there's no real evidence of wrongdoing.'

'It's all right, I understand. Thanks for listening.' She didn't blame Simon, but she was disappointed.

He sensed it, and looked contrite. 'I haven't been much help, but you should consider the outcome. From a selfish point of view, I'd hate you to leave. You and Rebecca are the colleagues I'm closest to. Katie calls you my daytime family.'

Joanna smiled. 'I enjoy working with you too – and I certainly don't want to leave First Clarence.' She glanced at her watch. 'Come on, or we'll be late.'

When they reached the desk, Jeremy advised them that their monthly password had been changed to Einstein. As Joanna took her place alongside him, he reached for his diary, flicked back the pages, and quickly keyed in the previous Monday's date. From the stealth in his action, she surmised that she wasn't meant to have noticed.

Oliver telephoned Joanna that evening, by which time she had begun to think that she had misread his enthusiasm to help her.

'I'm sorry I couldn't ring before, but I had to go to Warsaw unexpectedly.' He paused, before asking, 'Now, what's worrying you? It must be important if you took the trouble to drive over to my house before work – and hit my gatepost, so I'm told.'

'Yes. I apologise. It was careless of me. You must let me pay for it to be repainted.'

'Joanna, don't offend me! Please! I want to know why you're so anxious. Is it First Clarence?'

'Yes. Something happened and . . .

'Stop! Don't tell me on the phone. Come to dinner tomorrow evening and we'll discuss it then. In the meantime, keep your concerns to yourself.'

'Of course I will.' She was relieved to know that his offer of help had been genuine.

On the following morning, as the analysts' meeting ended, Jeremy pulled up a chair close to Joanna. 'I've looked into your doubts about Kathpeach again,' he told her quietly, 'and I've also had a word with the head of the Regulatory Section.'

She was so surprised that she couldn't think of a response.

'We both feel that Kathpeach's deal was on the level,' he went on. 'However, you were right to bring your concern to my attention. Please always do so.'

'Er . . . thank you.'

He looked solemn. 'It's the duty of all of us to stamp on any hint of dishonesty.'

'Yes . . . of course.' She felt very uneasy when she recalled the seriousness of her accusations. Maybe she'd jumped to conclusions. After all, she had no proof. As Simon had said, why would Jeremy risk prison when he already earned a great deal of money?

A short while later, she saw Simon heading towards the coffee machine and she joined him there.

'Thanks for listening to me yesterday,' she whispered. 'I'm still not convinced about the client, but as for the . . . person, I may have been adding two and two and making fifteen.'

Simon's face broke into a broad grin. 'Thank God for that!'

They returned to the desk. The market was quiet ahead of the release of Government inflation figures. Joanna arranged a lunch with Harriet, spoke to Mr Sternhold, and took a buying order from Hugo Porter. Before close of trading, she checked her fax machine and the contents of her in-tray. The former was clear and the latter contained only confirmation orders. At six o'clock she checked again and left work promptly.

'Have a nice evening,' said Jeremy, with a friendly smile.

'Thank you.' She wondered what he'd say if he knew with whom she was to spend it.

Joanna arrived at Oliver's house to find only the red E-type Jaguar parked outside. As she walked towards the front door, it opened.

'Good evening, Miss Templeton,' said Withers, giving a stiff bow. 'I'm afraid that Mr Safarov has been delayed by traffic, but he shouldn't be long. Do come in.'

'Thank you.' She entered the mirrored hall.

As she did so, a door at the far end opened and a youngish man appeared. He was slight, with immaculately styled blond hair and, although he was casually dressed, he wore an expensive designer jacket.

'Don't let me detain you, Stuart,' said Withers, giving the young man a fond smile.

'Oh, I'll keep you company a little longer.' The man had a

slightly nasal voice. He retreated into what Joanna assumed to be the butler's quarters. She couldn't help wondering who he was.

'That's my nephew,' said Withers, sensing her curiosity.

'Oh . . . how nice.' Whatever the nephew did, he earned good money.

'Yes, Stuart's a fine lad.' Withers ushered her into the drawing room and poured her a glass of champagne. 'It's thanks to him that I came to work for Mr Safarov. After my dear wife died I was at a loose end, so Stuart suggested I went back to work. I was in the army and I like to keep busy.' They were interrupted by the sound of tyres crunching on gravel. 'That'll be Mr Safarov. I recognise the car.' Withers hurried to answer the front door.

Joanna waited in the drawing room.

'Is Miss Templeton here?' she heard Oliver enquire.

'Yes, sir.'

'Good. And your nephew?'

'He's in the back parlour, sir.'

'Thank you. Please tell Miss Templeton that I'll be with her shortly.'

Ten minutes later Oliver greeted Joanna with a kiss on both cheeks. 'I'm so sorry to have kept you waiting,' he said.

'Mr Withers looked after me very well.'

'I knew you'd be in good hands.' He pulled up a chair opposite her. 'You were absolutely right to contact me. I'm only sorry that I took so long to respond. Now, tell me what you've found out.'

Joanna gave an embarrassed laugh. 'I feel an awful fool. Since we spoke I've come to the conclusion that my suspicions were unfounded – at least so far as First Clarence is concerned.'

'I'm encouraged to hear that, but you must've had a reason for these doubts.'

'I overreacted.'

'Joanna, you're clever and astute. You wouldn't become suspicious without a reason.'

She hesitated. 'I . . . suspected a colleague of being involved in something shady, but I now believe that I was wrong.'

'Was it someone more senior?'

'Yes, but I was mistaken. At least, I'm pretty sure there's no cause for alarm.'

'But you're not one hundred per cent certain?' he persisted.

She took a sip of champagne and thought for a moment. 'You're right. I'm not convinced that the client is law-abiding, but I am fairly sure that the person whom I suspected is innocent. That is the truth.'

Oliver was silent and thoughtful. Then he leaned back in his chair, smiling. 'I'm very glad your fears proved unfounded. You couldn't work for a better bank than First Clarence.'

She nodded. 'I know.'

They went into dinner. Oliver talked of his mother and his worries about her health, whilst Joanna made polite comments. Only at the end of the meal, when Withers withdrew, did he touch her.

'I've missed you,' he said, reaching for her hand.

She couldn't bear him to continue. At the same time, she didn't want to offend him, not after he had put himself out to help her.

'Oh, dear!' she exclaimed, consulting her watch. 'It's half-past eleven. Unfortunately, I have to go. My little sister, Alice, is staying with me and she's nervous of being on her own in London.'

'What a shame.' He released her hand. 'But of course you must look after your sister.'

When Oliver escorted Joanna out to her car, she noticed that the E-type had gone and concluded that it must belong to Withers' affluent nephew.

'I may base myself in France for a week or two so as to be near my mother,' Oliver told her as they said goodbye.

'Please send her my best wishes.'

'I will. Thank you.' He kissed her on both cheeks, but they were the kisses of a friend.

Joanna drove away, hoping Oliver would never discover that Alice was safely at home in Somerset.

XV

AT AROUND NINE o'clock next morning Jeremy took a call on his yellow telephone, the one which Rebecca swore was unrecorded.

Sitting next to him, Joanna was in the middle of telling Harriet Cunningham that the head analyst had tipped Fact-Select as the likely winner of a contract to supply software to a Middle Eastern government. Harriet asked a few pertinent questions, then bought 100,000 shares.

Joanna turned to Jeremy, who was still on the phone, and mouthed the size of Harriet's order. He nodded. Pleased with her morning so far, she went to the coffee machine.

On her return she found Jeremy standing by her desk holding a sheaf of papers. 'Could we have a private word?' he asked, indicating one of the side offices.

'Of course.' She hoped that he intended to allocate her a new client, wishing only that it wouldn't be a colleague's account. She knew how painful it was to lose a client.

Ushering her into the nearest office, Jeremy closed the door. 'Why didn't you place this order from Società Hadini?' he demanded, holding out a fax.

She took the sheet of paper and stared at the writing. 'I've never seen it. When did it arrive?'

'Yesterday. Four twenty-eight p.m. Can't you bloody read?'

She turned white when she saw the time and date. 'I've never seen this. I checked my fax and my in-tray before I left. I remember doing so.'

'Joanna, look at the fax number. It's yours.'

'That order wasn't there last night. I promise you.'

'I just found it on your desk, when you went to get your coffee.'

'But I checked my tray this morning as well.'

'Joanna, Mr Lawrence of Società Hadini phoned me to find out why you hadn't confirmed their order. He is furious – and I don't blame him.'

She felt sick. 'I'm . . . I'm so sorry. I can't believe I missed it. I'm so careful.'

Jeremy appeared to soften. 'I realise that you would only have had two minutes to place the order before the market closed. I told Mr Lawrence that he was cutting it fine.'

'Thank you. I promise you it won't happen again.'

Jeremy frowned. 'I'm . . . afraid there won't be another time, Joanna. First Clarence cannot employ a salesman who has failed to fulfil instructions from two clients in one month. I regret to inform you that I have instructed personnel to terminate your employment.'

Joanna slumped into a chair. She was stunned, almost unable to breathe. She couldn't believe that this was happening, that she could have been so careless as to miss an order. She wanted to scream and cry and beg him to reconsider, to give her one more chance: she had to bite her lower lip to prevent herself.

Jeremy studied her crumpled face. 'If you hadn't been in such a rush to reach your hot date last night, you would have done your job properly.'

She thought back to the previous evening. 'I checked twice. You were there. You must have seen me.'

'I was occupied.'

She stared at him. 'Jeremy, none of us was busy. The market was dead.'

'I was busy,' he repeated.

'But . . . that's not true. You were just sitting there. We all were.' She rose and took a step towards him.

To her astonishment, he backed away as though afraid of her. 'Leave quietly or I'll call security.'

He looked so ridiculous that Joanna would have laughed if she hadn't been so distressed.

'Jeremy,' she said, 'I don't know what your game is, but you're a liar.'

She marched out of the office. He hurried after her. She went straight to her desk and began to collect up her bag and briefcase.

'What's going on?' asked Rebecca, looking from Joanna's shocked anger to Jeremy's tight-lipped wrath.

'I've been fired for failing to act on a fax which I never received.'

'Oh, no!' exclaimed Rebecca, visibly distressed.

Simon forsook his screen. 'It's not Kathpeach again? They complain about everyone.'

Joanna shook her head. 'No, a similar client.'

'But you won back Sternhold. We'd all failed with him.'

'Your figures are among the best,' cut in Vikram. 'Why are you getting rid of her, Jeremy? You're mad.'

Jeremy was scarlet with anger. 'If I were you I'd mind my own bloody business,' he snapped. 'Just remember, there are many hungry, highly qualified people out there who'd jump at the chance to work for First Clarence.'

Before any of her colleagues replied, Joanna intervened. 'Thanks for your support, all of you, but don't risk your jobs for my sake.' She tried to smile but it was impossible. She was choked with rage and misery.

Simon and Rebecca hugged her. Vikram and Karen shook her by the hand. Joanna could only nod in response. Her words stuck in her throat.

She picked up her belongings and, forcing her head up high, walked the length of the trading room. Jeremy followed. As she passed through the electronic doors, she removed her bar-coded name tag and dropped it on the floor so that he was obliged to bend to retrieve it. It was a petty act, but she didn't care.

At the lift, he pressed the bell for the personnel department. 'I'm sure you'll find another job soon, Joanna,' he said, in an attempt to regain his power over her.

She turned to him. 'Jeremy, that fax did not arrive at my desk – and you haven't heard the last of me.'

His eyes narrowed and he glanced quickly around to make sure no one was watching. Then he seized Joanna by her arm, digging his fingers into her flesh and pulling her towards him.

'Let the matter drop, Joanna, if you want a reference,' he hissed.

At that moment the lift arrived and the doors opened. The people inside stared in astonishment when they saw Jeremy, Head of Sales, clasping a reluctant Joanna. He blushed, adding further fuel to their suspicions, and released her.

She leaped into the lift, obliging its occupants to make room for her. She knew what they suspected – and they could not have been more wrong.

XVI

BY CLENCHING HER jaw, Joanna managed to stop herself from giving way to tears in the taxi, but, once inside her flat, she dropped her briefcase and bag on the floor, put her hands to her face, and cried. Leaning her forehead on the cool wall, her shoulders shaking, she cried until she had no tears left inside her. They were tears of disappointment, humiliation – and anger. Then, suddenly, she stopped, wiped her face on the sleeve of her jacket, and hurried to the telephone.

Oliver answered on the second ring. 'Joanna, how lovely to hear from you.'

'I've been . . . sacked.' Her voice trembled. 'I was accused of not acting on a client's instructions.'

'I am *so* sorry. When did it happen?'

'This morning.' She stammered out the story of the fax, adding, 'I know I didn't miss it. I checked.'

'First Clarence are fools,' he said. 'But don't be too distressed. You're clever. Through my contacts, we'll soon find you another, better position.'

'You haven't understood,' she protested. 'I'm upset – but I'm also incensed. Jeremy is lying. He saw me check my tray and he denied it. Don't you see, he wanted to get rid of me. You should've seen him by the lift. When I said he hadn't heard the last of me, he grabbed me and threatened to refuse me a reference.'

'That's appalling.'

'Oliver, it was Jeremy whom I suspected – and now I know I was right. Why else would he act that way if he wasn't guilty?'

'Have you any proof?'

'None,' she answered ruefully. 'But I'm damned well going to get it.'

'Joanna, be careful. Remember, you need that reference to impress a future employer.'

'You're not suggesting that I should kowtow to a crook?'

'Absolutely not!' he replied vehemently. 'I've always maintained that fraud must be stamped out.' He paused, and continued in a more hesitant tone. 'Only that was before someone . . . I care about risked being hurt.'

She was slightly embarrassed by his confession. 'Thank you, but I have to fight this. I refuse to be dismissed unfairly.'

He was silent for a moment. 'Joanna, I admire your courage.'

'Oliver, your approval means a great deal to me.' She spoke the truth.

'We need to talk it through,' he went on. 'Dine with me at my club tonight. I have a meeting nearby but it should be over by seven.'

She thanked him again. With Oliver's support, Jeremy wouldn't dare try to intimidate her.

Joanna occupied the intervening hours by jotting down her suspicions against Jeremy. She wished that she could speak to Felicity. Together, they would have analysed each twist. But Felicity was uncontactable. She was still with her father on his houseboat.

At lunchtime, Rebecca and Simon telephoned from a public call box.

'Everyone on our desk is shocked,' said Rebecca.

'We're all on your side,' added Simon.

'Thanks.' Their words touched Joanna deeply.

She reached The Archimedes a few minutes early to find that Oliver had not yet arrived. She gave her name to the porter and took a seat on the stiff leather sofa in one corner of the hall. Opening her bag, she checked her notes, confident that Oliver would be impressed with the amount of detail she had recalled. She couldn't wait to unburden herself to him. Each time the front door opened, she looked up expectantly.

The grandfather clock struck quarter past seven. Joanna fiddled with the strap of her bag. Another ten minutes passed. She caught the porter looking at her. Normally, she would have shrugged off his curiosity. Today, she felt vulnerable and conspicuous, a woman alone in a gentlemen's club.

She walked over to the desk. 'Mr Safarov is always so punctual. Are you sure there's no message for me?'

The porter checked the messages for the second time, but there were none.

She returned to her seat, selected a copy of *Country Life* from the nearby table and flicked through the pages, but she was unable to concentrate. After forty minutes, fearing that Oliver had been taken ill or had had an accident, she telephoned his home.

Withers answered. 'I'm afraid Mr Safarov is out for the evening, Miss Templeton.'

'If he phones, please tell him I'm waiting at his club, as arranged.'

It embarrassed Joanna that upright Mr Withers must think that she was pursuing Oliver, when nothing was further from the truth.

She remained at The Archimedes for a further hour, by which time she was anxious, frustrated and deeply embarrassed. Unable to stand it any longer, she left a message with the porter to tell Oliver that she had gone home, and went outside to find a taxi. Even as she settled into the back seat, she searched the street, hoping to see him.

She expected to find a message from Oliver at home, but there was none – just one from Felicity to say that she wouldn't be back till next Friday when Tom was arriving; she'd decided to go straight from her father's to next week's sales conference. Joanna couldn't help being disappointed.

Pacing up and down, she waited for Oliver to phone. She felt sick. Or was it hunger? She couldn't tell the difference. Opening the fridge, she reached for a plate of cheeses but the smell of food made her nauseous.

The phone rang. She grabbed the receiver.

'Hello, Jo,' said her father. 'Glad to catch you at home.'

'Oh . . . hello.' She tried not to sound deflated.

'I'm finalising the arrangements for your mother's sixtieth.' He lowered his voice to a whisper. 'She's in the bath so I decided to ring whilst she can't overhear.'

'Yes . . . of course, Daddy.' Joanna didn't tell him that her mother knew all about the party but was pretending to be oblivious so as not to spoil his enjoyment.

'Would you mind collecting Virginia on your way down?' he asked. 'I know she's an awful old busybody, but it would be a kindness.'

'Of course.' Joanna's heart sank at the prospect of her mother's elder sister.

Her father carried on talking about the party. 'You sound tired, darling,' he said, at the end. 'Been working hard?'

'I'm fine . . . thanks.'

Joanna couldn't bring herself to distress him by admitting that she had lost her job. Her parents were so fragile.

It was long after midnight by the time she finally went to bed. Even then, she couldn't sleep. She tried not to cry but she couldn't hold back her tears, burying her face in the corner of her duvet. She felt abandoned by Oliver, by everyone. When she eventually dozed off she kept waking, imagining that she'd heard the telephone ring – but it was merely a police siren wailing in the night.

In the morning she rose early out of habit, showered, drank a pint of coffee and tried to gather the strength to plan her day. She was still in her dressing-gown when the front doorbell rang. Assuming it was the postman, she answered on the intercom.

'Joanna?'

'Oliver!' She could hardly say his name, she was so relieved that she hadn't been abandoned.

A moment later he stepped into the flat and took her in his arms. 'I'm sorry about last night.' He hugged her fiercely. 'I was in a meeting which ran till after midnight and I couldn't get away, not even for a second. When I finally rang the club, of course you'd left.'

She clung to him for comfort. 'I came home. Didn't they tell you?'

'Yes, but I decided it was too late to call you. You'd had such an awful day, I thought you'd be exhausted. Then I received a message to say that my mother has had a stroke. I'm on my way to France now – my chauffeur is waiting outside – but I wanted to see you before I left.'

'I'm sorry about your mother.' She did her best to mask her disappointment that he was leaving so soon.

Oliver took her face in his hands. 'Joanna, First Clarence have treated you appallingly. Last night I decided to remove my business from them.'

'You did?' She was astonished when she recalled how, previously, he had thought only of himself.

'I refuse to deal with them again.'

'Thank you. I can't tell you how much your support means to me.'

'But I'm worried about you.' He smoothed her hair back from her face. 'I think it might be wiser for you to forget First Clarence and concentrate on your future.'

Joanna looked up at him. 'Oliver, last night I was on the point of giving in, but you have renewed my determination to fight. I intend to consult Max. He's my lawyer, and a close friend from university. I've been unfairly dismissed and I want justice.'

Oliver frowned. 'Have you considered how taking legal action would affect your career chances? Of course I'll help you find another job, but it may not be so easy if you're known as a trouble-maker.'

'I'll only tell the truth,' she protested.

'Well . . . of course you must do what you feel is right. But, Joanna, please promise me that you won't make any rash moves whilst I'm away. Promise me that you won't discuss this with anyone. Wait till I'm back, then we can confer properly.'

She hesitated.

'Please,' he went on. 'I shall be so worried if I think you're trying to take on First Clarence single-handed.'

She was loath to agree, but Oliver had removed his business from First Clarence. In the face of such a step, it seemed churlish to refuse.

'Very well,' she acquiesced, reluctantly.

He kissed her on the forehead. 'I must go now. I'm sorry to leave you. I'll be back as soon as I can.'

'When will that be?' she asked, feeling terribly abandoned as he moved towards the door.

'In a week or two.'

'A week or two!' She was horrified. 'Oliver, I can't wait that long before I take action.'

'My return depends on my mother's health.' His voice was cold and distant.

She suppressed her impatience. 'Yes. Of course. I understand. It's just that . . . I can't hang around doing nothing. I need to find another job.'

'You will. You're clever.' He paused. 'Maybe too clever.'

'What do you mean?'

'Oh . . . that you don't suffer fools. You have the courage to speak out where others would turn a blind eye.'

'You have courage too, Oliver.'

He shrugged off her compliment. 'Goodbye, Joanna.'

'Goodbye – and thank you.' She smiled bravely, but as soon as Oliver had closed the door behind him, she gave way to tears. She couldn't help remembering how much she had wanted that job at First Clarence.

As the day progressed, Joanna became increasingly uneasy about not discussing her predicament with anyone. When she had given her word to Oliver, it hadn't occurred to her that he'd be away so long. During a sleepless night, she decided that she had to take legal advice. Much as she disliked breaking her promise to Oliver, in the morning she telephoned Max.

He was sitting in his garden, engrossed in the Sunday papers. Putting them aside with a rustle, he listened to Joanna's story.

'Jeremy sounds a real bastard,' he said sympathetically, when she had finished speaking. 'But I'm afraid it's his word against yours – and he has the fax as proof.'

'Max, there was no fax in my tray and I refuse to be sacked for a mistake I didn't make. This is very wrong.'

'It's what we'd call unfair. Wrongful dismissal means your dismissal was not handled in accordance with your contract. Unfair dismissal means you have been dismissed for an unfair reason. Unfortunately, as the law stands today you need to have been employed for two years.'

'You mean, Jeremy gets away with it?'

'Er . . . Jo, hang on a sec. I'll take this inside. It's more private.' The line went dead. Shortly afterwards, Max picked up another extension. 'Why would the respected Head of Sales, who earns a great deal of money, lie about a fax to one of his salespersons? It doesn't make sense.'

'He knew I was suspicious and he wanted me out.'

'Have you any proof?'

'No, but . . .'

'Then for goodness' sake keep quiet. You don't want to be sued for slander.'

'Max, he threatened to withhold my reference.'

'Jo, an employer is not obliged to give a reference.'

'I know – but surely Jeremy isn't allowed to bribe me with it?'

'Did anyone overhear him?'

'Unfortunately not. The people in the lift assumed he was making a pass at me.'

'In any case, I doubt that they'd stick their necks out and risk their own careers – and you must think about your future. You should write to First Clarence asking for a written reason for your dismissal.'

'Wouldn't the letter be more effective coming from you?'

'Not at this stage. A lawyer's letter would make them think you're litigious – and you need that reference.'

They discussed the wording of Joanna's letter, and finally Max said, 'Emma and I are going to Copenhagen tomorrow for a couple of days. I'll phone you as soon as I get home. Once again, I'm really sorry about your news.'

They said goodbye, and it seemed to Joanna that no sooner had she replaced the receiver than Max rang back.

'Emma tells me that Felicity is away all next week.'

'Yes. She's hyping up the sales reps to sell next season's books.'

'Then come with us to Copenhagen. We're catching an afternoon flight. I've just checked and there are spare seats. We're borrowing a flat belonging to some cousins of Emma's, so there'll be no hotel expenses.'

'It's very kind of you but . . . surely you two would prefer to be on your own?'

'We wouldn't invite you if we didn't mean it.'

Joanna still hesitated.

'If you're anxious about money, let me treat you to the flight,' he added.

'No, it isn't that. I'd love to come but . . .' She feared to leave the safety of home, her sole anchor now everything else had been turned upside down.

'Jo, you need a break. I'll book your flight whilst you draft your letter to First Clarence. Then you can read it to me when I phone you with the travel details.'

The prospect of escape seemed suddenly very appealing. 'I'd love to come,' she said. 'You're a true friend.'

Late that evening, as Joanna was packing her suitcase, Oliver telephoned.

'I'm glad you caught me,' she told him. 'I'm off to Denmark with some friends for three days.'

'What friends?'

'Max and Emma.'

'Max the lawyer? So you consulted him after all?'

'I phoned him because I wanted to know my rights. He told me to ask for a letter of dismissal.'

'Joanna, you promised me that you would speak to no one.'

'I know, and I'm sorry, but I hadn't realised you'd be away so long. Max is totally trustworthy. He's one of my oldest friends.' She paused, and continued in a more conciliatory tone, wondering if Oliver was jealous. 'Max is not a boyfriend.'

'You gave me your word.'

She was becoming irritated. 'Oliver, I cannot get fired from the job I love, then sit at home on my own for two weeks, without speaking to my close friends. I'd be suicidal.'

'A promise is a promise,' he said, coldly – and the line went dead.

XVII

JOANNA CONTINUED TO be incensed by Oliver's attitude, but she didn't confide in Max and Emma when they collected her, since they knew nothing of her affair.

It was evening when they reached Copenhagen but the sun was still shining and there remained several hours of daylight. The streets were thronged with cyclists and the pavement cafés along the Nyhavn – the old harbour – were crowded with people talking, laughing and drinking lager.

Emma's cousins lived on the fourth floor of a newly restored building just off the harbour. As soon as they had deposited their luggage, they went out to look for a restaurant where they could dine outside. They found one beside the harbour. It served fresh fish and white wine, so expensive that Max thought there was a printing error in the menu. As they chatted over their meal, putting the world to rights like they used to do at university, Joanna realised that between her long hours at First Clarence and her on-off affair with Oliver, she'd missed spending time with her friends.

She woke next morning to see cars being loaded on to the ferry for Sweden. It was a world away from her problems with First Clarence and she was very glad that she'd come.

'Thanks for inviting me,' she told Max and Emma as they studied a map over the breakfast table.

'We're delighted to have you.' Max ran his finger down the list of attractions. 'Oh, look! The Museum Erotica! We must visit that.'

They set off to explore the old city. Max walked between the two women, linking an arm with each of them as they made their way through the cobbled pedestrian streets of the Strøget. They found the Museum Erotica, giggling as they climbed the stairs past an enormous plastic phallus. Joanna would have left Max and Emma to themselves but she felt conspicuous on her own among the pornographic photographs and paintings. At the same time she was conscious of being alone, and of them being a couple, of their desire for each other perhaps being stimulated by their surroundings.

At one point she wandered on ahead, studying the daguerreotype photographs of nineteenth-century prostitutes awaiting their clients. The girls' faces were sad, their expressions resigned. Just before the exit, she walked into a mini-cinema showing nine blue movies simultaneously on television-sized screens. A dozen solitary businessmen watched from the back of the room. Had Joanna been with a lover she might have felt differently but, surrounded by these strangers, she was embarrassed.

Max and Emma caught up with her.

'Just the sort of place where you bump into an old school friend,' said Max.

Laughing, they hurried out of the museum into the busy shopping precinct.

They continued to explore the old centre of the city, stopping for lunch at an outside café in one of the old cobbled squares. Nearby there was a group of students, perched on their bicycles, drinking beer straight from the bottle. One was playing a guitar.

In the afternoon, they hired bicycles and pedalled out to the Little Mermaid, dodging buses full of middle-aged American tourists. On their return to the harbour, they found it once again thronged with people taking an evening stroll, the hum of their voices mingling with the sound of jazz.

'Tomorrow we want to go to Elsinore to see Hamlet's castle,' Max told Joanna. 'We can hire a car. It's only about an hour away.'

'You two go. I'll stay here.' Joanna was determined to allow them some time on their own.

'You must come,' protested Emma.

'No . . . really . . . it's very kind of you, but I wouldn't mind a day on my own to think about . . . my future.'

They didn't press her.

Max and Emma set off early. As soon as they had gone, silence descended on the flat. Joanna stood in the sitting room, feeling like an intruder as she looked around at the possessions of the Danish family who had no idea she was in their home.

It was raining hard, but she slipped on her jacket, picked up her bag and went down to the street. In the doorway, shielded from the weather, she studied a street map. Then she set off, along the harbour, towards the Queen's Palace, bowing her head against the wind and the driving rain.

She cut through the cobbled square beside the palace and up into the King's Gardens. The trees dripped on her as she muttered to herself, reliving her last afternoon at First Clarence. Was it possible that she had overlooked the fax? She was sure she hadn't, but for the first time she had niggling doubts.

By the time Max and Emma arrived back from Elsinore, Joanna was greatly relieved to see them. She'd had enough of her own thoughts and company in a rain-swept foreign city.

They flew home next morning. Joanna tried to keep up a cheerful front as they neared London, but it was an effort to return to her empty flat. With Felicity still away, the mail had piled on the doormat and the answering machine pulsed a dozen times. There were calls from Simon, Rebecca, Vikram – but the rest had hung up without leaving a name.

As she opened her letters, the phone rang.

'Joanna Templeton?' said an unfamiliar man's voice.

'Yes,' she replied.

'I am from the *Interrogator.* Have you any comment to make on our article concerning your affair with Oliver Safarov?'

Joanna gasped. 'What . . . what article?'

'How do you respond to the suggestion that you have been sexually harassing Mr Safarov?'

'I . . . I don't know anything about it.' She slammed down the receiver.

The phone rang again, but Joanna didn't answer. She let the machine intercept. The caller didn't leave a message.

Picking up her purse, she hurried from the flat and down the road to the newsagent's, where she bought a copy of the *Interrogator.* Walking back, she flicked through the pages. It was a tabloid-size magazine, not very substantial, but she couldn't find any article referring to herself.

As she neared the house, a man approached. He had a camera slung around his neck. 'Sorry to disturb you,' he said, 'but do you know Joanna Templeton?'

Joanna stared at him.

'Smart lady banker, about your height,' he continued.

'No . . . er . . . sorry.' She hurried up the steps to the front door, her hands shaking as she turned the key in the lock.

Realising his mistake, the photographer raised his camera. 'Joanna! Joanna!' he shouted.

She refused to look round, but darted into the hall and slammed the door behind her. Only when she was safely inside her flat did she feel secure. Even then she closed the curtains, both front and back – the latter in case he gained access to her garden.

Joanna checked the magazine again, scanning each page until she came to the *At the Stake* City gossip section near the back, where her attention was caught by a paragraph.

What is behind the dismissal of high-flying Joanna Templeton who until this week raised the testosterone level among traders at First Clarence? Could it be linked to her pursuit of well-known City personality Oliver Safarov, one of First Clarence's most valued private clients? Surely the luscious Joanna could not possibly be harassing the newly appointed chairman of Invest-Est Europe?

Joanna slumped down on the sofa. She read the article three times. With each reading, her humiliation deepened. She could not imagine how they knew about her affair with Oliver.

As she was reading the article for the fourth time, the phone rang. She waited for the machine to answer, only lifting the receiver when she recognised Rebecca's voice.

'Oh, Rebecca, thank God,' she said. 'I thought you were another journalist.'

'Joanna, you must sue the *Interrogator.* It's appalling that they should be allowed to publish such rubbish.'

Simon joined in. 'Come to supper tonight. Rebecca will be there. It'll just be something simple. Katie will be feeding the twins, and I'll be cooking.'

'I'd love to come.' Joanna wondered how they would react when she admitted that she did know Oliver.

Even if Oliver was still angry about Max, she needed to speak to him. She knew he'd be outraged about this tacky disclosure of his private life.

Withers answered her call. 'I'm sure Mr Safarov wouldn't mind you having the number, Miss Templeton, but I'm not at liberty to divulge it,' he explained apologetically. 'I do hope you understand.'

'Yes . . . of course.' She should have asked Oliver for the number. 'Please tell him to contact me urgently.'

'I will, Miss Templeton.' The butler sounded so sympathetic that she almost confided the reason for her call, but she stopped herself. Oliver would not like that.

Unsure what to do next, she made herself some coffee. With the mug in one hand, she tiptoed to the front window and peered out between the curtains. There were now two photographers. She backed into the kitchen.

Feeling trapped and hounded, she paced up and down, waiting for Oliver to return her call. Surely the butler must have got hold of him by now? Surely Oliver wouldn't refuse to speak to her in order to punish her for confiding in Max? She made more coffee and decided that when this mess was over she'd invite him to dinner and introduce him to her friends. In the meantime, if he asked her to join him in France, she would go. She thought wistfully of the beautiful white villa, the sunshine, the swimming pool, the escape. No journalist would dare harass her there.

The phone rang. She answered it eagerly, no longer caring if Oliver admonished her about Max.

'Miss Templeton?' enquired a polite voice.

She was instantly wary. 'Yes.'

'This is Kevin Cardwell from the *London Evening Post*. I apologise for disturbing you but . . .'

She cut across him. 'I have nothing to say. Please don't phone again.'

'Miss Templeton,' he said, still courteously, 'we have proof that you pursued Mr Safarov to his villa in France.'

'I didn't chase him! He invited me.' She stopped, realising that she'd revealed too much already.

'Miss Templeton, this is very unfair on you. We journalists are making your life a misery solely because Mr Safarov is a prominent international figure.'

Joanna kept silent.

'Let me give you some advice,' he went on. 'It would be much better if you told me your side of the story. Then our readers won't think you're just some bimbo chasing a rich and famous client – which, of course, I know you're not.'

Joanna thought for a moment. Her instinct was never to trust a journalist, but maybe Cardwell was right. Perhaps she had no alternative, if she wasn't to be permanently labelled a fool.

'I do know Mr Safarov,' she said, selecting her words with care. 'I did visit his house in France, but only at his invitation. I did not pursue him there. I know Mr Safarov will gladly support me.'

'I never believed you did harass him,' admitted Cardwell.

'Thank you.'

'Just one other question, Miss Templeton. Whilst you were in France, did you offer to sell Mr Safarov information about which shares your other First Clarence clients were buying?'

She was outraged. 'Certainly not!'

'Did you offer to tell him for free?'

'I did nothing of the sort. I wouldn't dream of betraying clients' confidence.' Her voice rose in anger as she recalled how careful she'd been not to mention names. 'I don't know where you heard that story but it is absolutely untrue and if you print such a lie, I shall sue.'

'Thank you very much, Miss Templeton.' The line went dead.

Joanna was appalled. She paced up and down, clenching her fists, incensed by the stigma of dishonesty. Cardwell must have been fed the story by Jeremy. There was no alternative. She felt enraged but so helpless, as if her skin had been peeled away laying bare her flesh.

She needed Max's advice. He'd know what she should do. With shaking hands, she tapped out his number – only to be told that he'd left for a meeting. Whilst she waited for him to call back, she tidied the flat – anything to keep herself busy. The telephone rang on eight occasions. She let the answering machine intercept, but none of the callers left a name. Her intercom buzzed. She ignored it. It buzzed again. She removed the handset.

Max rang her on his car phone. 'Emma has just told me about the article. I'm between meetings. Shall I pop in?'

'Oh, yes! Please do!'

Twenty minutes later she unlocked the door and Max slipped inside.

'Poor Jo! How ghastly for you!' He engulfed her in a bear hug.

'It's a pack of lies.' She buried her face in his shoulder.

'Do you mean . . . you don't even know Safarov?'

Joanna took a deep breath and stepped away. 'I do, Max, but I didn't harass him. He made all the running. And I certainly didn't offer to sell him information about other clients' share deals.'

Max looked shocked. 'Who accused you of that?'

'A journalist asked me if the rumour was true. I was furious.

I'll never find another job if people think I committed fraud – as well as everything else.'

'I expect he was just trying it on,' said Max, in an attempt to comfort her. 'No paper would print such a story without proof. If they did, we'd demand huge damages – and they know it.' He paused. 'But . . . you were . . . seeing Oliver Safarov?'

She nodded.

'Good heavens! You aim high.' He looked at her in a new light. 'I had no idea.'

Joanna perched on the arm of the sofa. 'Only Felicity knew – and she was sworn to secrecy. But, Max, this had nothing to do with me losing my job. No one at First Clarence knew. Oliver made certain of that. He was anxious to protect me from gossip – and himself, I suspect.'

'Well, someone let the cat out of the bag. Do you have any idea who?'

'None. But I expect Oliver will have his suspicions. I'm waiting for him to ring me now.'

'Could it have been Jeremy?'

'He's the most likely culprit – and the most obvious inventor of scurrilous rumours – but I'm surprised that he'd dare upset Oliver.' She grimaced. 'This isn't going to help my career prospects, is it?'

'It's the rich and powerful Mr Safarov whom the press are interested in, not you. Most people will forget your involvement once the story dies – especially if First Clarence give you a first-rate reference. Just keep your head down and remain out of sight.' He gave her an encouraging smile. 'I must dash now. I'll phone you later. If you can escape from the house tomorrow, come to the office and I'll take you to lunch.' He enveloped her in another comforting bear hug and hurried to his meeting.

By the time Joanna was due to leave for Simon's house, there were five journalists outside in the street. Not wanting to run the gauntlet or to give them an opportunity to take another photograph, she arranged with Bertrand and Sylvie to climb over the wall into their back garden.

'If you need any help, you can depend on us,' said Bertrand as he accompanied Joanna through their house.

'Shall I tell those wretched reporters that a man only sends his Bentley for a woman he desires?' asked Sylvie.

Joanna shook her head. 'Thanks, but the sooner the story dies the better.'

Keeping her face turned away from the journalists, Joanna slipped out of the adjacent front door and headed for her car. Then she realised that might give away her identity. So she walked on, into the nearby square, where she hailed a taxi.

She arrived at Simon and Katie's large Victorian house and as soon as she touched the bell, they opened the door, welcoming her with sympathy and ushering her through to the friendly kitchen where Rebecca was waiting.

'What hell for you!' She hugged Joanna.

'It is – a nightmare.' Tears pricked Joanna's eyes.

'These journalists should be shot.' Simon handed Joanna a large glass of wine. 'They ought not to be allowed to claim that you allowed them into your house.'

'What do you mean?' Joanna was nonplussed.

'Haven't you seen the *Post*? It says that you gave an interview.' Rebecca passed Joanna the article by Kevin Cardwell, which was printed alongside an unrecognisable photo of the back of her head, taken as she had hurried into her building.

'Joanna Templeton confessed to me today that she did spend a weekend in France with multi-millionaire Oliver Safarov – but it wasn't financial advice she was giving!'

On the opposite page there was a feature headed '*The New Predator – the Young Career Woman*'.

Joanna lowered the paper to the table and looked at her former colleagues in despair. 'How could I have been so stupid? I spoke to Cardwell because it seemed the only way for me to defend myself. What a fool I am to have trusted a journalist. I hope my parents don't hear about this. They'll be so ashamed. It's the last thing they need – after my brother.' She buried her face in her hands.

Distressed, her friends gathered around and tried to comfort her.

'So it is . . . true about Oliver Safarov?' Rebecca ventured when Joanna was more composed.

'Yes, but I didn't chase him. He pursued me.' She looked up, and from the expression on their faces realised that they had thought the whole story a lie. 'It began at the Merantum Building launch. Remember the gorgeous lilies? They were from Oliver. I did go to France, but at his invitation. But I did not harass him. I am not in love with him. I just . . . like him. He's great company. We were . . . friends more than lovers.' She was too loyal to Oliver to tell them that sex had been a fiasco.

'If he's a good friend, why isn't he here now, defending you?' asked Katie with customary frankness.

'He's in France with his mother. She's had a stroke.' Joanna paused. 'Mind you, she always seems to be ill whenever he wishes to be out of the country.'

'Just like Bunbury, the conveniently sick friend in *The Importance of Being Earnest*.'

'So useful it's France, where he's protected by their privacy laws.' Simon stirred a carton of pesto sauce into the pasta. 'At least the article publicly discounts the other rumour,' he added, trying to sound optimistic.

'You mean, about me selling information?'

'Joanna, we all know you wouldn't do it. Even Vikram said it was untrue.'

'It's a total lie.' Her voice shook with anger. 'If anyone dares to print or repeat it, I shall sue.'

'And we'll all support you.' Simon turned off the gas. 'Please sit down, everyone. Help yourselves to garlic bread. Joanna, here's your plate. You look as though you haven't eaten all day.'

'Thanks. I haven't.' Joanna had always known that Simon was kind.

They sat at the long kitchen table.

'At least the photo in the paper is unrecognisable,' said Katie in an attempt to console Joanna.

'That's something,' she agreed, twisting tagliatelle around her fork. 'What I can't understand is how this story reached the press.'

'Oliver Safarov is a major player,' said Simon. 'He's rich, suave, famous, and enigmatic. He's newsworthy.'

'But who told the *Interrogator*?'

'Charlotte's the obvious choice,' said Rebecca firmly.

Simon shook his head. 'Charlotte wouldn't talk to a journalist. She'd never endanger her career – or her future reference.'

'Is she leaving?' Joanna was momentarily deflected from her own problems.

'Rumour says yes. Jeremy never liked Charlotte, and now that she has lost Sebastian's patronage, he doesn't bother to hide it.'

'And Vikram?' said Joanna. 'I bet he's overdosed on scandal mongering.'

'Yes, but he wouldn't talk to the press. He liked you, in his cynical way. No, I think the leak has come from Safarov himself.'

'But Oliver hates publicity.' Joanna recounted how he had gone out of his way to avoid the press at Sotheby's and how, after Goodwood, he'd purposely taken her home first.

'What about his butler?' asked Rebecca.

'Withers wouldn't risk his job. He's devoted to Oliver.'

'He could be secretly disgruntled.'

Joanna recalled Withers' story of how he had come to work for Oliver. 'I don't think so.'

'I reckon we are all missing the point,' said Katie, fetching the cheeseboard. 'This story is not just about a well-known man and a much younger woman. It taps into the whole issue of mixing business and pleasure – with the added ingredient that the predator is a woman.'

'So what do I do? Pray for a new royal scandal?'

'It'll blow over,' Katie assured her. 'I used to work in public relations. No story runs without further fuel.'

'I hope you're right.' Joanna wanted to believe her. 'The trouble is that dirt sticks – and sexual dirt sticks worst of all. Until this is dead and forgotten, I don't stand a chance of finding another job.'

It was late, and Joanna realised that Simon and Rebecca hadn't mentioned their early start in order not to rub salt in her wounds.

She rose. 'Thanks for this evening. I'd have been suicidal on my own. But it's late. Could you call me a cab, Simon?'

'I'll give you a lift,' offered Rebecca.

'You live in Hampstead. It's out of your way.'

'No, it isn't. Anyhow, you can't go home alone, not after such a horrific day.' Rebecca picked up her bag. 'I insist.'

They thanked Katie and Simon, and went out into the night.

When Rebecca drove into Joanna's street, she braked whilst they checked that no reporters were hanging around. To their relief, it was deserted.

'I'll phone you at lunchtime tomorrow to make sure you're all right,' Rebecca told Joanna.

'Don't worry. I'll survive. I'm lunching with an old friend from university and my flatmate will be home in the evening.'

'Then I'll call you on Monday – I'm visiting my grandmother in Brighton at the weekend.'

'Thanks – for everything.' Joanna forced a smile, fighting back her dread of the lonely flat which awaited her, comforting herself that tomorrow Felicity would be home.

She took out her key and raced up the steps to her front door, unlocked it, then turned to wave goodbye. As she watched Rebecca drive away, she felt a stab of envy. Tomorrow Rebecca and Simon would be in the hustle and excitement of First Clarence – where she, Joanna, was no longer welcome.

It was long after midnight but Joanna couldn't sleep. She sat at the kitchen table working out her finances. She had some money saved, but not a lot, perhaps enough to last six months – more if she was careful. Working at First Clarence had proved expensive. It had meant high spending on clothes, taxis, and after-work drinking.

She recalled Fittertons. Maybe she should have stayed there, played safe, and not yearned. She wondered if old Mr Fitterton had heard of her downfall, and knew with a pang of fondness how upset he would be for her.

There was a sharp knock on her flat door. Joanna froze. She listened intently, not making a sound, hardly daring to breathe. She couldn't imagine who it could be. There was no access to the building without using the intercom.

Another knock and a muffled voice called, 'Joanna.'

She tiptoed to the door. 'Who is it?' she whispered.

There was no reply. Whoever was outside could not – or would not – hear her. Keeping the chain in place, she cautiously opened the door and peered out through the crack.

There was a man in the dimly lit hall. He seemed familiar but she couldn't place him.

'I'm Adam Hunter,' he reminded her. 'I want to talk to you about Oliver Safarov.'

'I have nothing to say, except that you have no right to be in this building,' she replied icily. 'I don't know how you got in but . . .'

'A journalist's ingenuity. Joanna, please listen to me. Just for five minutes.'

'Absolutely not.' She shut the door in his face.

'I'm not interested in your sex life with Safarov,' he called to her.

'I've trusted one journalist – and that was enough. If you don't go away, I'll phone the police.'

He was silent for a minute. 'All right. I'll leave. You'll find a present on your doormat. I suggest you read page fifteen.'

The street door clicked and Joanna heard his footsteps descend the outside steps. She crept to the front window, and watched as he retreated along the pavement to his car and drove away. Only then did she open her door. On her mat was a newspaper. Without removing the chain, she stretched her hand through the gap and pulled it inside. Across the top Adam had written his work and home telephone numbers.

Joanna opened the paper. Halfway down page fifteen there was a picture of Oliver leaving an exclusive French clinic.

> *'I know Joanna Templeton,' Mr Safarov admitted today. 'She is a charming girl who, unfortunately, misinterpreted our relationship. But I am a gentleman and I do not discuss the ladies in my life – even those who only feature briefly.'*

Joanna felt sick with rage and mortification. Oliver's words punched her in the stomach, sucked the air from her lungs, crushed her and humiliated her. How dare he imply that she was just a fling. How dare he turn her into a laughing stock in order to make himself appear more virile.

She relived the occasions on which she'd felt guilty in case she was using Oliver for his contacts. She recalled how earlier that evening she'd refrained from recounting the fiasco of their love-making. She remembered assuring Simon that Oliver would never speak to the press. What a fool she'd been!

She made some coffee and re-read the article. Was it possible that the journalist had twisted Oliver's words, as Kevin Cardwell had edited hers? She wanted to believe it, but she was afraid of deluding herself. Oliver was rich and powerful. He would sue over the slightest distortion. Therefore, no newspaper would dare misquote him. She was an unemployed saleswoman. What paper would worry about tweaking up her words in order to produce a better story? She studied Oliver's statement. He was too clever not to be aware of what he'd said. It was only her – stupid and gullible – who fell into journalists' traps.

XVIII

THE MORNING POST brought two letters. One was from First Clarence stating that she had been dismissed for 'neglect of duty'.

The second was a handwritten note from Harriet Cunningham.

Sorry to hear of your troubles. Never liked Safarov. Get in touch when the dust settles. Will do my best to help.

Harriet was one of the last people whom Joanna expected to bother with her now, and she felt shyly grateful as she penned an appreciative reply.

The morning dragged past. The only contact was from a journalist who rang her intercom until she threatened to call the police if he didn't stop. At noon, she peered out through the front curtains. To her relief, the street was deserted.

Not wanting to waste money on taxis, even though rain threatened, she took the tube to Temple and walked up through Lincoln's Inn Fields to Max's smart, busy offices. He was in a meeting, so she waited in the chrome and leather reception. On the table in front of her were several newspapers and magazines, including the *Interrogator*. Joanna eyed the receptionist, wondering if she knew.

Max burst out of his office. 'Hello, Jo. Sorry to keep you. I've booked an Italian restaurant. Hope you like it.' He gave her his usual bear hug, and ushered her into the lift. 'Shitty business about that article,' he said, once the doors had closed. 'They must have misquoted Safarov. He wouldn't be so ungentlemanly.'

'I wish I could believe that!'

'You mean . . . you think he really said it?'

'Yes. Vain bastard. God, what a fool I was to get involved with that man.'

Joanna handed him First Clarence's letter. Max glanced at the page, then placed it in his pocket.

'What do I do now?' she asked anxiously.

'I'll tell you when we reach the restaurant.' The lift stopped and he took her by the elbow, escorting her out into the street. 'We'll find our table, order a drink, then we'll discuss it.' He glanced up at the darkening sky. 'Quick, before it pours!'

They dashed down Chancery Lane, dodging the barristers and clerks from the High Court. Only when they were settled at their table, with the wine poured and their crudités in front of them, did Max re-read First Clarence's letter, taking an inordinately long time to do so – or so it seemed to Joanna. From experience, she knew that it was impossible to hurry him. Max had always been meticulous.

'They have a perfectly valid reason for dismissing you,' he said eventually. 'You failed to fulfil instructions – twice.'

'I didn't receive the fax.'

'It's your word against Jeremy's.' Max laid the letter on the table.

With a sharp crack, Joanna broke a stick of grissini. 'I have lost my job. I've been threatened. I've been accused of sexual harassment and dishonesty. Are you telling me that there is nothing I can do?'

'To be sensible – yes.' He munched on some raw cauliflower. 'The wild rumour that you offered information to Safarov has died of its own accord. If it hadn't, we'd have had to take action. As it stands, your best best is to forget about it. If you keep speaking about it, you'll resuscitate it. And people will start to wonder.'

'You mean, they'll think there's no smoke without fire.'

He nodded. 'Yes. I know it seems unfair, but my advice is to put this behind you as quickly as possible. Even if you did sue, First Clarence wouldn't give you your job back – which is what you'd really like.'

'I know – unfortunately.' She made no attempt to hide the anguish in her voice.

'So we have to try for the best achievable result. Let me argue for a good reference – not just a 'To Whom It May Concern' testimonial – but something which will impress a prospective employer.'

Joanna sighed. 'Max, I appreciate your advice but this is unjust. Jeremy lied. So did Oliver. He's probably in on it too.'

Max eyed the nearby tables. 'Jo, keep your voice down. You'll be sued for slander. Safarov may not be chivalrous but that doesn't mean he's crooked. He's far too big a player to participate in some racket. Why would he take such a risk, for goodness' sake? He's fabulously wealthy already.'

'I know – but Jeremy isn't.'

'Be careful.'

'Why?' She jabbed her fork into her steak. 'I have nothing to lose.'

'You have your life. If what you suspect is true, big money is involved.'

'Jeremy should be stopped.'

'If – I say *if* – he is committing fraud. But you have no proof. You don't even have enough to warrant going to the police. If you start making wild accusations, you'll end up dead.'

'The way I feel today it would be a blessing.'

'That's not true! You have a great future, so long as you don't get bogged down by desire for revenge.'

Joanna looked at him with deep anguish in her eyes. 'Max, I don't want revenge. I want justice.'

He smiled sadly. 'I know – and I wish I could help you obtain it. In a perfect world, we'd fight. In this world, we have to be practical.'

Joanna reached across the table and squeezed his hand. 'In a perfect world, Max, there would be no Jeremys.'

They parted on the pavement outside the restaurant.

'You can't spend the weekend on your own,' Max said worriedly. 'Emma and I are off to Wales tonight. Come with us.'

Joanna kissed him on the cheek. 'Thanks – but no. You've done more than enough already, inviting me to Copenhagen. I'll be fine. Felicity is back tonight.' She mustered up a cheerful smile, thanked him for lunch, and set off down the road.

As she was on the point of crossing Fleet Street, a portly young man in a cheap, tight suit pushed into her. She stepped aside. He elbowed her again. She started to protest.

'You're Joanna what's-her-name,' he said, with an unpleasant snigger. 'The girl in the newspaper.'

Joanna felt a flush creep up her neck. For a moment she was paralysed, unable to think how to act. Then she dodged past him, ran into the middle of the road, and hailed a taxi. His laughter followed her.

She was still shaking when she reached home, her hands trembling so much that when the taxi driver gave her her change she dropped it in the gutter. She left it there and ran inside.

Once in the flat, Joanna bolted the door and slipped on the chain, tugging at it to ensure that it was properly secured. Even then, she didn't feel safe. She tiptoed to the front window and peered out through a crack in the curtains. There were two men talking in the street. Were they waiting for her? Was she their prey? She recalled the stag trapped in the quarry, clambering up the steep earth as it tried to escape from the hounds. She remembered how it had lost its footing and, with eyes rolling in terror, had fallen backwards into the pack, to be torn to pieces.

The telephone rang. She backed away from it, into the kitchen, as though afraid that the caller could see her. The machine intercepted with a series of clicks.

'I'm meeting Tom in Paris for the weekend. See you Sunday night. Bye.'

Joanna grabbed the receiver but Felicity had cut the connection.

She sank into an armchair and buried her face in her hands. She was selfish to be upset that Felicity was going to Paris, especially when, until recently, she'd had little time for her friends, but she couldn't help her disappointment. She'd been looking forward to Felicity's return, to the sympathy and support which formed part of their friendship. Now she was faced with a weekend alone.

Her father telephoned as soon as it turned six o'clock. When Joanna heard the quaver in his voice, she knew that he had been informed of her downfall.

'Virginia brought us a newspaper,' he began.

'I know, Dad. I'm sorry.' Joanna cursed Virginia, picturing her bossy aunt hurrying over to her parents, revelling in someone else's bad luck.

'Why didn't you tell us you were in trouble?'

'I didn't want to worry you.'

'Jo, we're your parents. We want to help. Come home for a few days. Come tonight. The break would do you good.'

She looked around the flat. Only here, behind the bolted door and the chain, did she feel safe. 'I'll be fine . . . thank you . . . and I'll be down for Mummy's birthday.'

They said goodbye. He hadn't asked if the stories were true and Joanna sensed that he didn't want to know about his daughter's sex life.

Furious with Virginia for interfering, and with Lindsay who hadn't even bothered to get in touch, Joanna changed from her suit into jeans and a shirt. Then she checked the fridge for provisions. There were plenty of precooked meals in the freezer, but no milk.

She went to the window and looked out. The two men had disappeared. Just a couple of neighbours ambled home from work, stepping over puddles which glistened in the sporadic shafts of sunshine. Picking up her keys and a handful of change, Joanna hurried out to the corner shop.

It felt good to be in the fresh air, to see people laughing and joking and going about their normal Friday evening routine. After buying the milk, Joanna kept on walking. She wandered down to the Fulham Road, into the bookshop near the cinema. No one looked at her. She was just another browser. They didn't associate her with the woman at the centre of the Oliver Safarov scandal.

Ambling on, she came to the cinema where she stopped to study the forthcoming features. Passing the corner shop for the second time, she bought an *Evening Standard*. She skimmed the pages as she walked, relieved to see no mention of herself.

When Joanna reached her street, she was perturbed to see the photographer from the *London Evening Post* outside the house. Irritated, she retreated to a nearby square, sat down on a bench, and waited.

Mrs Applegate, an elderly neighbour, was walking her poodle in the gardens. 'Enjoying the fresh air, dear?' she asked Joanna.

'Yes . . . er . . . I am.'

'Quite right too. I can't stand being cooped up. Mind you, one has to be careful with all these strange men hanging around. Someone told me they're from the newspapers, but I think they're burglars. Not that I have anything worth stealing. My pension barely covers the two of us. Come on, Nancy! Time for supper.' She tugged gently on the poodle's lead. 'Goodnight, Joanna. Enjoy your evening.'

Joanna wondered what Mrs Applegate would say if she knew the reason why she was lurking in the gardens.

She returned to her street, keeping to the far side where a large tree arched out over the pavement. There were now two photographers. She wished she knew what had happened to renew their interest. She longed for her home, but feared their barrage of questions. So she retreated to the bench, and read her newspaper.

Joanna spent the next two hours in the square, leaving it only to check her street at regular intervals. But the photographers did not move. She became desperate. Dusk was falling, and the air grew colder. The sky darkened, threatening rain.

She found a phone box and, using a precious 20p from her handful of coins, she telephoned Simon and Katie.

Their nanny answered. 'They've gone to Katie's parents for the weekend.'

Joanna thanked her – and cursed the wasted 20p.

She tried Rebecca, hoping to catch her before she left for Brighton, but the answering machine cut in. Another 20p wasted.

Hungry and thirsty, she walked to the corner shop and bought a bar of chocolate – she no longer cared if it was fattening. Back in the square, she wolfed the chocolate and drank the milk. The men still hadn't moved.

It began to drizzle. The wet drove her out of the gardens. She returned to the Fulham Road, wandering in and out of all the shops which stayed open late, pretending that she was a serious shopper, whereas in reality she was keeping dry and killing time.

Needing to go to the loo, she went into a pub, slipping through the crowds of drinkers to the ladies' room. She remained there for a while, warming her arms beneath the automatic hand dryer.

Two girls entered, discussing a film they'd seen. One left a copy of the *London Evening Post* beside the basin whilst she went into a cubicle. Joanna glanced at the front page. There was nothing about her. Then she looked inside – and bit her lower lip as she read:

BANK GIRL IN THE RED

When wealthy City figure Oliver Safarov was pestered for sex by bank employee Joanna Templeton, colleagues say it wasn't just a power suit she wore to entice him but pure silk scarlet underwear.

Joanna clutched at the basin for support. No wonder the press was on her doorstep. But what colleague had talked? Could it be Charlotte? Others at First Clarence were tough; Charlotte was a bitch. Except, Simon was right, Charlotte would not endanger her own position.

The cubicle opened and the girl stepped out. 'That's my paper,' she said accusingly.

'Sorry.' Joanna dropped it and fled.

She returned to her street. The photographers were sheltering under one giant umbrella. They were smoking and chatting, and showed no sign of moving. Again Joanna backtracked to the square. This time she hovered in the shelter of the trees, the bench being far too wet for her to sit on.

She started to panic. She didn't know what to do. She couldn't stay out all night and she had no money for a hotel or even a taxi fare.

The drizzle turned to rain. Her jeans and shirt were plastered to the lines of her body. She shivered violently. Whatever the consequences, she had to go home. Steeling herself to run the gauntlet, she made her way along the pavement beside the iron railings which surrounded the garden. She had almost reached her street when the low-slung door of a red MG sports car swung open, blocking her path.

With a sharp intake of breath, she jumped backwards.

'Joanna! I want to talk to you.' It was Adam Hunter.

'Please leave me alone.'

'I can't.'

Realising that he was about to get out of his car, she turned and ran, away from her house and back down towards the bright lights of the Fulham Road.

Adam ran after her. 'Joanna! Wait!'

She ran on, past the pub, and almost catapulted into the traffic when he caught up with her, seizing her by the arm.

'Don't kill yourself for Safarov,' he said.

She pulled away. 'Stop bothering me or I'll call the police. I mean it this time.'

He released her. 'Joanna, I can help you.'

She laughed cynically. 'A journalist! Don't give me such crap!'

'I'm working on a story and you are my source.'

Joanna raised her chin and looked him in the eyes. 'I have nothing to say to you – or to any other journalist.'

She started walking back to the flat, her feet slopping inside her wet trainers.

Adam followed. 'I'm not interested in your sex life with Safarov,' he said. 'I'm interested in Safarov.'

Joanna didn't reply.

They drew level with his car. Now she could see five photographers and reporters outside her house. She slowed down, hesitant, taking refuge from the rain under a large tree.

'Bad tempered though you are, you may shelter in my car,' said Adam, opening the passenger door.

Joanna ignored him.

'You'd be wiser to trust me than to throw yourself on the mercy of the wolf pack,' he went on.

She continued to watch the house.

'You'll catch pneumonia.' He settled himself in his car and wound down the window, calling out in an irritatingly jokey voice, 'Oliver Safarov is not worth dying for.'

Joanna didn't reply. She realised that he was trying to make her retaliate in order to get her talking.

Adam turned on some music and lit a cigarette. Joanna shivered beneath the dripping tree, wondering what to do next.

The rain became heavier. It came down like stair rods, straight through the tree and on to Joanna's head. She clutched her newspaper for warmth, its print coming off on her arms and her shirt. She refused to look at Adam in the comfort of his car. She wouldn't give him that satisfaction.

Watching her, Adam was astonished by her resilience. She was soaked. Her clothes stuck to her body and her hair hung like rats' tails, but she refused to give in. He recalled the sleek, confident saleswoman he'd met at First Clarence. There was no resemblance. Instead, he was reminded of the half-drowned puppy he'd found in a weighted sack on the edge of a gravel pit when he was eight. He remembered how he'd attempted to revive it, cuddling it under his sweater, trying to impart some of his own warmth – but it had died in his arms.

He stepped from the car and marched over to Joanna. 'Shall we negotiate a ceasefire?' he suggested.

'Only if you promise not to interrogate me.' Her words were spoken through chattering teeth.

'I promise – until it stops raining.'

'That is not long enough.' The end of her sentence was lost in a sneeze.

'It will be, if you die of cold.' He took off his jacket and placed it around her shoulders. 'Get into the car, you obstinate woman!'

Joanna was too cold and wet to argue further. She allowed herself to be ushered into his car, relishing the comfort of the leather seat and stretching out her legs into the warmth of the heater, which he turned up so as to dry her.

'Cigarette?' He offered her one.

'Don't tempt me! I've given up.'

He smiled. 'I said you were a mule.'

'If you'd experienced what I have this week, you too would be wary,' she responded sharply.

He held up his hands in surrender. 'I offered a ceasefire and I stick to my promise. But you're cold and wet and I'm starving. So why don't we go back to my place, dry off, eat and then I'll bring you home.'

'And you won't question me? Come on, Adam, I may have made mistakes but I'm not a complete moron. Please drive me up to my house. I'll run inside.'

'Do you really want to give them the chance to take a recognisable picture?'

Joanna stared at him. 'That man! How could he have known my face?'

'What man?' asked Adam eagerly.

'I was accosted in the street today, after I saw my lawyer.'

'You saw a lawyer? Why? For God's sake, you must tell me.'

'I don't *have* to do anything,' she reminded him.

'I know. The ceasefire. No questions.'

The injustice of her dismissal and the strain of the past days flooded into Joanna's face. 'Do you really believe I pursued Oliver Safarov?' she asked.

Adam took her by the shoulders and turned her to face him. 'No – and I don't believe that you offered him information on other clients' shares either.'

Joanna flinched.

'I heard that rumour and discounted it, as did most people,' he went on. 'Their reason was lack of proof. Mine is that I don't think you're a cheat. You were a bloody fool to play with a man like Safarov. But so what? We've all had unwise love affairs.'

'Most don't cost you your job,' she said bitterly.

'Joanna, there's much more to this story. That's why I need to talk to you.' He saw the mistrust in her expression, and continued quickly, 'I only want you to listen to me. I won't ask you a single question. You don't have to say anything. Just hear me out. At the end, if you choose, I'll drive you home – and I'll never contact you again.' There was deep emotion in his voice and real anguish in his dark blue eyes – a torment similar to that which Joanna had been suffering.

'So long as you promise not to interrogate me,' she said.

'I have given you my word.'

He held out his hand and she shook it – ignoring the inner voice which warned her that Adam Hunter was just another untrustworthy journalist.

XIX

ADAM OWNED THE top two floors of a large Gothic-looking house in Bayswater. He had his own front door at the side of the building. A wide oak staircase led straight up into an enormous hexagonal space, with a high, arched ceiling and windows looking out towards Hyde Park. The room was sparsely furnished, with just two expensive-looking but uncovered sofas, a grandfather clock, a couple of oil paintings, some piles of books and a stack of packing cases. It could hardly have been more different from Oliver's ornate London home.

Adam disappeared through a closed door and returned with two dry sweaters.

'Put this on,' he said, offering Joanna the smaller, in navy blue.

'It's all right, thanks. My shirt has dried.'

'You'll catch cold.' He held it over her head. 'Do I have to dress you by force?'

'No.' She took it from him. The wool smelled faintly of his aftershave.

He led the way up a spiral staircase to his spacious attic office-cum-kitchen. At one end, there was an antique leather-topped desk with his computer, fax, files and telephone. The walls alongside were lined with books, whilst more books waited in boxes to be allocated shelf space. At the other end there was a kitchen, with a door opening on to a roof terrace. On the kitchen table were piles of magazines. Underneath it were more packing cases full of books.

'When did you move in?' asked Joanna.

He looked slightly embarrassed. 'Four years ago.'

She laughed.

'My sister nags me to unpack each time she visits,' he confided. 'But I always find something more important to do – such as work. I refuse to buy furniture which I don't like, just to make do, so I end up with nothing.'

'The minimalist office?'

He grinned. 'That's what I'll tell Sarah – my sister.'

He went into the kitchen and placed some French bread in the microwave. 'Wine or coffee – or both?' he asked.

'Wine first. Coffee later.'

'Good.' He opened a bottle of claret and poured two glasses, saying, 'This will warm you up. Shame it won't have time to breathe, but we can't be fussy.'

Adam was right, the red wine was too cold, but it heated her veins and made her feel mellow. Whilst he raided the fridge, producing cheeses, pâté and the remains of a salad, she studied a photograph of a boy aged about six or seven. He had dark brown hair, like Adam, and the same intense blue eyes, but a chubbier face and a rounded urchin hair cut.

'Your son?' she asked.

Adam's face lit up. 'That's Toby. He's my little devil.'

Joanna assumed that Toby was asleep downstairs, behind one of the closed doors. There were numerous pictures of the boy, as a baby, as a toddler, playing football, but none of a woman – although Joanna noticed a pair of pearl stud earrings on a shelf.

She wondered if their owner would appear, and if she would be perturbed to find her husband with a strange woman wearing one of his sweaters. Or perhaps they were so confident in each other that she had no insecurities. Joanna couldn't help feeling envious. She had never been that sure of any man – not even Peter.

The delicious smell of warming bread filled the room. Adam cleared the magazines and books from the table, glancing at the titles, asking if Joanna had read them, and recommending some but advising against others.

'Let's eat,' he said, pulling out a chair for her. 'Sorry it isn't more exciting.'

'It looks wonderful.' She cut a slice of brie.

They ate quickly, tearing at the French bread and covering it with lashings of pâté or cheese. Between mouthfuls, Adam talked.

'It was because of Richard Holdfast, my first editor at the *Sunday Chronicle*, that I bought this flat, put down roots and became a staff reporter.' He paused to top up Joanna's glass. 'Until five years ago I'd never considered being anything but freelance.

I loved the liberty, although it was bloody hard graft touting my ideas, hassling for columns, fighting to obtain a byline. Then, one afternoon, the *Sunday Chronicle* offered me a permanent job. Without even considering it, I turned it down. I didn't want to lose my freedom – even though the *Sunday Chronicle* was my favourite paper and I longed to work on one of its in-depth investigations, which were always allocated to staff reporters.'

Adam rose to place more bread in the microwave. 'Later that day, I stepped into the lift and found myself alone with Richard Holdfast, the editor. The Great Chief! I was like a lowly mercenary sharing a lift with the head of the armed forces. Richard had only ever spoken to me twice – once to disagree with an article I had submitted, and another time to congratulate me. On this occasion, he stared at me from under his bushy eyebrows. "You're a bloody fool, Hunter," he said. "You have potential, but you're without discipline."

'At that moment we reached the ground floor. Without another word, he marched through the reception and into the street. I hurried after him to ask what he meant. We were standing on the corner of Fleet Street and Ludgate Hill – this was before the paper moved to Docklands – and he pointed his huge finger at me – he had these huge hands – and told me that only by committing myself to one newspaper would I become a better journalist.' Adam smiled at the memory. 'I changed my mind on the spot and accepted the job.'

The microwave pinged. Adam extracted the bread and sat down again.

'Did you ever regret your decision?' asked Joanna.

He grimaced. 'Every day for the first few months. Richard made me rewrite and rework until I never wanted to see another story. But, gradually, I grew to appreciate him. I loved him. We all loved him. He taught me to seek perfection. He smoothed my rougher edges. He gave my writing structure.' Adam glanced at Toby's picture. 'Other aspects of my life did not go so well, but you can't have everything.'

Joanna remembered her conversation with Jeremy. 'Didn't Richard Holdfast write that article about Carthew Instruments?'

Adam frowned. 'Richard killed himself because of Carthew.'

'Of course. I'm sorry. I shouldn't have mentioned it.' She reproached herself for having been so tactless.

'He suffered from depression but, in spite of what people said afterwards, his moods never clouded his judgement.'

'Adam, I didn't mean to criticise. In any case, if Carthew couldn't meet their commitments, which they clearly couldn't, then Richard was correct to write the article – however painful the repercussions. He had no reason to blame himself.'

'Carthew weren't in serious trouble.' Adam left the table to open a second bottle of wine. 'They were struggling because of the recession, but they could have survived. Their product – precision scales for weighing pills – was excellent. People always need medicines. Richard's article not only caused their bank to panic and foreclose, but their suppliers also lost confidence and demanded instant payment.'

'Then why did Richard write what he did?'

'He believed he had evidence.' Adam walked over to the shelves, extracted a book and removed two letters secreted amongst the pages. 'Read that!' he said, handing one to her.

The letter, marked 'Confidential', was from the Chief Executive of Carthew to the company solicitor, Nigel Kirkpatrick at Rawdale's – Bryan Rawdale's firm. It asked Kirkpatrick for advice on the best way for Carthew to inform their bank that they could not meet the next instalment of their loan.

'It's a fake,' said Adam, as Joanna finished reading.

'How do you know?'

He handed her the second letter. It was an angry missive from the Chief Executive of Carthew to Richard. He strenuously denied having written the letter to Kirkpatrick to which Richard had referred in his article – although he admitted that the signature was a perfect copy of his own. He accused Richard of not checking his facts, saying he alone was responsible for the 2,000 Carthew employees who had lost their jobs. At the bottom of the letter Richard had written, '*He is right. I am to blame. Oh God, what have I done?*'

'Five days later, Richard shot himself.' Adam took the letter from Joanna's hands.

'I'm so sorry,' she said. 'What a tragedy. But why didn't he quickly write another article, correcting his mistake?'

'By the following Sunday the damage was done.'

'How awful that he blamed himself.'

'He couldn't help it. You see, he understood all too well the black despair of being laid off. His father was a miner who never worked again after his pit was closed.'

'Where did you obtain the letters?'

'From Mary Holdfast, Richard's widow. In the note which he left for her, he asked her to give them to me.'

'Who gave them to Richard?'

'If I knew that, I'd be halfway to solving the mystery.'

'Do you think it was that creep Rawdale?'

'Much as I dislike Bryan Rawdale, I can't believe he'd risk his lucrative career.' Adam replaced the letters inside the pages of the book. 'If he were found to have released a confidential client letter, he'd be struck off. The same applies to Kirkpatrick. They are greedy animals, but they're not fools.'

'If the Chief Executive of Carthew is to be believed, there was no letter to Kirkpatrick.'

'Exactly! Someone forged it.'

'Someone with access to Carthew headed paper and the ability to copy the Chief Executive's signature.' She looked at Adam. 'Any employee or shareholder could have copied that from the annual report.'

'Except that no employee or shareholder would have wanted Carthew to go bankrupt.' Adam rose and paced the floor, then he turned and fixed Joanna with his intense blue eyes. 'On the day when Richard began to draft that article, he met Oliver Safarov at a lunch.'

'So that's why you wanted to speak to me?'

'I swore I'd solve the mystery for Richard's sake – and for Mary.'

Joanna thought of what Max had said. 'I wish I could believe that Oliver was involved,' she replied, 'but greatly as it irks me to defend him, I'm not so blinded by desire for revenge as to claim he's a forger – or that he'd get mixed up in a sleazy little deal.'

'How can you be so sure?'

'Because he doesn't need to. He's extremely rich, and respectability means everything to him.'

'That didn't stop him from disparaging you to the press.'

She pulled a face. 'You don't need to remind me.'

'I'm sorry.'

She returned to the subject. 'What could Oliver possibly gain from bankrupting Carthew?'

'I don't know.' Adam spooned coffee into the cafetière then added boiling water.

'Was he the only person Richard spoke to at the lunch?'

'Of course not. Richard was a journalist. He would have worked the whole room. But I have checked the guest list and, of the thirty people there, not one was connected to Carthew.'

'Was there anyone present from First Clarence?'

Adam seized on her question. 'No, but you haven't told me why you consulted a lawyer. Did you suspect something there? You did, didn't you? I can see it in your face. Joanna, you have to tell me!'

She stiffened. 'I only agreed to listen.'

He held up his hands in surrender, a habit she had noticed earlier. ' I didn't mean to bully you. It's just that . . .' He gave her his most appealing smile. 'I'm due to be posted to New York in January. You are my best – and probably my last – chance to discover what really happened to Richard. By the time I come home, in two years, the trail will be even colder than it is now.'

They were silent for a few minutes, whilst Adam poured the coffee. Joanna deliberated between her desire for justice and her mistrust of Adam as a journalist. Then she thought of Oliver. What an idiot he'd made her look. And Jeremy. She could still feel his fingers digging into her arm and hear his threat to deny her a reference.

'This afternoon, when I left Max, my lawyer, I was in a fighting mood,' she said. 'On my way home a man accosted me. He claimed to recognise me from the papers. Now I realise that was impossible. The picture was too blurred.'

'Someone is determined to humiliate you – and I think that person is Safarov.'

'For what reason? He has already satisfied his inflated ego.'

'Then who else?'

'It has to be Jeremy, my boss. He set me up in order to sack me.'

'Do you have proof?'

She shook her head.

'Then we'll find it.'

Joanna rose. 'No, Adam, I can't.'

'So you'd let him get away with it?' he said despairingly.

'I have to! My father phoned this evening. My busybody aunt had shown my parents the stories in the press. They are distraught.

If I don't back down, I risk more publicity. I can't inflict that on them.' She crossed to the door, then stopped. 'I'm sorry about Richard.'

She started down the spiral staircase.

'Joanna!' Adam called after her. 'Whoever is trying to shut you up wants you to forget about First Clarence because your suspicions are correct.'

Joanna stopped in the curve of the spiral. 'Don't you think it drives me wild that I lost the job I loved because I suspected my boss was a crook?'

'Then tell me all you know. Help me to ascertain that Richard fell foul of an insider-trading ring and I will do everything I can to prove that you were unfairly dismissed – and that you did not pursue Safarov.'

'Adam, who would believe you? People prefer to think the worst.'

'I'll make them . . . we'll make them. I promise!'

She hesitated.

'Come back,' he said, holding out his hand to her. 'However long it takes, I won't give up. I make the same promise to you as I gave to Mary at Richard's funeral.'

They stared at each other in the gloom. Then she raised her hand to touch his long, slim fingers with her own.

'For as long as it takes.' She repeated his words.

He did not release her fingers, but led her back up to the office, gripping her tightly as though afraid she would change her mind.

'First we need to establish a link between those under suspicion,' he explained, pulling up a second chair behind his desk. 'Then we must discover the system by which they commit the fraud – and, finally, we need concrete proof of the fraud itself.'

Joanna spent the next two hours outlining the doubts which she believed had led to her dismissal. Initially, she omitted the names of the offshore companies, still feeling bound by the rules of client confidentiality, until Adam pointed out that unless they pooled all their information they would never succeed.

Whilst she spoke, he keyed in the names of the funds and the dates of transactions – most of which she remembered without assistance from a diary.

'Could Società Hadini have previously dealt through another salesperson and sent that fax to him or her in error?' he asked.

'The fax number was mine.'

'Do you have a copy of it?'

She shook her head. 'I wish I had. I wish I'd copied all the data whilst I had the opportunity. If only I could break into the trading room. The password won't be changed for a month, but of course I no longer have an electronic pass to the door.'

'You can't go back to First Clarence,' said Adam firmly. 'It's too dangerous. You'd put Jeremy on guard. And it would all be for nothing. A newspaper can't use information obtained by illegal entry. The Press Complaints Commission allow us some subterfuge if a story is in the public interest and the material cannot be obtained by other means, but that doesn't include breaking into office premises and stealing information.'

'If illegally obtained evidence gives you a lead to a legitimate source, can you use that?'

'Yes.' He thought for a moment. 'What about your colleagues? Were any of them sufficiently disgruntled to access the computer for us?'

Joanna was shocked. 'Adam, I couldn't ask them. It wouldn't be fair.'

He shrugged. 'It was just an idea.'

Adam's proposal reminded Joanna that he belonged to a hustling profession. Whilst he questioned her about the offshore companies and the people with whom she had dealt, she resolved that he would never gain access to her friends.

He keyed in Bilsham at Kathpeach, Lawrence at Società Hadini, Frederick at New Aldren Fund, and George at the Redrey Trust. 'Any connection between these people?' he enquired.

'Not as far as I know.'

'Did you speak to them or just fax them?'

'I only spoke to Mr Bilsham that once. I told you, Jeremy was furious.'

'Was Bilsham angry?'

She thought back. 'Not at all. He didn't even sound surprised to hear from me. According to Jeremy, Kathpeach were about to place an order.'

Adam leaned back in his chair and stretched his arms above his head. 'Why the hell would a client, who didn't complain when you disobeyed his instructions, subsequently ask for you to be taken off his account for a far lesser misdemeanour?'

She sighed. 'I don't know – but I'd like to.'

The grandfather clock struck three.

She pushed her chair away from the table. 'I must go home.'

'I'll accompany you in a cab to make sure you get home safely,' he said, adding apologetically, 'I know I promised to drive you, but after the wine we've drunk I'm over the limit.' He hesitated. 'Or else you could stay the night in Toby's room.'

Joanna looked doubtful.

'No. You're quite right. Why should you sleep in a strange bed when I agreed to take you home?'

'Oh, it isn't that.' She was suddenly filled with dread at the prospect of her lonely flat. 'Won't Toby mind?'

'He lives with his mother and only stays here on Sunday nights. I take him to school on Mondays – Monday is a home day if you work on a Sunday paper.'

'Then I'll stay – if that's all right.'

'Good.' He smiled, and she decided that he was really quite attractive in a hawkish way, though not a type she had ever been drawn to – Peter had a boyish face. Nevertheless, his attitude to her colleagues continued to shock her.

Adam led her downstairs to a small bedroom which was decorated with pictures of Thomas the Tank Engine.

'The bathroom's next door,' he said, handing her a towel and a new toothbrush.

'Thank you. Goodnight.'

As they faced each other in the darkened corridor outside the bathroom, Joanna felt increasingly awkward. She began to wish she'd made him take her home. She must be mad to stay in a strange man's house. After all he'd read about her in the newspaper, he probably assumed she was offering sex.

He took a step towards her.

She froze.

He put his hand inside the bathroom. 'The light is here,' he said, pulling the cord. 'But the door doesn't lock. Toby lost the key.'

Joanna reproached herself for being so presumptuous. 'Thank you . . . very much.'

'Goodnight. Sleep well.' He started up the spiral staircase, calling over his shoulder, 'I wouldn't have asked my colleagues to compromise themselves either.'

She was inexplicably relieved.

She washed her face and cleaned her teeth half-undressed, and slid under Toby's Peter Rabbit duvet. From upstairs she could hear the click of Adam's keyboard.

Joanna woke early, to the sun streaming through the window and the drone of a printer in the office. Feeling jaded from too much wine and lack of sleep, she dragged herself out of bed, under a shower and into her clothes. When she studied her reflection in the mirror, she decided that she had seldom looked worse. Her clothes were rumpled, her shirt had a smear of chocolate on one sleeve, and her hair had matted in the rain. She couldn't even disguise the dark rings under her eyes with make-up – she had none.

She ran her fingers through her hair and went upstairs. Adam was hunched over his computer.

'Good morning,' she said.

He glanced up. 'Oh . . . hello. Umm . . . do you mind making yourself breakfast? Coffee's made.' He waved his hand towards the kitchen and returned to his screen.

Joanna poured herself a mug of coffee, then asked, 'Would you like some?'

He frowned. 'Er . . . no, thanks.'

Joanna tried not to let Adam's offhand manner annoy her, but she began to have doubts. She'd told him everything about First Clarence and her affair with Oliver. On top of that, she'd spent the night in his house.

'I'd like you to get your facts straight,' she said angrily.

He looked up, surprised by her tone. 'What are you talking about?'

Joanna pulled down the shoulder of her shirt to reveal the strap of her bra. 'My underwear is white, not scarlet. Shall I spell white for you?'

Adam rose from his chair, seized her by the arm, and frog-marched her over to his computer. 'I'm not writing an exposé of my night with Joanna Templeton, if that's what you fear. I don't write that kind of rubbish.' He pushed her closer to the screen. 'See for yourself!'

Joanna looked. He was updating an article on the Maastricht treaty.

'I'm a newspaperman,' he went on. 'I work for a Sunday paper. Saturday morning is our busiest time.' He released her abruptly. 'Do I get an apology?'

'Yes. I'm sorry, I really am, but I can't help being suspicious.'

He sat down at the computer. 'We have to trust each other if we're going to work together.'

'I know.' She looked bleakly at him, wondering if she would ever trust anyone again.

Whilst Adam finished his article, Joanna sat out on the roof terrace, eating toast and marmalade and relishing the morning sun.

'Where can we find the offshore company fax numbers?' he asked, joining her.

She reeled them off.

He stared at her. 'I'm impressed.'

'Numbers are what I'm good at.' She pulled a face. 'At the moment they seem to be the only thing I'm good at.'

'Wallowing won't help.'

'I am *not* wallowing!'

He laughed. 'That's better. Every time you feel crushed, I shall provoke you until you fight back – even if that means you fight me.'

They were interrupted by the telephone.

Adam returned to his desk. 'I bet that's the office.' He picked up the receiver. 'Yes, Malcolm. Good, you received it. No, I'm working on something. It could be the break we need, a major scoop, but not for this week. Of course I'll tell you! You're my editor!' Adam listened and started to frown. 'What's wrong with Maastricht? You have to reduce it? No, don't cut that line, it's the whole point of the argument. I'll do it. Fax it back to me. No, I'll come in.' He came off the line and turned to Joanna. 'I have to rescue Maastricht from Malcolm's cowardice. Malcolm Burke – Burke by name and berk by nature.'

Joanna laughed. 'Is he that bad?'

'Malcolm used to be Richard's deputy. Paola, one of my colleagues, says he was born to deputise, and she's right. Initially, the board of directors only promoted him as a stop-gap. A newspaper editor needs flair and courage. Malcolm's too cautious. After Richard died, I wrote a piece about all he'd achieved for the *Sunday Chronicle* – his brilliance and his downfall. I mentioned the last City lunch he'd attended and listed those present, including Oliver Safarov. Within an hour of the first edition hitting the streets, the chairman of the board asked Malcolm, as a favour, to omit Safarov's name.'

'Why – if you hadn't libelled him?'

'Because Safarov is a friend of the chairman and they sit on the same boards of various big charities.'

'Did Malcolm acquiesce?'

'Yes – the coward! He cut all the names. He extracted the teeth from my piece.'

Joanna recalled what Sebastian Deveraux had said about the *Sunday Chronicle* losing its bite.

'Why isn't he fired?' she asked.

'Because we cover for him.' Adam collected his papers together. 'Malcolm's not unpleasant, he's just not editor material, and he's compared unfavourably to Richard, which understandably enrages him.' He closed his briefcase. 'Anyhow, who wants to be responsible for a man losing his job?'

'Jeremy would.'

'I'm not Jeremy,' he said firmly. 'Come on!'

As they went down the oak staircase to street level, Adam explained the workings of a weekly newspaper. 'It's run like an army, with a strict hierarchy. Producing a Sunday paper is to plan a weekly battle. It only works if the editor is in full control. Each Tuesday morning we have an editorial conference when stories and features are discussed and allocated. If a big news story breaks, of course, it takes precedence. So, come Saturday, some features have to be shelved. A journalist who's spent days working on a feature fights hard for his or her story. The editor has to be decisive. Malcolm makes the mistake of trying to pacify everyone by reducing each article – as if Wellington had tried to win the battle of Waterloo without sacrificing a single foot-soldier.' He unlocked the front door and they stepped out into the bright morning sunshine.

Adam offered to drive Joanna home but she refused. She could tell that he was in a hurry, whereas she had nothing to do. Before they parted, they arranged to meet at Companies House on Monday morning to check if any of the offshore companies had obvious subsidiaries in the UK.

'It's a long shot,' said Adam, 'but investigations are a mixture of hard slog, tiny details – and a dose of luck.' He stepped into his car and drove away.

The moment he disappeared, Joanna remembered that she only had 40p – not even enough for a bus fare. She set off to walk home across Hyde Park, where joggers sweated up and down the paths and dogs gambolled on the grass. As she drew near to her flat, she kept a cautious eye out for photographers, but the street was deserted. Thankful, she hurried into the safety of the house.

But when she slotted her key into her flat door, she found it unlocked. She froze, terrified, her imagination racing between armed burglars, reporters, and the man who had accosted her in the street.

The door flew open.

She gasped with fear.

'There you are!' exclaimed Felicity. 'We've been so worried. We came back to find your bed untouched, your bag and purse on the table – but you were gone.'

Joanna could not speak. She put her hands up to her face and cried with relief and exhaustion.

Whilst Tom poured her a stiff brandy, Felicity explained that she'd known nothing of Joanna's problems until she'd read a newspaper on the flight to Paris. On landing, she'd tried to phone Joanna from Charles de Gaulle airport but received no reply from the flat. Then she'd tried Max and Emma, who were away. Finally she'd rung Joanna's parents, who had sounded devastated. Worried at the thought of Joanna being on her own, Felicity had hardly slept. In the morning Tom had suggested they fly home.

'I can't thank you enough – both of you,' whispered Joanna. 'This week's been hell. First I lost my job then . . . the press stories. I've been hounded by photographers and reporters. They were on the doorstep last night. I couldn't get in. I could kill Oliver.'

Tom was astounded.

'Surely a man like Oliver Safarov wouldn't have revealed your affair to the *Interrogator*?'

'No, I think it was Jeremy, though I am surprised he'd risk displeasing Oliver – unless he got wind that Oliver intends to take his business away from First Clarence, or so he promised. Not that his word means much, as I've discovered to my cost.'

'Didn't Safarov try to head off the press?' Tom persisted.

'Did he hell! He told them that I was just a fling.'

'That man is a bastard.' Felicity put an arm around Joanna. 'He may be a respected figure in the City, but he's a bum and he didn't deserve you.'

Joanna smiled weakly. 'Thanks.'

'At least you weren't in love with him.'

'Yes. It's bad enough to be humiliated by someone who claimed to be a friend.'

They made coffee and sat out in the garden in the sunshine. With the warmth on her face and on her limbs, Joanna began to feel better.

'I don't know how I'll ever trust any man again,' she confided, watching two courting sparrows on a nearby roof and wondering if birds also deceived each other.

'You haven't told us where you stayed last night,' said Felicity.

'I was with Adam Hunter.'

Felicity looked blank.

'I'm sure I told you about him. He's the journalist from the *Sunday Chronicle.*'

'You stayed with a reporter?' Felicity stared at Joanna as though she'd gone mad.

'I slept at his house – not *with* him! He's going to help me exonerate myself. He has been trying to solve the mystery of Richard Holdfast, his editor who committed suicide, and he thinks there's a link.'

Tom and Felicity exchanged doubtful glances.

'I hate to interfere,' said Tom, 'but are you certain you can trust this guy? Once he has his scoop and clears this Richard character, why should he give a damn about you?'

'I have to believe in Adam,' replied Joanna, looking from one to the other. 'Don't you see, he's my best chance – my only chance.'

XX

ON MONDAY MORNING Joanna waited on the steps of Companies House in City Road, watching the buses and cars belch fumes into the hot summer morning. The pavement was thronged with people, hurrying to their offices – but there was no sign of Adam.

Fifteen minutes passed. The sun beat down on her face. The smell of petrol and diesel penetrated her nostrils and her throat, and made her eyes sting. She shifted from foot to foot, reminded of the evening when she had waited for Oliver at his club. It was more than a week since she'd been fired from First Clarence, but the wound was as raw as if it had happened yesterday.

Another ten minutes ticked by. Joanna became angry. She recalled the exchange of glances between Felicity and Tom. Were they right? Was she being a fool – again?

Suddenly, a huge black Norton Commando motorbike roared up to the steps.

'Sorry to keep you,' Adam called to Joanna. 'I had to take Toby to school by car. Then I decided to go home for the bike. It's so much quicker in this traffic.' With a cheerful wave, he drove off to find a parking space.

A moment later he sauntered along the pavement, his helmet under his arm. When he saw Joanna's expression, he stopped smiling.

'You thought I wasn't coming, didn't you?' he said, astounded.

'I don't like to be kept waiting.'

'You assumed I'd changed my mind?' He repeated his accusation, shaking his head in disbelief. 'Joanna, are you crazy? Do you think I'd jeopardise my best opportunity to vindicate Richard?'

'It would sound more courteous if you included your desire to exonerate me,' she said crisply, irritated by his attitude.

'Proving you were set up is part of our bargain. It's the price I have to pay for your help.'

She stiffened. 'Are you always so rude?'

'I'm being honest,' he replied. 'I like you. I find you attractive. I enjoyed the way you fastened my cufflinks, as though it was the most natural thing in the world to go to City parties where strange men asked you to help them dress. But Richard meant the world to me – whereas you and I have just met. There can be no comparison in my feelings. To say otherwise would belittle the strength of my affection for him – and suggest that you're fool enough to believe me.' He paused, and added, 'If you want saccharine lies, you need Oliver Safarov.'

She flushed. 'That was cruel.'

'It's the truth.' He opened the door of the building for her.

'Have you read *Pride and Prejudice*?' she asked.

He looked puzzled. 'A long time ago. Why?'

'To quote Elizabeth Bennet, "Honesty is a greatly overrated virtue; in some cases silence would be more agreeable".' She stepped haughtily past him and into Companies House.

Adam laughed. 'That's what I like about you, Joanna. You have spirit.'

She gave him her most withering stare. 'It was meant to be an insult.'

They sat down at one of the terminals in the large open-plan offices, calling up the company names on the screen. Although there were many companies with similar names, it was clear that none was linked to the offshore funds. They checked Bilsham, Lawrence, George and Frederick among the names of directors. Again, there were directors with those surnames but none was connected to companies called Kathpeach, Società Hadini, the Redrey Trust or New Aldren Fund. Nor did they appear to have any link with Liechtenstein, Grand Cayman, Bermuda or Monte Carlo.

'It always was unlikely,' said Adam, as they left the terminal and went out into the stuffy, airless day.

'What now?' Joanna tried not to feel deflated by their lack of immediate success.

He glanced at his watch. 'Eleven o'clock. Let's separate. We'll get more done. We'll meet at your place at seven. I'll go to the commercial sections of the embassies or consulates which represent Monaco, Liechtenstein, Grand Cayman and Bermuda to see if I can obtain actual addresses for the funds – not just box numbers. You go to the Westminster City Library and check every Bilsham, George, Frederick and Lawrence in the telephone books for London and the Home Counties. Look for smart addresses, like Mayfair, Kensington, Hampstead, or The Manor, The Old Rectory, The Grange, The Hall.'

'Shall I include the fashionable counties like Gloucestershire and Cheshire?'

'Definitely. I refuse to believe that one of them does not have a UK residence.'

'You mean, having made a fortune abroad they can't resist the temptation to lord it at home?'

He smiled. 'You've got it!'

They had just started down the road towards his motorbike when a taxi swerved into the gutter and a blond, bespectacled man, whose face was vaguely familiar to Joanna, stuck his head out of the window.

'Adam! You rogue!' he shouted. 'What kind of friend are you? Why didn't you answer my call on Friday? Melissa is visiting her mother and I wanted to go drinking.'

Laughing, Adam approached the taxi. 'David! What the hell are you doing here?'

'I'm on my way to interview the Governor of the Bank of England.' David studied Joanna. 'Aren't you going to introduce me – or are you having a secret assignation? Monday morning in the City Road! Adam, couldn't you find somewhere more romantic?'

Joanna giggled.

'I know what you're up to,' said David. 'You're on the trail of some hot story.'

'Would I tell you if I were?' joked Adam.

'No, you bastard, you wouldn't. How's Toby?'

'Very well.'

'Are you still going to New York?'

'Unless Malcolm can be persuaded I'm indispensable in London.'

'Or unless he can be convinced that your popularity is not a threat to his editorship.'

'Which it is not!'

'Of course not – with a stronger editor.' David glanced at his watch. 'I must dash. Can't keep the Governor waiting. Come and see us soon, Adam. I'm off to California tomorrow to join Melissa and the boys. We'll be away a week. Bring Toby over on Sunday when we get back.' He eyed Joanna again. 'Goodbye, mystery lady. Be nice to Hunter. He's a good friend.' He tapped on the dividing glass and called to the driver to continue.

'He's most entertaining,' said Joanna, as the taxi disappeared. 'I've seen him before, but I can't think where.'

'On television. He presents *Weekly Money* every Saturday morning.'

She clicked her fingers. 'Of course!'

'I'm always at work, so I video it,' Adam went on. 'David's one of my closest friends. We met when we were cub reporters on a chaotic provincial newspaper. Our editor was the most heartless man I've ever known. His stock instruction was "Get me an N and D sob", which translated as us having to hang around the streets in order to waylay the nearest and dearest of a bankrupt or fraudster so as to capture their distress.

Joanna couldn't help laughing at his ghoulish story. 'Supposing they wouldn't talk?' she asked.

'We bribed them.'

'And if they still refused?'

'They never did.'

They had reached the big black Norton Commando. 'I'll give you a lift,' he offered. 'I have a spare helmet.'

Joanna shook her head. 'No, thanks.'

'Scared? he teased, as the engine throbbed into life.

'My brother was killed in a motorbike accident ten years ago. For my parents' peace of mind, my sisters and I promised never to go on a motorbike again.'

'I'm sorry if I touched a raw chord,' he said gently.

'It's not your fault. That's the disadvantage of barely knowing someone, isn't it? You say things which hurt them because you're unaware of their past wounds.'

'The disadvantage of knowing someone well is that if you want to hurt them, you know what to say. You know how to turn the knife.' A bleak expression came into his narrow face, making it appear older and harder. He swung his leg over the seat of his bike and roared off in the direction of the City.

Joanna assumed that he had been referring to Toby's mother.

She spent the rest of that day checking the directories at the Westminster Library. In London alone, there were six Bilshams, three columns of Georges, a dozen Fredericks and a page of Lawrences. In the Home Counties she discovered a further ten Bilshams, thirty Georges, eight Fredericks and seven pages of Lawrences. She photostatted the entries and went home, thankful that when she reached her street she found it free of reporters.

She opened the French windows to let in fresh air, then checked the messages. There were words of encouragement from Rebecca and Simon. She wished she could tell them about her quest for exoneration, but she couldn't: it would put them in an invidious position.

As she was watering the pot plants, Max phoned. 'I've been worried about you,' he said. 'How are you?'

'I'm a little better, thanks.'

'Have you decided if you want me to negotiate with First Clarence over your reference?'

'I'm . . . umm . . . thinking about it.'

'Jo, you're being ambiguous. I know that tone. What are you up to?'

'Max, please don't ask me. You wouldn't approve. But I appreciate your concern.'

She carried on watering the plants. Then she cleaned the flat, not because it was dirty but to keep herself occupied. The day was warm and close. By the time she had finished, she was dripping with perspiration. She showered and changed into a sleeveless dress in dark pink Indian cotton, a garment she'd only ever worn on holiday.

Adam arrived late, but she was getting used to that. He'd discovered the addresses of the offshore companies, but didn't know if they were real offices or glorified post boxes. Joanna showed him her lists of names and addresses. He glanced down them.

'Have you tried any?' he asked.

She shook her head.

He sat down at the table. 'Let's start dialling. May I use the phone?'

'Of course.' She was surprised that he had thought to ask.

'We'll do the county Bilshams first.' He indicated to Joanna to pick up the kitchen extension, and dialled the first name.

'May I speak to Mr Bilsham?' he enquired politely.

'Er . . . who's calling?' replied a quavering elderly woman.

'An old friend of his.'

'But . . . my husband has been dead for ten years.'

'Oh, I'm so sorry. I must have the wrong Bilsham.' He replaced the receiver, crossed out that Bilsham, wrote 'deceased', and tried the next name.

'Mr Bilsham?'

'I'm sorry, he can't come to the telephone. Can I help?' This woman's voice was brisk and businesslike.

'I met him in Vaduz and . . .'

'Where?'

'Liechtenstein.'

'You're mistaken. Mr Bilsham has never been out of England.'

'Oh, I'm sorry. I must have the wrong Bilsham.' Adam crossed off the second name, and tried the third – again without success.

It took him half an hour to telephone fifteen Bilshams. The sixteenth was on holiday, according to the gardener who answered the phone.

'Could you tell me where he is?' asked Adam.

'Somewhere in Austria, I believe.'

'Austria!' Adam repeated giving Joanna the thumbs up. 'When will he be back?'

'Tomorrow morning.'

'Thank you. I'll phone again.' Adam came off the line, smiling broadly. 'I think we've struck gold. Liechtenstein borders both Switzerland and Austria. Joanna, I'll be tied up in our Tuesday meeting, so you phone him tomorrow.' With a flourish, he circled the last Mr Bilsham in red.

Felicity returned from work. 'Don't let me disturb you,' she said.

'You're not.' Adam made room for her at the table. 'I was about to invite Joanna out to supper. Why don't we all three go?'

The two women exchanged glances and nodded.

They went to a nearby bistro and sat at a table in the window. When they had updated Felicity on their progress, and discussed their next moves, Adam made a point of talking of other subjects. He asked Felicity about her job and they all discussed their favourite writers.

After dinner, Adam walked them home and waited until they had safely unlocked their flat door. Then he turned to Joanna in the darkness of the hall. 'Phone Bilsham at lunchtime. I'll check with you later.'

'Fingers crossed he's the right one.'

'If he isn't, we'll keep trying.'

'I want results – now!'

'Patience, Miss Templeton!' He smiled, and said goodnight.

Joanna closed the flat door behind him. She felt oddly deflated.

'I like Adam,' Felicity called from the bathroom where she was cleaning off her make-up. 'He's quite different from what I expected. It's very noble of him to spend his free time trying to clear Richard's name.'

'He has to do it,' said Joanna.

Felicity stuck her head round the bathroom door. 'Why?'

Joanna recalled the way Adam's face had softened when he spoke of people for whom he cared. 'He promised Richard's widow.'

In the morning Joanna telephoned Mr Bilsham, putting on her most businesslike voice.

A woman answered. 'What are you calling about?' she enquired.

'I'm Mr Hunter's secretary. Mr Hunter recently met Mr Bilsham in Liechtenstein and he'd like to arrange a lunch meeting.'

'Who? What? But my husband's never been to . . . Liech . . . wherever.'

'But he has just been in Austria?'

'We've been on a coach tour with our local art history society.'

In spite of her disappointment, Joanna nearly burst out laughing at the highly respectable explanation. 'I'm sorry,' she spluttered. 'There's been a mistake.'

When Adam phoned, he shrugged off the setback, saying they were bound to have false leads.

'I have to go to Brussels,' he said. 'It's a bloody bore but Malcolm wants me to cover some damned conference.'

'Didn't you tell him about our investigation?'

'Of course.'

'Isn't he interested?'

'He's slavering at the thought of it. To be in on a big scoop is the dream of every newspaperman. The nightmare is to be duped.'

'Like the Hitler diaries?'

He chuckled. 'Exactly!'

'If Malcolm is keen, why do you have to waste time in Brussels?'

'God only knows! But that's the way it is. Malcolm insists I continue to work on other stories.'

It was Joanna's turn to be positive. 'Brussels is only about four hundred miles from Liechtenstein. You could go there and check the address for Kathpeach. You might even find Mr Bilsham. If he lives in Liechtenstein, someone must know him. It's a tiny place.'

Adam bounced back. 'Good idea! I'll fax the Brussels article on Friday, then fly to Innsbruck and hire a car. I used to have a contact in Vaduz, the capital – a retired telephone engineer. He's bound to know Bilsham.' Adam paused. 'Why don't you meet me there? It would be fun – and we'd get much more done.'

'I wish I could.' She meant it. 'But it's my mother's sixtieth birthday on Saturday. My father's giving a party for her. I couldn't possibly miss it.'

'The tenth anniversary of your brother's death must be a poignant time,' he said sympathetically.

'It is.' Joanna was astonished that he remembered.

The last thing Joanna felt in the mood for was a family celebration, with all her relations and her mother's friends aware that she had made such a mess of her life.

It was the first Saturday of a predicted hot spell and the traffic leaving London was heavy, with acrid fumes belching up into the motionless air. The sun beat down on the roof of Joanna's car as she crawled along the M4. North of Bridgwater, an accident held her up for an hour. She thought of Virginia and Lindsay, waiting impatiently, and of her parents who were alarmed by the slightest delay, but there was nothing she could do. She turned on the radio, laid her arm on the open window ledge, and tried to relax.

She arrived to find Virginia and Lindsay fretting on the doorstep of Virginia's pretty wisteria-covered cottage. They were checking their watches and looking anxiously up and down the lane. Virginia, a formidable grey-haired woman, wore a lilac silk dress she'd bought fifteen years earlier, when she was two sizes smaller. Lindsay was in wistful pale blue. Her shoulder-length auburn hair, the same shade as Joanna's, was looped back in a loose plait. Her face, not dissimilar to Joanna's but lacking the determined chin, was devoid of make-up.

'Sorry to be late,' Joanna called to them. 'The traffic was awful.'

'Since you're out of work I can't see why you couldn't leave

London last night,' said Virginia, easing her bulk into the front seat. 'Your poor father will have had to organise the caterers all on his own.'

Resolved not to lose her temper, Joanna didn't reply.

In the back seat, Lindsay was also silent.

'I must say, Joanna,' Virginia went on, 'of all Margaret's daughters, you're the one I least expected to fall by the wayside. You're meant to be clever.'

Before Joanna could explode, Lindsay intervened. 'Virginia, we've decided not to discuss it. Mummy doesn't want us to,' she added to give weight to her words.

Joanna was surprised and grateful for Lindsay's intervention. She caught her eye in the rearview mirror and smiled.

They completed the remainder of the journey in frosty silence. When they reached the house, Virginia stepped from the car without a word of gratitude and marched across the lawn to the orchard, where the buffet lunch was being arranged on trestle tables in the shade of the old apple trees.

Joanna turned to Lindsay. 'Thanks for sticking up for me. I could have strangled the old bitch.'

'I don't blame you. It's none of Virginia's business.' Lindsay fiddled with her hair. 'I'm sorry I haven't been in touch. I kept meaning to phone, but I didn't know what to say. You must've had an awful time, being betrayed so publicly. I don't know how I'd cope if it happened to me, I really don't.'

Joanna grimaced. 'Bloody men!' she said through gritted teeth.

Lindsay laughed. 'That's right, Jo! You show him what you're made of. If anyone can fight back, you can.'

They walked slowly up the garden path, savouring their new-found intimacy.

XXI

JOANNA WAS RELIEVED when the party was over. Although all the guests had avoided the subject of her disgrace, she had been acutely aware of their sympathy for her parents – and a certain smugness from those whose daughters had never ventured beyond Taunton.

She spent the remainder of the weekend taking long walks over the Quantocks with Lindsay and Alice, breathing in the fresh air, relishing the smell of bracken and heather. From time to time they stopped to eat bilberries or to watch the wild ponies grazing in the wooded valleys.

She had planned to return to London on Sunday night but she couldn't face the flat and the possibility of reporters on her doorstep, so she remained with her parents. In the morning she departed later than she'd intended, dawdling over breakfast, dreading the moment when she would have to launch herself back into the world.

It was noon when she drove into her street, thankful to find it deserted. She parked her car and hurried inside. The house was oppressively silent. Everyone was at work. On the hall table were a couple of letters for her – both bills. In the flat she found yesterday's newspapers neatly stacked, and the remains of a bar of Felicity's chocolate.

There were two messages on the machine. Joanna stared at the winking light, trying to fathom her reaction if one of the callers proved to be Oliver. Would she ring him and savage him – or had she the self-control to wait for her triumph in the *Sunday Chronicle*?

She pressed the button.

The first message was from Adam. It had been left on Saturday. He'd found Kathpeach's registered office but it was closed till

Monday. He was remaining in Vaduz for the weekend and hoped to see his engineer contact.

There was a series of clicks, then the second message.

'I'm home. Where are you? You told me you'd be back in London on Sunday night. We need to talk.'

It was Adam again. She breathed a sigh of relief. His voice cheered her. As she dialled his number, she pictured their scoop on the front page of the *Sunday Chronicle.* Herself exonerated. Jeremy imprisoned. Oliver abashed and humiliated. Yes, she needed that last victory.

'Where the hell have you been?' he demanded.

'With my parents,' she snapped back.

'I've been hanging around all damned morning.'

'Then hurry up and tell me what happened in Vaduz.'

He gave an impatient sigh. 'It was a waste of time! It was a solicitors' office and they refused to divulge any details – except that it is Kathpeach's registered address. Bloody lawyers! I was furious.'

'And you still are,' she said. 'Did you meet your contact?'

'He was on holiday.' He paused. 'How was your mother's party? Did the relations burn you at the stake – or commiserate quietly with your parents?'

She laughed, and her temper abated. 'The latter. But the good thing was that I talked to my sister, Lindsay. I mean, we really talked, something we've never done, and we realised that we don't . . . dislike each other. We're different, that's all. Discovering Lindsay was the best part of the weekend.'

'I'm glad.' He was suddenly very gentle. 'Why don't you come over now? I'm about to make lunch – or rather the delicatessen made the sauce. Spaghetti *alle vongole.*'

'Put the water on to boil. I'll be there in fifteen minutes.'

When Joanna arrived at Adam's house he didn't come down to the door but let her in via the intercom. 'I'm in the kitchen and I need help!' he called down.

She hurried upstairs to find him attempting to drain the spaghetti into a sieve which was too small. Much of the pasta had already slithered down the sink. Amused by his predicament, Joanna took over.

'You still haven't told me why you didn't come back last night,' said Adam, thankfully relinquishing the sieve.

She didn't look at him. 'I couldn't . . . face it.'

'That Monday morning feeling?'

She nodded. 'But I'm better now that I'm here.'

'I'm glad.'

He opened a bottle of white wine and poured them each a glass. Then they sat down to eat.

'I used to have that sinking feeling at the end of the school holidays,' he said, between mouthfuls. 'When I was eleven, my father had his first stroke. Mother was busy looking after him – and I ran wild.' He broke a stick of French bread and handed half to Joanna. 'I played truant and started shop-lifting. I was an angry little boy, desperate for attention. Eventually I was picked up by the police – which caused my poor mother yet more worry.'

'What happened?' she asked, pushing aside her clean plate.

'A well-meaning social worker found me an assisted place at a boarding school designed to discipline uncontrollable boys. It was one step away from Borstal. I'll never forget the dread of going back for a new term.'

'How long did you stay there?'

'One year.' He lit a cigarette. 'I was expelled for selling cigarettes. They threw me out so fast that I had no time to collect my stock – ten packets of Gitanes hidden under the awnings. I expect they're still up there, blocking the gutters.'

She smiled at his story. 'You should stop smoking.'

He blew a ring of smoke towards the open terrace doors. 'Yes, Boss.'

Joanna leaned towards him, her elbows on the table, a flirtatious gleam in her eyes. 'You need controlling.'

He studied the set of her face, her large grey eyes, her generous mouth. 'No. You do.'

They held each other's gaze, challenging, provocative, enjoying the game, each determined not to back down. Then Joanna remembered Oliver, who'd always had to win.

'We'd better get to work,' she said, in a businesslike voice.

'You're right.' He copied her tone. 'We're wasting my precious free Monday.'

They telephoned all the remaining names whose addresses sounded monied, but none had any connection with the companies in Liechtenstein, Grand Cayman, Bermuda or Monte Carlo.

'This is going to take forever,' said Joanna, with a groan.

'We'll succeed in the end.' Adam gave her an encouraging smile. 'Investigations can take months.'

She was even more dismayed. 'I can't kick my heels for that long!'

'Joanna, we cannot write our story until we have proof that the law has been broken. Malcolm wouldn't print it – and for once he'd be right. We have to ascertain that at least one of these funds not only bought shares just ahead of takeover announcements but that they did so on the basis of insider information. That is the crime.'

She sighed. 'If only I could access that list of offshore clients' transactions in Jeremy's computer. Then we could line them up with the public announcements.'

'If only!' repeated Adam, leaning back in his chair.

She rose. 'I must go. I have . . . things to do.'

'What things?'

'Oh . . . personal stuff.'

'Can't it wait?' he asked impatiently. 'Today's my only free day. We'll never succeed if you give up so easily. We have to follow every lead. Go to the newspaper library at Colindale. Check the back issues of the *Financial Times* for the past three years and make a chronological list of announcements of bids and takeovers. The ring are bound to have bought shares in some of the companies concerned. Somewhere, somehow there is a clue – and we have to find it.'

Joanna retrieved her bag. 'I'll phone you tomorrow morning.'

Adam didn't bother to hide his irritation. 'I thought you had more guts. I'd never have suggested we team up if I'd known you were so spineless. You don't stand a chance in hell of exonerating yourself, even with my input – and you don't fucking deserve to.'

'You can't absolve Richard without my help,' she retorted, stung by his accusations. 'You had accomplished nothing in two years.'

'Your help! You're as useless as Malcolm.'

She raised her chin. 'Maybe you'll have to eat your words.'

He took a step towards her. 'I very much doubt it!'

'We'll see.' Joanna stalked out of the attic.

As she left, she noticed that the pearl studs were no longer on the shelf. Their owner had returned.

She walked up to Notting Hill. She didn't blame Adam for being disappointed. She just wished she could have told him what she planned to do, but he might have tried to prevent her – and she couldn't risk that.

She stopped at a phone box to check a number and confirm an address. Then she took the underground to St Paul's. After consulting her *A–Z*, she crossed under Holborn Viaduct, doubling back several times before she found the dead-end street. Halfway along, on a bright blue door, was a sign: 'BetterClean Office Services'.

She opened the door and stepped into a large shabby office with a desk at one end and a row of chairs along one wall. It was empty. Joanna hesitated.

An inner door opened and a plump, bosomy middle-aged blonde appeared. 'Good afternoon,' she said, seating herself behind the desk and putting on the turquoise-rimmed spectacles which hung on a chain around her neck. 'Do sit down. I'm Mrs Hollingsworth, manageress of BetterClean. How may I be of service?'

'I'm looking for work,' said Joanna, taking one of the chairs.

Mrs Hollingsworth registered surprise. 'Cleaning?'

'Office cleaning.'

'Are you sure, dear? My girls work very unsociable hours.' Mrs Hollingsworth eyed Joanna's worn but clearly expensive black linen jacket. 'They start at one a.m. and finish at five a.m. No time for parties and boyfriends. Have you cleaned before?'

'When I was at university, I worked in a pub and we had to clean the offices next door.'

'University!' Mrs Hollingsworth looked even more doubtful. 'Why do you want to be a cleaner, if I may ask, which I feel obliged to do. Our clients expect me to know everything about all our girls. After all, you'd enter their offices when the staff are home in bed, and there's a lot of confidential information lying around.'

'I've been made redundant and I . . . need money.' Joanna didn't like to lie, but she had no alternative.

'What about references?'

'Would character references be all right? A solicitor and a publishing editor?'

'I'd prefer the name of your last employer.'

Joanna had visions of Vanessa, First Clarence's rule-bound personnel officer, receiving a call from BetterClean. 'I'd rather not, if you don't mind,' she told Mrs Hollingsworth, adding by way of explanation, 'I . . . er . . . don't want them to know that I've had to resort to being a cleaner.'

Thankfully, Mrs Hollingsworth didn't take offence. 'Very well. I'll accept character references so long as they verify your honesty.'

'Oh, they will.'

Joanna began to fill in the application form, but when she came to *Name* she hesitated, her pen poised. She was afraid to give her real name in case First Clarence were issued with a list of cleaners entering the premises, something which she had no way of checking. On the other hand, she couldn't ask Felicity and Max – especially Max, a lawyer – to perjure themselves by giving a reference for a name they knew to be false. She glanced up. Mrs Hollingsworth was watching her. She wrote Jo Temple and gave an address in Maida Vale where she and Felicity had shared a soulless flat when they first came to London. It was safe, because the building had since changed hands.

'I never contact referees in front of an applicant,' said Mrs Hollingsworth. 'And I don't normally accept telephone references but . . . well . . . you seem a pleasant girl and we're very short staffed. It's always the same in the summer.'

'When would I be able to start?'

'Tonight, if I'm satisfied.'

Joanna stood up. 'Thank you. I'll check with you later. Where . . . will I be working?'

'In one of the City banks.'

Joanna longed to ask which bank, but she couldn't without arousing suspicion. Why would a cleaner care?

She hurried from the office, down the street to the nearest public phone box. Guessing that Mrs Hollingsworth would phone Max first because he was a solicitor, she dialled his number. His receptionist put her through.

'Max, it's Joanna. Please don't ask me any questions, but a Mrs Hollingsworth from BetterClean, the office cleaners, is going to ring you for a reference for a Jo Temple. That's me.'

'What?' he gasped.

'I've applied for a job as an office cleaner but I . . . er . . . decided not to use my full name – my proper career name.' She stretched the truth because she couldn't ask Max to lie for her.

'Jo, listen, you don't need to do that.' Max was dismayed. 'If things are difficult, I can lend you some money. I'll put a cheque in the post tonight.'

'Max, you're a brick, but I don't need it. I just . . . need the job. Please!'

'All right.' He hesitated. 'I suppose it's no good asking what you're up to?'

'Better not to. Thanks.'

Next she phoned Felicity, who was equally horrified and also offered money.

'I just want that job,' explained Joanna.

'But why? What are you up to?'

Lack of coins saved her from having to reply. The line went dead.

On her way home, Joanna stopped at a chemist. 'I want to make my hair go temporarily blond,' she told the shop assistant as she studied the rows of hair colourants.

The girl eyed Joanna's auburn hair. 'A semi-permanent rinse won't make much difference. You'll just be a little lighter. To go blonde, you'd have to bleach it – permanently.'

'Oh, no!' Joanna envisaged herself with auburn roots growing through platinum hair.

'You could try this.' The assistant handed her a tin of spray. 'Blonde streaks. You'll have to do them every day.'

Joanna purchased the rinse and the can.

From home she telephoned Mrs Hollingsworth, who informed her that she could start work that night.

Felicity returned that evening to find Joanna with her head over the basin combing the blonde rinse through her hair.

'What are you doing?' she asked, reading the name on the package. 'Light Golden Blonde! Jo, what is going on?'

'I'm changing my image.'

'But why?'

Joanna straightened up. 'Please don't ask me.'

'I know this has something to do with that woman from BetterClean,' Felicity persisted.

'Please!'

'All right. I shall stifle my curiosity.' Felicity opened her handbag and took out her cheque book. 'Let me pay the next three months' rent in advance, to tide you over.'

'Thanks, but I can manage and I know you've set your heart on that MaxMara dress to impress Tom's parents.' Gently Joanna pushed Felicity's cheque book away. 'Only please don't tell Adam about BetterClean.'

'Why not?'

'He'd try to stop me.'

'Jo, you're up to something . . . risky. I know you are.'

'I'll be perfectly safe, so long as it remains a secret,' replied Joanna, making herself sound braver than she felt.

Just after midnight, Joanna put on an old pair of jeans and a sweat shirt, scraped her hair back into two short blonde bunches, and slipped out of the flat. She would have driven to Smithfield and parked a few streets away from BetterClean but she was afraid the police, finding her car supposedly abandoned at night, might remove it on suspicion that it contained a bomb.

She arrived at BetterClean to find the office packed with some thirty or forty exhausted-looking women, mainly foreign. They slumped in chairs or leaned against the walls, talking and smoking. Many spoke in Spanish. Joanna glanced cautiously at the faces, praying that the girl to whom she'd given the twenty pounds wasn't present. Then she decided that no one would associate the new cleaner with a First Clarence Bank employee.

'Here's your uniform, Jo.' Mrs Hollingsworth handed Joanna a bright blue overall. 'You have a clean one every Monday. I hold a ten pound deposit from your wages in case you disappear without bringing it back. I have to do it or I'd be bankrupt.' She beckoned to a sprightly black woman who was chatting animatedly to a group of women. 'Sheila, this is Jo, your new girl.'

Sheila smiled broadly, revealing several gold teeth. 'Hi, Jo, I'm your team leader.' She peered out of the window. 'Ah, the Broadgate minibus is here. Follow me.'

The bright blue minibus had backed down the street until it was level with the office. The women climbed aboard. Joanna followed. The remainder of the women joined buses for Bank or Leadenhall. At least she was going in the right direction.

The bus set off through the dark, empty streets. With no traffic to hold them up, they rattled along at a fair pace. As they approached Broadgate Circle, Joanna felt increasingly nervous. She crossed her fingers. Please let it be First Clarence.

In Liverpool Street, the bus halted and they filed out.

'Come on team!' called Sheila, punching her hand into the air as she strode towards Broadgate Circle.

Joanna had all fingers plaited as they headed for the First Clarence Bank Tower. When the swing doors came into sight, her stomach lurched. Simultaneously, she felt exhilarated. She was fighting back. She couldn't wait to tell Adam.

But Sheila didn't stop at First Clarence. To Joanna's intense disappointment, she marched on to the black granite entrance of the St Leonard's Commercial Banking Group, showed her identification card to the night porter, and ushered her team inside. Joanna could only rage silently – and hope for better luck tomorrow.

She was allocated to the accounts department and spent four frustrating hours emptying waste bins, dusting desks and hoovering. By the end of the night, she was exhausted. In the breaking dawn, she followed the other cleaners out of St Leonard's Commercial and down through Broadgate to the minibus.

As they passed the angular iron sculpture outside Liverpool Street Station, Joanna noticed Jeremy stepping from a taxi. He was barely twenty yards away. Horrified, she turned her head to one side, pulling her hair over her face like a veil. He walked towards her. She didn't want to look at him, and yet she couldn't prevent herself – his fleshy face, pale amber eyes, red curly hair. She shivered at the memory of his hand gripping her arm, his threatening tone, the way he had pulled her closer.

Jeremy glanced at Joanna – and the blood drained from her face. Her jaw seized up with fear. She could hardly breathe. But he walked on without a second look, leaving her weak with relief. Then she realised how silly she'd been to be afraid. Jeremy wouldn't notice a cleaner.

The minibus dropped Joanna at St Paul's and she took the underground home. She was so tired that she didn't even bother to check her street for journalists. Luckily, there were none. Careful not to wake Felicity, she washed away the grime of the night then fell into bed, asleep as soon as her head touched the pillow.

She was woken by the telephone. Semi-conscious, she reached for it. 'Yes,' she mumbled.

'You were meant to phone me this morning,' said Adam.

'Sorry. I . . . umm . . . forgot.'

'Are you still in bed?'

'Er . . . yes, I am.'

He gave a sigh of annoyance. 'Joanna, for God's sake! We'll never get anywhere if you spend all day lazing around.' He paused before continuing in a more sympathetic tone. 'Look, I know you've had a difficult time but you mustn't give up so quickly.

Come over this evening. I'll be working from home. We'll talk it through and decide a plan of action.'

'I'd love to . . .' Joanna remembered her dyed hair. 'But I can't. I think I'm getting a cold.'

There was silence. She pictured him gritting his teeth, biting back a scathing retort.

'Very well. I hope you feel better tomorrow.' He clearly thought she was pathetic.

'Thank you.' She couldn't wait to see his face when he learned the truth.

For the next three nights, Joanna cleaned the accounts department at St Leonard's Commercial, curbing her frustration that she had got so near to First Clarence – but not near enough.

Each morning Adam telephoned, becoming increasingly annoyed to find Joanna still in bed.

On the third occasion, he lost his temper. 'You don't bloody deserve to clear your name,' he shouted at her, slamming down the receiver.

Simon and Katie invited Joanna to supper. She longed to see them but she couldn't, not without arousing their curiosity over her dyed hair. Rebecca invited her to the theatre. Again, Joanna was forced to invent a prior engagement.

On Thursday evening when Joanna arrived at BetterClean, Mrs Hollingsworth beckoned to her. 'I'm taking you away from Sheila tonight. We're short on Big Pam's First Clarence team. Michelle is missing. Sorry, dear, I know how you girls hate to be moved.'

'Oh, that's all right.' Joanna tried to appear nonchalant as she boarded the minibus with Big Pam, but she had to grip her hands together to prevent them from shaking.

The bus driver shouted, 'Everyone on board?'

There was a chorus of, 'Yes.'

As he reversed away from the office, a tiny blonde in tight leggings whom Joanna had noticed before came running down the road, waving her arms and calling, 'Stop! Wait for me!'

The driver opened the door and the woman climbed on board. 'Sorry I'm late, Pam,' she said.

'Honestly, Michelle! I suppose your new boyfriend stopped by?' chided Big Pam.

Michelle giggled. 'He can't get enough of me. He wants me to give up night work.' She eased past Joanna to join the First Clarence team.

'You're back with us, Jo,' said Sheila, smiling.

Joanna nodded. She couldn't speak, she was nearly in tears with disappointment. There remained just one more night before the password was changed.

Joanna spent Friday afternoon alternating between despair and optimism. Her whole scheme hung on whether Michelle's new boyfriend wanted sex with her all night. If Joanna had known his identity, she would gladly have paid him to keep Michelle at home.

Leaving a note for Felicity to wish her luck with Tom's parents, Joanna took the night bus. During the journey, she became so desperate that she considered asking Mrs Hollingsworth to put her on the First Clarence team, but she could think of no good reason for making such a request.

She arrived at the office and scrutinised the other women. Michelle was missing. Joanna crossed her fingers. The clock ticked on. At five to one, the bus arrived. Still no sign of Michelle. Joanna tried not to let her hopes soar.

'Michelle and Tracy are missing,' complained Mrs Hollingsworth. 'That makes the First Clarence team two short. Jo, would you join them?'

'Of course.' Eagerly, Joanna stepped towards Big Pam.

'Don't take Jo!' protested Sheila. 'She's a good worker and Tracy often goes straight to Broadgate.'

Silently, Joanna cursed Sheila.

'Oh, very well, said Mrs Hollingsworth. 'Big Pam will make do with one less.'

Joanna nearly screamed. It had all been for nothing. Despondently, she followed the other cleaners into the minibus, wondering if she could slip away into the darkness and go home.

As they were about to set off, Mrs Hollingsworth hurried out of the office and tapped on the side window. 'Michelle's rung. She isn't coming. Nor is Tracy. I'm sorry, Sheila, I'll have to take one of yours.' She glanced around the bus.

Joanna seized her chance. 'I'll move,' she offered, ignoring Sheila's outcry.

'Oh, thanks, Jo. Just for tonight. Sorry, Sheila, but you can have her back next week.'

Joanna was sorry to deceive Mrs Hollingsworth who was kind in her bossy way.

Again, she gripped her hands together to prevent them

trembling as the bus approached Liverpool Street. Her knees knocked when she followed Big Pam through Broadgate Circle. Beads of cold sweat formed on her forehead as she neared the First Clarence Tower. When she stepped through the swing doors into the pink marble atrium, she could hardly believe she'd made it. She longed to drink in the familiar surroundings but, aware of the security cameras, she kept her eyes fixed on the floor.

She recognised the two night porters. They'd been on duty the night when the Hong Kong market had fallen. As they counted the cleaners, she half-expected them to shout, 'That's Joanna Templeton. Get her out!' But they merely checked Big Pam's card which listed the number of girls. She had a moment of fear when one porter gave her a closer look, but he showed no sign of recognition. She was merely a new face, more attractive than most, and he was bored.

To Joanna's frustration, Pam sent her to the sixth floor, to Corporate Finance, whilst a Spanish girl called Fernanda was allocated to the trading room. As they went up in the lift, she considered asking Fernanda to swap, but again she was afraid to provoke suspicion.

Since Joanna was the sole person on the sixth floor, she gave it a perfunctory clean, running the Hoover between the desks but not bothering to vacuum underneath. As she flicked a duster over Sebastian Deveraux's desk, she wondered what he'd say if he knew.

With half an hour to spare, she took the lift down to the trading room. Fernanda was still wiping the desks. Joanna tapped on the closed door and beckoned.

'I've finished,' she said when Fernanda released the door. 'Would you like some help?'

Fernanda gaped at Joanna in astonishment. 'Yes . . . thank you. Can you finish the desks while I hoover?'

'No, I'll hoover.'

With an empty rubbish sack over her arm, Joanna seized the vacuum cleaner and raced down the aisle towards her old desk, keeping her head down to avoid the security cameras. She didn't know if they were switched on at night but she couldn't risk them capturing her face. At the podium she turned sharply, to maintain her distance from the overnight salesmen dealing on the Far Eastern markets.

As she approached her desk, a lump came into her throat. It was poignantly familiar – and yet different. Another salesman's pens were lined up beside the telephone. Unfamiliar handwriting covered a notepad. Pretending to adjust the Hoover, Joanna bent to read the name '*Jane Dixon*'. Neither Simon nor Rebecca had mentioned a new salesman. She realised they had wanted to spare her feelings.

With no time to waste, Joanna vacuumed along the aisle, past Simon's desk, around the corner, and behind Rebecca's. She longed to leave them a message, but couldn't – for their sakes as much as her own. Positioning herself so that her back was turned to Fernanda, she opened up the empty plastic sack and draped it over Jeremy's in-tray, engulfing the contents. As though by mistake, she knocked the lot on to the floor. Swiftly, she knelt and searched through the papers – but her fax was not present.

Refusing to give way to disappointment, Joanna replaced the papers in the in-tray. Again, she laid her plastic sack over Jeremy's desk. Mindful of the security cameras, she used the sack as cover, sliding her head underneath it towards Jeremy's computer.

'Do you fancy a smoke?' Fernanda called to her.

With a start of fright, Joanna withdrew her hand. 'I've . . . er . . . given up.'

'I have to smoke. I know we're not allowed to. Mrs Hollingsworth says we'll set off the fire alarm. But I always sneak one. I need it for my nerves.' Looking for a gossip, Fernanda wandered down the aisle towards Joanna, adding, 'My husband's . . . difficult. You know men, nothing's ever right. He's more trouble than all my children.'

To discourage Fernanda, Joanna bent down to clean under Jeremy's desk, relishing the thought of his shock if he could see her. A few yards away, Fernanda hovered. When Joanna took no notice, she retraced her steps.

Quickly, Joanna reached under the sack and switched on Jeremy's computer. She held her breath as the machine buzzed into life. The screen turned from black to bright blue.

Password?

With one hand on the Hoover and the other on the keyboard, Joanna typed 'Einstein'.

The date and time appeared, followed by *Password?*

She repeated 'Einstein' plus 'enter'.

It repeated *Password?*

Horrified, she recalled that Jeremy's computer, with access to the central system, required his own code. In spite of her careful planning, she had somehow overlooked this essential information.

Nearly crying with dismay, Joanna stared at the screen. She refused to believe that fate could let her get this far, and all for nothing. She tried to think logically, to focus on Jeremy, the kind of person he was – greedy, dishonest, arrogant, and yet not so totally sure of himself that he could accept being a younger brother. What was it Vikram had said on her first morning at First Clarence Bank? Something about vain men never using their birthdays.

Thinking of dates jogged her memory. Swiftly, she manoeuvred Jeremy's diary underneath his desk and flicked back the pages to the Monday prior to their code being changed.

'Jo!' called Fernanda.

Joanna tore the page in fright. 'Yes?'

'I'm going to the toilet.' Fernanda waved a packet of cigarettes. 'Don't tell Mrs Hollingsworth.'

'Of course I won't.' Joanna gave Fernanda the thumbs up, and decided that fate did love her – at least for tonight – so long as Fernanda didn't set off the fire alarm.

With fingers so nervous that the keyboard felt as though it had been electrified, Joanna typed in the relevant date. She held her breath, terrified in case a wrong code triggered a secret warning. Nothing happened. With increasing desperation, she watched the screen. Two seconds passed. Three. Then, suddenly, it filled with data.

She felt a surge of triumph. Swiftly, she called up Kathpeach. A list of their transactions appeared – date of purchase, number of shares, price, date of sale, selling price. She called up the Redrey Trust, New Aldren Fund and Società Hadini. All their information was present. Jubilantly, she reached for the print key. Then she stopped. She couldn't risk the sound of the printer attracting attention. In a panic, she began to jot down all the transactions.

There was a click as the trading-room doors opened and Fernanda called, 'Jo, aren't you ready? It's five to five.'

'Almost.'

Joanna was only partway through Kathpeach. She stopped writing. She'd have to copy the disk. Pretending to retrieve her duster, she opened Jeremy's drawers. No disks. She tried Rebecca's, then Simon's, but there were none. With no time to re-access the program, she laid her duster over the data on Jeremy's screen and hurried out to the back office, to the stationery cupboard. Leaning against it as though to adjust the laces of her trainers, she tried the handle. It was locked. She cursed, and tried the nearest desk, perching on the end, still pretending to tie her laces. In the second drawer she found a box of used disks. She removed one, wishing she could leave a note for the unfortunate secretary who'd be blamed for its loss.

Joanna raced back to Jeremy's desk, slotted the disk into the computer terminal, and pressed 'copy'. The green light came on as the disk began to copy. But Joanna couldn't stand next to the terminal without looking shifty, so she dusted the nearby desks while Fernanda waited impatiently by the trading-room entrance.

'Just the rubbish and I'm finished.' Joanna pretended to empty Jeremy's wastepaper basket. Simultaneously, she removed the disk from the terminal, exited the program and switched off the computer. With the disk tucked inside the waistband of her jeans, the rubbish sack in one hand and the Hoover in the other, she joined Fernanda.

'You clean too thoroughly,' said Fernanda accusingly. 'You'll show up the rest of us.'

'Sorry,' Joanna bowed her head but not in apology – she was avoiding the camera inside the trading-room door.

She was forced to curb her impatience whilst they waited by the lift for Big Pam, and again when they trailed down to the minibus. She was frantic to get away, but she couldn't disappear without causing comment. So she returned to BetterClean to receive her pay. Not to have done so would certainly have courted suspicion.

'See you all on Monday night.' Mrs Hollingsworth smiled at Joanna, pleased to have found such a hard worker. 'You'll be with Sheila's team as usual.'

'Yes, Mrs Hollingsworth.'

Joanna followed the other girls down the street, said goodnight, and walked on until she was out of sight. Then she ran, skipping and dancing down the centre of the road, exhilarated by her success and the night air. On Holborn Viaduct, she hailed a cruising taxi.

'Won the pools, luv?' asked the driver, grinning at her animated face.

'*Much* better than that!' She gave him Adam's address.

XXII

ADAM'S STREET WAS quiet. The houses slept. The curtains were drawn.

After settling the taxi fare from her pay packet, Joanna hurried up the path, past his motorbike chained in the parking bay, to his door, and pressed the bell. She heard it ring upstairs and waited for him to wake and answer on the intercom. A minute passed. Nothing happened. She rang again and counted to sixty. Silence. Was he out? Away? Working late? She scrutinised the street. His car was parked on the far side. She pressed the bell a third time. As the sound echoed upstairs, it occurred to her that he might be in bed with a woman. She hadn't considered that – and she was suddenly conscious of how much she wanted him to be alone.

There was a noise on the stairs. She heard muffled footsteps. The bolt was pulled back and the key grated in the lock. Unaware that she was doing so, Joanna clasped her hands tightly together.

The door opened. Adam stood in front of her, dishevelled, sleepy, bare chested, in just a pair of jeans. He stared at Joanna in astonishment – at her blonde-streaked hair, at her BetterClean overall.

'I have a present for you,' she said. With a flourish she removed the disk from her waistband and held it out to him.

He took it, turning it over in his hand. 'What is it?'

'Our evidence,' she replied proudly.

'Joanna, where have you been? What have you done?'

'Copied Jeremy's data.'

He looked stunned. 'You're joking.'

'Try it in your computer.'

'But . . . how did you get into First Clarence?'

She pointed out at the BetterClean label. 'Legally.'

For a moment, Adam was speechless. Then he took her in his

arms, lifted her off the ground and swung her round in a circle. 'You are brilliant!'

She laughed, with happiness, relief – and nervousness. 'I couldn't tell you before. You might have tried to dissuade me.'

'Of course I would. Joanna! The security cameras.' He lowered her to the ground. 'Are you sure they didn't capture you on film?'

'I was careful. I kept my head down.' She touched her blonde bunches. 'And I am disguised.'

'What a risk you took!' He checked the street, fearing she had been followed. Then he hurried her inside, bolting the door, surprising himself by his concern for her safety.

They raced upstairs to the office, switched on his computer and slotted in the disk. The screen flickered.

'Supposing I've used a dud,' said Joanna, horrified at the thought. 'I copied so quickly I had no time to verify.'

'Give it time.' Adam took her hand in his, crossed her fingers, and crossed his own on top of hers.

Joanna couldn't bear to look. She raised her eyes to the ceiling. 'Tell me the worst,' she said.

He laughed. 'No, the best. Look!'

As she tentatively lowered her gaze, Kathpeach's data filled the screen. Adam gave a cheer. Immediately, he called up Società Hadini, New Aldren Fund and several other companies. Not one of them had done business more than three times, spread over several years, but each deal had resulted in a profit. Individually the transactions had not earned eye-catching sums, but the total amounted to nearly six million pounds.

Adam took Joanna by the shoulders. 'I apologise for accusing you of cowardice,' he said, kissing her first on one cheek and then on the other.

'You provoked me into doing it. I thought, I'll show him, damn him!'

He chuckled. 'You're the best partner I've had.'

She raised an eyebrow. 'Have you had many?'

Her words seemed to take on another meaning – no longer referring to work, but to Toby's mother and to any other women he might have had in his life, including the owner of the earrings.

They stared into each other's eyes. She thought how sensuous his bare chest was, with its triangle of dark, curly hair; how soft his skin; how endearing his sleepy eyes and ruffled hair. She wanted to caress his hawkish face and to make his blue eyes soften. She wondered how she could have been attracted to Oliver, who was so perfect, when it was the raw imperfections in Adam which she found so sensuous, which made her want him – and want him to desire her.

'I admire you for refusing to be defeated,' he said softly.

Joanna's smile slipped. Oliver has said something similar at their last meeting.

Adam read the misgiving in her eyes and drew away.

'We must copy this disk and print out the information,' he continued in a friendly but detached voice. 'It would be tragic to lose the data.'

She nodded, wishing she could find the right words to explain that it wasn't him whom she'd retreated from, but the past.

Adam made five copies – one for Joanna, one to lodge in the bank, one for himself and two spare.

'What about the fax from Società Hadini?' he asked, continuing to maintain his distance.

'I searched, but I couldn't find it.'

'That's bad luck.'

'Yes, but I think I know what happened. It occurred to me on the way here. Heaven knows why I didn't think of it before. Jeremy could divert calls and faxes to himself from any salesman, if he saw that salesman was busy with another client.'

'What about the number?'

'It would remain the same.'

'Obtaining the fax isn't crucial,' he said.

'It is for me,' she answered sharply.

'No, it isn't. You can't prove you never received it – but if we demonstrate that Jeremy is a crook, we'll have established his motive for getting rid of you.' He smiled at her. 'You must be hungry if you've been cleaning all night.' He walked over to the kitchen, switched on the percolator and placed four croissants in the oven.

Joanna followed him. 'I am – now that you mention it.'

'I'll cook. You lay.' He cleared a space on the table for breakfast, reached into the cupboard and handed her two plates, two knives, some butter and marmalade – careful not to brush her hand as he did so.

Joanna wished they could return to their former closeness. At the same time she reproached herself for being perverse. Had Adam not backed off, she would have withdrawn even further.

She stepped out on to the roof terrace, relishing the early morning sunshine as she rested her elbows on the parapet and looked along the street to the trees of Hyde Park. He came out and stood behind her, almost touching her, until she was so conscious of him, of his body, of his breath on the back of her neck, that when he moved away, into the house, she felt physically bereft.

Over breakfast, he enquired exactly how she had gained access to First Clarence and she regaled him with an amusing description of BetterClean, Mrs Hollingsworth and the other cleaners.

'I spent all yesterday praying that Michelle's new boyfriend still wanted her,' she told him.

Adam laughed. 'To think that your success depended on his libido.' He stirred his coffee, watching the grains swirl around in his cup. 'If I'd known what a risk you were taking, I'd have insisted on coming with you.'

She eyed his unpacked tea chest. 'Adam, I don't think you'd make a good cleaner.'

He grinned. 'And you wanted to make me eat my words – of course.'

'You bet I did!'

The intimacy was restored, and she felt ridiculously happy.

They returned to the computer, sitting side by side, sipping strong coffee as they worked their way through the offshore funds, seeking a link between them.

'If only we could track down one signatory,' said Joanna.

'Yes. Just one of them. It wouldn't matter which. George . . . Frederick . . . Lawrence . . . I've got it!' he exclaimed excitedly.

'What? Where?'

'G. F. L. Bilsham. Joanna, don't you see? George Frederick Lawrence.'

Joanna looked doubtful. 'Both New Aldren Fund and Società Hadini purchased shares in Fact-Select on the same afternoon. How could one man travel from Grand Cayman to Monte Carlo in three hours?'

'It's obvious. He has contacts who place the orders for him.'

'Or he turns into Superman and flies?'

'Joanna, I'm serious.'

She held up her hands in mock surrender, unconsciously copying Adam's gesture. 'Sorry, I didn't mean to joke.'

'I have a gut instinct about Bilsham,' Adam went on. 'He's

fabulously wealthy. He owns a private jet and visits each place, say, once a month, where he has a trusted accomplice looking after each fund. On receiving insider information about a public company, Bilsham decides which of his funds he'll use and instructs the relevant accomplices to buy or sell shares in said company. It is those accomplices who place the orders with First Clarence – and other banks.'

He keyed in George, then Frederick, then Lawrence, and finally Bilsham. A list of ten more companies appeared. He moved the cursor through the unfamiliar names, pressing 'retrieve'. Each company had dealt three times in five years and on every occasion had made a profit.

'No one gets it *that* right,' said Joanna, as they studied the transactions. 'He's buying across all the sectors – communications, building, computers. Where on earth is he getting such a spread of information?'

Adam shrugged. 'I'd love to know – but, with this data, we won't need to prove his source. These facts speak for themselves. This could not be mere coincidence. He must be using inside information. But I'm puzzled. If Bilsham's prepared to risk prison, why doesn't he deal in larger sums?'

'Because he doesn't want to draw attention to himself. If he made a million on each deal, the salesmen would gossip.'

'You realise that Safarov could be Bilsham,' he said, studying her reaction to his words.

'It's possible,' he acquiesced, 'but First Clarence check their new clients very carefully. They might realise.'

'Not if Jeremy's part of the ring and he authorises the accounts.'

'Credit Clearance sanctions new clients.'

'You think I'm wrong, don't you?' he said.

'I'm playing devil's advocate.' She reached for the telephone list of Bilshams and ran her finger down the initials.

'Any with that combination in London?' he asked.

'No.' She picked up the country pages and skimmed the Bilshams. 'Wait a minute! Look!'

He read over her shoulder. 'G. F. L. Bilsham. Summer House, Summerford, Oxon. Eat your words, Miss Templeton.'

She was conscious of his breath on her cheek. 'Yes, Mr Hunter, but this is the Bilsham who has never been outside England.'

'Maybe that was a cover-up?'

She passed Adam the telephone. 'Try him again and see if you get the same response.'

'Not yet.' Adam handed back the phone. As he did so their hands touched. This time they parted slowly.

'Why not?' she asked, reliving the sensation of his skin caressing hers.

'If he's our Bilsham and he's in England, we don't want him to flee the country. If he's overseas, whilst pretending he never travels, we don't want him afraid to come back. Our Bilsham must be a multi-millionaire, have a heavily alarmed house, probably a helicopter and possibly bodyguards. The slightest hint that we're on to him and he'll disappear. Undoubtedly he has a secret way of slipping in and out of the country. We have to be patient.'

She pulled a face. 'How I hate that word!'

'We need facts, concrete evidence that he's our man – our Mr Big. Even then, it may be better not to confront him.'

'Adam, I want a show-down. I want to win – and be seen to win.'

He took her hand in his. 'Joanna, you deserve your victory. But we can't risk Bilsham slapping an injunction on the story. If that happened, we might never get into print.'

'I suppose you're right.' Her sigh became a yawn.

'You're falling asleep.' He stood up. 'Come on, I'll drive you home.'

'Are you going to the *Sunday Chronicle*?' she asked, stifling another yawn.

'Unfortunately, yes. It's my turn to be "late man". If last-minute news breaks, it's the late man's job to adjust the front page and ensure that the final edition makes its nine o'clock deadline.' He placed a copy disk and the print-out in his briefcase, adding, 'Afterwards, I plan to consult the *Sunday Chronicle*'s reference library. By comparing the transactions on Jeremy's disk with the financial information stored by the library, I'll be able to see if the offshore funds bought shares just ahead of public announcements of bids and takeovers.'

'I'd like to help,' said Joanna as they set off downstairs.

'Impossible!'

'Why? We're in this together.'

'Joanna, I'm sorry, but I can't take you into the *Chronicle* – and certainly not on our busiest day.'

She felt excluded. She'd risked so much to obtain the disk and she wanted to be part of each step.

As they set off across Hyde Park, Adam asked, 'Won't Better-Clean be suspicious when you don't report for work on Monday?'

'I'll leave a message on their machine to say I've found another job and I'll post back the uniform.'

He glanced at her face, at her clenched jaw and the dark rings beneath her eyes. 'Joanna, I'm worried. You could be in danger. Are you sure you can't be traced?'

His solicitude made her ashamed of being resentful. 'Better-Clean only know me as Jo Temple. Mrs Hollingsworth has Max and Felicity's work numbers, but Felicity has gone to stay with her fiancé's parents for a fortnight and Max is a solicitor. He'll have given my reference "without responsibility". In any case, BetterClean have a constant turnover of cleaners. By Tuesday, they won't even remember my existence.' She paused, and added, 'Thanks for being concerned.'

He smiled. 'I don't want to lose my best partner.'

They drew up outside Joanna's flat. Mrs Applegate was walking her dog. She waved to Joanna.

'I'll see you safely inside,' said Adam.

'Oh, don't worry! I'll be fine, thanks.' Joanna opened the car door. 'The story seems to have blown over, and I have excellent neighbours.'

Adam clasped his hands together as though in prayer. 'Lord save me from argumentative women.'

She laughed. 'Strong women are good for you.'

He insisted on accompanying her into the house, unlocking her flat door and scrutinising the sitting room and kitchen to ensure that none of the windows had been tampered with.

'You're making me nervous,' she said, watching him.

'I want you to be careful.' He touched her cheek. 'You did brilliantly to obtain that disk. Perhaps you'd better change careers and become a sleuth.'

'And alter my name to Templeton-Holmes?'

'No, you have to be Watson. I'm Holmes.'

'Why?'

'Because Holmes was in charge.'

She raised her hand, pretending to hit him, and he caught her arm. They laughed. He stroked her neck, and she leaned towards him.

Felicity's bedroom door opened and she stumbled out, yawning, tying her dressing-gown cord around her waist. She stopped dead when she saw Joanna and Adam, who jumped guiltily apart.

'Sorry to interrupt,' she said.

Joanna turned pink. 'I thought you were with Tom's parents.'

'I've changed my flight to go via Paris because Tom's there on business. I leave tomorrow morning. I thought I told you.'

'I must have forgotten.'

'You've had a lot on your mind.' Felicity's eyes twinkled as she looked from Adam to Joanna. 'I'm going to have a shower. I'll leave you two to . . . umm . . .' With a cheery wave, she disappeared into the bathroom, calling over her shoulder, 'I shall go shopping in half an hour. I'll be out all day.'

'Unfortunately, I have to go to work.' Adam gave Joanna a quick kiss on the cheek. 'I'll phone you later.' He stepped out into the hall. 'Don't answer the door to strangers.'

Joanna gave him a mock salute. 'Yes, sir.'

He came back and cupped her face in his hands, looking deep into her eyes. 'Please be careful, Templeton-Holmes.'

'I will.' She felt the blood rush through her veins.

Adam held her for a moment – then he released her.

After he had gone, Joanna wandered out into the garden. The sun had disappeared behind a humid haze. The white geraniums in their terracotta pots drooped from neglect and lack of water. She filled a can and watched the parched earth bubble as she doused each plant.

'Sorry to barge in on you like that,' Felicity called through the bathroom window.

'It doesn't matter.'

'I thought you liked Adam?' Felicity sounded disappointed.

'Yes, I do. Very much.' Joanna turned her attention to the jasmine which had fallen away from its trellis. 'But I don't want to fall into another mess. I must clear my name and find another job. I can't bear this hanging around, not knowing. If Adam and I become lovers, it's bound to ruin our partnership.'

'It might make it into something much better.'

'Sex changes things. It always does. I can't afford to lose his help.'

'You like him. He likes you. It's obvious that you're deeply in lust with each other. You can't wait to get into bed together – it's written all over your faces. Take a chance, Jo!'

'I've taken enough chances. Look what happened with Oliver.'

'Adam isn't Oliver.'

'He's being posted to New York for two years in January.'

'Tom lives in Washington and we've survived.'

'I know, but . . .'

Felicity came out of the bathroom, her head wrapped in a towel. 'Remember how self-protective I was when I met Tom? I'd had five disastrous affairs, one after the other, all with men who didn't care about me. They just wanted sex and an occasional girlfriend to take to the office party. Then I met Tom, and he made all the running. So I thought there was something wrong with him. There isn't. He's simply a man who, when he likes a woman, isn't afraid to show it. Adam is the same.'

XXIII

JOANNA REFLECTED ON Felicity's words many times that afternoon as she mooched around the flat in a sleepy haze. If she'd been sensible she'd have gone to bed, but she was too restless.

She was disturbed by the intercom.

'Miss Templeton?' asked an unfamiliar man's rough voice.

She froze, recalling Adam's warning. 'What do you want?'

'Flower delivery.'

'Can you leave them on the doorstep?'

'I need a signature.'

She hesitated. 'You'll have to leave them. I can't open the door at present.'

There was a silence, then a muttered, 'Bloody stupid female.'

Joanna crept to the window in time to see a very fat, heavily tattooed man step into an unmarked van and drive away.

Fear gripped Joanna so tightly that she could hardly breathe. Swiftly, she tapped out Adam's number.

'Adam Hunter's phone,' answered a woman.

'May I speak to Adam?'

'He's in a meeting.'

'Do you know when he'll be free?'

'No idea. This *is* Saturday. But if you leave your name, I'll do my best.' The tone was brisk. It told Joanna that she was interrupting a busy office.

'Don't worry,' she replied, taking a deep breath to quell her nerves. 'I apologise for troubling you.' She replaced the receiver.

The day had become even more humid. She longed to shower away the grime of office cleaning, but the prospect of being naked made her feel vulnerable. Supposing the man returned. Supposing he gained access to the house – or, worse still, to her flat. She locked the windows and doors, and secured the safety chain.

Then she stripped off her clothes, turned on the shower and stepped quickly underneath the cascade of water, furiously shampooing her hair to remove the blonde dye while she tried not to dwell on the shower scene in *Psycho*.

Within ten minutes, she was slipping on a pair of cool linen shorts. She felt refreshed, but still apprehensive.

She heard a noise at the front door.

'Who's there?' she called.

'Me – of course,' replied Felicity.

Joanna removed the chain and opened the door.

'Why Fort Knox?' asked Felicity, staggering inside, burdened with carrier bags.

'A strange man came. He claimed to be delivering a bouquet for me, but he was in an unmarked van. I was . . . scared, so I wouldn't let him in and he refused to leave the flowers without a signature.' Joanna gave a self-deprecatory laugh. 'Silly, aren't I?'

'No, just over-tired,' said Felicity sympathetically.

With Felicity's return, Joanna felt safe. She opened the garden doors.

'I'll make some tea,' she said. 'Let's have it outside. We'll share a Mars bar. Who cares if we get fat!'

'I do – or I won't get into my new dress.' Felicity disappeared into her room, calling over her shoulder, 'I'll show it to you, but please don't say if it doesn't suit me. It's too late to take it back.'

She returned wearing a very plain, elegant slate blue dress with a boat neckline and a panelled skirt.

'What do you think?' She gave a twirl. 'Am I the daughter-in-law of their dreams – or some tart who's stolen their baby boy?'

Joanna giggled. 'The former. Definitely. You look perfect. I'd hug you but I don't want to cover you in chocolate.'

Watching Felicity parade around the sitting room, Joanna was aware how much she would miss her when she went to live in America.

The telephone rang. They stared at it.

'Why are we being scared rabbits?' Felicity lifted the receiver. 'Hello? Oh . . . er . . . Hello.' She covered the mouthpiece with her hand. 'It's Oliver.'

Joanna turned pale. 'What!'

Felicity kept her hand in place. 'Shall I say you're out . . . occupied . . . ill?'

'And give him the satisfaction of thinking I'm crushed? Hell, no!' Joanna took the receiver. 'Hello, Oliver.' She spoke in a cool tone which belied her shaking hands.

'Why did you refuse my flowers?' he asked. 'I'm most offended.'

'I thought the delivery man was a fake.' She tried not to be affected by the sound of his voice but she couldn't help it. This was a man who had betrayed her.

'Why should a man delivering flowers be an impostor?'

'He was in an unmarked van. I have to be so careful. I've had a lot of strange people hanging around my front door – thanks to you, Oliver. How dare you turn me into a laughing stock? How dare you belittle me to inflate your own ego?' She was angry but gaining control.

'I don't know what you're talking about.' He sounded genuinely puzzled.

'That interview you gave.'

'But, Joanna, I was only trying to minimise our relationship to protect you.'

'Balls!'

'It's true. I promise you.'

'Oh, come on! I'm not that gullible. What about the lurid details?'

'Those did *not* come from me,' he said firmly. 'They must have been leaked by one of your colleagues. What about that woman who tried to steal your client? Charlotte? It was probably her.'

Joanna hesitated. She was sure that she'd never discussed any of her colleagues with Oliver, and now she asked herself the true motive behind his call.

Oliver interpreted her silence as uncertainty. 'So . . . what have you been doing?' he asked in a friendly, chatty voice.

'Having a short holiday.' She decided to respond as though partially won over by his protestations of innocence.

'Not still planning to sue First Clarence?'

'My lawyer has advised against it.'

'How sensible.'

Joanna said nothing.

'Even if you were in the right,' he added.

She remained silent.

Oliver was becoming irritated. He'd expected to find Joanna angry or tearful, but not self-possessed. 'What do you intend to do now?' he asked.

'Get on with my life.'

'You *are* being secretive.' In spite of his annoyance, there was a hint of respect in his manner.

For the sake of investigation, Joanna knew that she mustn't arouse his suspicions. 'I haven't been doing very much, that's all,' she replied meekly, although it infuriated her to do so.

'Oh, my poor Joanna, you must allow me to cheer you up. I'll be in London next weekend.'

'For *Tosca?*'

'How clever of you to remember! You must come.' He was at his most patronising and she longed to tell him what she really thought.

'No, thank you,' she replied politely.

'What a shame! A night out would do you good.' It didn't occur to him that she might not want to go.

Unable to keep up the pretence any longer, Joanna gave an audible gasp. 'Oh, dear! I've just noticed the time. I have to go. Thank you for the flowers. Goodbye.'

She replaced the receiver, and turned to Felicity. 'The bastard! How I longed to tell him that I faked an orgasm.'

'Why didn't you?'

'Because I could jeopardise our scoop – and because that would mean sinking to his level.'

Shortly afterwards, the florist returned with a bouquet of white lilies exactly like those which Oliver had first sent Joanna. She felt sick when she remembered how flattered she'd been.

There was a plain white envelope nestling amongst the blooms. Joanna extracted it. Inside was a card, with a typed message. *'Missing you. With love.'*

'Love! He'll soon wish I was dead,' she exclaimed angrily. 'That man was responsible for the most humiliating days of my life. I feel like stamping on his flowers, but they're too beautiful to waste. I'll give them to Mrs Applegate.'

'Have you noticed something odd?' Felicity was examining the Cellophane. 'The card has no name, the wrapping doesn't identify the florist, and the van was unmarked. You have no proof that Oliver sent these flowers.'

'And no proof that he phoned.'

'So what did he want?'

'I don't know,' replied Joanna, picking up the bouquet to take to Mrs Applegate. 'But I can't wait to tell Adam.'

Joanna and Felicity settled down to a cosy evening at home. They opened a bottle of chilled white wine and drank it in the garden, snacking on olives and hot pitta bread dipped into taramasalata. The night was sultry. They lay on sun-loungers, looking up at the indigo sky as they chatted.

Just after ten o'clock, Adam telephoned. 'You sound nervous,' he said. 'What's wrong?'

'Oliver rang.'

'You're joking!'

'He'd sent me some flowers but I'd refused to answer the door to the delivery man. I remembered your warning. I tried to contact you, but you were occupied. Then he phoned, demanding to know why I wouldn't accept his bouquet. As you can imagine, I let rip.'

'I can. What did he say?'

'That I'd misunderstood and he was only trying to protect me. I tackled him about the smutty details, and he blamed Charlotte – you know, the bitchy one at First Clarence – but I'm sure I never discussed Charlotte, or any of my colleagues, with Oliver. I was too conscious of him being a client.'

'He must want something,' said Adam. 'Why else would he send you flowers now?'

'I agree – though it isn't very gallant of you to say so.'

'I'm being truthful. Safarov does nothing without a reason. What else did he ask?'

'If I was still suing First Clarence. I told him Max had advised against it. Felicity and I reckon that the flowers were an excuse to check on me.' She described their lack of identification.

'You didn't tell him about us?' said Adam.

'Of course not! But he was suspicious – not when I was angry, but later when I was non-committal. He accused me of being secretive. So I pretended to be meek and miserable – and he invited me to the opera next Saturday.'

'He what?'

'Isn't it extraordinary? The ego of that man!'

'Joanna, I know you find it hard to believe that Safarov would risk being involved in fraud, but if I were a cynic . . .'

'Which you are!'

'I'd say he either knows about us, and was hoping you'd let slip something, or he wants to find you a new job so he can deal illegally through you because you'll owe him a favour.'

'You make him sound like a first cousin to the Mafia.'

'He is.' Adam paused. 'What did you feel when you heard his voice?'

'I was angry.'

'But not indifferent?'

'No,' she replied truthfully. 'I'm too enraged with him to feel nothing.'

Adam was silent for a moment. When he spoke again his tone was brisk. 'I'm in the *Sunday Chronicle* library. If you want to, come over.'

'Of course I do.' She was excited. 'I'll be right there – but I thought I wasn't allowed inside.'

'I'll handle Malcolm. Our investigation is more important than petty rules.'

She reached for pen and paper. 'Give me the address.'

He dictated directions, telling her where to turn and which narrow street to follow. Then he stopped. 'Forget that. I don't trust Safarov. It isn't safe for you to drive around London on your own so late. I'll send a car. The driver's name is Reg Cooper. Don't go outside till he rings your intercom and identifies himself.'

'All right . . . thank you.' She was glad not to brave the night alone.

She changed into her smartest white linen shorts, which emphasised the pale glow of her legs, and draped a white cotton sweater around her shoulders. Then she dabbed her favourite scent on her wrists and neck, squirting some behind each knee for good measure. When the intercom rang, she wished Felicity good luck for the second time, and hurried out.

Reg Cooper was a small cheery man with a wrinkled face and bright eyes. He chatted nonstop as they drove along the Embankment and through the silent, sleeping City.

'It's very kind of you to fetch me,' said Joanna, squeezing in her thanks when Reg was forced to draw breath.

'I'd cross Antarctica for Adam. He has a rough edge sometimes, I know, and God what a temper, but he has a good heart. When my missis was in hospital having a . . . you know, er . . . women's problem, it was Adam who sent her flowers, Adam who remembered to ask how she was doing. I won't forget that.'

'Did you know Richard Holdfast?'

'Know him? I was his driver. Poor Mr Holdfast, such a shame.

The *Sunday Chronicle* hasn't been the same since.' Reg chatted on about the deceased editor.

When they drew up outside the modern, glass *Sunday Chronicle* building, Adam was pacing up and down in reception. He hurried out to open Joanna's door, thanking Reg as he quickly ushered her inside, shielding her from prying eyes with his body.

They crossed to the reception desk.

'I'm not signing the lady in,' Adam informed the night porter. 'I don't want her name to appear.'

The porter looked anxious. 'Mr Hunter, everyone has to sign. Mr Burke will blame me if he finds out. You know how he is about rules.'

'I'll take the rap if there's any trouble.' Adam picked up a pad of paper and wrote, '*Malcolm, I was requested to sign in my guest, but I refused to do so. I alone am responsible for breaking this rule.*' He signed and dated it.

The porter visibly relaxed. 'That's the kind of thing Mr Holdfast would do, but nowadays everyone passes the blame.'

Adam and Joanna took the lift up to a large open-plan office crowded with computers, telephones, fax machines, and desks spread with copies of tomorrow's paper. He led her through the back to the reference library, which was lined with fireproof cabinets.

He unlocked one cabinet and selected those disks which contained financial information for the previous three years. 'These'll give us share prices for each day, as well as news of bids, takeovers, mergers and acquisitions.' He smiled at Joanna. 'Now we'll see when the funds struck gold.'

They sat down at adjacent terminals. Into Joanna's, they inserted the copy disk from Jeremy's computer. In Adam's they placed the *Sunday Chronicle*'s information disk. Adam typed Carthew Instruments.

His screen showed that on 21 October – the day when Richard had met Oliver at lunch – Carthew's share price stood at 180. On the following Monday – the day after Richard's article appeared – the shares opened at 130. By close of business, they stood at 80p. By the end of the week, they'd fallen to 20p.

'See if any of the offshore companies held Carthew shares,' said Adam.

Joanna checked her screen. 'None. Kathpeach weren't dealing

through First Clarence then. Nor were New Aldren Fund. Società Hadini were, but they didn't buy Carthew.'

'There has to be a connection.' Adam read over her shoulder. 'Maybe Safarov or Jeremy is Bilsham.'

Joanna was very conscious of his face close to hers. 'Oliver is heading up a new investment trust,' she said. 'He spends most of his time in Eastern Europe. He couldn't fly in and out of there to Grand Cayman, Monte Carlo and Bermuda without being noticed.'

'You're defending him again.'

'*I am not!*'

'All right. You're not. Supposing Bilsham is Oliver's partner.'

'Oliver's too clever to have a partner. He only has pawns.' She grimaced. 'Like me.'

Adam took her by the shoulders and shook her gently. 'Stop that – or I'll have to make you angry.'

She smiled. Then her eyes widened. 'I've just remembered! Rebecca had a client who bought ahead of a bid.'

'Did they complain about her?' asked Adam, scenting a pattern.

'No, they're the ones who folded. Oh, heavens, what was their name?' She clicked her fingers as though the sound would trigger her memory. 'It sounded slightly exotic – possibly Italian or Spanish – and began with Don.'

'Don Giovanni?'

She laughed and shook her head. 'Not that exotic!'

'Donna?'

'That's it? I think. If not, it's close.' She was so excited that her voice rose to a squeak, which made Adam laugh.

They keyed in Don. Donia & Co appeared, filling the screen with data. The signatory has been a Mr Summer. They looked at each other.

'Summer House!'

There were two transactions listed in the early Nineties, both through different salesmen, and one sub-entry which read '22 October 1991 – 700 Nov 70 CI p @ 10'.

'The first date is the day after Richard met Safarov at lunch, when the shares stood at one eighty,' said Adam. 'The second could be a typing error. CI has to be Carthew Instruments.'

'Twenty-two October 1991 – 7 November 70? That date span doesn't make sense.'

'I know, but this can't be coincidence. Whoever was behind

Donia knew that Richard had been passed the fake lawyer's letter and that he'd swallowed the bait.'

Joanna laid a hand on Adam's arm. 'Why would Donia buy shares in Carthew if they had inside information that the company was going down the drain?'

He studied her screen. 'God knows!'

'Because they didn't!' In her enthusiasm, Joanna dug her fingers into his arm. 'Donia bought put options. They gambled that the price would go down. They spent seventy thousand pounds buying seven hundred contracts of a thousand shares each, on the basis that the price would drop below seventy pence by the end of November.'

'Because they knew it would.' Adam accessed the Futures price on Carthew on 22 October. The premium for November puts stood at ten pence.

Joanna totted up the profit. 'Donia cleared seven hundred thousand pounds. How they must've kicked themselves. If they'd realised Carthew would crash, they'd have doubled it.'

Adam rested his hand on top of Joanna's. 'Each time I see your fingers imprinted on my arm, I shall remember this breakthrough.'

She laughed. 'Sorry. I was so excited.'

He smiled. 'So was I.'

They swapped computers in order to bring a fresh eye to their search, and continued to examine the dates on which the offshore companies had purchased shares. Painstakingly, they followed every lead and scrutinised each transaction. Since Joanna had left First Clarence, the Redrey Trust had dealt once – through her replacement, Jane Dixon. She stared at the entry. If Oliver was Bilsham, he had not moved his business. But was he Bilsham? She still couldn't believe he'd risk prison and disgrace.

Whilst she was checking the news headlines for 1989, whizzing the cursor through page after page, her eye was caught by a name. She stopped, and read aloud, '*Ponary, Latvia. Trial of elderly camp guard accused of war crimes halted by defendant's suicide.*'

There was a brief paragraph, followed by a statement from the representative of an institute in Central London saying that some Latvians, in their desire to free their country of Russian domination, had sided with Germany – Russia's old enemy.

'That's the camp where Oliver's father died,' she explained to Adam. 'His mother showed me a picture of him.'

'What was his father like?'

'Handsome and swarthy.'

'And his mother?'

'Oh, she's very different from what I'd have expected. She's dainty and reserved, and quite simple in her tastes. Oliver has a fabulous villa, with staff, but she does all the cooking. She adores him.'

'Is he fond of her?'

'Very. She's probably the only person with whom he is completely unselfish. When he's with her, he changes. In London, he was distant and sophisticated.' Joanna thought for a moment. 'I've just realised how odd it is that his London house should be so very Russian, when he wants to be considered so Establishment – at least, he says he does.'

'How was he different in France?' Adam persisted.

'He was prickly and defensive, like a boy attempting to protect a young widowed mother – which is how they must have been after the war. Yet, peculiarly, the villa where his mother lives has nothing of Russia – except in her room.'

'I wonder why he took you to meet her, if he loves her so much and you were just a fling?'

'I've asked that question myself, and I don't know.' Joanna returned to her screen.

Adam watched her face for a few moments, trying to ascertain her emotions. Some time later he pointed at a name on his screen. 'Who was Rosalind?'

'A salesman who was fired before I arrived. Jeremy said she couldn't sell, but Simon told me she was argumentative and queried every deal.'

'Maybe she suspected.'

'That's what I wondered.' Joanna sat back in her chair. 'Simon told me he'd bumped into Rosalind. She was working the night shift on a garage till. That bastard Jeremy had refused to give her a reference, so she couldn't get another job in the City.'

'Then she'll be angry enough to talk. Where is this garage?'

'Near Simon's home. I can't ask him the name, I don't want to involve him, but I know where he lives. There can't be that many all-night garages nearby.'

'We'll find her, but first we need some coffee. This could be a long night.' He smiled at Joanna. 'Another night without sleep for you. Can you bear that?'

'Yes – if the alternative is being left behind.'

He touched her cheek gently. 'You have to come. You're my partner.'

He went to the coffee machine on the far side of the financial section. Joanna swivelled round on her chair to watch him, swinging her bare legs, staggered that she could have thought Oliver more attractive.

When he returned, carrying two cups of coffee, he looked serious.

'Is . . . anything wrong?' she asked.

'No.' He put down the cups. 'I was wondering how Safarov first approached you.'

'He phoned, invited me to lunch at his club – and sent me lilies afterwards.'

'How ostentatious!'

'The bouquet was beautiful.' She gave him a teasing smile. 'Don't you pursue women with flowers?'

'No – with croissants for breakfast.'

She arched her eyebrow. 'How very to the point.'

'That's the way I am. If I meet a woman I like, I want her in my bed. I want to make love to her. I don't send flowers and I don't talk for hours on the telephone. I can't be bothered to play games – and I refuse to pretend I don't want to be with someone, saying I'll be in touch but leaving it for days so as not to appear too eager. That's all balls. If I desire a woman, I want to get to know her at home, alone, naked, making love, talking, sharing, exploring.' He fixed Joanna with his stare. 'Don't you agree?'

She blushed and turned his question into a joke, although that was not what she really wished.

'Oh, I expect at least five dozen red roses,' she replied flippantly.

'From me, you'd get croissants.'

She looked at him. He held her gaze. Was he teasing – or did he mean it?

'Now, drink your coffee and let's find Rosalind,' he said. 'It's nearly six o'clock and I have to collect Toby at noon.'

'Yes, sir!' She raised her cup to her lips. She still didn't know the answer.

They drove to Clapham and cruised the streets near Simon's house. The first petrol station was shut. The second was operated by a man.

'Maybe Rosalind has left,' said Joanna. 'I'll go in and ask. He's more likely to give her address to a woman than to a man.'

She crossed the forecourt, the cold air on her bare legs making her shiver. At the kiosk, she spoke through the grill to the young Asian cashier who was studying a geometry text-book.

'Sorry to bother you but I'm looking for Rosalind. Someone told me that she worked here on the night shift.'

The cashier shook his head. 'No women here – unfortunately!' he added with a boyish grin.

'Is there another garage nearby?'

'Half a mile down the road. Turn right at the lights.' His eyes drifted back to his text-book.

Joanna reported back to Adam and gave him directions.

The next garage was operated by an older man.

'I'm looking for Rosalind.' Again Joanna had to speak through a grill.

'I'm the night cashier now.' He was defensive, as though Joanna was after his job.

'Did Rosalind work here?'

'Why do you want to know?'

'She was an old friend and we've lost touch.'

He shrugged. 'There was a girl called Rosalind but she left.'

'Could you tell me where she lives?'

'I could – but it's against regulations.'

'Please! It's terribly important.' Joanna tried to look her most appealing.

The man stared back through the grill, impassive, waiting.

Adam joined her. 'Any problem?' he asked.

'This . . . gentleman knows Rosalind's address but he isn't allowed to tell me.'

'Perhaps this would help.' Adam slipped a fifty pound note through the grill.

The man eyed the money and licked his lips. 'If I give you her address, you won't tell anyone where you got it?'

'Of course not,' Adam assured him.

In a flash, the cashier trousered the money. He opened a drawer, took out a notebook, and pointed to an address in Pimlico.

Jubilant, Adam and Joanna returned to the car.

'It's seven o'clock,' said Adam. 'We'll have to kill an hour. We can't wake her this early on a Sunday morning or she'll certainly refuse to talk.' He switched on the engine. 'Let's have breakfast. I'll introduce you to my favourite café.'

'Croissants already?' She gave him a mischievous smile.

He grinned. 'Not till you've earned them.'

They drove through the damp, deserted streets of south-east London to a brightly painted café nestling under the blackened arches of a disused railway bridge. Parked nearby were a dozen lorries, many with continental number plates. Inside, the café was cheerful and cosy, full of lorry drivers tucking into enormous plates of food. The sizzle of frying sausages mingled with talk and laughter.

A smiling red-haired woman came towards them, wiping her hands on her apron. 'Hello, luv,' she said, recognising Adam. 'Been working late again?' She winked at Joanna. 'Newspapers! Who reads 'em? Not me. I don't have time.' She started to clear a table for them.

'No one reads them, Cherry, but you mustn't tell my editor or I'll be out of work,' replied Adam.

Cherry chuckled. 'Glad you haven't lost your sense of humour. Well, what can I get you?'

'A pot of coffee and two of your specials, please.'

They sat at a trestle table covered with a red and white checked plastic cloth.

'This is the best breakfast in town – and you deserve it,' said Adam.

'We both do.'

Cherry bought two plates piled high with eggs, sausages, bacon, mushrooms and tomatoes. Adam and Joanna didn't talk much whilst they ate, they were too hungry, but their silence didn't make Joanna feel uneasy, as it had with Oliver.

They left the café just after eight and, thirty minutes later, drew up outside Rosalind's purpose-built first-floor flat. The curtains were open and they could see a figure moving around inside.

'Fingers crossed,' said Adam.

Joanna smiled. 'And toes!'

They hurried up the path to the front door, and pressed the bell.

'Yes?' came the response from the intercom.

Joanna spoke. 'Rosalind, my name is Joanna Templeton. I used to work at First Clarence and I need to talk to you.'

'Why? What about?' The voice was anxious.

'Could you let us in? I don't want to shout it down the intercom.'

Rosalind hesitated. 'I'll come down.'

'She's even more defensive than I expected,' whispered Adam as footsteps approached.

The front door opened a few inches and a young woman peered out. She had short brown hair and a thin, querulous face. 'Yes?'

'May we come in?' asked Joanna.

'No. Tell me what you want, then please go.'

'Rosalind, I worked at First Clarence after you did. Like you, I was unjustly fired. That's why I want to talk to you.'

'I can't say anything.'

'Please! We have to fight back. It's the only way we'll ever find jobs again.'

'I have a job.' Rosalind's eyes would not meet Joanna's. 'A good job – at last.'

'I thought Simon said . . .'

'Jeremy relented. He gave me a reference after all.' Rosalind glanced at Joanna's tired, drawn face. 'Look . . . I'm sorry, I wish I could help you, but I can't afford to jeopardise my career a second time. I'm never going to stick my neck out again. If I'd been out of work for one more month, my flat would have been repossessed. I've learned my lesson. Turn a blind eye and keep your mouth shut.' Rosalind closed the door in their faces.

Joanna bent down and called through the letter box. 'Rosalind! When did you receive the reference?'

Rosalind started up the stairs. 'Please go away!'

'Just nod if it was the past month.'

Rosalind hesitated.

'I was sacked in the past month,' Joanna went on. 'If Jeremy relented, it was to stop you talking to me. Did he make the reference conditional on your silence?'

Rosalind carried on up the stairs. Watching her, Joanna felt as though she were talking to a statue. Then, as Rosalind was on the point of disappearing into her flat, she gave a brief nod.

Joanna straightened up. 'Jeremy bought her silence.'

'And scared her to death,' said Adam.

They were too exhausted to discuss Rosalind further. Adam drove Joanna home, whilst she fought to remain awake. They arrived to find the lights on in the flat and Felicity waiting for a cab to take her to the airport.

'Our next step is to prove that G. F. L. Bilsham is not the stay-at-home he wanted us to believe,' said Adam. 'On Monday we'll drive out to Summerford.'

She nodded. Monday seemed a very long way off.

'I don't know what you're doing today – apart from resting,' he continued, 'but Toby and I will be in the Natural History Museum, next to the big dinosaur, at around three o'clock. Why don't you join us?'

'Wouldn't Toby prefer to have you to himself?'

'He likes people. It's I who am the loner.'

She smiled. 'If you're sure, then I'd love to come.'

She was so tired that she could have slept for a week, but she couldn't imagine not seeing Adam until Monday.

XXIV

IT WAS RAINING softly as Joanna walked along the busy Cromwell Road but she barely noticed. She was in a glow of anticipation at the prospect of being with Adam. The museum was proving popular with families on a wet Sunday afternoon and she was obliged to queue for a ticket. The delay seemed like an eternity.

She made her way to the central hall. Adam and Toby were standing side by side, staring up at the dinosaur's massive skeleton. Neither of them noticed her approach, they were so engrossed in the huge beast.

Seeing Adam brought a smile to Joanna's face. She wanted to wrap her arms around him and feel his lips on hers. At the same time, she felt ridiculously shy – like a teenager on a first date.

Adam glanced around. 'There you are!' His face lit up.

She blushed. She was so pleased to be with him again.

'Toby, this is Joanna,' said Adam. 'We're working on a story together.'

Toby studied Joanna solemnly.

'Hello, Toby,' she said, trying to sound friendly but not gushing.

Toby continued to stare at her.

'When I was just a little older than you, I came to see the dinosaur with my brother and sister,' she told him, hoping to break the ice. 'My brother and I were very naughty. We pretended to my sister, Lindsay, that the hamburgers we ate for lunch were made from this big dinosaur and the grapes in the fruit salad were baby dinosaurs' eyes. She screamed and was sick – and she never ate meat again.'

'Never, ever?' he asked, fascinated.

Joanna nodded. 'Never.'

Toby insisted that Joanna repeated the story. This time he bombarded her with questions.

'He loves the gory details,' Adam confided in her. 'The gorier the better!'

'And you?' she asked, laughing up at him. 'Are you bloodthirsty too?'

'I only eat female dinosaurs.' He pinched her cheek as though testing it for tastiness.

At Toby's insistence, they visited all the prehistoric skeletons.

'How will you manage to see him when you go to New York?' she said, when Toby was out of earshot.

'With difficulty. That's the main reason why I don't want to go. I'll lose the weekly contact, which is so important at his age. I'll miss a huge chunk of his childhood which I can never recapture.'

She nodded. She was going to miss Adam, too – a great deal.

They returned to his house for tea. Whilst Toby watched television, Adam and Joanna discussed Rosalind.

'I wonder if Jeremy told her specifically not to speak to me or simply not to talk to anyone,' pondered Joanna.

'The latter.' Adam broke a digestive biscuit in half. 'To name you would be too incriminating.'

'Let's hope she doesn't tell Jeremy we've been in contact.'

'I doubt she will,' said Adam. 'She wants nothing more to do with First Clarence. But in case she does, and Jeremy warns Bilsham, we'll drive out to Summerford tomorrow, as soon as I've dropped Toby at school.'

They talked excitedly in low voices in order not to alarm Toby. Time ticked by. Joanna thought of her flat, empty now without Felicity. She had no desire to go home.

Toby dragged his eyes away from the television. 'Is Mummy bringing my school uniform today?' he asked.

Adam didn't look at Joanna. 'Yes, she'll be here in an hour. She forgot to pack it.'

'But am I staying with you tonight?' he asked anxiously.

Adam smiled reassuringly. 'Of course. You always stay with me on Sundays.'

Soothed and happy, Toby returned to the television.

Joanna was tense. Why hadn't Adam warned her that his ex-wife was about to arrive? She waited for him to offer an explanation, but he didn't. In any case, he couldn't say much with Toby in the room.

After a few very long minutes, Joanna rose. 'I must go. I have things to do. Could you call me a cab?' She tried to sound as if she had always intended to leave now.

'Yes, of course.' Adam didn't try to persuade her to stay.

He phoned for a minicab whilst she said goodbye to Toby. Then he accompanied her down to the front door. She walked ahead of him, rapidly, wanting to get well away before the arrival of the woman who had once called this house her home.

'Joanna, wait!' said Adam, in the darkness of the hall, out of earshot of Toby.

She raised her chin. 'What for?'

'I want to tell you something.' He laid his hand on her shoulder and pulled her back against the wall so that she was obliged to look at him. 'Val and I have been over for years, but we have a bond because we share a child, and we still like each other.'

'How long were you married?' she asked.

'We weren't married.'

'Why didn't you warn me she was coming today?'

'I hadn't intended you to come back to the house.'

Joanna flushed. 'Then why did you invite me?'

The doorbell interrupted them. Reluctantly, Adam released her and opened the door.

'Minicab?' said the driver, looking from one to the other.

'I'm coming.' Joanna turned to Adam. 'I'll expect you tomorrow morning.'

'If I invited you, it was because I wanted to,' he said.

She hurried out without replying. She had so wanted to believe in Adam, but now she was unsure. The only thing she knew for certain was that – after Oliver – she would rather be alone for the rest of her life than be with a man she could not trust.

Her flat seemed unnaturally quiet. The only sign of life was the remnants of Felicity's packing – abandoned shoes and discarded bags. Joanna felt deflated. She tried to forget about Adam and Val, but her thoughts kept returning to the house in Bayswater.

To keep herself occupied, she went to the newsagent's to buy a paper. Walking home, she studied the headlines. As she crossed the square where Adam had persuaded her to shelter in his car, she noticed two men standing stock-still beneath the trees on the far side of the gardens. Their faces were hidden in the shadows. Her first thought was that they were reporters, but that seemed unlikely because they were too reticent. In any case, her story was no longer news.

She walked on. Then, some reason made her look back. The men were following. She could see them moving through the trees. She stopped. They halted whilst one lit a cigarette, the flame from his lighter flaring in the gloom. She hurried on. The men increased their pace.

Joanna's skin prickled. Had Jeremy been to work on Saturday? Did he know already that she'd accessed his computer? Had he seen the security video? Or was it mere coincidence that these men were walking her way?

She hastened across the road and up the street, almost running now.

'Hello, Joanna,' said a voice from behind a hedge.

Joanna started with fright. 'Oh . . . Mrs Applegate, I didn't see you.' She glanced around.

The men had halted before the crossroads. They were standing with their backs to her.

'Are you feeling unwell, dear?' asked Mrs Applegate, dead-heading a rose. 'You're as white as a sheet.'

'I'm fine, thank you.' Joanna forced a smile. 'What lovely roses you have.'

Mrs Applegate glowed with pride. 'That's because I feed them regularly. They need it, poor dears, especially with all the pollution in the air.'

'I'm sure you're right.' Joanna glanced back again, but the men had disappeared. Nevertheless, she said a quick good evening to Mrs Applegate and hurried up the steps, into the safety of her flat.

She had been frightened, she couldn't help it. The men might be quite innocent, but she'd felt threatened. Why had they followed her? Why had they stopped?

She picked up the phone and stared to tap out Adam's number. Then she stopped. Adam had not intended her to go back to his flat. He'd told her so. He'd been expecting Val. She pictured them sitting at the table, eating a family supper with their son. She imagined Val, fiercely glamorous, fashionably skeletal and oozing confidence, asking, 'Who on earth is that hysterical woman on the phone?'

After checking the locks on the windows and doors, Joanna sat down and attempted to read the newspaper. But she couldn't concentrate. The print swam before her eyes, her head buzzed from lack of sleep, and every noise made her jump. Eventually she went to bed, but it was hours before she slept.

She didn't wake until Adam rang the intercom.

'Sorry,' she mumbled sleepily as she let him in. 'I don't know what happened.'

He wagged an admonishing finger at her. 'You were out on the town, you wicked girl.'

'No, I was not.'

'Joanna, I phoned and phoned, but you didn't answer.'

'I was here . . . honestly.' She shivered as she recalled the men.

Adam picked up her telephone and listened. 'It's out of order.'

The men. The phone. Joanna tried not to panic.

'I'll report it on my mobile while you dress,' said Adam. 'Wear something inconspicuous and bring a sweater. We may have to hang around. Hurry up!' He gave her a gentle shove towards the bathroom. 'We don't want Bilsham to escape.'

His cheerfulness infuriated her and she could not help wondering if it was due to Val.

She showered quickly, returned to her room, and slipped on a pair of jeans and a dark red sweater.

'Coffee's ready,' called Adam.

'I'm just coming.' She touched her eyelashes with mascara and sprayed her neck and wrists with scent. As an afterthought, she removed her copy disk from its hiding place amongst her books and dropped it into her bag: she couldn't bear to be separated from her hard-won evidence.

'You look and smell delicious,' said Adam as she stepped out of her room.

He handed her a mug of coffee, perfectly at home in her kitchen.

'Thank you.'

Joanna decided not to tell Adam about the men. She'd probably overreacted, exhausted after six sleepless nights. They could simply have been walking in her direction. In the bright sun of a new morning, this seemed the most likely explanation.

They drove out along the M4 and turned off at Theale, following the Thames valley through Pangbourne and the other small towns which straddled the river. The meadows were glossy green and the water sparkled in the sunshine. Gleaming white motorboats churned upstream, rocking the swans and the moorhens in their wake.

A few miles short of Oxford, they came to Summerford. It was a small, well-maintained village of bow-fronted Georgian houses built around a crossroads, with a narrow twisting main street leading down to the ancient stone bridge where the original ford used to be.

'Look! There's a driveway.' Joanna pointed at a pair of imposing wrought-iron gates.

Adam slowed. But the sign next to the entrance said Summerford Manor.

They drove on to the end of the village, where the houses gave way to rolling cornfields. Puzzled, they stopped to study the map in the forecourt of a garage.

'I'll ask directions,' said Joanna, calling to the attendant.

'Summer House?' he repeated. 'You're on the wrong road. Go past the pub, over the bridge and take the first left.'

The road which he had indicated ran parallel to the Thames. On its river side, there were a number of spectacular properties with sweeping lawns running down to private jetties.

'Fit for a millionaire,' said Adam, peering through the heavily alarmed gates of one mansion.

'Or an insider trader.'

They drove slowly, halting at each imposing entrance, but not one was called Summer House. Again, the houses gave way to countryside. They stopped at a crossroads.

'We must have missed it.' Adam turned the car.

They drove back even more slowly. Overlooking the river there was a beautifully converted Elizabethan barn. On the other side of the road was a high cypress hedge.

'Summer House!' cried Joanna, seizing Adam's arm in her excitement.

Adam braked. 'Where?' He scrutinised the barn.

'There.' She pointed at a modest gateway, set in the cypress hedge.

Adam reversed, angling the car so as to give them a sight of the house, but they could see nothing. Beyond the gate a gravel drive curled away, hidden by the hedge.

'The house must be set right back,' said Adam.

'Or this is the rear entrance.'

They returned to the crossroads and took the right turn, which they assumed ran parallel to the side of the property. This too was flanked by the cypress hedge which continued to block their view. To their surprise, after barely a hundred yards, the lane took a sharp turn. There was now a deep ditch as well as the hedge separating them from Summer House.

'We must be behind it,' said Adam. 'But there's not much space for a large estate.'

'Maybe it really is just a summer house, where Bilsham comes to work.'

'An address he uses whilst he lives elsewhere.'

'A hangar for his helicopter.'

'Only one way to find out.' Adam drew into a gateway.

They scrambled out of the car and darted across the lane. The bank was steep and the ditch was full of water. Adam jumped first, then he turned, holding out his hand to help Joanna. She followed, clutching at his arm to prevent herself from falling into the water.

'Here goes,' he said, carefully lowering a branch to create a window in the cypresses.

Beyond the hedge were high iron railings, then an expanse of lawn surrounding a pleasant double-fronted Edwardian house. It was a comfortable family home in an acre of well-manicured garden, but not the residence of a man who had made millions in illegal trading. Joanna and Adam stared at it, then at each other.

'If that's Bilsham's house, he can't be our Mr Big.' Adam was unable to mask his disappointment.

'He certainly isn't Oliver,' said Joanna, thinking of the ornate house in London and the glittering white villa in France. She was relieved to know that he wasn't crooked, not for his sake but for her own.

'Bilsham could be just a glorified courier,' suggested Adam.

'Maybe he isn't in it for the money?' She laughed. 'How silly! Of course he is. Why else would he be involved in crime?'

As they watched the house, a van came up the drive. A man stepped out and rang the doorbell. It was answered by a middle-aged woman wearing a white apron. They exchanged a few words and the man handed her a box. She carried it into the house and closed the door. The man drove away. Stamped across the back of his van were the words 'Video Game Delivery Service'. The address was a trading estate on the outskirts of Oxford.

'Wife, cook or housekeeper?' asked Adam.

'I don't know – but I'm starving.'

He smiled. 'So am I.'

An upstairs window was opened, and they could see the shadow of someone moving behind it.

'We mustn't get caught acting suspiciously,' said Adam. 'Come on! Let's discuss our next move over lunch.' He jumped back on to the road, then held out his hand to help Joanna.

They returned to the old, black-beamed pub beside the bridge where they ordered a ploughman's lunch and sat at a table in the window, well away from the other customers congregated around the bar.

'Since we're here, we should try to talk to Bilsham,' said Adam, once the barmaid had brought their meal. 'At least then we can cross him off our list.'

'How do you suggest we meet him?' asked Joanna, spreading duck pâté on her French bread.

'We wait for his wife – or whoever she is – to go out.'

'Maybe she does a school run.'

'Her children would be old enough to travel alone.'

'They're teenagers. The video delivery is for them.'

'I don't think so.' Adam cut a slice of Cheddar. 'That doesn't look like a house with children. It's too quiet. I think the videos are for Bilsham. I just wish he had come to the door to receive them.'

'I've had an idea.' Joanna laid down her knife. 'We go to Video Game Delivery Service, tell them we're visiting Bilsham and want to buy him a present. Then we deliver the game to the house.'

'Two strangers turn up with a present? Joanna, he'll be highly suspicious.'

'So we find out what type of videos he likes, tell him we're doing market research, and with luck he'll invite us into the house.'

Adam's face lit up. 'You're brilliant!'

'We both are.' Her eyes sparkled.

They wolfed their lunch and hurried from the pub. Video Game Delivery Service occupied a modern warehouse on a small trading estate. Outside were a number of vans, similar to the one which they had seen at Summer House. Inside, the walls were lined with video games. By the entrance there was a large notice stating that the weekly delivery round was only available to account customers purchasing a minimum of three videos.

'Can I help you?' asked an eager, pony-tailed young man.

As they had agreed, this time Adam did the talking. 'We're visiting a friend, a customer of yours, a Mr Bilsham at Summerford, and we want to take him a present.'

The young man's eyes brightened. 'Mr Bilsham's our best customer – but you have a problem.'

'What do you mean?' asked Joanna.

'He receives every new game.'

'For his children?' enquired Adam.

The assistant looked puzzled. 'I thought you knew him?'

'He's a friend of my parents,' Joanna explained quickly. 'They asked us to call on him – and we remembered he always liked video games.'

'You can say that again! He's a fanatic.'

The young man appeared satisfied with the explanation. He took them into a storeroom and ran through a shelf of newly arrived games, describing their differences, none of which meant anything to Adam and Joanna, who tried to conceal their impatience.

'Here's one Mr Bilsham hasn't seen.' Triumphantly, the assistant lifted it from the shelf. 'He's on our delivery list and he becomes angry if we don't have at least five new games, so sometimes we keep a game in reserve.' He looked worried. 'Please don't tell him.'

'Of course we won't,' Adam assured him.

The assistant led the way to the till. 'Mr Bilsham will like this game,' he said. 'He's brilliant at chess. He can remember the twenty moves in each opening sequence, just like the grand masters.'

'I can't remember more than half a dozen,' said Joanna, impressed. 'But, of course, Mr Bilsham is very clever,' she added quickly, remembering that she was meant to know him.

'I suppose he is – in a way.' The young man gave her a curious glance.

During their return journey, they rehearsed what they would say to Mr Bilsham. When they reached Summer House, they parked the car in the road to facilitate a rapid escape, and tried the gate. To their surprise, it was unlocked.

The drive was shorter than they had imagined. It twisted round behind the cypress hedge, through a small spinney, and into a circle outside the front door. They walked briskly, their shoes crunching on the gravel, aware of the noise and conscious that they were most likely being watched.

At the front door, Joanna crossed her fingers whilst Adam pressed the bell.

Heavy footsteps hurried to answer. A bolt was scraped back and the door swung open.

The man on the threshold reminded Joanna of the boffins. He had a fuzz of grey hair and wore tortoiseshell-rimmed spectacles which gave his smooth, chubby face the appearance of an overgrown schoolboy. He stared blankly and silently at Adam and Joanna.

'Mr Bilsham?' asked Adam.

'Mr Bilsham,' he repeated.

'We're doing market research and we would much appreciate your opinion of this game.' Adam held out the video.

Mr Bilsham's eyes lit with eager anticipation. Without a word of thanks, he snatched the game and hurried inside, leaving the front door wide open and Adam and Joanna on the doorstep. They hesitated, but only for a moment, before they followed him across a wood-panelled hall and into a spacious study where five very expensive computers, all switched on, were showing video chess games in various stages of play. In front of each computer was a chair.

As they entered, Mr Bilsham pulled out one game, tossed it aside, and slotted in their video. Within seconds he had the new game on the screen. But he didn't remain with it. Instead, he hopped between one chair and the next, playing each of the five games simultaneously, knowing exactly where he was in all of them, so totally engrossed that he was unaware of his visitors.

Adam and Joanna exchanged glances and shook their heads.

'He can't be our Bilsham,' she whispered.

Adam nodded.

'Goodbye, Mr Bilsham,' said Joanna gently. 'Thank you for your time.'

He didn't reply. They moved to leave, but he didn't turn round.

Someone was coming down the stairs and they had no time to escape undetected. It was the woman. She was not wearing an apron, but a nurse's uniform.

'What are you doing here?' she demanded.

'We brought another video for Mr Bilsham,' Adam answered quickly.

'But you've already delivered his weekly order.'

'This is an extra game.'

The nurse sighed. 'Mr Bilsham, I've asked you before not to let people into the house. You should call me. That's what I'm here for.' She chided him gently, as though he were a small child.

Mr Bilsham took no notice.

Adam and Joanna backed away, embarrassed to have disturbed an already troubled household.

'Sorry to have bothered you.' Adam followed the nurse out into the hall.

'We didn't realise.' Joanna gave Mr Bilsham a sympathetic smile.

She turned to follow the others, but as she reached the door her attention was caught by a black and white photograph of a teenage boy on the table beside the telephone. She stopped, and bent to look closer.

'Oliver!' she gasped as she stared into the unmistakable dark, hooded eyes.

The name activated Mr Bilsham like a trigger. He abandoned his video games and grabbed the telephone.

'Ollie!' he shouted, animated in a way that he had not previously been, even when they'd handed him the video game. 'Laurie's ready, Ollie. Laurie's ready.'

Adam hurried back into the room. He looked from Joanna's white, shocked face to Mr Bilsham, and then at the photograph.

'Safarov?' he whispered.

She nodded, sickened with anger as she realised that, once again, she had been deluded. Oliver was a crook. There was no getting away from the fact.

The nurse returned. She looked accusingly at Joanna. 'What on earth is happening?'

Adam cut in quickly. 'Something has disturbed Mr Bilsham.' He placed a protective arm around Joanna. 'We'll go.'

'Yes, you had better.'

But Mr Bilsham didn't want them to leave now. He forced his way between Joanna and the door. 'Is Ollie phoning today?' he asked her excitedly. 'Is Ollie coming?'

'I don't think so, Mr Bilsham, but I'm sure he'll telephone,' the nurse answered in a soothing voice. She took him by the arm and steered him towards the bank of computers. 'Why don't you play with the game these nice people brought you?'

He sat down – and immediately forgot the existence of his visitors.

Adam hurried Joanna out of the study.

The nurse followed. 'I don't know what set him off talking about his brother, but he'll be hyperactive all day now – as well as up all night. He hardly goes to bed before dawn as it is,' she complained. Then she adjusted her uniform, and added in a kinder tone, 'Mind you, he's no trouble, playing with his games.'

'What exactly is wrong with him?' asked Adam.

'He was starved of oxygen at birth, poor man. One of those unfortunate accidents.'

'But he can beat those video games, which is difficult.'

'He remembers the sequences. He can follow instructions to the letter, but he can't work things out for himself. They used to think he was autistic, because he's able to complete repetitive tasks and he has a brilliant recall for numbers, but he's too friendly . . . too open.'

'How comforting that he has a brother to care for him,' remarked Adam in a tone which invited further confidences.

'Indeed! Mr Bilsham's brother is an important figure. Not even a brother, a stepbrother. I can't tell you who, of course, but if it weren't for him, poor Mr Bilsham would be in a home. He couldn't live alone. He's so trusting that he'd open the door to anyone. He really shouldn't have allowed you inside. His brother would be horrified.'

Adam gave the nurse an understanding smile and wished her goodbye. Even in her shocked state, Joanna noticed that he didn't promise to keep their visit a secret.

She walked ahead down the drive. She couldn't bear it if Adam said I told you so – even if he had reason.

He followed. He did not try to catch up with her.

'How could I have been so gullible?' she raged aloud, kicking at the gravel. 'How could I have given him the benefit of the doubt, even after he disparaged me? When I think how that bastard wheedled information from me. I was so reluctant to break client confidences, but he kept assuring me that it was our duty to fight crime. Because he's the great Oliver Safarov, I trusted him.

Throwing open the gate, she strode out into the road. 'On the morning when I was fired, Jeremy received a call on his unrecorded phone. I bet that was Oliver telling him to get rid of me because I'd become too suspicious.' She turned to face Adam. 'When I phoned Oliver to say I'd lost my job, he must have already known. When he came to the flat and promised to remove his business, it was a smoke-screen to placate me. No wonder that bloody crook didn't want me to contact Max.'

Her fists were clenched with rage as she paced up and down beside the car. 'The first time Oliver phoned me at home, I was so flattered. I took the call in the bath. He offered to ring back. I said no. It was during the Fact-Select takeover. Both Società Hadini and New Aldren Fund had bought shares ahead of the public announcement. I thought Oliver . . . desired me. I even encouraged him. But he was merely trying to discover if I was suspicious.'

She thought back, to the very beginning. 'At the Merantum party, when Jeremy beckoned me over, do you know what he said? May I introduce Joanna Templeton, our newest star. I was so pleased, so eager. I'd been singled out to meet an important client. But you know what he really meant? This is the unsuspecting dupe we'll use as our pawn. Oh, what a fucking idiot I've been!'

Adam put his arms around her and held her very tight. 'We're all fucking idiots at some time in our lives.'

XXV

ALL THE WAY back to London, Adam and Joanna discussed Oliver's involvement, speculating on how his system worked and where he obtained his information. Although a man in his position would hear endless gossip, they agreed that he dealt too regularly to rely on mere chat.

When they reached the end of the motorway, Adam turned towards Kew.

'Where are we going?' she asked.

'I want you to meet someone who means a great deal to me.'

'Adam, I don't want to see Val, not today of all days.'

'Do you really believe I'm that insensitive?'

'No, I don't.' She hadn't intended to offend him. 'But I can't face a stranger, not at the moment, I feel so . . . foolish.'

He glanced at her taut face. 'Stop reproaching yourself.'

'I can't help it.'

'You are not stupid.'

'I *am*.'

'All right. You are.'

Her eyes blazed. '*I am not!*'

He smiled. 'I warned you that I'd always make you angry.'

Just before the river, they turned down a pretty, twisting road which ran parallel to the towpath. Adam parked outside a wisteria-covered cottage.

He touched Joanna's clenched fists. 'We've arrived. I know you didn't want to come, but I hope you'll change your mind.'

A woman opened the front door. She was tiny, with a round, smiling face framed by grey-flecked red hair which was scooped into a wispy bun. Her brightly coloured patchwork skirt and embroidered blouse reminded Joanna of the ethnic clothes her mother had worn twenty years earlier – the style which Lindsay still loved.

'I'm Mary Holdfast.' She took Joanna's hands in hers. 'I've been longing to meet you. I'm so sorry about your troubles and so grateful for all you're doing to clear poor Richard's name.'

The kindness in Mary's voice brought sudden tears to Joanna's eyes. She blinked them back, but they glittered on her eyelashes.

'There's no need to say anything,' Mary continued gently. 'Words get stuck sometimes, don't they? I was often that way after Richard . . . died. I still am. Probably always will be.' She led the way into a tranquil, sun-filled sitting room with a beautiful view of the Thames.

'How restful to be so close to the water,' said Joanna, watching a family of swans swim sedately upstream.

'Yes. Richard and I bought this house when we first married. We fell in love with the river. He loved to fish. We always spent our holidays in Scotland.' Mary's glance fell on a photograph of herself and a very tall, thin, balding man proudly displaying a salmon. Then she straightened up. 'I'll make some tea. I'm longing to hear how the investigation is going – if you're able to tell me. I promise not to interrogate. I learned that from Richard.'

'I think we can brief Mary?' Adam turned to Joanna for confirmation.

She nodded. Despite not having wanted to come, she had warmed instantly to Mary.

They settled down in the bay window, with the swans feeding nearby and the river sliding past. Adam recounted their visit to Mr Bilsham. When he reached the point where Joanna had recognised Oliver's photograph, he omitted her earlier rebuttal, stating merely that this was the proof they had lacked of Safarov's involvement. True to her word, Mary asked no questions.

They discussed the Carthew letter.

Mary repeated how she had found it in Richard's desk with a note asking her to give it to Adam. 'I assumed he'd been passed it by someone at Carthew's solicitors, but that seems too obvious.'

'I'm convinced it was Safarov – only God knows how we'll prove it,' said Adam.

'Richard met him at that lunch.'

'Yes, but Joanna doesn't think he'd get involved in small fry like Carthew.'

'I could be wrong.' Joanna looked from one to the other and

gave a self-deprecatory sigh. 'I've been wrong about everything else.'

Adam reached across and squeezed her hand. 'Stop it!'

Joanna turned to Mary. 'I feel so humiliated – and very, very angry.'

'I was furious too when Richard died,' said Mary. 'I raged at him for leaving me, at myself for not realising how anguished he was, and at the people who drove him to despair. Anger is part of grief. I know that now. Initially I raged, but I could not cry.' She gave Adam a fond glance. 'Now I cry often, and I'm better for it – except that I ring poor Adam to talk about the past.'

'You know I don't mind,' Adam assured her. 'I owe any success I have to Richard.' He smiled at Joanna. 'Come on! It's time I took you home. You look exhausted.'

'I am.' She was conscious of feeling utterly drained.

Mary accompanied them to the front door. 'I hate to fuss, Adam,' she said, 'but aren't you worried that Safarov will hear you've visited his stepbrother?'

'I don't think he will. The nurse is clearly afraid of Safarov's wrath and I doubt that Bilsham will remember us.'

'At least, we hope he won't,' said Joanna. She pictured the bright-eyed overgrown schoolboy who'd seized the video from Adam's hand and she wondered if Oliver had, from the outset, cold-bloodedly plotted to exploit Laurie – as he had herself.

Dusk was falling. The dying light cast ominous shadows across the street.

'Do be careful,' said Mary, standing on tiptoe to kiss Adam on the cheek. 'I couldn't bear something to happen to you.' She turned to include Joanna. 'Either of you.'

Joanna thought of the men lurking in the street, her telephone out of order, and Oliver's surprise phone call after weeks of silence – and she pressed her lips together and shivered.

Sleep was, as always, Joanna's healer. Her eyelids drooped in the warmth of Adam's car and she did not wake until they were in London, stationary at traffic lights.

'Sorry to doze off,' she mumbled.

Adam laid his hand on hers. 'There's no need to apologise.'

She opened her fingers wide to let his slip between them. 'I'm glad you made me meet Mary. I like her.'

He caressed the backs of her knuckles. 'She likes you.'

Joanna was acutely conscious of his skin on hers, of the strength in his grasp – and her own reaction to his touch. Desire coursed through her veins. She stretched out her legs under the long bonnet of the sports car, and gave Adam a sideways glance. Did he feel the same? She thought so, but she wasn't sure. After Oliver, she was afraid to believe in her instincts.

They drove to her flat.

'I'll see you safely inside,' he said.

'Thank you.' Did he hope to stay the night? No matter how tired she felt, she knew that she wouldn't be able to resist him.

He accompanied her into the house and across the hall to her flat. At each moment she half-expected him to say goodnight and leave, but he didn't. She smiled at him, and slipped the key into the lock. As she did so, the door swung open of its own accord, separating from the splintered frame.

She gasped, her eyes wide with alarm. 'I've been burgled.'

'They may still be inside.' Swiftly, he pulled her away from the entrance, protecting her with his body. Then he opened the door further, and listened. There was silence.

Inside the sitting room, Joanna could see her grandmother's antique overmantel mirror lying on the floor, its gilt frame split in half, its glass shattered.

'Stay here!' said Adam. 'I'll check the rooms.'

'No. I'll come.' She was afraid to be alone.

She followed him, sickened when she saw the destruction. All the pictures and mirrors had been pulled off the walls. Each drawer and every cupboard had been forced open, their contents strewn round the rooms. Even her photograph of Christopher had been torn from its silver frame. She bent to retrieve it.

'My brother.' She attempted to smooth the picture. 'The bastards! Why rip his photo? Of what value is it to anyone but me?'

Adam was moved by the sadness in her face. 'This is so damned unfair, after all you've suffered.'

'Why don't burglars simply remove things? Why smash my flat?'

'They were searching for money and jewels.'

'Felicity's jewellery!' She hurried towards Felicity's bedroom.

'Don't touch the door knobs! The police will need fingerprints.'

'I must check her valuables.'

Felicity's bedclothes and mattress were on the floor and her cupboard was open, but the rest – the chest of drawers, the books, the ornaments – appeared untouched. Joanna stepped on to a chair and ran her hand along the top of the cupboard, crying out with relief when she encountered a small iron box. 'They haven't got her jewels. Thank God for that!'

'What about yours?' he asked, surprised that she hadn't checked her own possessions first.

'I don't have much – and my mother is still alive. Felicity's mother died when she was a child. The jewellery is all she has to remember her.' Joanna opened her own bedroom door and turned pale. 'Oh hell! Look at that. Everything is on the floor.'

'I wonder why they hardly touched Felicity's room?' said Adam, looking thoughtful.

'Maybe they had no time.'

He clicked his fingers. 'We're ignoring the obvious. These weren't ordinary burglars.'

'You mean . . . Oliver?'

'Who else?'

'Jeremy – in a panic.'

'You're defending Safarov again.'

'*I am not!*' she snapped, her anger and fear misdirected at Adam.

'You're giving him the benefit of the doubt. He's a crook, Joanna.'

'Oliver wouldn't break into my flat. He wouldn't be involved in something so . . . petty. Adam, don't look at me with such disbelief! I know I defended him before, and I was wrong, but he wouldn't dirty his hands in this way.'

'I meant, he'd pay to have it done.'

'But why? What would he be after? Not the disk. We could've made a thousand copies by now.'

Adam pointed at the wall where the telephone had been ripped from its socket. 'Perhaps he's trying to scare you into silence. Maybe it wasn't an accident that your phone was out of order last night.'

'Or the men,' she said, suddenly feeling very frightened.

'What men?'

'Yesterday evening, after I came home, I went out to buy a paper. As I was walking back through the square, I noticed two men standing under the trees. They followed me. At least, it felt that way.'

Adam crossed the room and seized Joanna by the shoulders.

'Why the hell didn't you tell me?' he demanded, shaking her gently.

'This morning I decided I'd overreacted. They could have simply been walking in this direction.'

'I mean, why didn't you phone me last night?'

She didn't look at him. 'You were with Val.'

'So what?'

'I didn't want to disturb you. It could have been a coincidence.'

'The men. The phone. The burglary.' He slipped his arms around her and held her tight, enclosing her in a protective barricade. 'Joanna, you're in danger. Once Safarov realises we're on to him – and his phone call proves that he's suspicious – he'll stop at nothing to silence you.' He released her just enough to extract his mobile phone from his pocket. 'I'm calling an old friend, a police contact.'

'Won't that blow our story?' She couldn't bear to think that all their hard work might be for nothing.

'You need protection.' He tapped out a number. 'Walter? This is Adam Hunter. Sorry to disturb you at home but I need your advice. I have a source who needs looking after. Her flat has been turned over. Yes, we're there now. We've just discovered it. No, I'm on a mobile. The land line's been cut. You'll come over now? Walter, I can't thank you enough.' Adam gave the number of Joanna's house and the postal district, not the full address in case his call was intercepted.

Then he put his hands on Joanna's shoulders. 'Forgive me.'

'For what?' she asked, nonplussed.

'I overlooked the obvious. When Jeremy accessed his computer this morning he would have seen that the previous logged entry was early on Saturday morning.'

'It's not your fault, Adam, it's mine. I worked at First Clarence. I should have remembered,' she said, thinking what a strange dichotomy he was, honest to the point of rudeness and yet generous enough to take the blame for her oversight.

'No,' he insisted. 'You took the risk. I should have focused on the details. Jeremy will have checked the security video and realised that the hacker was a girl from BetterClean. One call, and he'll have discovered it was you – Jo Temple or Joanna Templeton.'

'I went in with my eyes open. No one forced me. And I don't

think Jeremy would ask to see the video. He wouldn't want to arouse curiosity.'

Before they could speculate further, they were interrupted by the intercom.

Adam answered. 'Walter?'

'Who else were you expecting?' replied a gruff voice.

A man walked in. Thick-set and swarthy, he was dressed in jeans, trainers and a worn leather jacket. To Joanna, he appeared more like a middle-aged football fan than a policeman.

'So what hornets' nest have you stirred up now, Hunter?' he asked, clapping Adam on the back so hard that he nearly sent him flying.

'Walter, I'm very grateful to you for coming – but I can't give you the details, so please don't ask me.'

'What? I play nanny but I don't get the glory?'

'You're a public servant. You shouldn't seek acclaim.'

'I should have known. Bloody journalist! Always chasing a scoop.' Walter eyed Joanna. 'So . . . you want me to keep this break-in quiet, check any fingerprints against known thieves, and tell you if it's an ordinary burglary or something more sinister?'

Adam smiled. 'How did you guess?'

'I'm a detective. I know how your scheming mind works – and knowing you, that's not all you want from me.'

'You're right. Walter, I'm worried about Joanna. She needs a bodyguard and the flat needs watching.'

'On taxpayers' money? You're joking! We don't have the resources, not without evidence that she's in physical danger – and I don't have that proof because you won't tell me what this is about.'

Adam held up his hands in mock surrender. 'But you could recommend the best security firm in the business?'

Walter grinned. 'Oh, I expect I could come up with a few names – if you promise to give me the file of evidence *before* your story appears in print.'

'I can't do that,' protested Adam. 'If these crooks found out about our investigation, they'd slap an injunction on the paper.'

'If they've turned this flat over, they know already,' Walter pointed out.

'Or they suspect, and are trying to frighten Joanna.'

Walter shrugged. 'All right. I'll compromise. I'll help you, if you help me catch these criminals. You'll owe me that file of evidence as soon as your story is published. Understood? Say yes, Hunter, or I shall go straight home to my wife.'

'You'll have the big fish but not the pawns. I have to safeguard my sources.' Adam didn't look at Joanna but they all knew that he referred to her.

Walter gave a dramatic groan. 'God save me from journalists! OK, Hunter, I trust you. Can't think why, but you haven't back-tracked on me yet.'

They waited whilst he rang a colleague, asking him to arrange a carpenter and to join them.

Then Walter turned to Joanna. 'Don't mind me. My bark's worse than my bite. Young Hunter and I go back ten years – and I went back even further with Richard Holdfast, God bless his soul.' He paused, and continued in a surprisingly gentle voice, 'You all right, luv?'

She nodded. 'Yes, thank you.'

'Is this your flat?'

She nodded again.

'Do you live alone?'

'I have a flatmate – Felicity – but she's in the States.'

'Anything missing?'

'I don't know. I haven't had a chance to look. But I did check Felicity's jewellery. It's all here.'

'The flatmate's room has hardly been touched,' said Adam.

'That's interesting.' Walter reached for his notepad. 'Let's take some details. Your name and address?'

Joanna answered.

'Do you work?'

She hesitated.

'Can we omit that – please?' said Adam.

Walter glanced at Joanna's name. 'I thought it rang a bell.'

'Then please ask no more.'

'OK – for now.' Walter looked at Joanna. 'If this is a straight burglary, the chances are we'll have had others reported in the building. So far, there've been none. This suggests that whoever broke in was after you or something you possess. They're unlikely to return unless you're here – which you shouldn't be.'

'Joanna will be with me,' said Adam.

'No . . . really . . . I'd prefer to stay.' She was afraid to abandon her home in such a defenceless state.

'Joanna, you can't remain in this flat on your own. It's too risky, even if it is properly secured.'

'But I have to check what's missing. I'll need to claim on my insurance. And I ought to warn Felicity. I can't leave her to find this mess.'

'Felicity doesn't come back for a fortnight. I'll help you clear up long before then.'

'But . . .'

'Where else could you go?' Walter intervened.

Joanna thought of Simon or Rebecca, but she couldn't involve them. That wouldn't be fair. She thought of Max and Emma, but they'd already done so much for her.

'You have a first-class degree in obstinacy,' said Adam, taking her firmly by the arm. 'You're coming home with me – and that is that. I want you safe.'

Joanna took one last look at the wreckage – and acquiesced.

Adam had to help Joanna pack a bag, because when she went into her room and examined the destruction at close quarters – every picture broken and both curtains ripped to shreds – she began to shake.

After some debate, they decided to place Felicity's jewellery safely in Adam's bank, and before they left he telephoned one of the private security firms recommended by Walter. On their way out, they met Walter's assistant, closely followed by a carpenter coming to mend the door. Despite these arrangements, Joanna was still loath to forsake her home.

She was hardly aware of the drive up to Bayswater, except that each time they stopped at traffic lights Adam covered her hand with his in a gesture of reassurance. By the time they reached his house, she felt so weary that she could hardly make it up the stairs. Her legs had turned to lead and she was freezing cold – so icy that her teeth chattered.

'Can you manage?' he asked, putting an arm around her.

'Yes, thanks.' She relished the comfort of his body. 'I'm just tired, but I'll be fine in the morning.'

'You need a hot bath and a large brandy,' said Adam, ushering her into the bathroom and turning on the taps. 'Here!' He handed her a white towelling dressing-gown. 'I forgot to pack yours. Now, get in the bath and I'll bring you that drink.'

Joanna undressed, wrapped a towel around her hair and stepped into the water.

There was a sharp knock. She glanced at the unlockable door, and quickly submerged her body.

'Your brandy's outside,' he called, and went back upstairs.

Feeling silly and presumptuous, and ashamed at having credited Adam with no manners, Joanna opened the door. On the threshold was a large glass of brandy. She sank back into the bath and sipped it, with the warm water lapping at her breasts. On a nearby chair there was an open guide book to New York. She covered it with her towel.

There was another knock on the door. 'I've ordered in a pizza. It'll be here in ten minutes. Don't fall asleep. You must eat.'

Wrapped in the white towelling dressing-gown, Joanna joined Adam in the attic. They sat at the table, as they had done before, but on this occasion they barely spoke. Joanna could hardly keep her eyes open.

'You've had a rough day,' said Adam sympathetically. 'Seeing Safarov's photograph was bad enough, without your flat being done over. I admire you for not cracking.'

Joanna rested her chin on her hand. 'I'm too stubborn. I want justice.'

Adam smiled. 'You deserve it. You have courage.'

'Thank you, but I don't feel very brave tonight.'

He leaned across the table and tucked an escaping tendril of her hair behind her ear. 'Time for bed.'

He led the way downstairs. Joanna followed, wondering if he would try to kiss her. Outside Toby's room, he turned to face her. She stopped. He moved closer.

'Goodnight,' he said, and he opened Toby's door.

'Goodnight.' She stepped inside, and shut the door firmly behind her. She had no intention of making a fool of herself.

Joanna woke next morning to find Adam shaking her arm. He was already dressed for work.

'An ex-policewoman called Claire will keep you company,' he said. 'She should be here in a few minutes.'

'Thank you.' Joanna sat up slowly, rubbing the sleep from her eyes. 'What time is it?'

'Ten to seven.'

'In films journalists always burn the midnight oil, with a glass of Scotch, a pile of discarded drafts and a cigarette hanging out of the corner of their mouths.'

He laughed at her description. 'I'm going in early because I need to speak to Malcolm before the editorial conference. I want to ensure he saves front-page space this Sunday.'

'The front page!' Joanna felt a surge of excitement as she imagined her former colleagues reading the truth behind her dismissal. 'Oh, I wish I could warn Simon and Rebecca.'

Adam looked horrified. 'You mustn't.'

'Don't worry. I won't – for their sakes as well as for ours.'

He crossed to the window and drew back the curtains. 'I plan to enlist Paola's help. She's brilliant at picking up inconsistencies. In the meantime, you run through our evidence. See if you spot any obvious errors. You'll find I've already started to draft the beginning of the story. Print it out and check my facts. When I get back tonight I want to carry on with it.'

'Who. . . . is Paola?' Joanna tried to sound casual but she felt irrationally jealous of this unknown, exotic-sounding woman, and resented the idea of a stranger being involved in their project.

'Paola's a features writer. I'm sure I've mentioned her before. We often collaborate.' He looked down at the street. 'A dark blue car has just drawn up outside. A woman has stepped out. I bet she's your bodyguard.' Adam picked up the phone and tapped out a number. 'Good morning, Walter, it's Adam. Thanks again for last night. Yes, Joanna's much better this morning. That firm is sending someone – Claire. You know her? She used to be in your squad? And she's first class? Well, I couldn't want for a better recommendation.'

The doorbell rang.

'I'll let her in,' said Adam.

'I'll be with you in a minute.' Joanna slipped out of bed, wrapped herself in Adam's dressing-gown, ran her fingers through her hair and followed him out into the corridor.

Claire was standing in the hall, questioning Adam about access to the flat. She was tall and lithe, with very short blonde hair and a cheerful face. In her navy trouser suit, she could have been a well-to-do Swedish tourist.

She spun round when she heard Joanna. 'Good morning, Miss Templeton.'

'Please call me Joanna. I apologise for not being dressed yet.'

Claire grinned. 'On my day off I stay in bed till noon.'

Whilst Adam showed Claire the layout of the flat, Joanna returned to Toby's room to dress. She was tucking her T-shirt into her shorts when there was a knock on the door.

'Come in,' she called.

Adam stepped inside, closing the door behind him. 'You'll be quite safe with Claire,' he assured her. 'She's tough, competent, head-girlish – and an expert in judo.'

Joanna swallowed hard. 'Let's hope that's not necessary.'

'These are just safety measures.' He tried not to alarm her without diminishing the danger. 'Always let Claire answer the door. Don't reply to the phone till you know who's calling. Allow the machine to intercept. Whatever happens, don't go out.'

'Do you really think . . . they'll come after me?' Joanna could not camouflage the tremor in her voice.

'No.' He gave her a comforting smile. 'These are precautions.'

Joanna raised her chin. 'Damn Oliver!'

'We'll nail him.'

'He'll rue the day he met me.'

'You bet he will!' Adam drew her gently towards him. 'I'll be home as soon as I can. Ring me if you have any cause for alarm. If my line is busy, call Walter.' He kissed her gently on the mouth, his voice hoarse as he whispered, 'Be careful!'

'I will.' She gave him a brave smile, trying to look confident for his sake – but she wished desperately that he didn't have to leave.

XXVI

AFTER ADAM LEFT, Joanna went up to the attic to make breakfast. Claire followed.

'We can sit outside in the sunshine.' Joanna threw open the French windows and stepped outside.

'Don't lean over the parapet,' said Claire quickly. Then she modified her tone when she saw Joanna's startled expression. 'If whoever you are hiding from suspects that you are staying with Mr Hunter, they could be watching.'

'Of course . . . sorry.'

Claire smiled. 'Don't worry. Most of the time nothing happens.'

'Do you . . . guard many people?' asked Joanna, busying herself with the coffee so as to stop her hands from shaking.

'Now, yes. But when I was with the force, I specialised in surveillance.' Claire positioned herself so that she could observe both the terrace and the stairs. 'You'll get used to me being here. Just carry on as though you were alone.'

Joanna wondered if any of Claire's previous cases had come to grief, but she didn't like to ask. In any case, she suspected that Claire wouldn't tell her.

After breakfast, Claire remained at the table, glancing through a pile of Adam's magazines, although she never allowed herself to become immersed in the articles. She stayed alert to every sound and movement.

Joanna carried her coffee over to Adam's desk, pulled out his chair and switched on his computer. But she didn't start work immediately. Instead, she leaned back in her seat and studied her surroundings.

She was conscious of Adam all around her – his past and his present. His pens and pencils filled a blue pottery jar brought back from somewhere in the Mediterranean. His reference books lined the shelf beside the desk. Toby's photograph hung on the wall. The desk diary lay open. Joanna couldn't resist glancing at the page, but the entries told her nothing. There were no names, just initials.

Angry with herself for being so nosey, she slotted in her disk and called up Jeremy's data. Once again, she checked Kathpeach's transactions, looking for any inconsistencies, but she found it hard to concentrate – not because of Claire's presence but because her thoughts kept drifting back to Adam.

She recalled the decisive manner in which he had taken charge in a crisis, how he'd known who to contact, helped pack her bag, and brought her here. She'd been surprised by his thoughtfulness, running her bath, lending her a dressing-gown and fetching her a brandy. She remembered the sympathy in his voice when he'd said, 'You've had a rough day.' But most of all, she relived the moment when he had kissed her on the mouth – the first time he had done so.

She stood up. 'I need to fetch a sweater.'

'Let me check first.' Claire hurried downstairs. Joanna could hear her opening the various doors. A moment later she called, 'You can come down.'

'Thanks.' Joanna felt a little foolish at all the fuss. At the same time, it was reassuring – like Adam's protection.

She slipped on a white sweat shirt. As she came out of Toby's room, she noticed that the door to Adam's bedroom was slightly ajar. Through the gap she could see his bed with a blue and white striped duvet tossed over it, a telephone and a lamp on a bedside table. Carefully, she opened the door a little further. On the far side, beneath the window, there was a perfectly scaled-down wooden tea clipper inside a glass case. On top of the case was part of a mast, held upright between two books, and next to it was a tube of Superglue. Joanna would not have credited Adam with the patience to mend something so intricate.

She returned to the attic, determined to concentrate on work, and spent the rest of the morning trying to find a link between the shares targeted. There appeared to be none. Not only were the companies spread across the sectors but, as far as she could tell from company reports, they had no common directors or locations.

At lunchtime she made sandwiches for herself and Claire. Whilst they were watching the television news, the phone rang. Joanna waited by the answering machine.

'Adam, it's David. We're back from holiday. Give us a call. By the way, who was that mystery woman?'

The phone rang again.

'Joanna, it's me.'

She hurried to reply.

'Are you all right?' he asked anxiously.

'Yes . . . fine . . . thanks. We're having lunch.' The sound of his voice reminded her of his whispered, 'Be careful'.

'The line was engaged when I tried a moment ago. I was worried in case you were attempting to contact me and my number was busy.'

'Your friend David phoned.'

'You didn't speak to him?'

'Of course not.'

In the background of his office she heard someone call, 'Adam!'

He cursed. 'I have to go. I'll see you later.' He added softly, 'I'm looking forward to it.'

She smiled. 'Me too.' She could not wait.

She rejoined Claire. They chatted about the news headlines, but Joanna's thoughts were of Adam. She imagined herself in his arms, kissing him, making love with him. She envisaged his body on hers, in hers – and she felt a surge of pure, raw desire.

The television screen showed queues of people waiting to visit Buckingham Palace.

'I was on duty on the night before the royal wedding,' said Claire. 'It was my first surveillance job. Do you remember the fireworks in Hyde Park?'

'Oh . . . er . . . yes.' Joanna blushed. In her mind's eye she'd been naked with Adam.

During the afternoon she had a long lazy bath, washed her hair, shaved her legs, cut her toenails, and dressed again – carefully but without looking too contrived. In any case, she was limited in her choice of clothes. Adam had only packed her jeans, her shorts, a pair of smart black trousers, a selection of shirts and a black Lycra mini-skirt which she seldom adopted because it was too short. Now, she wore it.

When Adam returned in the late afternoon, Joanna was sitting at his computer. On hearing the front door lock turn, she forgot about danger and security and, before Claire could prevent her, she raced down the spiral stairs. Then she stopped dead, blushing as she realised that he was not alone.

'Paola has come to help us.' Adam introduced his colleague, an elfin-faced, black-haired woman of Mediterranean appearance who was dressed in a very expensive navy trouser suit.

'Hello, Joanna.' Paola had a smile which suggested some deeper amusement. 'Heavens, what a short skirt! It's the kind of thing that Holly wears – but only in the house. No wonder Adam keeps you locked up.'

'I'm here for security.' Joanna bristled. She objected to being dismissed as some bimbo. She wouldn't have worn the skirt if she'd known Adam would be accompanied.

Paola chuckled. 'Oh, don't mind me! I'm envious. I'd love to show my legs but they're like tree trunks!' She started up the stairs, making it obvious that she was well acquainted with Adam's flat.

Joanna thanked Claire and said goodnight. Then she followed Paola and Adam up to the attic, determined to mask her disappointment. She didn't want to share her evening with this woman. She'd waited all day to be alone with Adam, and had believed he felt the same way. If he didn't, why had he kissed her?

'Malcolm doesn't deserve our scoop,' Adam was raging to Paola. He stopped talking and smiled when Joanna appeared in the doorway. 'Is everything all right? Are you happy with Claire?'

'Yes, thanks. She's very nice.'

'Have some wine.' He handed her a glass. 'I'll tell you why I'm so angry. Malcolm insists that I interview a banker about what the twenty-month delay in ratifying the Maastricht treaty will mean to the British economy. I'll waste a whole blasted day of our precious week.'

Paola cut across him. 'Adam, you're Malcolm's obvious choice for the interview. You did the last Maastricht article – and you're our best writer.'

'Balls!'

Paola gave Adam a fond, almost maternal smile. 'It's true, Joanna. Everyone says so.'

Deciding that she'd been over-sensitive about Paola, Joanna joined her at the table.

Adam was refusing to be pacified. He paced up and down the attic. 'What the hell is the point of all our hard work, of Joanna being at risk, if these criminals have time to slap an injunction on the story and our investigation never sees the light of day?

Anyone would think that Malcolm doesn't want our scoop to succeed.'

'He does – and he doesn't,' replied Paola.

Adam stopped pacing. 'What do you mean by that?'

'Malcolm lives in Richard's shadow and your story will establish Richard as an old-fashioned hero. Richard took the gentlemanly way out, accepted the blame, and went into the next room with a revolver! That kind of *Boy's Own* glamour is impossible to trump.' Paola downed her wine and held out her glass for a refill. 'At the same time, Malcolm is desperate for a scoop. The *Sunday Chronicle* has suffered under his editorship and he needs a big story.' She pointed her finger at Adam. 'Or the board may vote to replace him and offer his job to you.'

Adam looked stunned. 'That's not true.'

'Oh, come on, Adam! Everyone at the *Sunday Chronicle* is convinced that one day you'll be our editor – including Malcolm. That's why he's sending you to New York. He's frightened of your popularity – and you do nothing to allay his fears. You make it so bloody obvious that you think he's ineffective. Don't deny that you'd like to be editor.'

'Of course I want to be – but not yet. I enjoy being a journalist. I like investigating.' Adam topped up Paola's glass. 'What's more, Malcolm may be a useless wanker but I have no intention of putting him – or anyone – out of work.'

'You know, Joanna,' Paola confided, 'Adam's worst fault is that he never listens to office gossip.'

'I don't need to, Paola. I have you, my Machiavelli reincarnated.'

Joanna chuckled. This was clearly an on-going office joke.

The local Italian restaurant delivered their supper. Adam went downstairs to collect it, returning with a pile of cartons containing *gnocchi al pesto,* parmesan, chicken with tarragon, and various salads.

'It's time you learned to cook, Adam,' said Paola, as she helped Joanna to lay the table.

'And catapult my local restaurant into bankruptcy? Paola, how could you be so heartless towards your fellow Italians?'

'I'm only half-Italian. My mother was a practical Lancastrian.' Paola took the chicken from Adam, placed it in the warm oven, and shooed him out of the way.

Over the gnocchi, Adam and Joanna detailed their evidence.

When they had finished, Paola sat back in her chair. 'Oliver

Safarov!' She rolled his name around her tongue. 'Good God! This is really going to rock the City! You two are brilliant.'

'It was a team effort.' Adam smiled at Joanna. 'I couldn't have done it alone.'

'Nor could I.' Joanna returned the compliment.

'But I'm going to play devil's advocate,' said Paola.

'That's why we asked you here,' Adam assured her.

'You lack proof,' she told them bluntly. 'This . . . Laurie may be Safarov's stepbrother but you have no evidence to say that Safarov receives insider information or that he instructs Laurie to deal in shares on the basis of that information – which is the crime you must prove. Are you sure Laurie is capable of dealing?'

Adam repeated what the nurse had said.

'It sounds as if he is, poor man.' Paola sipped her wine, and thought.

Adam and Joanna waited.

'With regard to Jeremy,' Paola went on. 'You have no corroboration of his involvement. Just because the names of shady offshore companies are stored in his computer that doesn't mean he's a fraudster. Even if you had Società Hadini's fax, Joanna, you can't show that Jeremy diverted it from your machine. It would be his word against yours. Why should he do it? At the very least you have to establish Jeremy's dishonest motive.'

'That's what my solicitor said.'

'He's right.' Paola looked from Joanna to Adam. 'I'm sorry.'

'Don't apologise. We need you to pick holes,' replied Adam. 'The last thing we want is for Malcolm to discount the entire investigation solely because of one missing piece in the puzzle.'

Joanna frowned. 'Surely he wouldn't do that?'

'Malcolm's not known for his bravery. He's already succumbed once to pressure to cut out Safarov's name.' Adam was still irritated about his lacerated article.

'But if Oliver knows we're on to him, how come he isn't putting the screws on Malcolm again?'

'I don't know,' Adam admitted. 'It's certainly out of character for Safarov not to wield his power.'

'Unless he's waiting to find out how much you know,' suggested Paola.

'Or setting a trap for us.' Joanna pictured her shattered possessions.

'You're quite safe here.' Adam gave her a reassuring smile,

placed the chicken in front of her and handed her a large spoon. 'You be Mummy.'

She pushed her fears to the back of her mind, as he'd intended her to. 'Yes, dear! Did you remember to wash your hands?'

He laughed and showed her his palms.

She plonked Paola's empty glass in them.

'What a subtle hint!' He reached for the wine.

Whilst Joanna served the chicken, the conversation turned to the disk.

'Such a bloody shame that it's inadmissible,' said Paola. 'Of course it doesn't prove Jeremy's a crook, but it's a link.'

Joanna looked from one to the other. 'Surely if the information is in the public interest and I couldn't have gained it any other way, it can be used?'

'Yes, but you'd leave yourself open to a criminal charge. You could go to prison.'

Paola helped herself to salad. 'What you need is proof of Laurie receiving instructions from Safarov and relaying those instructions to his contacts in Grand Cayman, Liechtenstein . . . or wherever.'

Adam forked up a slice of tomato from the bowl. 'The question is, who are his contacts if they're not George, Frederick and Lawrence?'

'Why would Oliver trust them with his secret life?' asked Joanna. 'It doesn't make sense. He'd never leave himself vulnerable to blackmail.'

'Laurie wouldn't blackmail him,' Paola pointed out.

Adam frowned. 'Why does Safarov involve Laurie at all? Why doesn't he phone his contacts himself?'

'Because he doesn't want the calls traced to him,' suggested Paola.

'Laurie's no safeguard. The contacts must realise he couldn't operate alone. I can't believe that he hasn't told them about his brother. He told us.'

'We're overlooking the obvious,' said Joanna. 'Oliver can't make the calls. He travels constantly to Eastern Europe. To fax or phone, he often has to use hotel operators. He wouldn't risk drawing attention to himself by phoning all these glamorous places.'

'But he can speak to his disabled brother as frequently as he pleases and people will merely think how caring he is.' Paola shook her head in disgust. 'How cynical can you become!'

They mulled over the problem of the missing information, arguing backwards and forwards.

Suddenly, Adam sat upright. 'I've got it! I know his system. There are no intermediaries – just telephones and fax machines. Safarov is using an international private telephone circuit. He instructs Laurie to fax an order to, say, the Liechtenstein number to buy X number of shares in Y company at Z price on behalf of Kathpeach. In Liechtenstein that fax is automatically recreated and returned to First Clarence.'

'But the Kathpeach orders only showed the Liechtenstein number,' Joanna pointed out.

'They would do. That's the beauty of it.'

She sat forward eagerly. 'So when I phoned Kathpeach in Liechtenstein, my call was answered by Laurie in Summerford?'

'Exactly.'

'How do we prove it?'

Adam raised his eyebrows heavenwards. 'That's the problem. We have to tap into the wire between Liechtenstein and London to prove that Laurie's fax has been recreated.'

'You'll need a copy of it as evidence for Malcolm,' Paola reminded him.

'I know. Our difficulty is that such circuits cost thousands of pounds in rental and the police in these countries will only tap a phone if they believe the line's being used for criminal activities, like drug dealing. They aren't going to act on our unsubstantiated suspicions – and certainly not in time for me to write my article by Friday.'

Joanna tried not to look disheartened but she couldn't help it.

'What about your policeman friend, Walter?' asked Paola. 'Could he help?'

Adam shook his head. 'I can't ask him to get involved in illegal phone tapping. He'd refuse – and probably never speak to me again. In any case, the second leg of the circuit will have originated outside the UK. But there is my contact in Vaduz – the retired engineer.' He rose. 'I'll phone him. He should be back from holiday by now.'

'How can you be sure that Safarov won't use a Grand Cayman fund?' asked Paola.

'We'll have to take a risk,' replied Adam, looking up the engineer's number.

'Oliver might not even deal at all this week,' said Joanna. 'It depends if he receives a tip-off.'

Adam stopped. 'Damn! I hadn't thought of that.'

'I know this sounds cruel.' Paola lit a cigarette. 'But one solution would be for you to originate the order and instruct the wretched Laurie yourselves.'

Adam turned to Joanna. 'We'd set them up – as Jeremy set you up.'

'Poor Laurie!'

Adam touched her hand. 'There is no other certain way – unfortunately.'

The engineer was out – he'd gone to the cinema – but he'd be back in two hours. Whilst they waited, Adam practised imitating Oliver's accent.

'Do I sound like Safarov?' he asked Joanna.

She couldn't meet his eyes. 'No, but you're close.'

As further proof for Malcolm, Adam taped their instruction to Laurie on a mini recorder, keeping the message brief since they all agreed that Oliver would want to limit the risk of being overheard.

The phone rang, and they all jumped. Adam picked it up. To Joanna's surprise, he spoke in German. It had never occurred to her that he spoke another language, especially so fluently. He talked for ten minutes, then replaced the receiver.

'Can he help?' she asked impatiently.

'I don't know. He's going to speak to a friend who works the night shift at one of the exchanges. He wanted a week to set it up, but I said it has to be tonight. He says they can't divert a circuit destined for First Clarence to my number. The best they can do is to repeat that fax to me. That means First Clarence get the order – which will immediately put Jeremy on red alert.'

Joanna remembered the delay between her unauthorised call to Kathpeach and Jeremy sanctioning their purchase of Merantum. 'Jeremy won't act till he's checked with Oliver.'

They sat around the table, so tense that they could barely speak. An hour passed. Then another. At midnight the phone rang again. Adam grabbed it, listened, frowned. When he replied in German, he appeared to be bargaining.

'Well?' said Paola, as he replaced the receiver.

'The friend can repeat the fax to my number, but only if it's sent between two and two-thirty tonight, our time. Let's hope Laurie doesn't make an exception tonight and go to bed early.'

Joanna reached across the table and laid a hand on his arm. 'Why are you looking so worried?'

'I've had to agree to pay twelve thousand dollars whether we succeed in activating Laurie or not.'

'Won't Malcolm refund you?'

'I hope so.'

'If he won't, I'll pay half.' If necessary, she'd sell her car.

'Out of the question.' He smiled at her. 'But you can make some more coffee.'

She switched on the kettle. Then she froze. 'Adam, we can't call Laurie from here. He might have the nurse with him. With so much at stake, we must be sure he's alone.'

He stood up. 'You're right. We'll have to ring him from his garden, where we can see the study. It'll take over an hour to get there. Come on! You too, Paola.' He hurried to his desk. 'Where's that print-out with the phone numbers? Ah, here it is. Paola, phone Holly to say you'll be late.'

'No, thank you, Adam. I shall escape before I get caught up in your mad schemes.'

'Then wait! We'll all leave together. Joanna, you'd better wear jeans and you'll need a thick sweater. It could be a long, cold night. Choose a dark colour, so you won't stand out. Oh, you probably haven't anything suitable. I'll lend you one of mine.'

They raced down the spiral stairs. Joanna went into her room to change.

When she came out, Adam handed her the same navy sweater she had previously borrowed. 'It's dark, so you won't be noticeable,' he said, smiling at her, expectant and excited.

She nodded, equally excited.

They hurried down to the street, insisting on accompanying Paola to her car although time was short.

'Thanks for supper,' she said, settling in behind the wheel. 'Adam, bring Joanna to visit us one day. I know Holly would love to meet her. And for heaven's sake be careful tonight.'

'We'll take care.' Adam laid a hand on Joanna's shoulder. 'I'd rather forget the whole thing than have Joanna get into more trouble.'

His statement astonished Joanna. She recalled his blunt comments on the steps of Companies House.

'Is Holly her daughter?' she asked, as they hurried across the road to his car.

'No, her girlfriend.' Adam saw the surprise in Joanna's expression. 'I didn't realise either – initially. I met Paola on the day I had my first article accepted by the *Sunday Chronicle.* I found her attractive, and gathered she was single, so I invited her out. She turned me down – and told me about Holly.' He chuckled at the memory. 'It was one of the few occasions on which I have been struck dumb.' He unlocked the passenger door. 'Let's hit the trail.'

As they headed west, out of London, with the night countryside flashing by, Joanna reflected on Adam's earlier admission. Once, he would not have thought twice about jeopardising her to clear Richard, and she would have sacrificed him to exonerate herself. Now, she too had changed. She still wanted justice, but she also wanted Adam – she wanted both.

XXVII

THEY DROVE ALONG the lane behind Summer House. It was very dark, with just the odd glimpse of moonlight behind thick clouds.

'We'll park here.' Adam drew into the same small gateway. 'We'll attract less attention than at the front.' He checked the time. 'Half-past one. We'd better hurry.'

They closed the car doors quietly and crossed the road, scrambling over the ditch to the cypress hedge, trying not to curse when brambles scratched their hands.

All the lights on the ground floor of the house were illuminated. They cast their beams in every direction.

'What about security?' whispered Joanna, as they peered through the branches.

Adam scanned the building. 'I can't see any cameras. Even if there are some, I don't believe the nurse checks the videos and by the time Safarov – or whoever – has done so, we'll be long gone.'

'With our evidence in hand.'

'Our scoop already published!'

'Jeremy arrested.' She couldn't wait for that day.

'Safarov in disgrace.'

'Richard's name cleared.'

'Joanna exonerated.' He touched her cheek. 'But first, we have to climb these railings. Can you manage?'

'If you can, I can.'

'Very good, corporal. I'll go first.'

She gave him an exaggerated scowl. 'I'm a field marshal – not a lowly corporal.'

'Joint chief-of-staff, please hold down this branch.'

'With pleasure.'

Joanna secured the hedge whilst Adam grabbed the top bar and pulled himself upwards. He swung his leg over the railings and jumped down on to the rough grass at the edge of the lawn. Impatiently, he waited as they watched the house for a reaction. There was none.

'Come on!' He beckoned her over.

Joanna lifted her foot to the cross rail but it was too high. She tried again. Still she couldn't reach it.

'I'll climb back and help you,' he whispered.

'No! I can do it!' She was furious with herself for holding them up.

Gritting her teeth, she kicked her leg upwards and managed to catch her heel on the bar. Then she seized the top of the fence and dragged herself upwards, almost splitting her jeans when she jumped over.

He caught her and held her. 'Well done, general.'

'I'm a field marshal – I refuse to be demoted.'

The air was damp. The dew had begun to settle, and there was a smell of warm mown grass. From the extremities of the garden came the occasional rustle of small animals searching for their food.

Joanna and Adam hurried along beside the hedge until they reached the study side of the house. The lights were on and the curtains were open. Adam gave Joanna the thumbs up and took a step forward.

She seized his arm and pulled him back, whispering urgently in his ear, 'We mustn't leave footprints in the dew.'

'You're right. I forgot.' He returned to the rough grass. 'Thanks for reminding me.'

From the relative safety of the hedge they searched for cover, but there were no trees between themselves and the study, just sunken flowerbeds. They crept on until they were directly behind a large rhododendron bush some forty feet from the study window. Adam nudged Joanna. She gave him a brief nod. Bending double, so that his face didn't reflect the light, he ran across the lawn and into the safety of the branches. Joanna waited for a moment. When no one appeared at the windows and no alarm rang out, she followed.

As she reached the shrub his hands sought hers, guiding her into the dark, dry, dusty bower. A cobweb dropped on to her face.

She brushed it away, disturbing more dust. Quickly, she stifled a sneeze.

'We can watch from the other side,' whispered Adam.

She nodded, afraid to speak in case she sneezed.

He went ahead, holding the branches and twigs so that they didn't hit her in the face. Each time a dead twig cracked underfoot, they froze. Every rustle of the dead leaves seemed like approaching footsteps.

At last they arrived at the far side of the bush. Adam lowered a branch and they looked out. The study was now some thirty feet away. The lights were on and one of the computer screens was illuminated, but there was no sign of Laurie.

Adam consulted his watch. 'Eighteen minutes to go. We'd better make ourselves comfortable.' He slipped off his jacket and laid it on the dried leaves.

They sat down, side by side, watching the study through a window in the branches. They waited, motionless, not daring to speak. Five minutes passed. A breeze picked up, rustling the leaves. The ground was damp, and Joanna shivered.

Adam put his arm around her. She leaned against him, savouring the warmth of his body, conscious of his masculine smell mingled with the faint hint of aftershave.

He tightened his hold, running his hand up and down her arm to warm her.

She turned her face to him, intending to whisper her thanks. As she started to speak, his mouth covered hers and he pulled her fiercely to him, gripping her so tightly that his arm was like a band of steel. Parting her lips beneath his, she slipped her arms around him – and drew him back with her on to the dry leaves. She wanted him to make love to her in the darkness of the garden. She craved the weight of his body on hers, to feel him deep inside her. She ached for sex, but not just sex – she also wanted his love.

Suddenly, a shaft of yellow light reached across the lawn. They froze, but didn't draw apart. They waited. No one came. Cautiously, they sat up and peered through the branches.

Laurie was sitting at one of the computers, his face rapt and eager as he competed with the video. Beside him was a desk lamp with a yellowish bulb. Behind him, the door was closed. As far as Joanna and Adam could see, there appeared to be no one else in the room.

'He's so defenceless,' Joanna whispered. 'I wish we didn't have to involve him.'

'So do I. Poor bugger.' Adam checked his watch again. 'Three minutes to two. Pray that he doesn't decide to go to bed now.'

The seconds ticked by. Laurie continued to play with his computers. Suddenly he stood up and walked towards the door.

'Oh, no!' Joanna gripped Adam's arm.

They stared, transfixed with horror. Laurie reached for the door knob. Joanna held her breath. He withdrew his hand, and returned to his computer. She relaxed her grip on Adam's arm. Weak with relief, they slumped against each other.

'Two o'clock. Here goes,' said Adam. 'Watch Laurie.' He handed Joanna the tape recorder, adding, 'Keep this ready. I'll need it in a minute.'

He took the mobile phone from his jacket pocket and tapped out Kathpeach's number in Liechtenstein. There was a brief delay, normal for an overseas call, then a ringing tone. They studied Laurie. He carried on playing his game, neither moving nor reacting in any way.

'I can't hear it ringing in there,' said Joanna.

'It must be.'

'Adam, we'd hear it.'

'Not if the volume was turned down low.'

'Or he has switched it off.'

'I don't believe he'd do that. Safarov wouldn't allow it.'

They let the phone ring for five minutes, but Laurie didn't move. Joanna could feel Adam tensing beside her. There was so much at stake – not just their scoop and his promise to Mary, but also his twelve thousand dollars.

'I'm going to check if it's ringing,' she whispered. 'Try him again once I'm within earshot.'

'No!' He reached out to stop her. 'It's too dangerous. I'll go.'

'Adam, you have to make the call. If the tape fails to activate, I couldn't imitate Oliver. Even Laurie wouldn't believe I was his brother.'

Adam hesitated. He didn't like it, but he knew that she was right.

'I'll just get close enough to hear if it's ringing.' She parted the branches and stepped out of the safety of the shrub.

Once outside, she experienced a moment of sheer panic, but she dug her fingers into the palm of her hand to steady her nerves and thought of Adam. He gave her confidence. He made her feel invincible.

Avoiding the yellow beam, she started to cross the lawn.

'The dew!' came Adam's urgent whisper.

She jumped back. 'Thanks. I forgot.'

Circling the rhododendron until she was a safe distance from the study, she made a dash for the shadows of the house. There, she slipped along the wall, keeping her body flat to the surface, till she was within a few feet of the study window. She looked towards Adam but she couldn't see him and she felt very vulnerable. A moment passed. Then, inside the study, she heard a very faint ringing. She ducked down, and turned back to safety.

'It's just audible,' she said, as she crawled thankfully into their lair.

He touched her cheek. 'You have guts.'

'She smiled. 'Thanks – but has Laurie moved?'

'No, damn it!' He's too absorbed.' Adam consulted his watch. 'We've less than fifteen minutes before our contact clocks off. Let's try again.'

Adam held the receiver so that they could both listen. The phone rang fifteen times. They exchanged glances of increasing desperation. Then, on the twentieth ring, Laurie raised his head. He looked around with an expression of bewilderment, jumped out of his chair and hurried to the back of the room – to the table where Joanna had seen Oliver's picture.

There was a click on the line.

'Ollie, Laurie here. Laurie ready.' His voice burst into the darkness beneath the rhododendron.

Swiftly, Adam reduced the volume. 'Laurie, ready?' he asked, hunting for the words which might belong to Laurie's routine whilst simultaneously attempting to imitate Oliver's accent.

'Ready.' Laurie didn't seem to notice a difference.

Holding the tape machine next to the phone, Adam pressed the *play* button. 'Use the Kathpeach number to buy one hundred thousand Merantum Building Company shares at maximum one hundred and eighty signed Bilsham.' With his exaggerated foreign accent, Adam sounded like a villain in a B movie.

Laurie didn't flinch. He repeated the message, enunciating each word, and placed the receiver on one side. Forced to control their impatience, Adam and Joanna watched as he carefully typed the order. With less than five minutes to spare, he dialled a number – and sent the fax.

'Let's hope our contact was successful,' said Adam, switching off the tape recorder.

'He has to be!' Joanna couldn't bear to consider the alternative.

Laurie had picked up his receiver. 'Laurie ready,' he said, standing to attention.

Covering the mouthpiece, Adam whispered, 'How do I sign him off?'

'Try saying goodbye.'

'Goodbye, Laurie.'

'Goodbye, Ollie.' He didn't move.

'What now?' asked Adam, watching Laurie with despair. 'We can't stay here all night. God, I wish we hadn't had to tamper with someone so helpless.'

Joanna nodded. 'I'll always feel guilty.'

'Safarov doesn't. He has no compunction about exploiting his brother.'

Or about using me, she thought ruefully.

'We'll have to leave,' said Adam. 'We must check if that fax's been copied to my machine. I just hope the nurse finds him soon.' He switched off his phone.

The click on the line made Laurie jump as though he'd received an electric shock. To their intense relief, he replaced his receiver and returned to his video game. Their last sight of him, before they retraced their steps across the garden, was his eager boyish face, smiling peacefully.

XXVIII

DAWN WAS BREAKING as they drove back to London, streaks of red chasing the night away. Adam and Joanna discussed the evidence they had – and that which they still lacked.

'We know the funds belong to Safarov and that he uses Laurie to place the orders,' said Adam, accelerating along the almost deserted motorway. 'We can show that those deals are done ahead of public announcements and that they're placed through First Clarence – where Jeremy allocates the funds to new salesmen, still on probation, whom he hopes won't dare query.'

She grimaced. 'Mugs like me!'

He pretended to punch her, stopping his fist just before her cheek and ending with a caress. 'No, you did question.'

'But I confided in the wrong person.'

'Safarov is highly respected. Why should you suspect him of being a cheat?'

She smiled. 'Thanks.'

The motorway ended and the three lanes reduced to two.

'What we haven't ascertained is whether he uses other banks as well,' said Adam, as they roared up on to the flyover.

'He once told me he didn't – but he was probably lying.'

'Another missing point is whether he receives his information from one person or a network. We don't *have* to prove this, but I'd love to know – and it would make a better story. Could it be Jeremy?'

Joanna shook her head. 'It can only be someone with knowledge of forthcoming bids and takeovers – like a mole at the SFA or the Stock Exchange.'

'An employee who suddenly leads a glitzy lifestyle arouses suspicion.'

'Then who else?'

He smiled at her. 'I wish I knew.'

When they reached Adam's house, he took Joanna by the hand. 'Fingers crossed that Laurie's fax has arrived,' he said, plaiting her middle fingers.

They raced up the stairs, into the flat and on up to the attic. A dozen faxes had arrived. Adam flicked through them.

'Here it is!' Triumphantly, he held up the page. 'Buy one hundred thousand Merantum Building Company at maximum 180 signed Bilsham, Kathpeach, Liechtenstein.'

Joanna studied the fax. 'There's no indication that it originated in England.'

'That proves their system. They're definitely using an international private telephone circuit.'

'But have we established the fraud?' she asked anxiously, removing her thick sweater. 'Do we have enough to convince Malcolm?'

'I damned well hope so.' Adam cupped Joanna's face in his hands. 'I could never have succeeded without you.'

'Nor could I, without you.'

She waited for him to kiss her but, to her surprise and disappointment, he detached himself and started down the stairs.

Nonplussed, Joanna stood alone in the middle of his study. Then she walked to the door.

'Adam!' she called after him. 'What's wrong?'

He had reached the bottom step. 'I don't want to have sex with a woman who's only in my bed because her flat has been burgled.'

She swung down the spiral steps and seized him by the buckle of his belt, pulling him towards her. Then she stood on tiptoe, so that her mouth brushed his, gratified when he stiffened against her. 'Make love to me!' she whispered.

He drew her into his bedroom. She kicked off her shoes. He unbuttoned her shirt and slid her bra straps from her shoulders.

'I've wanted you since I first saw you,' he said.

She removed his leather belt. 'When you told Rawdale to . . .'

'To fuck off.' His mouth was on her face and neck, his arms were around her.

Her breasts were bare against the rough wool of his sweater. Her nipples were hard with desire. She wanted him. She ached for him. She moved against him, her legs pressed to his. He held her tight, almost lifting her on to him. Their mouths were pressed together as she reached down, unbuttoned his jeans and held him.

He undressed her quickly – her jeans and the wisp of white

silk. As he threw off his remaining clothes, she was conscious of his body being hard and lithe and far more muscular than she had envisaged. Naked, they fell back on the bed. The duvet came between them, and they kicked it aside. He pressed her down into the pillows, framing her face with his arms. She sank her teeth into his shoulder, then kissed the mark she'd made. He ran his mouth down her throat to her breasts, taking her nipples in his mouth, rolling them between his teeth until she gasped with a mixture of pain and pleasure. He kissed her stomach and the soft insides of her thighs, touching, stroking, probing.

She laid herself on top of him and massaged his body with her firm breasts, wanting to please him as much as he aroused her. She kissed his neck and chest, licking his brown curly hairs and enjoying the taste of him. Her hair covered her face as, slowly, she slid down his body until she knelt between his legs and took him gently in her mouth whilst he snaked his fingers through the silky mane of her hair.

'I want to be inside you,' he said, pulling her up to him. 'I want to see your pleasure.'

'I want to give you pleasure.'

She spread her legs, wanting him to penetrate every corner of her body, gasping with pleasure as he entered her. He made love to her slowly, holding back so that she was always one step ahead of him. He aroused her until she begged for more. He framed her face with his arms so that he could look into her eyes and see her enjoyment.

She relished the feel of his body on hers, around her, deep inside her. She revelled in his strength, in his muscles. He blocked out the world, the recent past, everything outside this flat, beyond this room. He thrust harder and she wrapped her legs around him, trapping him inside her. She began to tremble and felt him quiver. She cried out in ecstasy and he thrust deeper. When her orgasm pulsated through her, he joined her, prolonging her pleasure with his own.

Sated and tender in the afterglow of their lovemaking, Adam held Joanna close. 'Would you like some champagne?' he asked, kissing the corner of her eyebrow.

'I'd love some.'

'So would I. It's in the fridge.'

She gave him an innocent smile. 'Oh, good, I prefer it very cold.'

'The glasses are in the cupboard.' He gave her a gentle nudge towards the edge of the bed.

She wriggled back towards him. 'I'm the guest. I expect to be waited on.'

'Well . . . just this once.' He swung his legs off the bed.

'If you're not nice to me I shall run away,' she told him, laughing.

'If you do, I shall pursue you and drag you back to my lair.'

She lay among the pillows and watched him from beneath her eyelashes. She could think of nowhere she would rather be.

Adam returned with a bottle of vintage Krug.

'A special treat.' He handed her a glass.

'Because this is the first time?'

'The first of many – I hope.'

'I hope so too,' she admitted, suddenly a little shy.

He leaned across and kissed the tip of her nose.

They snuggled together under the duvet, drank champagne and talked.

Joanna found herself telling Adam about Peter, although she hadn't intended to. 'We should have separated years earlier,' she admitted. 'We would have if we'd been unhappy, but we weren't. We were good friends. It's so hard to make the break when things are almost right.'

'But not quite right?'

'Yes.' She glanced at him. 'Were you and Val the same?'

'Similar. We met, sparked, and had fun. I gave up my rented flat and moved into her house. We argued, but it worked because I was away a lot, chasing stories. When I began to concentrate solely on the City, I travelled less – and we argued more. We'd already agreed that I should move out when Val discovered she was pregnant. I'll never forget coming back to the house one night to find her sitting at the kitchen table with a bottle of gin in front of her.'

'Were you shocked when she told you?'

'Horrified. So was she.'

'Did you consider getting married?'

'I suggested it, but Val was sensible enough to turn me down.'

'Did you think of . . .'

'An abortion? Val wouldn't contemplate it. She was brought up a Catholic and, although she calls herself lapsed, she couldn't conceive of taking such a step. At the time, I wished she would.

But now . . .' He smiled with a fondness which touched his whole face. 'I'd be bereft without my Toby.'

He refilled their glasses and they lay back among the pillows.

'Were you in love with Safarov?' he asked after a few minutes.

Joanna shook her head. 'No. But he was charming, amusing, powerful, and fascinating. I suppose it started as an . . .'

'Adventure?' He supplied the word.

'Yes.' She could never have admitted that to Peter.

'An adventure into hell!'

She nuzzled the hair on his chest. 'You could say so!'

He took her glass from her hand and looked into her eyes, kissing their lids and the soft sloping corners to her eyebrows. They made love again, slowly, but with no less pleasure, their long limbs entwined, the light from the bedside lamp reflecting on their bodies.

'So you . . . didn't live here with Val?' Joanna asked some time later. She meant, did you make love to her in this room, in this bed?

'Val has never even stayed here.'

Joanna laid her cheek on Adam's shoulder. She didn't feel threatened by Val nor was she jealous of the bond they shared in Toby. She assumed that Adam had had other girlfriends since, but sensed that none had been important. Like Adam, she had a past – and hers was far more notorious. If he could accept hers, then she could accept his. But she was glad that he hadn't lived here with Val – that this had not been another woman's home.

She woke to the sound of the shower. A few minutes later Adam returned to the bedroom, a towel around his waist, his hair wet and tousled.

He smiled when he saw that she was awake. 'I have to go to the office,' he said, with an unenthusiastic expression. 'I need to prepare my Maastricht interview. I should've done it last night.' He bent to kiss her. 'But I discovered something much more important on my agenda.'

She linked her arms around his neck. 'I have a very serious complaint.'

He raised an eyebrow. 'What?'

'Where are my croissants?'

'You'll have them on Sunday morning – when we lie in bed, reading our investigation.' Reluctantly, he began to dress. 'I'll be home as soon as I can. I have to take the banker out to lunch, so it won't be before mid afternoon. Claire will keep you company.'

Joanna slipped from the bed and into Adam's towelling robe. 'What can I do to help?'

'Key in all the data from last night – where we went, what time, what was said. I've sketched out some sections of the story, but I want to draft the entire article tonight.'

The phone interrupted them.

Adam answered. 'Good morning, Malcolm. Yes, we have the evidence. I'll give you all the details this morning. Yes, I am interviewing the banker at midday.'

Adam was still talking when Joanna went into the bathroom. She had a quick shower, standing under the cascade of warm water whilst the soapy bubbles of shampoo poured through her hair and down her naked back. As she turned off the water, she heard the buzz of the intercom heralding Claire's arrival. She wrapped herself in the robe, with a towel around her head, and slipped on her watch.

It was eight o'clock. She visualised the busy desk at First Clarence and her replacement, Jane Dixon, finding their fax. She imagined her consulting Jeremy – and Jeremy reaching for his yellow phone. She saw Oliver in his bright white villa taking the call. He might even be in bed with a woman and break off from his lovemaking to hear that she, Joanna, had rumbled his game. She pictured his disbelief – and felt triumphant. She envisaged his rage – and was afraid.

Adam was waiting for her in the bedroom. He slipped his arms around her and drew her close. 'How I wish I could stay – even for five minutes.'

She leaned against him and tried to forget about Oliver.

He nibbled the lobe of her ear. 'Damn Maastricht!'

She stroked his sleeve. 'You're wearing the same cufflinks that you had at the Merantum Building party. I haven't seen you use them since. Was R.H. your father?'

'No. They belonged to Richard. He left them to me. They were in the envelope with the Carthew letter. Until now, I've always been uneasy wearing them. I never felt I'd earned the right.'

Joanna reached up and kissed him. 'Richard would be proud to see you in his cufflinks.'

He touched her face, gently, fleetingly. 'Be very careful.'

'I will.' She wished she could confide in him what she planned to do, but she was afraid that he would try to stop her.

Within an hour of Adam's departure, Joanna was dressed and ready. She hovered in the bedroom, undecided what to do about Claire. The simplest solution would have been to creep out without saying a word, and hope that Claire didn't hear her. Only that would bring trouble on Claire's head, which would be unfair.

She went upstairs. Claire was sitting at the table.

'I have to go out for a couple of hours,' Joanna told her.

Claire looked alarmed. 'It isn't safe.'

'I must.' Joanna paused. 'I'm sorry, I really appreciate all you're doing for me, but I have to go somewhere this morning.'

'Where?'

'I can't tell you – not yet.'

Claire rose. 'Joanna, your safety is my responsibility. If you go out, I'm coming with you.'

Joanna started to protest, then she stopped. After the trouble and expense which Adam had taken to keep her safe, it seemed ungrateful to refuse Claire's offer.

'Very well . . . thank you. But please don't tell Adam.'

Claire looked even more concerned.

'I want to tell him myself,' Joanna explained. 'But not till much later.'

'As you wish,' said Claire. 'But we must take sensible precautions. We'll travel by taxi. It'll be more anonymous than my car and will leave me free to defend you, if needed.'

'Whatever you say.' Joanna hid her nervousness behind a smile.

They departed some ten minutes later.

'You still haven't told me where we're going,' said Claire, as they stepped outside into the uncomfortably hot morning sun.

'To buy a ticket and check on an old photograph.'

Claire positioned herself on the outside of the pavement. 'It must be important.'

Joanna nodded. 'It is.'

They found a cab immediately. It whisked them through the stifling streets, jinking along behind Oxford Street to Bloomsbury. They asked to be dropped on the southern tip of Russell Square. Claire kept a wary eye out whilst Joanna paid the fare. Only as the driver drew away did Joanna realise that she had misread the street numbers.

'It can't be very far,' she said, stepping off the pavement to cross the road.

At that moment, a car came from behind them. It drove straight at Joanna. She stared at it, transfixed by fear, unable to move or scream. Claire seized her by the arm, pulling her roughly backwards as the vehicle mounted the pavement. Joanna staggered and almost fell, grabbing at the nearest lamppost as the car scraped the other side of the post with its offside fender. She caught sight of a man crouched in the back seat, his head hidden by his arms. Then the car drove on.

'Are you hurt?' asked Claire anxiously.

Joanna shook her head. 'Thank you for saving my life,' she whispered, so terrified that her lips would barely move.

'Thank goodness I was here. Now, please, let's go home.'

Joanna took a deep breath to quell her nerves. 'I can't. Not yet.'

'But you're in danger.'

'It'll be worse if I fail to accomplish what I set out to do.'

The two women looked at each other.

'Very well.' Claire acquiesced. 'It must be even more important than I imagined.'

'It's life or death,' replied Joanna quietly.

It was early afternoon before they returned to Adam's flat. As they walked in through the door, they could hear his worried voice on the answering machine.

'Joanna, where are you? This is the second time I've called. Please answer!'

She hurried into his bedroom and picked up the receiver. 'I'm here.'

'Where have you been? Are you all right?'

'I'm fine.' She attempted to sound calm and relaxed, and to blot out the memory of the car.

'Where were you?'

'I . . . wanted to go out. Claire came with me. Don't worry.'

'I can't help it. I don't like you taking risks. Please promise me you won't go out again.'

'I promise.'

To Joanna's relief, Adam didn't persist with asking where she had been. He seemed to assume that she'd merely gone for a walk.

Conscious that Claire couldn't help overhearing, Joanna pushed the door shut. 'What did Malcolm say?' she asked.

'He can't wait to see the article – and I couldn't wait to hear your voice.'

'I like to hear yours.' She sprawled across his bed.

'I was so worried when you didn't answer.'

She thought of the man crouched in the back seat – and shivered.

'Just the sound of you makes me . . .' he went on.

'Then hurry up and come home!'

'Where are you?'

She rolled over on her stomach. 'Lying on your bed.'

'Stop tempting me!'

'I want to tempt you.'

'When I was seventeen,' he said, 'I was desperate to buy a motorbike. To earn money during the holidays, I packed bags of frozen fruit. I spent all day watching the clock, begging its hands to move faster. I was like that at lunch today.'

'You could come back early,' she suggested.

'And have you distract me?'

'I might ignore you.'

'You'd damn well better not!'

She chuckled. 'How was the Maastricht interview?'

'Long and dull. The banker guzzled his way through the entire menu, including a steamed pudding. I kept thinking of you.'

She feigned outrage. 'Because of the steamed pudding or the dull banker?'

'I mean that if the name Joanna suddenly appears in the middle of Maastricht it will be because my mind had drifted.' He paused whilst a package was delivered to his office, then continued, 'How are you progressing with our data?'

Guiltily, she recalled his untouched computer. 'Oh . . . I'm . . . er . . . still organising my notes.'

'Don't worry about that. Just key in the facts and I'll arrange them.' Another phone rang on his desk.

'That'll be Malcolm. I have to go. I'll be back soon.' He added in a barely audible whisper, 'I'm looking forward to tonight.'

'Me too,' she replied. 'Very much.'

After Joanna had spoken to Adam, she stood in front of his long mirror. Her face glowed, her eyes shone and her lips seemed more full. As she held her arms together she could almost imagine that his skin caressed hers. When she looked around his room, she felt secure – or as safe as she could be with Oliver out there, stalking her.

XXIX

AT SIX O'CLOCK Joanna heard a key turn in the front lock and Adam called her name. She hurried down from the attic. She had no doubt that this time he would be alone. When he stepped into the hall, he saw her standing at the bottom of the spiral staircase, happy and waiting for him.

She smiled.

He dropped his briefcase and engulfed her in his arms, swinging her round as he had that early morning when she had come to him, dressed in her BetterClean uniform, carrying the stolen disk – the morning when she'd realised how much she wanted him to be alone and he'd realised how concerned he was for her safety.

Claire came downstairs, carrying her bag and jacket, and they wished her goodnight.

'Thank you for . . . everything,' Joanna added in an undertone. She didn't need to elaborate.

As the door closed behind Claire, Adam kicked off his shoes. 'This must be the hottest, stickiest day of the summer,' he said, walking into his room and throwing off his tie and shirt. 'What a relief to be home.'

Joanna stretched out on the bed to watch him undress.

'I was thinking about you whilst I was driving back,' he went on. 'Thank God we don't have to go anywhere or see anyone. We have the evening . . . the night . . . and in the morning we'll wake up together. I like that.'

Joanna smiled. 'So do I.'

Adam ran himself a bath and lay in it, drinking ice cold lager. Joanna sat on a low rattan stool, sipping white wine.

'Shall I wash your back?' she offered, admiring his hard body.

'No, just chat to me.'

She told him about her afternoon, making it expand to cover the whole day. They discussed the data.

'As soon as I've polished Maastricht, I'll start on our scoop,' he said, adding with feigned innocence, 'I told Malcolm I'd be working from home tomorrow morning, with you, and that no one must interrupt us – unless it's urgent.'

'Nothing is that urgent.' Joanna swung her leg into the bath and traced a line down his chest with her big toe.

He seized her by the ankle. 'I said work, not play.'

'That's tomorrow.' She took off his hand and moved her foot further down, across his stomach, titillating him with her toes. He slid his hand up her thigh.

'You're not wearing any knickers,' he said, stroking her.

She leaned forward and licked a drop of water from his upper lip. 'There didn't seem much point.'

'Let's go to bed,' he murmured against her mouth.

She nodded.

They made love in the warmth of the early evening, with the dull gold light of the dying sun caressing their naked bodies. Eventually, hunger drove them up to the attic, where they snacked on pâté and strawberries. Later, Adam reworked the final paragraph of his Maastricht piece whilst Joanna used the kitchen table to spread out all their evidence, checking it for the final time.

When he had finished the article, he handed it to her. 'I want your opinion.'

She took the pages. 'My honest view?'

'I never wish for any other.'

She read it carefully, flattered to be consulted. 'It's terrific,' she said as she reached the end, 'but there's one topic I'd elaborate.'

'Tell me.' He was interested, not defensive.

She read aloud. ' "Analysts believe the Footsie will fall soon, regardless of Maastricht or GATT".'

'Interest rates are bound to rise.' He justified his statement.

'Yes, but we're also nearing the end of a bull market – at least people fear we are – so nervous trading will automatically drag shares down.'

'Good point.' He returned to his computer to insert a line.

Joanna watched him. She enjoyed being part of his work.

As soon as he had faxed Maastricht to the *Sunday Chronicle*, he joined her, linking his arms around her as he nuzzled the back of her neck.

'Let's go to bed,' he whispered. 'We'll work tomorrow.'

She leaned back against him, relishing the feel of his hard body and the knowledge that he desired her. He untied the belt of her dressing-gown and slid his hands underneath the towelling material, caressing her until she whimpered with pleasure.

Early next morning they chivvied each other out of bed.

'It'll be worth it on Sunday morning, when we see our investigation in print,' said Adam, the first to rise.

'You mean, when you're buttering my croissants?'

He laughed, and pulled the duvet off her. 'Come on! Up!'

She rose reluctantly. 'May Jeremy rot in prison!'

'And Safarov?' he asked, watching her reaction.

She bent down, not intending to appear furtive but to retrieve her hairbrush. 'I wonder if he'll risk coming back to see *Tosca* on Saturday?'

'He wouldn't dare.'

She thought of the car. 'I'm not so sure. He can't bear to concede defeat.' She straightened up, and her expression froze when she saw the look on Adam's face. 'What's wrong? Why are you staring at me like that?'

'Will you ever be indifferent to him?'

'He betrayed me too deeply.'

Adam frowned and fell silent.

'But it wasn't love,' she hurried to assure him. 'It wasn't trust. There was no depth, no fondness, no laughter. It was never anything like you and I have shared in these few days.'

He shrugged. 'We'd better get down to work.'

'Of course.'

Joanna tried not to let his tone upset her. She hated things left hanging in the air, but she sensed that regardless of what she said, Adam would only be convinced by her actions.

He spent the morning drafting the article whilst she fed him information in chronological order. It was a dull, overcast day, much colder than recently, and they needed all the electric lights in the previously sun-filled office.

At around noon, Joanna searched through the freezer and found a packet of uncooked mince. With the help of an onion, some frozen vegetables and several large potatoes she rustled up a cottage pie, grating Cheddar cheese on top of the mashed potato before she browned it under the grill.

'You can cook too,' Adam remarked appreciatively, after the first taste.

'Oh, nothing elaborate. Just nursery food.'

'I like it.' He forked up a second mouthful. 'I'm tired of restaurants where you're given half a quail's egg balancing on a lettuce leaf.'

She giggled at his description of nouvelle cuisine. 'So you're a "meat and two veg" man?'

'As are most men.'

'Not Lindsay's boyfriends. She only goes out with vegetarians. She broke up with one man because he ate meat in secret.'

Adam looked amused. 'What about your little sister? Does she have a boyfriend?'

'Alice is still at school. She lives at home with my parents, in a tiny village on the Quantocks. She doesn't have much chance to meet boys. My mother is very over-protective since Christopher's death.'

'Understandable.' He helped himself to more cottage pie.

'What about your sister?' she asked, aware that although they knew much about each other, they also knew nothing at all.

'Sarah's married to a sheep farmer. They have two children and live in Yorkshire. He's solid and practical and she has a heart of gold but is terribly vague. When she stayed here before Christmas, she left her watch. In July, she forgot her pearl earrings.'

At last, Joanna knew the identity of their owner.

By early afternoon, Adam had drafted the entire article. Joanna read it with increasing excitement. Seeing the story spelled out in his clear prose, she finally allowed herself to believe that the nightmare might be coming to an end.

'I'll be able to hold up my head . . . carry on with my career . . . see my old colleagues,' she told him, with tears of emotion in her eyes.

Gently, he stroked them away. 'Didn't you think we'd succeed?'

She leaned against him. 'Yes – but I was afraid to depend on it.'

The telephone interrupted them. Reluctantly, he turned away to answer it.

'Hello. Yes, Malcolm, I'm working on the story now. What? Postpone it to next week! That's out of the question. It *has* to appear this Sunday. My source is in considerable danger. Her flat has already been broken into and I've had to hire a bodyguard to protect her.' Adam looked at Joanna and rolled his eyes in frustration. 'Malcolm, I told you all this yesterday. Yes, I know we have to be careful about libel but we agreed that, so long as I had the article ready by tomorrow, the house lawyers would have time to check it.' He paused to listen. When he continued, he did not try to mask his impatience. 'For God's sake, this is the scoop of the year. It deserves front-page exposure. It's just what the *Sunday Chronicle* needs.' He paused again. 'Very well. I'll see you in an hour.' He slammed down the receiver. 'What a wanker!'

Joanna laughed.

'I have to go in,' he said, putting his arms around her.

'I realise that.' She nuzzled his cheek.

'I'm sorry.'

'So am I – but the scoop comes first.'

He brushed her mouth with him. 'Only until Sunday.'

Adam called Claire. Whilst they awaited her arrival, he tinkered with the final paragraph and Joanna telephoned her parents.

Her father answered. 'Darling, how lovely to hear from you at last. We left two messages. Your mother was worried.'

She explained about the burglary.

'How ghastly!' he exclaimed. 'Are you all right? Why didn't you tell us?'

'I didn't want to worry you.'

'But we're your parents, Jo.'

Once again, by trying to protect them she'd made matters worse.

'Was much taken?' he went on.

'I . . . er . . . don't think so, but Felicity is away, so I decided to stay with a friend.' She glanced across at Adam. 'Er . . . no, no one you've met. Yes, please don't worry. Things are fine . . . in fact, going well. That's what I wanted to tell you. This friend and I – he's a journalist – have been investigating an insider trading ring. It's the reason I was dismissed from First Clarence. No, Dad, of course I wasn't involved. I was falsely set up and sacked because I voiced my suspicions. Yes, well, I want to warn you that the true story should appear in the *Sunday Chronicle* this weekend.' She listened to his fears, then replied, 'No, I can't forget the whole thing. I was wrongfully dismissed. Daddy, please believe me, I have to do it – even if it means more publicity. Yes, I do intend to warn Lindsay. I'll speak to her straightaway. Of course I'm sorry about Mummy. I don't want to upset her. But I have to clear my name.'

She came off the line and sank back in her chair, drained by guilt and apologising.

Adam looked up from the screen. 'Don't blame yourself.'

'He doesn't understand why I can't let it blow over.'

'He loves you and wants to protect you.'

She pictured her father climbing nervously up the ladder to trim back the ivy because he wanted to look after his garden – as he tried to take care of his family.

Adam left as soon as Claire arrived. Since their article was completed, Joanna had no work to do, so she spent the afternoon chatting to Claire and thinking about Adam.

Every aspect of his home had now taken on a sexual meaning. In his bedroom, they had made love. In the attic, he had walked away from her – and she'd run after him. At the bottom of the stairs, she'd seized him by the belt. At the kitchen table, they had talked.

He telephoned as soon as he'd spoken to Malcolm. 'We're on for Sunday.' His voice was brimming with excitement.

She laughed from sheer relief.

'I just have to rewrite one section, then go through it with the lawyers,' he continued. 'I'll be back for supper. I've invited Mary, Paola and Holly to celebrate. The off-licence will deliver a crate of champagne in an hour. Can you phone Il Pesto and ask them to send us something delicious? You'll find their card on my desk.'

'Don't you think we should celebrate after publication?' asked Joanna, afraid to tempt fate.

'Don't be a pessimist!'

'I'm a realist.'

'So am I – and I'll explain all this evening.'

She was impatient to know what he meant but realised that he would not – or could not – elaborate. 'I'll see you later,' she said.

'I look forward to it – very much.' His tone was soft.

'So do I.'

Adam didn't return until after his guests had arrived. He hurried up the spiral stairs, full of apologies, relieved when he saw that Joanna had made everyone welcome. Mary and Paola were chatting to her as though she were an old friend. Holly, a very pale, pretty blonde, was curled up on the sofa, listening.

Joanna sensed that Adam was worried. He didn't say so, but he was nervous, almost angry, and he talked very fast. 'To a successful scoop,' he said, topping up their glasses.

Mary squeezed his hand. 'I could cry with gratitude. I only wish Richard was here.'

'What will you do if Malcolm is too scared to print?' asked Paola.

There was a sharp intake of breath as everyone stared at her.

Adam turned to Joanna. 'I didn't have time to warn you but I'm having a problem convincing the house lawyers.'

She lowered her glass as the champagne acidified in her mouth. 'Why? Because we haven't identified Oliver's source?'

'No, although that would help. The problem is that Malcolm's afraid to point the finger at Safarov in case he upsets the board – and loses his job.'

'Don't the directors want a scoop?' Joanna tried to keep the anxiety out of her voice.

'They don't like a friend to be labelled a criminal. But if we prove that Safarov is guilty, they'll drop him like a hot brick and back Malcolm all the way.'

'So . . . what will happen?' she asked.

'I've made some cuts and the lawyers are reading it again.' He glanced at his watch. 'I have to check in with them shortly. Don't worry! This story will run. Malcolm *has* to publish it. He can't afford to chicken out. The entire newspaper scents that I'm working on something big.' He raised his glass. 'And that we're celebrating tonight.'

'So that's what you meant by being a realist?'

He nodded. He didn't need to elaborate for her.

'But what'll you do if Malcolm loses his nerve?' Paola persisted.

'Swap with the late man tomorrow night and alter the final edition.'

Paola looked horrified. 'Adam, you wouldn't insert your scoop against the editor's instructions?'

'I was only joking – unfortunately.'

'Thank God for that! You'd lose your job.'

'I might leave anyhow.' He started towards the door. 'I haven't told Malcolm, because I'm not a petulant child making threats, but the truth is that if he fails to publish the Safarov story I shall hand in my notice.'

'You're not serious?' said Paola.

'I can't work for an editor I don't respect.' He went down the stairs to use the bedroom telephone.

Mary was visibly distressed. 'Adam loves his job.'

'And the paper certainly needs him,' said Paola. 'If he goes, the financial pages will lose half their readership. Moving him to New York is bad enough.'

Joanna felt physically bereft at the prospect of being separated from Adam. 'Could Malcolm cancel the posting?' she asked.

'Of course. He could send Sean, who has family there and longs to go, but I can't see Malcolm backing down – unless he's a better man than we've given him credit for.'

'Does he suspect Adam might leave?'

'Probably. Malcolm may not be forceful, but he is intuitive.'

'That still wouldn't make him print our story?'

'Only if he's hovering on the borderline – not if the house lawyers advise against it. You see, if Safarov sued successfully, the damages would ruin the *Sunday Chronicle.* No editor wants to be blamed for closing a newspaper.'

'I understand.' Joanna tried not to sound defeatist.

Adam reported that he had to make one further alteration. 'They're frightened to accuse Safarov outright of Carthew's downfall,' he told Mary, gritting his teeth in frustration. 'I'm so sorry, but Malcolm won't print as it stands because we haven't proved it. We can only say that Donia profited – which implies, but doesn't point the finger.'

Mary patted his hand. 'It'll come out in the criminal investigation. Richard will just have to wait a little longer.'

'Don't worry,' he assured her. 'I'll make certain that Walter knows the whole story.'

Whilst the others continued to discuss Malcolm, Joanna was quiet and thoughtful. She recalled her job, her hopes, and the morning when she'd been dismissed. She pictured her burgled flat, the men hidden among the trees and the car which had almost crushed her. Why hadn't Oliver tried again to silence her? He must know where she was. She glanced out through the terrace doors at the night sky. What was he waiting for?

XXX

ON THE FOLLOWING morning, after Adam left for work, Joanna lay in bed listening as his MG roared into life. Then she drifted back to sleep.

She rose late and took a long, luxurious bath before joining Claire in the attic. In the corner of the room, below the television, the VCR glowed red. Remembering that Adam always recorded *Weekly Money*, Joanna switched on the set.

David's face filled the screen. He was talking about Twinberrow's recent success in acquiring competitor companies. Listening with interest, Joanna poured herself some coffee.

'Twinberrow were advised by the eminent QC, Quentin Brocklebank, who always seems to be retained by one or other side in major takeover battles,' David told the viewers.

The camera cut to Carey Street, behind the High Court, and Joanna recognised the unmistakable tall figure of Quentin Brocklebank striding diagonally across the road. He was trailed by a gaggle of junior barristers and two clerks laden with books, all scurrying to keep up like chicks after a mother hen. As David detailed the outcome of the previous week's proceedings, Brocklebank swung under the old stone arch into Lincoln's Inn, and his entourage raced after him. Bringing up the rear was one of the clerks. Before he disappeared, he looked back, straight into the camera.

Joanna gasped.

'What's wrong?' asked Claire, ever alert.

'I . . . thought I recognised someone.'

'Who?'

She was saved from the need to reply by the telephone. As soon as she had ascertained it was Adam, she picked up the receiver.

'We have a problem,' he confided.

Her mouth went dry. 'What . . . is it?'

'Malcolm's still hesitating because the lawyers say our evidence isn't watertight. He wants to meet you and hear your story. I'm sorry to ask you to come in but it's our only hope.'

'Do I tell him about BetterClean?'

'Everything.'

'But . . . I thought you said that must remain confidential.'

'Yes, but not from my editor. Malcolm may be a jerk but he's a newspaperman. He would never reveal my sources. This is solely to put his mind at rest. If I send Reg, can you come straightaway? He's delivering in the West End. He could be with you in ten minutes.'

'I'll be ready.' The prospect of leaving the flat was alarming but Joanna couldn't tell Adam about the car now, not when their success depended on her.

'Ask Claire to come with you.' He paused, and added, 'Do I repeat myself if I say you're my best partner?'

'Yes, but I like it.'

'Then I'll say it again – tonight.'

As soon as they said goodbye, Joanna hurried downstairs. Deciding that Malcolm, a man bound by rules and anxiety, wouldn't be impressed by a casually attired woman, she selected the only smart clothes which Adam had packed – black tailored trousers and a yellow silk shirt.

She was applying her mascara when Reg rang the bell. Scooping up her lipstick, comb and scent, she followed Claire down to the car, glancing apprehensively up the street before she slid into the back seat.

Reg took the same route as their taxi, jinking along behind Oxford Street, after which he turned down through Holborn. To avoid a burst pipe in Kingsway, they were diverted around Lincoln's Inn Fields. As they passed close to Max's office, Joanna decided to telephone him as soon as the scoop was published. She hoped he wouldn't be too upset that she hadn't confided in him beforehand.

The reception area at the *Sunday Chronicle* was very different from her previous visit. Then, she had been the sole visitor. Now, the porters' desk was a hive of activity and all the lifts were in constant use.

Adam was waiting for them, and Joanna hurried to him. He

looked at her quizzically. She nodded, but said nothing. He didn't question her, but took her by the elbow, the pressure of his fingers telling her he understood.

'Thank you for taking such good care of Joanna,' he told Claire.

'It's been a pleasure.' Claire turned to Joanna. 'Good luck! You deserve it. Hit him where it hurts.'

Joanna laughed and shook her warmly by the hand. 'I won't forget what you did for me. Please keep in touch.'

'I'd like that.' Claire looked pleased. She gave a half salute and strode out through the revolving doors.

Adam ushered Joanna towards an empty lift. 'What did Claire mean?'

'That we mustn't back down.' She didn't like to lie.

'Is that what you were trying to tell me?'

'No.' She waited till the doors closed and they were alone. 'Do you remember I told you that Oliver had an elderly butler?'

Adam nodded.

'That butler has a nephew – he's Quentin Brocklebank's clerk.'

'You mean . . . Brocklebank, the QC who does all the big takeover work?'

'Exactly! I was watching your *Weekly Money*. David was doing a feature on Twinberrow. There was a clip showing Brocklebank. The nephew was carrying his books.'

'So . . . what are you suggesting?' Adam pressed the tenth floor button. 'That Brocklebank is Safarov's source? Joanna, I don't believe it. That man is honest.'

'No, the nephew,' she spoke quickly. 'A clerk in a top chambers has a very powerful position. He has access to all the briefs.'

'Good God. If that's true, this is an even bigger story.' Adam stared at the overhead panel, where the floor numbers were flashing past. Swiftly, he thumped the eighth floor button. 'We must talk. Malcolm will have to wait.'

They stepped out into a wide corridor, deserted except for one porter.

'What else do you know about the nephew?' he asked, drawing Joanna to one side.

'His name's Stuart, he's about thirty, and he's a big spender. He has an E-type Jaguar and he dresses in designer clothes.'

Adam looked less convinced. 'A clerk in a chambers such as Brocklebank's earns big money.'

'I know, but it was Stuart who found the butling position with

Oliver. Withers – the uncle – told me so. He also told me that his nephew often visits him. He kept saying how unselfish Stuart was, what a good boy, all that kind of thing. But, Adam, if you saw Stuart you'd know that he's not the type to visit an elderly relative without good reason.'

'Supposing they planted Withers there.'

'To give the nephew a reason to call frequently,' she added eagerly.

'In order to pass on information, gleaned at work, to Safarov?' Adam put his hands up to his head. 'This is huge. The nephew's sitting on a gold mine. Brocklebank is the leader in his field.' He thought for a moment. 'Could the butler be involved too?'

Joanna shook her head. 'No.'

He raised an eyebrow. 'Sure?'

'Adam, I'm not being deluded again. Poor old Mr Withers is as straight as a die. He's ex-army and all that – and devoted to Oliver. He'll be devastated.'

'If Safarov could misuse his disabled step-brother . . .' he began.

Joanna pulled a face. 'And me.'

'He wouldn't give a damn about his unfortunate butler.'

'Do we have time to prove it?'

'Not before Sunday.' Adam glanced at his watch. 'We'd better go. Malcolm will be in a panic.'

He called the lift and they continued to the tenth floor. As they stepped out into a bustling hi-tech office where three hard-pressed secretaries were fielding calls to the editor, Adam touched Joanna's shoulder.

'Tell Malcolm everything – except about the nephew,' he said very quietly.

'Why hold it back?'

'Please. I need to think.'

'Adam, Malcolm's waiting.' One of the secretaries gave him a broad grin. 'You're to go straight in.'

'Thanks, Penny.' Adam opened the door marked *Editor.*

A large, jovial, pink-faced man with short grey-blonde hair and the physique of a rugger forward was sitting at a leather-topped desk surrounded by telephones. Opposite him were two men in dark suits.

'As we have already stated, Malcolm, from a legal point of view . . .' The more senior of the two was speaking in the controlled, precise words of a lawyer.

Joanna was astonished. Malcolm was completely different from the physically weak mouse she had pictured.

He rose when he saw her. 'Good of you to come in, Miss Templeton.' He had a booming, bluff voice and when he shook her hand his grip was firm.

'I want Adam's investigation to appear on Sunday,' she replied.

'Er . . . yes . . . we all hope for that. Do sit down. I'd like our house lawyers to hear your story as well. It's not that I don't believe you, Miss Templeton but . . .' He gave her a jolly smile.

'You don't wish to be sued?'

'Spot on!'

She took one chair. Adam took another.

'Coffee?' asked Malcolm politely.

'Yes, please.'

He smiled encouragingly, like a judge taking evidence from a child. 'Time is a bit pressed, but would you prefer to begin your story now or wait for your coffee?'

'I'll start straightaway.'

Joanna commenced with her first day at First Clarence, when Jeremy had allocated her the Kathpeach account. By the time her coffee arrived, she'd reached the morning when Kathpeach had complained about her performance. She explained the reason why Jeremy diverted calls and faxes to himself – and the fax which he claimed she had overlooked. She described the suddenness and misery of being sacked and Jeremy's threat to deny her a reference. She spoke of the humiliation of being labelled a sex pest, shaking with rage as she recalled the rumours that she had offered to sell information. She described her harassment by the press, the effect of Oliver's belittling statement, and the rough man in the street. She gave Adam a quick smile when she came to the night when he'd suggested they join forces. She related her interview with BetterClean, but omitted the names of Max and Felicity. The greatest detail she reserved for the moment when she had accessed Jeremy's computer.

The senior lawyer raised his hand. 'Hold it there, please. Miss Templeton, we can't use evidence gained in such a way.'

'I know, but that disk led us to Mr Bilsham.'

'Whose name you would both prefer to omit?'

'Yes.' She smiled at Adam, glad that he'd remembered.

They continued to question her for nearly an hour, by the end of which she was exhausted.

Finally, Adam interrupted. 'You've met Joanna. She's told you her story. What is the problem?'

The lawyers exchanged glances.

'Safarov is a very powerful man,' replied the senior. 'You have proved *how* he could commit fraud, but not that he actually *does* so – at least, not beyond doubt.'

'Don't tell me that twenty deals, all in profit, could be luck or coincidence?' said Adam impatiently.

'Of course not. Those facts speak for themselves. Twenty frauds have taken place. But can you prove that Safarov committed even one of them?' He looked from Adam to Joanna.

She remained silent, wondering if Adam would tell them about Withers' nephew – but he didn't.

'Not identifying Laurie is acceptable, because in the event of legal action we could name him,' continued the lawyer. 'But referring to accessed information from a bank computer, without giving any details of how you came by it, is asking for trouble. First Clarence will instruct their lawyers. Jeremy will deny everything. Safarov will slap on a writ. The *Sunday Chronicle* will fold in the face of crippling damages. And you, Miss Templeton, will be found hanging from Blackfriars Bridge.'

'For heaven's sake, that's a bit dramatic!' exclaimed Malcolm.

'Why do you think Joanna had to have a bodyguard?' said Adam. 'She was followed in the street, her phone was cut and her flat was turned over.'

'Do you have proof that Safarov was behind these acts?' asked the senior lawyer.

Adam shook his head. 'Unfortunately not.'

'Then it could have been ordinary burglars and other pedestrians.'

'Perhaps, but I'm not prepared to risk that.'

'Of course not.' Malcolm hurried to placate his star reporter.

Adam glanced at his watch. 'We have less than two hours to second page deadline.'

'I . . . er . . .' Malcolm turned to the more senior lawyer so as to avoid Adam's gaze. 'What's your advice?'

'Too dangerous.' The lawyer looked at Adam. 'Sorry. It's a terrific piece of journalism and I'd love to advise Malcolm to publish, but I can't. There are just too many loopholes.'

Adam was tense with disappointment.

'How can we make it acceptable?' enquired Joanna, intervening before he gave vent to his frustration.

'Persuade one of the ring to incriminate the others. Jeremy seems the weakest.'

'Impossible!' Adam didn't bother to hide his impatience. 'He might tip off the others. They'd either skip the country or get an injunction slapped on the paper – or both.'

'What else could we do?' Joanna persisted.

'It would certainly help if you were prepared to admit in court that you gained the information by accessing Jeremy's computer.'

'That's out of the question,' said Adam firmly. 'Do you realise what you're suggesting? Joanna could go to prison.'

'Adam, I wasn't saying Miss Templeton *should* do it,' the lawyer hurried to explain. 'That would be her choice. I don't blame you for being disillusioned. Your investigation would nail Safarov – and clear Richard. I wish I could advise Malcolm to print it, but I can't. The *Sunday Chronicle* would run too great a risk.'

Malcolm watched Adam with increasing apprehension. Although Joanna was deeply disappointed, she couldn't help feeling a little sorry for the wretched editor caught between his board of directors, his cautious lawyers and his forceful, money-generating journalist.

'Adam, you've done a brilliant job,' he said, selecting his words with care. 'I assure you, I'm not rejecting your investigation. I'm merely postponing it. Find new evidence – and we'll publish. We'll refund you the twelve thousand dollars. If you need more, tell me. Forget everything else. Concentrate on this. Call on my help any time. All the resources of the *Sunday Chronicle* are at your disposal. Let's see if we can run it next Sunday.'

There was silence. Joanna glanced at Adam. He was deep in thought. She knew he did not want to leave the *Sunday Chronicle*, but he would not work for an editor for whom he had no respect.

She waited for him to mention Withers' nephew, but he didn't. She would have done so, if he hadn't specifically asked her not to. It seemed insane not to play their last trump card.

She stood up. Adam glared at her – but she looked directly at Malcolm.

'I am prepared to state how I obtained the disk,' she said in a clear voice, 'but only if you run the story tomorrow.'

'No!' Taken by surprise, Adam laid a hand on Joanna's arm,

not caring that his colleagues witnessed his affection for her. 'You've endured enough.'

His words made her even more determined. 'Adam, I have to do it – for me, you, us.' She turned to Malcolm. 'If necessary, I'll stand up in a court of law and repeat my statement.'

She had expected Malcolm to seize on her offer but, to her surprise, he didn't.

'Are you absolutely sure?' he asked.

'Yes. I need you to publish this investigation so that I can hold up my head, silence people's sniggers – and continue my career.'

'Miss Templeton, you could be prosecuted.'

'So could those crooks who set me up – and for that, it's worth the risk.'

Malcolm was thoughtful. His silence infuriated Joanna. She'd offered herself as a sacrifice, and he was still indecisive. No wonder Adam couldn't work for him.

'Miss Templeton,' Malcolm spoke at last. 'I had to believe your story one hundred per cent.' He paused whilst the others waited anxiously for him to clarify his position. 'I had to be doubly sure, because it's obvious that you and Adam are . . . er . . . fond of each other and when people are . . . er . . . fond of each other they tend to be biased.'

'Are you suggesting that my judgement is influenced by sex?' Adam asked quietly.

Joanna blushed. She was livid with him for embarrassing her.

On the far side of the desk, Malcolm turned scarlet. 'No more affected than the rest of us would be,' he replied, determined to hold his ground.

There was a deathly hush. No one dared to breathe.

Then Adam laughed. 'I'd have asked the same question.'

Visibly relieved, Malcolm rose. He looked at their expectant faces. 'My decision is that we publish,' he announced with a broad grin. 'Congratulations, Adam! This is exactly what the *Sunday Chronicle* needs. Let's get this thing moving – then I shall inform the Chairman of the Board that we are publishing a major exposé.' He pressed the intercom and spoke to production. 'Hold the front page! We have a scoop. Yes, we're going with Hunter's story. It's big . . . It's huge. And for God's sake make sure we use a recent photograph of Oliver Safarov.'

The atmosphere in the office had changed the instant Malcolm gave the go-ahead. There was excitement, anticipation and smiles – even from the lawyers.

Joanna flopped back in her chair, too drained to do anything but listen to the infectious clamour around her.

Malcolm was talking to Adam. 'We want seven hundred words on the front page, two thousand words with pictures on page two, a picture of Safarov and a thousand words on the front of the City Pages and a further five hundred words on recent City scandals on the inner pages.'

The senior lawyer collected up his papers. 'Adam, I'm delighted,' he said. 'As soon as you're ready, we need to check copy again. I'll be in my office. No hard feelings, I hope?'

'Of course not. It's your job to pick holes.'

Unnoticed, Joanna slipped out of the office and asked Malcolm's secretary to put her through to Paola. When she returned, Malcolm was on the phone and Adam was sorting through his papers.

He touched her cheek. 'I apologise for embarrassing you, but I had to make the point.'

She linked her fingers around his wrist and squeezed hard. 'You'll pay for it – later!'

'I'll enjoy that,' he answered softly.

She released his wrist. 'Don't be so optimistic!' she said with mock severity.

His eyes sparkled. 'I am! I am!' He paused. 'You didn't have to agree to incriminate yourself.'

'It was my choice.'

'I know. And if the worst happens, we'll fight it together.' He nodded his head towards the door. 'The lawyers are waiting for me. I'll be tied up here till around eight, in case we need to make adjustments to the final edition. After that, we'll celebrate – on our own.'

She could almost feel his body on hers. 'I look forward to it – very much.'

He gave her a warm, intimate smile. 'So do I. But in the meantime, shall I call for Claire to take you home or would you prefer to stay? You can read in my office. This place is stacked with books and magazines.'

'Don't worry about me. I'm joining Paola for lunch.'

The lawyer reappeared at their side. 'Miss Templeton, we need you to sign a statement.'

Joanna experienced a stab of unease, but she couldn't back out now. 'Of course.'

'Hold on!' called Malcolm, covering the mouthpiece with his hand. 'We don't need a statement.'

They stared at him in surprise.

'The fact that Miss Templeton was prepared to stand up in court gave me the confidence to publish,' he explained. 'If Safarov sues, we'll use other evidence to prove our case. If need be, we'll identify Bilsham. But I'm convinced Safarov won't sue if he knows we have Miss Templeton. Her verbal offer is enough for me. I don't require her to sign an incriminating statement.'

Adam walked across to Malcolm. 'Thank you.'

'No. Thank you – both of you.' Malcolm hesitated. 'Adam, you and I must talk. This story has legs, not only now but when those crooks stand trial. I'm going to need you here, in London, but I'd prefer you kept that to yourself for the moment.'

'This could have longer legs than we imagined.' Adam kept his voice low. 'Joanna was watching *Weekly Money* this morning. Quentin Brocklebank, the QC, appeared in a feature. They filmed him being assisted by his clerk. That clerk is the nephew of Safarov's butler. Joanna had seen him at the house. What's more, it was the nephew who placed his uncle with Safarov. We've had no time to check this out, but we believe the nephew is the source and that he's obtaining the information from the papers he sees in Brocklebank's chambers.'

'Holy shit!' Malcolm's face expressed excitement and shock in equal measures. 'Brocklebank is involved in every major takeover.'

'We have no proof – yet,' Joanna reminded him.

'I realise that. But if it's true, this story is huge. God knows how Brocklebank will react. He'll be apoplectic with rage. He'll murder that clerk. As for his clients! They're all major international companies.' Malcolm shook his head. 'What a scandal! Adam, we must get on to this nephew angle immediately. Can you come to lunch tomorrow? Come to my house. We'll be more private.' He smiled at Joanna. 'Both of you, of course.'

Adam turned to Joanna, who nodded.

'We look forward to it,' he told Malcolm.

As the two men spoke, Joanna sensed the beginning of a new, working respect.

XXXI

NEWS OF THE scoop had spread like wildfire through the offices. The whole newspaper buzzed with excitement, although only a select number knew exactly who was to be exposed. As Adam escorted Joanna to Paola's office on the floor below, people gave her interested stares.

'Did you think I'd ignore your wishes and mention Stuart?' she asked, when no one was within earshot.

'Yes . . . no.'

She laughed. 'Yes, you did! I could see it in your face.'

'I needed to think it through,' he explained. 'As we had no evidence, it wouldn't have swayed the lawyers.'

'And it gave you something new to offer another paper, if Malcolm failed to publish?'

'Or to give Malcolm if he did print.'

She smiled. 'You're more canny than I thought, Adam Hunter.'

He gave her a playful pinch. 'I need to be – to hold on to you, Joanna Templeton.'

They entered Paola's office. 'Everyone's gaping at Joanna as if she'd arrived from Mars.' Adam told Paola.

'I expected as much, so I've ordered sandwiches.' Paola pointed to some covered plates.

'Thanks.' Adam smiled at Joanna. 'You'll be quite safe here.'

'Of course she will, Adam. Stop fretting. I'll look after her.' Paola shooed him out of her office and waved Joanna to a seat.

She placed the sandwiches on her desk, opened a small fridge, and removed a bottle of white wine – but Joanna opted for mineral water: she needed a cool head.

'I'm delighted you called me,' said Paola, pouring Joanna a large glass of water and herself an equally large glass of wine. 'I'm thrilled about the scoop. We all are.' She sat down on her side of the desk. 'You said you needed my help. What can I do?'

'I intend to confront Oliver Safarov at the Royal Opera House tonight.'

Paola lowered her glass. 'Joanna, you can't. It's too dangerous.'

'That man betrayed my trust, cost me my job and turned me into a laughing stock. I refuse to let him believe that he crushed me.'

'He might harm you.'

'Not with a whole audience of witnesses.'

'What about the scoop? I hate to sound selfish but Safarov could slap an injunction on the paper.'

'Don't worry! I've worked it all out.' Joanna extracted a ticket from her bag and laid it on the desk. 'The performance starts at seven-thirty. I'll arrive for the second interval, at nine-thirty, by which time the final edition will have gone to press. I can't tackle him earlier or he could halt publication. The interval lasts twenty-five minutes – quite long enough for me to say my piece.'

Paola continued to look concerned. 'Safarov is clever and powerful. He may be unaware that your story is to be published this Sunday, but he must know that you and Adam have been tracking him. I can't believe he'll come to England now. He wouldn't walk into a trap.'

'I think he'll come,' said Joanna. 'Oliver has to win. He couldn't allow himself to be scared off – especially by one of his pawns.'

'Supposing he receives a warning about the article during the first interval – and he runs?'

'Then I'll have wasted the sixty-five pounds I've had to spend on a ticket in order to gain entry to the auditorium.'

'You have thought it all through.' Paola spoke with admiration.

'This is important to me.' Joanna ate a cress sandwich.

'Does Adam know your plan?'

'No – and I don't want him to.'

'Because he'd try to prevent you?'

'Exactly.'

Paola frowned. 'He may find out. After all, you are in this together.'

'I hope he won't. If he does, I'll do my best to explain.'

Paola chewed thoughtfully on a piece of wholemeal bread. 'So? How can I help?'

'I need a dress. Something elegant and provocative.'

'Don't you own one?' asked Paola, perplexed.

'Yes – but at my flat. I have nothing suitable at Adam's, and I can't risk returning home until after the paper comes out. By then it'll be too late.'

'Of course! You're right. But we have a problem. I don't possess a dress. I always wear trousers.'

'You told me that Holly wears short skirts.'

'Oh, yes!' Paola grinned. 'On the first occasion we met. You were annoyed because you thought I was putting you down. But I wasn't. It's just my way of speaking.'

Joanna smiled. 'I know that now – or I wouldn't be asking for your help.'

'That's true.' Paola reached for the phone, saying, 'Holly has just the thing. It cost her a fortune and she's barely worn it.' She tapped out a number. 'Hi, it's me. We have a crisis. No, darling, not you and I – Joanna.' She explained Joanna's predicament. 'So she needs a smart, sexy dress. Would you lend her that short black tube you wore the other night? You would? You're a love. It's at the cleaners? Ready this evening? That's fine – if you could send it over in a cab.'

'I also need shoes,' Joanna whispered. 'High heels.'

'What size?' asked Paola.

'Six.'

'Holly takes five and a half. Could you fit into them?'

'If Holly doesn't mind.'

Paola spoke to Holly again, then nodded at Joanna. 'The clothes will be here by seven.'

'Please thank Holly. I'm so grateful. I'll try not to stretch her shoes.'

Over the sandwiches, they discussed every detail of Joanna's plan. Then Paola escorted her down to the small parade of shops on the ground floor, where Joanna selected some deep red lipstick and sheer black stockings.

'Surely you don't have to dress up for Safarov,' said Paola, pursing her lips with disapproval.

Joanna swept up her purchases. 'You need honey to trap a hornet.'

'That's just the kind of reasoning Adam would adopt. No wonder you two get on well.'

'Yes, we do.' Joanna smiled. 'We really do.'

They returned to the office. Whilst Paola continued with her work, Joanna read a magazine. From time to time, Adam put his head in to check that she was safe. She dreaded to think what he'd say if he knew her plan.

Holly's dress and shoes arrived promptly at seven. Whilst Paola stood guard to keep away curious eyes, Joanna changed in the ladies' cloakroom. The dress was black and plain, not unlike the one which Joanna had worn for her first dinner with Oliver, except that Holly's was shorter and tighter. The high-heeled shoes were tight and uncomfortable, but they flattered her legs, making them look longer and slimmer. The effect was stunning.

Laying out her make-up on the ledge below the mirror, Joanna applied extra mascara to her lashes and the bright red lipstick to her mouth. Then she doused herself in a cloud of scent, ran her fingers through her hair to fluff it out, and turned to face Paola.

'What do you think?' she asked.

'He'll be drooling for you.'

'Serve him right.' Joanna snapped her bag shut.

With her head held high and her shoulders straight, she strode towards the door. Then she stopped, suddenly hesitant.

'Adam has been my saviour,' she said. 'He's given me back my confidence. Without his help, I'd never have cleared my name so unequivocally. I'd still be fighting that bully Jeremy for a decent reference. No, I don't want to sneak off to meet Oliver behind Adam's back. He deserves better than me.'

'Thank goodness for that!' Paola looked relieved. 'It wasn't my business to interfere, but I'm glad you've changed your mind. Adam never forgives those who deceive him.'

She accompanied Joanna upstairs. The building was now almost deserted, with just a skeleton staff remaining to oversee the final edition.

Adam glanced up from his screen as Joanna entered his office.

'Good heavens!' he exclaimed, staring at her short tight dress and red lips. A slow, sensuous smile came over his hawk-like features. 'You look wonderful. Different, but . . . well . . . extremely glamorous. Where did you get that dress? I don't remember packing it.'

'That's what I've come to explain.' Joanna was aware of Paola retreating diplomatically.

'What do you mean?' he asked, picking up on her apprehensive tone.

She took a deep breath. 'I intend to confront Oliver at the Opera House tonight.'

He stared at her in disbelief. 'You can't. It's out of the question. He's dangerous.'

'I want to.'

Suspicion came into his eyes. 'Why?'

'Because I'm bloody well going to tell that bastard exactly what I think of him.'

'Joanna, our scoop will send Safarov to prison. He'll be enraged with you. I won't let you go. He could hurt you.'

She raised her chin. 'You can't stop me. I've made up my mind.'

'I could lock you in here.'

'But you won't, will you?'

He sighed. 'No – though I'd like to. I'd manacle you to the floor if I thought you'd ever forgive me.'

His reply made her laugh. 'I just want to show Oliver that he didn't destroy me.'

Adam refused to give up yet. 'But he'll know he's defeated when he reads the paper.'

'I want the satisfaction of him hearing it from me.'

He was silent for a moment. 'I don't want you to go because I'm frightened for you. But if you must, why do you have to dress so provocatively?'

Joanna took a step closer to him. 'Because he's a man who doesn't listen to a woman unless he's attracted to her and I'm determined he's going to hear me out.'

Adam laid his hands on her shoulders. 'I'm coming with you.'

'No! I must see Oliver alone or he'll think I'm scared.'

'I insist. You can't stop me. I'm afraid for you.'

She smiled softly. 'Thank you.'

From a cupboard behind his desk, Adam selected the smallest of several mobile phones and handed it to her. 'I'll wait outside the Opera House. If you need me, press *one*.'

She linked her arms around him. 'Thanks for being so understanding.'

'I'm not – but just this once, I won't fight you.' He held her very tight. 'Only this once.'

Before they left his office, Adam checked that the final edition had gone to press. Then he phoned Walter, keeping his side of the bargain.

By the lifts, they met the office boy carrying a pile of first editions. He handed a copy to Adam, then he grinned at Joanna.

'One for you too, Miss Templeton?'

'Yes, please.' She took it, avidly scanning the front page. Beside the heading '*City Ring Broken*', there was a large photograph of Oliver and a slightly smaller one of Jeremy. At the sight of them, she felt a surge of triumph. Then, she read on:

> *When Joanna Templeton voiced her suspicions concerning Kathpeach, one of her offshore clients, she was dismissed. When she threatened to take action, stories appeared in the press that she had sexually harassed Mr Safarov.*

'Satisfied?' asked Adam.

'Thank you.' Her face was alive with excitement. 'I can't wait to speak to Rebecca and Simon again – and to all my friends. I want you to meet them. I know you'll like them.'

'I'm sure I will.' Adam took her chin between his thumb and forefinger, and smiled tenderly. 'I'd kiss you, but you have an inch of gunge all over your face.'

She laughed. 'Don't you like my vamp look?'

'No,' he replied. 'I like you at home, alone, naked, with me.'

XXXII

IT WAS AFTER nine when Adam and Joanna drove through Covent Garden. The evening was warm and humid and the streets around the piazza were thronged with people.

As they came within sight of the Opera House, Joanna felt a stab of fear. Adam was right. Oliver was dangerous.

'Shall we wait in the car?' he asked.

'Just . . . just for a few minutes.' She tried to conceal the trembling in her voice.

He took both her hands in his. 'Joanna, we have our scoop. We've won. You don't *have* to face Safarov.'

'I want to.'

She glanced at the dashboard clock. 'Half-past. The interval should start soon. I'd better hurry.'

He touched her cheek. 'Brave lady!'

She forced a smile. 'Not as courageous as you think.'

At that moment, the doors to the Opera House opened and the audience drifted out into the summer night, sipping cooling drinks and chatting about the performance.

Adam opened the car door for her. 'Have you got the phone?' he asked as she stepped out.

She nodded and tapped her bag.

'If that bastard hurts you, call me.'

'He won't.'

'How can you be sure?'

She shrugged.

He cupped her face in one hand and touched her reddened mouth with his forefinger. 'Promise you'll be careful.'

'I will.' She had to force herself to break away from him.

Teetering in Holly's high heels, she walked along the pavement.

'You're my bravest partner, Templeton-Holmes!' he called after her.

She raised her hand to show that she had heard, but she didn't look back. She was afraid that she might lose her nerve.

At the Opera House, she showed her ticket and went up the red-carpeted stairs. But instead of heading for her seat, she followed the corridor to Oliver's box. The door was closed. It hadn't occurred to her that he might have company, and she had no time or means to find out. She had to hope that he was alone.

She took a deep breath and reached for the door handle. As she stepped inside, her fear receded. It was replaced by anger. In front of her sat the man who had betrayed her.

Oliver spun round. When he saw Joanna, he looked astonished. But he recovered quickly, the folds of his face breaking into his most charming smile.

'What a pleasant surprise. I'm so glad you could come after all. Such a shame you've missed the first two acts.' He registered her provocative dress, wondering if his informants were wrong and the silly girl still didn't realise what he had done to her.

She looked at him but didn't answer.

'You're even more beautiful than I remember,' he went on, deciding that he'd have sex with her that night. 'Come and sit down. Have some champagne.' He held out his hand to her. 'I'm longing to hear your news. I've missed you. What have you been doing?'

Joanna reached into her bag, took out the *Sunday Chronicle* and placed it in his outstretched hand. 'Exposing you as a crook, Oliver,' she replied coldly.

His face froze. 'What?'

She savoured his bewilderment. 'Read it!'

His eyes focused on the paper and the colour drained from his complexion. As he began to read Adam's text, his jaw tightened.

'So *you* initiated that last Kathpeach fax?' His voice was full of menace.

'Yes.' She recalled his sudden flash of brutality when they'd been in bed – the brief change of mood which she had subsequently wondered if she'd imagined.

'I knew it was false, but that fool Jeremy insisted that Laurie had created it.' He read on.

Only when he reached the end did he look up. When he did so, his appearance had altered. His face was coarser, his neck thicker and his suntanned skin had turned to an angry red. 'You stupid bitch!' he hissed.

Determined not to be intimidated, Joanna didn't even flinch. 'Oliver, you milked me of information, pretended to help me, cost me my job and ridiculed me in the press. Did you really believe that I wouldn't fight back?'

'You'll regret this.'

'You can't silence me by breaking into my flat, trying to run me down or cutting off my phone.'

He rose. 'You'll wish you'd never heard of First Clarence.'

She met his gaze. 'Don't threaten me, Oliver!'

'Threaten you?' He took a step towards her. 'I'm going to fucking kill you.'

'And be a criminal just like your father?'

He stopped dead. 'What do you mean?'

'If you hadn't threatened me, I wouldn't have shown you this – but you leave me no option.' She reached into her bag for the second time and produced a photostat picture of five men in uniform, smiling as they walked towards the camera.

He barely glanced at the page. 'How did you find out about my father?'

'Your mother showed me a photograph, identical to the right section of this one. It had "Ponary 15.3.1944" written on the back. I remembered the place, the date and your father's uniform. I went to a specialist reference library, gave them those details, and they showed me this picture. They told me that your father was a prison guard who'd sided with the Nazis and that he was executed as a war criminal after being identified by prisoners he'd mistreated.'

Oliver's face was flooded with bitterness. 'I hate that man. All through my childhood, I couldn't wait to return to Latvia, to meet his wartime friends and see my hero father through their eyes. But when I went back, I learned the truth – a fact which my mother still doesn't know.' He tore the photostat into tiny, precise strips. 'Nor will she do so.'

'I have lodged a copy of that picture with my bank and with my solicitor,' said Joanna.

'If you harm my mother, I'll kill you.'

'Hurt me – and my lawyer will release that picture to the press and police.'

'You fucking little blackmailer!'

'No, Oliver, I'm not blackmailing you. I am defending myself. I would not have produced the photograph if you hadn't threatened me. But it – and my knowledge – are my protection against you. If you persecute me, I'll ensure that both your mother and the press know about your father. If you leave me in peace, your secret will be safe.'

'Why should I trust you?'

'You have no option.'

'I could kill you here.'

'Don't be so ridiculous!' she replied, now fully in control. 'Do you wish to commit a crime in front of an audience? Do you want to rot in jail for the rest of your life? How do you think the press would treat the wife of a war criminal and the mother of a crook? I can tell you. They'd camp outside the villa, telephone her constantly and use telephoto lenses to take pictures of her bedroom. I know what it's like to be hounded. It's hell. I could barely cope. Your mother would be destroyed.'

'What is your price?' he asked abruptly.

'I've told you. Stay away from me.'

'Does your rough journalist know about my father?'

Joanna shook her head.

'Will you promise not to tell him?'

She hesitated. She didn't want to have secrets from Adam. But Oliver had inherited a hideous burden. She tried to imagine the horror of discovering that her own father had been a war criminal – the shame, the guilt, the disgust.

'Very well,' she replied, 'but only so long as you keep your side of the agreement. Whatever happens to you, Oliver, you deserve your fate. Your mother doesn't. For her sake, this will remain my secret.'

Oliver studied Joanna as though meeting her for the first time. 'You play rough. I would not have expected it of you.'

'In a vicious game, dirty tools are necessary – and you played a very deceitful game with me.' She turned to leave.

'If I'd known you were made of such steel, I'd never have let you go,' he said, his voice reverting to the suave, velvety tones of the Oliver she had first met.

Joanna didn't answer. She stepped out into the corridor and walked rapidly away. She wanted Adam, with his honesty and sanity, not a dangerous narcissist who even now was trying to trap her with a compliment – or was it another threat?

At the far end of the corridor, she noticed a door marked *Ladies*. Inside, she took a tissue and swiftly wiped the excessive make-up from her face.

She'd assumed that Oliver would leave immediately – not that it would do him much good. Already, Walter would have tipped off the airports and the ferries. But to her consternation, when she came out of the cloakroom, she saw him standing in the corridor outside his box. He had his back to her and he was hissing into his mobile phone. She only caught one sentence. 'If you open your mouth, Stuart, you're dead.'

Quickly, she removed Holly's shoes and darted down the carpeted stairs, out into the street.

Adam was pacing anxiously up and down outside the Opera House. Naked relief flooded his face when he saw Joanna.

She ran to him and threw her arms around him.

He held her tight. 'I've been so worried. I was about to come in and find you. Are you all right? What happened?'

'He was livid. But we were correct – about everything, including Withers' nephew. Oliver's on the phone to Stuart now, promising to kill him if he talks.'

'You mean he hasn't made a move to leave?'

'I know. Isn't it unbelievable? He must be mad – unless he plans to mingle with the audience.' Then she remembered how he hated crowds. 'No, I think he'll come out soon.'

'We'd better get out of the way. You're in danger here.' Adam ushered her into the safety of his car. 'What did he say? Did he threaten you?' he asked, settling into the driver's seat.

'Only at first.'

'Oh God, how will you ever be safe from him?'

'I will be.'

'How can you be sure?'

She thought of the photograph. 'I just am.'

Adam cupped her face in both his hands. 'When you walked away, I realised how much you mean to me – and how I'd hate to lose you,' he said.

'I'd hate to lose you too,' she replied.

He stroked her cheek. They looked into each other's eyes. Joanna remembered how he had offended her with his bluntness on the steps of Companies House. She was glad he'd been honest on that occasion. It meant that she believed him now.

'Let's go home.' She blushed in case she sounded presumptuous. 'I mean . . . to your flat.'

'I like it when you say home.' He ran his finger around the neck of her dress, caressing her with his touch. 'But first I have to make a call. You may want to witness something here – or you may not.'

He tapped out a number on his mobile phone. 'David,' he said. 'Joanna's safe. Safarov is all yours. He's still in the building, so far as we know. But watch the back exit.'

'I have news for you.' David's voice crackled slightly. 'Jeremy's holed up in his house, with our reporter camped in the street outside. His solicitor's just arrived and I wouldn't be surprised if Jeremy offers to spill the beans in the hope of a lighter sentence.'

'What have you done?' Joanna asked, as Adam put away his phone.

'I've given David a tip-off so that Safarov will have a taste of his own medicine – and you will have the triumph you deserve.'

Even as he spoke, a television outside broadcast van appeared at the top of Bow Street. A dozen men jumped out. Among them, Joanna recognised David.

'Let's go home,' she repeated, this time without embarrassment.

'Don't you want to see Safarov face the wolf pack?'

She shook her head. 'I've done what I set out to do.'

'Do you mean to say that after all that man did to harm you, you can walk away when he's about to get his just deserts?'

'Yes.' She was surprised by her own response. 'We defeated him, Adam, and he knows it. I have no need to see him torn apart.'

Adam took her face in his hands. 'I'm glad you feel that way. But why?'

She clasped her hands around his wrists. 'Oliver doesn't matter to me any more. I dislike and despise him, but I'm no longer eaten up with hatred. You helped me exonerate myself. Because of you, I can put it behind me – and move on.'

'We did it together – the two of us. I've paid my debt to Richard. Without you, I'd have no right to wear these.' He touched his cufflinks. 'Come on, Templeton-Holmes, let's go home.'

They drove slowly past the Opera House. The television crew had already set up on the pavement, their cameras and lights pointing at the main entrance. Joanna didn't expect to see Oliver. She felt sure he'd use another exit.

But suddenly there he was, holding her copy of the *Sunday Chronicle*. He halted when he saw the cameras, his face registering astonishment and anger. Joanna realised she'd been mistaken. Oliver was too egocentric to scuttle away like a rat. Despite Adam's article, he couldn't believe that he was no longer revered and respected.

David stepped towards him, holding a microphone. He spoke, but Oliver did not reply. Instead, he waved David away like an irritating fly and searched over the heads of the cameramen for his chauffeur. Then he caught sight of Adam's car – and Joanna. He stared at her. She met his gaze squarely. In his expression, she saw something akin to admiration and she recalled what he'd said about her being made of steel. In his eyes, she read the slow dawning of reality – *you* did *this* to *me*.

Her last view was of his defiant features captured in the bright white of the arc lights.

Joanna was not afraid that Oliver would persecute her even when his mother died. He would not harm his mother alive, or further sully his own name when she was gone. Nor was she sorry for the disgrace in store for him. She hoped he went to prison. He deserved it.

As time went by, she concluded that conceit had distorted his judgement to such an extent that it had all been just a game of power to him – one he'd never dreamed he'd lose. But that didn't explain the inconsistencies, such as why he had taken her to meet his mother.

As for her memories of the sinister man who had briefly been her lover – it was as if the Joanna Templeton who had known Oliver Safarov was another person, someone she used to know.